GRAND OPENING

Jon Hassler

BALLANTINE BOOKS • NEW YORK

Copyright © 1987 by Jon Hassler

All rights reserved under International and Pan-American Copyright Conventions. Published in the United States by Ballantine Books, a division of Random House, Inc., New York, and simultaneously in Canada by Random House of Canada Limited, Toronto.

No part of this book may be reproduced or utilized in any form or by any means, electronic or mechanical, including photocopying, recording, or by any information storage and retrieval system, without permission in writing from the publisher. Inquiries should be addressed to Permissions Department, William Morrow and Company, Inc., 105 Madison Ave., New York, N.Y. 10016.

A portion of this novel appeared originally in *Twin Cities* as a short story entitled "Dodger's Return."

Library of Congress Catalog Card Number: 86-28654

ISBN 0-345-35016-2

This edition published by arrangement with William Morrow and Company, Inc.

Manufactured in the United States of America

First Ballantine Books Edition: September 1988

20 19 18 17 16 15 14

For Betsy

The author is grateful for the fellowship
awarded him by the Minnesota State
Arts Board from funds provided by
the Minnesota Legislature.

AUTUMN

—◆—

1

A S T H E Y F O L L O W E D T H E Mississippi out of the
Twin Cities on U.S. 6l, Brendan wondered why his parents and
his grandfather seemed not to share his dread. Year after year
he had listened apprehensively to his mother and father talk
about moving to a small town and going into business for themselves, and now it was happening. Tomorrow he would begin
the school year among strangers in a village he had never seen.
The lawn mower was strapped to the roof of the car and his bike
rode the front bumper. The moving van was some miles ahead.
It was Labor Day. A light rain was falling.

His parents sat in front, his father gripping the wheel tightly,
fighting the car's tendency to wobble into the left lane, and his
mother reading *For Whom the Bell Tolls,* which she had promised to return to the city library by mail. The book was causing
her to gasp repeatedly as she read the final pages. Grandfather
and Brendan sat in back, separated by a pile of coats and coathangers. Brendan was twelve, born the year Roosevelt defeated
Hoover; Grandfather was nearly eighty, a baby when Lincoln
was shot. The car, a 1928 De Soto (black, square and noisy),

was propelled quite literally by the river, for the engine leaked coolant, and every thirty miles or so Hank had to pull off the highway and divert a gallon of the Mississippi through the coils of the steaming radiator.

"Hank, look at these hills, how awful," exclaimed his mother the instant his father switched off the ignition. She had closed the book on her lap, marking her page with both thumbs, and was shrinking back from the forested bluffs rising on her right. Brendan opened his door, handed his father the pail at his feet and watched him carry it down a long path to the wide, slaty river. The path was muddy. The rain was dwindling.

"Plum has hills around it, but they're gentle, rolling hills." She turned in her seat to reassure her son and her father. "They don't rise up and slap you in the face the way these do."

Brendan was sorry to hear it. These bluffs looked like fun.

"There!" shouted Grandfather, startling her, clutching the back of her seat, pulling himself forward and peering past her through the windshield. "Look there, the *Hiawatha*!" At the base of the bluffs, a green train came snaking north beside the highway. "Seven passenger cars," he said. He reached across the coats to nudge Brendan. "See how smooth she rides, lad? You know who laid that track, don't you, level as water?"

Brendan nodded. He counted the passenger coaches going by, pleased to see eight, not seven. Adult error was reassuring. Small error, that is. Large error, of course was frightening. For weeks it had been his secret prayer that uprooting themselves from the city was not the large error he felt it to be.

Don't think of the move as scary, his mother had told him. If we're a little lonesome at first, remember we've got each other.

Kids make friends fast, his father had said.

"*I* was the one," said Grandfather, easing himself back into his seat, sighing, feeling behind him for the wooden hanger poking him in the spine. The train slipped around a curve and out of sight, leaving behind a stream of soot slanting down with the raindrops. "I laid that track."

It was true. Not this selfsame track, of course, but the original track on this roadbed had been spiked down by Grandfather and

Grandfather's father, two of the construction hands of the 1880s who led the railroads west. Brendan had heard all about it.

His mother said, ''These are as close to mountains as anything I hope to lay eyes on.'' In her past—a railroader's daughter after the tracks had grown out of the deep river valleys—were the flat fields and rolling swells of western Minnesota and the Dakotas. She loved flat earth. She abhorred restricted vision.

Grandfather said, ''When I was sixteen they made my father foreman of a section crew and right away he let me quit school and go with him.'' His hand trembled as he felt his pockets— suitcoat, vest, shirt—for his pipe and tobacco pouch. ''That was the spring of 'eighty. We were laying track to Aberdeen when Aberdeen was nothing but a city of tents.''

Only by an act of will could Brendan stand to hear the rest of the story, the part about ice cream. He'd heard it, along with the rest of Grandfather's stories, a hundred thousand times.

''We headquartered in Aberdeen that summer and I thought I'd die for lack of ice cream. You couldn't buy yourself even a spoon of ice cream anywhere in South Dakota . . .'' His voice drifted off with his memory. His eyes narrowed as a glimmer of sunlight filled the car, highlighting his silky white hair and his pale, blue-veined temples. On his chin were the purple wounds of a shaky shave with a new blade. He murmured, ''Holy smut, how I loved ice cream in 1881.''

Brendan saw sunlight flashing here and there along the valley as the wind opened the low sky and folded it shut again. Down at the water's edge, his father's white shirt was momentarily agleam.

''How far now?'' he asked.

''It can't be much further to Uncle Herman's farm, and Plum is about forty miles beyond that.'' His mother looked at her watch. ''Eleven-thirty? Is that all? It seems like we've been on the road forever.''

Grandfather asked, ''Where did you say we were going?''

''Plum!'' they answered together, their voices, their impatience in tune. She added, ''We're stopping to say hello to Uncle Herman on the way.''

''I never heard of a town named Plum,'' Grandfather insisted, aware that he was on the verge of being scolded by his daughter, a sensation he rather enjoyed. He packed his pipe expectantly, scattering tobacco across the coats and coathangers. He added, asking for it, ''I've laid track in three states of the union and a province of Canada and I've never once heard of a place named Plum.''

''There *is* a Plum,'' she said precisely, peevishly, ''and our house is on the west edge of town. Upstairs you and Brendan will have the two bedrooms at the back, and Hank and I will have the bedroom at the front. And there *are* railroad tracks, just half a block from the house, I've told you a dozen times.''

Closer to two dozen, but it hadn't sunk in, Grandfather having aged to the point where change was unimaginable. Though briefed at every stage of this move, he had never truly believed moving day would ever dawn. He had said fifty or sixty times during August, ''There's not a mile of rail I haven't ridden in the state of Minnesota, and I've never heard of a place named Plum,'' and it was only at seven o'clock this morning when two strangers backed a truck up to the house and came in and took apart his bed that he agreed to pack his grip. ''I'll tell you one thing sure,'' he had muttered to the movers as he gathered up his hairbrush and handmirror from his bureau, ''there can't be a railroad running through it, or I'd know about it.''

Hank came up the path carrying the pail in one hand and flowers in the other—daisies bunched around a frond of wild fern. Brendan jumped out to take the bouquet and act as his father's emissary. His parents were linked by a love as direct and mute as a beam of light, and very few of Brendan's joys equalled that of coming between them and feeling himself pierced by that beam. He opened the driver's door and handed the bouquet across to his mother. She chuckled.

''Catherine, will you start the engine?'' Hank asked. He stood at the front bumper, removing the radiator cap. She slid over behind the wheel and stepped on the starter. As the pistons idled busily, Hank poured slowly, mixing the cool water with what remained of the warm. ''It's a wonder the way this old clunk putts along, overloaded like she is. I expected at least two flat tires by now.''

"But we've got only one spare."

"One'll do. The way it works you can usually get the first one patched before the second one goes flat."

"But what if you can't?"

"It's a chance you take."

Hank, the eldest son in a family of nine, was accustomed to taking chances. He had quit school at twelve and gone to work for a drayman, delivering ice in summer, coal in winter. Now he had a son of twelve, and during the intervening years he had held at least a dozen jobs, each one an improvement over the last by a dollar or so per week. From his most recent work as a streetcar motorman, he had saved enough money for a down payment on what was surely the least promising grocery business ever offered for sale in the classified ads of the *Minneapolis Star Journal*. A month ago Hank and Catherine had gone twice to Plum, the first time to see the trashy store behind the attractive newspaper ad, and the second time—after the price had dropped—to sign the papers that would make them grocers and to find a house to rent. Both times they were gone a full day, and old Aunt Nancy was brought to the house to watch over Brendan and Grandfather, particularly Grandfather, who sometimes wandered away and got lost.

This morning they had left Minneapolis by way of St. Paul in order to say goodbye to Aunt Nancy, who lived in an overheated apartment on Grand Avenue. She had delayed them by insisting they stay for tea and muffins and then by accompanying them slowly and arthritically down the steps and out to the curb, where there was a ceremony of kisses under umbrellas. Aunt Nancy's age was a guess—ninety-one probably. She was Grandfather's aunt. She was stronger of mind than Grandfather, but she was fearfully shriveled and frail. Every time she made a move Brendan held his breath, expecting one of her bones to snap. "Remember this," she called in her weak, reedy voice, watching them get into the car, sensing their uneasiness, "I've lived enough of life to know it works."

"What works?" asked Catherine.

"Life works. Now be sure to give these to Herman and tell

him he owes me a letter.'' She handed Catherine a small bag of muffins tied shut with a red ribbon.

Hank tipped the last drops into the radiator and handed Brendan the can. They got into the car, clouded now with the eye-smarting fumes of Grandfather's pipe. Hank sat poised with his hand on the ignition and waited for Catherine to finish talking. She was telling Grandfather that their house in Plum needed paint but there was no chance of painting it before winter set in, what with all that needed to be done at the store.

''The old dame will need convincing about the paint,'' said Hank, referring to their landlady-to-be, a woman named Ott-mann who lived with her retarded son in a small house facing theirs across Corn Street.

''Yes, I know what you mean,'' said Catherine. ''She has that nasty way of pursing her lips whenever you bring up money.''

Hank nodded, switched on the ignition and stomped with both feet on the starter and the accelerator. The engine clattered, the exhaust pipes thundered like guns and the car moved off down the highway.

It had been Aunt Nancy's idea, seconded by Catherine, to stop and see Uncle Herman, who years ago had become attached to the family by marriage, but not very securely. They assumed that Grandfather and Uncle Herman would enjoy renewing their neglected relationship as brothers-in-law. Turning in at his driveway near the town of Flensboro, they saw rusty machinery scattered across his yard, they saw the crumbling foundation and swayback roofline of his unpainted house, they saw Uncle Herman himself standing in the barnyard to receive them. He wore a shiny black suit, an uncertain smile, and a pair of glasses with a diagonal crack across the right lens. He was an earth-colored man, his complexion and eyelashes the color of sand, his hands, neck and ears burned a permanent bronze, his eyes green as agates. He was about fifty-five and handsome in a weatherbeaten way. Being shy, he avoided looking through the windshield as the DeSoto came toward him; he kept his eyes on the radiator cap. When the car came to a halt, he opened Catherine's door and said without preamble, ''Could we drive into town? I'd like to buy you all the dollar dinner at the St. Charles Hotel.''

''We weren't expecting a meal, Uncle Herman. We're only stopping to say hello—it's our moving day.''

''So Aunt Nancy wrote.'' He took two steps backward and looked meekly at his feet. ''I don't want to delay you, but I can't take you into my house—it's a mess. The neighbor lady says I'd be better off trading places with my pigs.''

''We'll take him up on the meal,'' said Grandfather from the back seat. ''We went pretty light on breakfast.''

''Please get in,'' said Catherine, making room for him in front.

He did as he was told, pulled the door shut and pointed through the windshield at his barnyard of puddles. ''You could make a U-turn there by the chicken coop and head into town. The St. Charles gives you a dandy meal for a dollar on Sundays and holidays.''

They had to raise their voices above the noise of shifting gears and clashing pistons:

''The neighbor lady says she'd have had us over for dinner, but she's got company from Iowa.''

''Uncle Herman, this is my husband, Hank Foster. I wasn't married when I saw you last.''

He shot a quick glance at Hank, then looked out his side window. ''How you been, Hank?''

''Just fine. Pleased to meet you.'' Hank turned onto the highway and picked up speed.

''And that's our son Brendan in back.''

Herman didn't look around; he kept his eyes on the ditch going by. ''How you been, Brendan?''

''Fine.''

''And did you see who else is back there?''

Herman nodded without turning to see. ''How you been, Michael?''

''Fit as two fiddles, Herman. How about yourself?''

''Can't complain.''

Sitting at a round table in the busy, noisy dining room of the St. Charles Hotel, they ate hamburger steak, fried potatoes,

mashed carrots, and pie. Throughout the meal Herman and
Grandfather exchanged the memories they held in common,
happy and sad. Grandfather's style of reminiscing was exuber-
ant, full of moans of regret and sighs and laughter. Herman's
was restrained. Happy, he emitted a whispery chuckle. Sad, he
lowered his head and shook it. They brought up names Brendan
had heard over and over at family get-togethers in Aunt Nancy's
apartment, names printed on the funeral cards the family used
as bookmarks in their missals, names mythical to Brendan because he had never seen the flesh they stood for. Margaret was
one such name. In 1919 Herman had married Grandfather's
youngest sister Margaret, and they had settled down on the farm
at the edge of Flensboro. Margaret died of cancer in 1928. Herman, childless, remained alone on the farm, working only hard
enough to support himself from harvest to harvest, allowing his
yard to become more cluttered by the year, his buildings to
become more dilapidated. Except for a field of oats and a field
of corn, he had let most of his acreage revert to brush. His
livestock, besides chickens, consisted of four or five cows and
a family of pigs.

By the time they finished dinner the sky had cleared. The
bluffs wore a mantle of sunlight. Leaving Flensboro, Uncle Herman pointed to what might have been the campus of a small
college and said it was the State Home School for Boys. "It's
bad what goes on there," he told them at the top of his voice.
"They try to hush it up, but it gets out anyhow. The guards are
rough on the boys. Break their arms sometimes."

"What boys?" Brendan asked. Above the hedge running
along the highway, he saw the upper half of the buildings—
yellowish brick, tall windows, red-tiled roofs.

"Criminal boys not old enough for the reformatory in St.
Cloud," Herman told him. "Eleven to sixteen, they say."

Through a gateway in the hedge Brendan caught a glimpse of
the grounds—yellowing elms standing like enormous umbrellas
over well-kept lawns, flowers growing beside the doorstep of
each building.

"Some years ago there was a killing. I never heard the details—just a killing is all anybody'd say."

Farther along, through a gap of dead hedge, Brendan saw a group of boys working in a garden, supervised by a guard. The boys wore brown caps and brown shirts. He saw the guard raise a stick as if to strike one of the boys on the head, and he saw the boy throw his arms up to protect himself, then the hedge closed off his view.

"Now this next place coming up is where the lady lives I told you about." This being the third mention of the neighbor lady, Brendan was reminded of the way boys sometimes dropped the names of girls they had crushes on.

"She's got eighty acres in corn and another sixty in barley."

It was a more prosperous farm by far than Herman's. The outbuildings were squared up and freshly painted. The large, pale-green house stood on a knoll commanding a view of the river and the town. Two large horses grazed in a pasture.

Letting Herman out in his yard, they all thanked him for the meal. Catherine said, "Come and see us in Plum."

"Might do."

"You'll find us in the grocery store on the south side of Main Street," Hank told him.

"Why Plum? . . . I have to ask. You're city people."

"That's what I'd like to know," said Grandfather, rolling down his window. "Did you ever hear of the place before?"

"Yeah, heard of it."

"Small town property's a lot cheaper," Hank explained.

"Makes sense. Funny name for a town, I always thought."

2

THE VILLAGE HAD BEEN named for a grove of wild plum trees which were said to have borne a biennial crop of delectable sweetness, but by the time Brendan and his family arrived the grove was long dead and so were most of the people it had warmed when it was chopped into firewood. The streets were now lined with enormous elms shading the houses of at least fifteen hundred people Brendan and his father didn't know as they stepped outdoors at sunrise on the morning after Labor Day. They slipped out quietly, so as not to waken Catherine and Grandfather. Hank and Catherine had been up until three, arranging furniture and pacifying Grandfather, who kept coming down from his bedroom to ask where he was. Hank hadn't slept at all. He had lain awake worrying about the house; there were salamanders in the dirt cellar, the loose window casements let in flies and drafts and the roof leaked. He worried about the store, which hadn't been properly cleaned for years; trade was down to nothing. He worried about his family; small towns, he'd heard, were hard for city people to fit into.

Brendan, too, was worried. This was the opening day of

school and he was leaving the house earlier than necessary in order to walk with his father, afraid that on his own he might get lost.

They stepped down off the front porch. Hank stopped and cocked his ear. "Listen."

Brendan listened. "What?"

"Silence."

After a few seconds they heard the faint barking of a farm dog. A few seconds more and a little breeze came along and rattled the cornstalks in the garden next door.

Hank gave the sky a long, suspicious look. It was much bluer and a lot broader than the sky over Minneapolis. "So this is the famous peace and quiet you hear so much about."

They looked at the small white house across the street where their landlady Mrs. Ottmann lived. They looked up and down the street at the white frame houses with wide gaps of high weeds between them. "It's quiet all right," said Hank, "but what's peaceful about it? It makes me nervous as hell."

Brendan understood. In Minneapolis, where he had been un-acquainted with a quarter of a million people, he had never felt so unknown.

Across the street a path led through a vacant lot and up to a railroad embankment that ran behind the Ottmann house and curved off toward the center of town.

Heading for the embankment, they saw a large, bony face smiling out through the Ottmanns' front window. Brendan re-coiled, for it resembled monster faces he had seen in movies, the eyebrows wiry and wild over hollow-looking eye sockets, the smile a great gaping mouthful of whatever the monster was having for breakfast.

"That's Rufus," said Hank. "He lives there with his mother."

Brendan shuddered and ran ahead a few steps. Passing through the vacant lot, he saw Mrs. Ottmann watching him from her kitchen doorway. Mother and son had the same dark, deep-set eyes, but only the mother's eyes appeared connected to a brain. Hank waved at her. She flourished a dish towel.

They climbed the embankment and set off along the cinder-buried crossties between the rusty tracks. Raised above the back

yards on their left and right, they noticed themselves being noticed by several people breakfasting in their kitchens. Who were
these strangers, Brendan imagined them saying, this man moving along at such a swift, tipped-forward pace and wearing a
white shirt and red tie, and this boy hurrying to keep up, both
of them squinting into the rising red sun?

The tracks ended behind Plum Feed and Seed. They walked
around the building and came out on Main Street. Hank pointed
to Plum School (two stories, twelve grades) down the street on
their left. They turned right, walked past a row of houses where
the lawns were groomed more neatly than those on Corn Street,
and came to Plum's two-block stretch of storefronts. They
stopped and regarded their store from across the street. It stood
between the Plum Theater and Gordy's Pool Hall. The mustard-
colored letters—KERMIT'S GROCERY—had partially flaked from
the glass.

"Kermit said he'd leave the keys under the mat on the doorstep," Hank said as they crossed over. There was no mat on the
doorstep. They went through the narrow passage between the
store and the theater and found no mat at the back door either.
They returned to the front, and while Hank pondered his next
move, Brendan read the decals on the glass of the door. USE
RED STAR YEAST. BUY WAR BONDS. CHEW COPEN-
HAGEN. Brendan tried the door. It was unlocked.

They stepped into the rank smell of old meat and festering
fruit. Following him through the building, Brendan watched his
father confront each disappointment with a nervous nod, as if
he had foreseen the worms in the sugar, the rat drinking from
the toilet in the basement (the rat and Brendan jumped back at
the same instant) and the man sleeping on a bed of flour sacks
in the back room.

"Who are you?" Hank touched the man's shoulder. He lay
face-up, snoring. He wore a green shirt, black suspenders, a
black beard.

"Out!" said Hank.

The man opened his eyes. He brought his hands to his face,
buried the tips of his fingers in his beard and slowly scratched.
"I work here. I come with the store."

"No, I'm sorry, I won't be hiring help."

He sat up, lazily. "Well . . ." He yawned. He was young, about twenty-five. He had gaunt eyes and a long nose. He wore blue socks with red arrows at the anklebones. No shoes. His black hair was clipped shorter than his beard. "I was Kermit's clerk for eight years and I know the ropes. I don't need much pay. I live with my mother, and we live very frugally." (Hank would tell Catherine later that he had never heard the word "frugally" spoken before.) "I'd never say a word against Kermit, he was a likable boss, but let's face it, he was a failure. Somebody with a thirst like his will never be anything but a failure. Kermit inherited this place from his father ten years ago, and his first day on the job was the high-water mark of his interest in groceries."

Brendan thought it remarkable the way this young man never paused to form his thoughts or choose his words. His voice was melodious, fluid. "In the ten years it took Kermit to bring his trade to a standstill, he taught himself to appreciate cheaper and cheaper booze. He drank Cutty Sark as recently as 1937, but he dropped down to a medium-priced rum after that, and last week he was guzzling white wine without a label the day he sent you that postcard saying the keys would be under the doormat."

He reached into his pocket and displayed two keys on a loop of dirty string. He put them back in his pocket. "He's gone off somewhere for the cure, and I wish him luck, but I'm not hopeful. Somewhere in Wisconsin, I guess. A sanitorium where they dry you out for a hundred dollars, he told me."

He stood and glanced about for his shoes. He was shorter than Hank by two or three inches. The back of his shirt was flour white.

"Here." Hank handed him a shoe. "Don't you have a bed at home?"

"Sure, but I wanted to be here when you came in." He yawned. "Isn't it awfully early? Kermit never had me open up till eight." He found his other shoe.

"It's seven thirty. I'm sorry, but there's no work for you here anymore."

"Well . . ." He sat down and put on his shoes. He stood and

tucked in his shirt. "The last year or so I've been practically running the place. I'm a steady worker. I've been here since high school. I hardly ever drink. Saturday was the first time in months. We locked up at noon, seeing it was Kermit's last day, and we went out and tied one on together. It's not good for me to drink, the doctor says. My epilepsy." He shook Hank's hand. "My name is Wallace Flint."

Hank had trouble being stern. "I'm strapped, Wallace. I cashed in my life insurance to make this move. My wife will be all the help I need, she's coming in later to help me clean. So let me have the keys."

Wallace ran his thumbs under his suspenders, untwisting them. "What about deliveries? I could at least deliver."

"My boy will deliver. This is Brendan. He has a bike."

Wallace didn't offer his hand, but gave Brendan a searching look, his dark eyes glistening. Under his intent gaze, Brendan wanted to squirm.

"What grade?" Wallace asked.

"Seventh."

"Mmmm, seventh. Your homeroom teacher is Mrs. Roberts, a crabby old bag."

Hank led them out of the back room to the front of the store, where they found a girl and boy standing near the cash register looking over the meager display of candy. They were older than Brendan. The boy wore a gold sweater with a maroon "P" stitched on the front and a maroon "45" stitched on the arm. The girl wore a green dress and a green ribbon in her hair. They chose a pack of licorice and handed Wallace a nickel. They left, holding hands.

Hank deftly crowded Wallace toward the door, explaining again how penniless he was.

Wallace gave up. He handed over the nickel, then the two keys on the string. "Ask around if you need me. I'm not hard to find." He opened the door, but before going out he turned for a last look at the interior. He reminded Brendan of the haggard and dying exiles of eastern Europe he had seen in newsreels and *Life*. Backing out, but still leaning in, Wallace put his fingertips delicately to his brow and said, "I don't have fits very often, if that's what's worrying you. As long as I get lots of rest I'm fine.'' He backed slowly outside, and a moment before the door went shut his eyes fell again on Brendan. They were watery eyes. Not tears, Brendan felt sure, nor the bleariness of fatigue or boredom such as he had often seen in Grandfather's eyes. This was a feverish gleam, suggesting illness.

They watched him go to the curb and look up and down Main Street, saw him wave at someone in a passing car, saw him tip his head to the sky, saw him return to the doorway and sit on the concrete step. Brendan wondered if his father sensed in Wallace the overdramatic manner of an actor.

''You'd better be off to school, Brendan.''

No, his father never speculated on people's expressions or mannerisms. He took people for what they said and did and never mind the subtleties. Brendan wished his mother had been here to meet Wallace; she would certainly have had something to say about his stagy movements and his spooky eyes.

Hank turned from the window and gazed at the discouraging interior. After a sleepless night he felt crushed by the toil ahead. Sunlight was falling in the window now, defining more clearly the cobwebs sagging from the ceiling, the dust fuzzing the cereal boxes, the dirt underfoot.

Brendan stepped outside and his father followed, bringing a second nickel out of his pocket and asking Wallace, ''Where can we get ourselves a cup of coffee?''

Wallace sprang to his feet. ''Next door.''

Hank locked the door and said, ''Come on.''

On his way to school Brendan looked back to see a very large man unlocking Gordy's Pool Hall from inside, pushing the door open, leaning forward for a moment as Wallace made the introductions, then shaking Hank's hand and ushering them in.

3

THE MOMENT HE SET foot in homeroom, Brendan was offered a stick of gum by a shifty-eyed boy named Dodger Hicks, who had been lying in wait for a friend. Among the twenty-four boys and girls of the seventh grade, Dodger had not even one friend, the parents of Plum having warned their children away from him because his father was a convict, his mother drank, and Dodger himself stole things from stores—crayons, comic books, candy.

Dodger was older and taller than the rest of the seventh grade, having taken nine years of school to get there. A poor reader, he was taunted for what his classmates assumed was stupidity and had spent every recess and noon hour of his life lingering at the edge of a game. His face was dark, his cheekbones prominent. He had the habit of nodding his head when he spoke, and of squinting and showing his long teeth when he listened. His dark hair, which hung unevenly about his ears, he trimmed himself, using a pair of small shears pilfered from art class. As he gave Brendan a stick of grape gum (the off-brand, crumbly gum of wartime) he said he had stolen it that very morning from Kermit's Grocery, the door being unlocked and no one inside.

"That's our store," said Brendan. "My mother and dad bought it."

"No kidding?" asked Dodger. He gave Brendan the rest of the pack.

Mrs. Roberts was a large, white-haired woman with a voice like a rasp and a propensity for threatening and shaming. The students' twenty-four names grated on their ears as she called them out and pointed to their alphabetical places in the room. A girl named Lorraine Graham took her place between Brendan Foster and Dodger Hicks.

It was a novelty to change rooms with each class. The day began with arithmetic, which was followed by art, current events, geography and health. At noon Brendan went home to eat with his mother and grandfather. He told them he had a new friend named Dodger. He asked if he could bring him home after school. Catherine said, "Yes, that's fine, but don't wake Grandfather if he's napping."

"Let's see your toys," Dodger said, arriving at Brendan's house after school, and he wasn't satisfied until he had examined every last gameboard and tin soldier. From a large box in a closet he drew out a boomerang—a beautifully curved piece of laminated wood, thick at the middle and tapered at both ends. It had been a Christmas gift from Brendan's Aunt Mae and Uncle Howard and had never interested Brendan because it returned only to throwers with stronger arms than his. Dodger had never seen a boomerang. "What is it?" He hefted it, turning it over delicately in his hands, obviously pleased by its smooth lines. His fingers were long and sensitive.

"A boomerang. You grab it by one end and throw. It's supposed to come back."

Dodger nodded eagerly. "Let's try it."

"Some other time, when my dad's home. He has to throw it."

"Let me throw it."

"No, you need lots of room."

Dodger pointed out the window. "More room than that?"

Brendan had momentarily forgotten that behind this house lay whole counties of open land. In the city his father had had to take him to a football field to show him how it worked.

"All right, see for yourself." They went downstairs and out the back door.

The field behind the house had undergone its fall plowing. Dodger carried the boomerang to the edge of the furrows, drew back his right arm, kicked up his left foot and accomplished a magnificent throw—all by sheer instinct apparently, for Brendan's only instruction had been to demonstrate the proper grip. The boomerang sailed up and away, spinning as it climbed, and at its apogee—incredibly high and small—it tilted almost vertical as it wheeled around and began its return flight, picking up speed and spinning faster and faster and heading straight for their heads and passing over them as they threw themselves flat and crashing through the kitchen window. At the sound of breaking glass, Dodger was up and running. He never glanced back or said goodbye.

The noise woke Grandfather, who called from his window upstairs, "Where are we, lad, and what was that noise like a china closet tipping over on its face?" This being Grandfather's second awakening in this unfamiliar house, he was of the opinion—as he had been for a while this morning—that he and his wife and two daughters were lodging in a tourist home en route West, retracing a trip he had made in 1921 to visit relatives. At breakfast it had taken three cups of coffee and a stern word from Catherine to convince him this wasn't a stopover in Billings.

"We live here," Brendan shouted up at him. Then softer: "And my friend broke a window."

"We live here?"

"Plum! Remember?"

Grandfather backed away from the window, smartly rapping his skull with a knuckle—usually a sign that a surge of fresh blood was making a swing through his brain and carrying off his delusions.

While Brendan swept up the glass in the kitchen, Grandfather dressed for dinner. He put on his green necktie and the darker of his two suitcoats. Then he picked his silver hairbrush and handmirror off the dresser and stroked over and over the tuft above his right ear that would never lie flat. Brushing, he thought of his wife. The brush and mirror were her gift to him on their twenty-fifth anniversary. The last year of the Great War, he thought, holding the mirror at several angles—1918. So if she had lived, this past summer would have been their fiftieth—and another great war going on. Their wedding day was June seventh. Or seventeenth, he could never recall. Where did you get money enough for a silver brush and mirror set, Sade?—I've admired this set in the window of Hudson Jewelry and I know it cost a fortune and a half. Her smile was her only answer. But later, after she died, he learned that she had earned the money by sewing and baking for the neighbors when he was out on his railroad runs. His daughter Catherine told him.

Their thirtieth anniversary was their last, 1923. One day that summer he came home from his run to Duluth (he was a brakeman by that time, no more pick-and-shovel work for a man nearly sixty) and Doc Hays was sitting on the front porch of their house on Clinton Avenue. It was hot. Doc was smoking a cigar. He said, "Morning, Mike." "Morning, Doc, don't tell me Sade's heart is fluttering again." Doc nodded, leaning forward and flicking a big ash over the porch rail. "She's dead, Mike. Died out back in the garden this morning. A neighbor saw her drop." Late June of 1923. Doc said that scattered around her were the radishes and green onions she had picked. Grandfather ran into the house and knelt at the sofa where she lay. She was covered to her shoulders by a blanket. Her face had dark spots. "Father Cullen!" He shouted back toward the front porch. "Call Father Cullen!" Doc came into the room: "He's been here and gone, Mike, I called him first thing. Said he'd be back later to see you."

She was cold. He couldn't get over how cold she was, and this during a heatwave, a stifling, sweaty morning. He backed away from the sofa and flopped into a deep chair. Doc fussed with the body, staightened the hair on her brow, adjusted the blanket. "You want the Moriarity brothers to make the arrangements, Mike?" Grandfather nodded, staring at the body, remembering he still had on his cap, taking it off, his visored brakeman's cap. Doc said, "I'll call Moriarity's," and while he was in the kitchen phoning, Catherine came across the porch and into the living room. Doc had called her before he called the priest, called her at Dayton's, where she clerked in the book department. She had to wait a long time for a streetcar. She and her father embraced. Then Mae, his other daughter, came in from playing somewhere. More embracing. They went and stood by the sofa, weeping freely.

Thirty years married and twenty a widower—Grandfather stroked and stroked his hair. Thirty years building railroad lines, then nearly twenty years as a brakeman. In those years a brakeman was exactly what his title implied. Besides throwing switches in the railyards and keeping tally of the boxcars dropped off and picked up, a brakeman scurried along the tops of the cars, often while they were in motion, to turn the wheels that set the brakes. Treacherous work. He had seen a brakeman killed one icy afternoon in the St. Paul yards. His own freight was pulling out, heading west; he was standing on the rear platform of the caboose and looking off to his left at another freight pulling in. He saw a brakeman standing on a cattle car of the inbound freight. The man wore a long black coat and black mittens. He noticed Grandfather and waved, and then as he turned and was about to leap the gap between cars he slipped. Down he went, striking his head on the coupling and then dropping to the track, and the wheels of the cattle car passed over his legs, or rather passed through them, for they were cut clean off just below the hip. Grandfather, riding away, signaled his engineer to stop and he jumped from his caboose and ran through the sleet to the other train, which continued to move, wheel after steel wheel rolling over the bloodsoaked pants and coattails. Grandfather pulled the man away. He was out cold, had been knocked out before he hit the ground, thank God. Grandfather waved and shouted but the train continued to crawl through the yard, and when the caboose finally rumbled by, there on the back platform stood the second brakeman looking down in disbelief at his dying partner, whose loss of blood was so lavish it spouted like a fountain from his stumps and he lost his life before he came to.

Ah, the damn trains. The wonderful damn trains.

In this strange house in this strange town named Plum, Grandfather, brushing his hair, heard the whistle of a locomotive. Short toots: crossing ahead, although on Grandfather's trains short toots sometimes meant the baked potatoes were ready. Hauling potatoes out of the Red River Valley, he and his crew always had themselves a baked potato feast. Delicious, huge, tender-skinned russets. He himself would buy the pound of butter in Fargo before they set out, giving half to the engineer and fireman in the locomotive and keeping the other half for himself and his partner in the caboose. The fireman was in charge of the baking; he would set the four potatoes in a covered pan next to the firebox, and when they were ready to eat—somewhere in the hills of Douglas County—the engineer would give five short toots to stop the train and the fireman would get down and set the pan beside the track—having removed two of the potatoes—and then the train would pull slowly ahead and stop again when the caboose reached the pan. Grandfather and his partner would pick it up, roll their potatoes out onto their tin plates, cut them open with their jackknives and cover them with salt and pepper and a quarter pound of butter apiece. Ah, what potatoes. To this day, short toots made Grandfather think of potatoes.

Another toot, this time accompanied by a bell. Grandfather stopped brushing. He heard the chuffing of steam. Noisy locomotives often moved through that part of Grandfather's life that was pure memory, but hardly ever this loud. He put down his brush and mirror and went to his window. Nothing there but farmland, no train. He went down the hallway to the front bedroom, Hank and Catherine's room. He looked down on the small Ottmann house. He saw an alley behind the house. Or no, not an alley but an embankment. Holy smut, a railroad. And there, drifting slowly into town from the north, emerging from a cornfield where the stalks stood nearly as tall as the letters SOO LINE on the caboose—drifting into town *backward*, of all things—was a train, by God. Caboose, three cars, coal tender, steamer. Another toot. More dinging. Chuff, chuff.

Grandfather took the stairs as fast as he dared and got to the front door in time to see the engineer leaning from his window before the locomotive disappeared behind the Ottmann house. Setting off at a hobbled run, Grandfather tried to recall the names of engineers he had met on the Soo Line; he might know this man. He angled through the Ottmanns' yard and through the vacant lot beside it, thistles and sharp-bladed grass nicking his ankles because he wore slippers and no socks and didn't notice the beaten path. He passed under some trees and came to the embankment. The headlight of the locomotive was moving slowly away from him now, rocking as the train rounded a curve. So Plum had a train after all. Where did it come from and where was it going? And why backwards for God's sake? He climbed the embankment. It was only ten or twelve feet higher than the thistly lot, but the slope was steep and when he reached the top and stood between the rails he felt his heart pounding in his temples and in the hollows above his elbows. He wiped his brow with the heel of his shaky hand.

He heard someone call, "Yoo-hoo." He turned. When Mrs. Ottmann saw him hurry past her kitchen door and scramble up the embankment wearing his suit, tie and slippers, she wondered if the old guy was dotty or in trouble. Now, waving a dish towel, she stood outside, calling like a loon. "Yoo-hoo, be careful of the train." She wore a black dress down to her black shoetops.

Grandfather turned to her and bowed from the waist, and then, straightening up, he put both forefingers to his brow in a double salute—the best he could offer since he had no hatbrim to touch. All his life, women inspired this sort of gallantry in Grandfather. He called to her, "Have no fear, my good woman, I laid track as a boy, and I have been around trains since 1881, when Aberdeen, South Dakota, was nothing but a city of tents. I was brakeman on freights much bigger than this puny puddle-jumper." He gestured down the empty track, the locomotive having backed around the curve and disappeared. "Now if you'll please excuse me, I wish to speak to the crew."

Grandfather was hot. He took off his suitcoat, hung it over his arm, turned and waved again at Mrs. Ottmann, his baggy shirtsleeve fluttering. He hurried along the oily cinders of the roadbed thinking, Imagine telling me to be careful of trains, as if I didn't know the dangers of walking in the right-of-way. He remembered 1925 and being on the train that struck a man around two o'clock in the morning and carried him on the cow-catcher, dead as a stovebolt, till dawn. That was on the run from Minneapolis to Brookings. At dawn a depot agent in South Dakota saw the body as the train sped by and he telegraphed the crew. The train stopped on a hilltop and a sheriff and a coroner showed up. From his stiffness and the address in his wallet they figured the dead man, who was dressed like a farmer, had been riding the ledge under the headlight for five hours, and was 160 miles from home. He belonged back in Carver County, Minnesota.

Some months later when Grandfather was laying over in Carver County he inquired about the dead man, met one of the dead man's cousins in a saloon, in fact, and learned that the man had been out on the tracks that night searching for a stray bull, that he had died a week short of his sixtieth birthday and that as a dead man he had traveled nearly five times as far as he had while alive. He had once been to St. Paul, according to the cousin, and he often spoke of crossing a state line some day just to see what it felt like, but he never did. The cousin said it took some of the edge off everybody's sadness to think that if he hadn't crossed a state line before he died at least he crossed one before he was cold. The cousin insisted that Grandfather meet the widow and took him out to the farm. The widow was a husky, friendly woman with a grown son to help her carry on. She served her visitors a meal. She, too, spoke of the solace of knowing her husband had crossed a state line, and Grandfather wondered if the whole family was a little bit cracked. "Actually, he crossed *two* state lines," Grandfather told her, "because that run we were on cuts through a corner of North Dakota before it gets into South Dakota." Leaving with the cousin after the meal, he bowed out the door with a flourish, kissing the widow's hand and feeling gallant and false. It wasn't true that the line cut through a corner of North Dakota, and he wouldn't have said it if it didn't seem to mean a lot to the family.

Panting, pulling at his tight necktie, Grandfather hurried along the embankment and came to an intersection where cars were crossing. He stopped traffic by raising his hands palm-flat to the drivers. Somebody honked. Somebody said, "Watch it, Pop, you could get flattened that way," and another voice, because he looked so bedraggled in the heat, called out, "Sir, are you all right?" This being a woman's voice, he turned in the direction of her car and without slowing down but with a grand sweep of his arm threw her a kiss.

Rounding the curve, he came face to face with the standing locomotive. It seemed to float on the hissing clouds of steam billowing out from its underbelly and obscuring the wheels. He passed through the steam, squinting and covering his ears. Gripping the handrail, he struggled up the steps to the cab. He grabbed the startled engineer by the shoulder and shook him. "Michael McMahon," he shouted, "brakeman on the Milwaukee Road through the teens and most of the twenties. Charter member of the Brotherhood of Railroad Trainmen."

The racket from the boiler was deafening and he couldn't hear what the red-faced engineer replied, but it must have been a warning or a curse, judging by his scowl.

Grandfather turned to the fireman, who looked friendlier. "Michael McMahon, brakeman on the Milwaukee Road. Why did you come to town backward?"

The fireman, smiling, took off his sooty glove and laid a brotherly hand on Grandfather's shoulder. He gently turned him around and guided him down the steps.

"Where does this spur lead to?" Grandfather spoke into the fireman's ear.

"It stops here in Plum." The fireman helped him off the last high step and pointed to where the track ended—a pile of ties serving as a buffer a few yards beyond the caboose.

Grandfather shook his head in disapproval: "No through train? I knew this was a no-account village. Where do you come from?"

"Winona."

"You live in Winona?"

The fireman nodded. He lifted his cap and drew his sleeve across his hot brow.

"And the engineer? Does he live in Winona?"

"Right."

"And both brakemen?"

"We make this run with just one brakeman. Yeah, he lives in Winona."

"Why backward?"

The man pointed again at the buffer of ties. "No turntable in Plum, no siding. If we come to town backward we can go home frontward. Sometimes we do it the other way around—leave Winona frontward and go home backward."

"Christ almighty, frontward, one day, backward the next—a hell of a way to run a railroad." He looked at the boxcar, the grain car, the empty cattle car. "What's your freight?"

"That there." The fireman pointed to the boxcar. "That's half a carload of feed."

"What's in the grain car?"

"We picked up a carload of oats in Pinburg." He gripped the handrail and swung himself up to the bottom step.

"Pinburg?" called Grandfather.

"Pinburg's about six miles down the track."

"You coming back tomorrow?"

"No, just once a week. Tuesdays." The fireman returned to his fire.

Taking out his handkerchief and wiping his throat, Grandfather walked past the open door of the boxcar and saw a man unloading it from the other side, wheeling large bags of something down a ramp and into the back door of Plum Feed and Seed. He passed the grain car and the empty cattle car and came to the caboose. He climbed aboard the front platform. Both doors were open and he could see through the caboose and out the other end. "Coming aboard," he called as he stepped inside so as not to startle the brakeman the way he had startled the engineer. The brakeman wasn't in the caboose. Grandfather hung his suitcoat on a peg and inspected the brakeman's tools—lanterns, oil cans, pry-bars. He looked at the papers on the brakeman's desk—timetables, bills of lading. He climbed up to the brakeman's high seat in the dusty window bay and sank into the dusty cushions. He took three dusty breaths and fell asleep.

Twenty minutes later, at the blast of the whistle, Grandfather began the strenuous work, for the third time that day, of collecting his wits. He had collected only a very few when the train began to move, bell ringing, whistle tooting, caboose rocking. He let himself down from the high seat and saw that he was alone (the brakeman was riding home in the locomotive), and although the caboose was unfamiliar and he couldn't remember which run he was making, he did recognize his coat hanging from a peg, so he assumed he was where he belonged.

Bracing himself left and right against the tilt, he made his way onto the rear platform, where the back yards of Plum passed slowly under his gaze. He waved at the motorists at the intersection. He waved at a man in coveralls who was kneeling in a garden pulling carrots. He waved at two women standing near the embankment, and both of them waved back—frantically, for they were Catherine and Mrs. Ottmann. Catherine, on her way home from the store to prepare dinner, had been detained by Mrs. Ottmann, who had barely begun tattling on Grandfather when they saw him go by on the outbound freight, his silky hair awry in the sun. He wore a grin of blissful mischief, and as he disappeared around a curve in the tall corn he threw Catherine a kiss.

In bed that night Catherine asked, "What will we do with him, Hank? How will we keep him out of trouble while we're at the store?" In the DeSoto she had raced the train to Pinburg, where she and the crew removed Grandfather from the caboose.

An enormous yawn from Hank, then: "Maybe we should bring him to work with us. Find him a comfortable chair."

"But he couldn't sit there all day. Where would he take his nap?"

"You could take him home in the afternoon. There's sure not enough to keep us both busy once we get the place cleaned up. I think we bought a tomb."

"Don't say that, Hank. It won't be long before we'll need all the help we can get. I can feel it."

Silence.

"You feel it too, don't you? The business we'll have?"

Hank snored softly.

Catherine lay awake for a long time. She heard the beginning of a soft drizzle of rain, and then she heard the beginning of a puddle on the bedroom floor. She got up and looked in at the other bedrooms. Brendan slept silently. Grandfather slept noisily, his nose whistling, his chest rumbling. She went downstairs for the dishpan, which she took to the bedroom to catch the water. She went downstairs again and put the kettle on for tea. She sat at the chipped enameled table at the center of the enormous yellow kitchen (she had not yet unpacked her tablecloths), and as she waited for the water to boil she thought about Wallace Flint.

One look at his quick, dark eyes and you knew he was a man of intelligence and humor. And something else besides. Something painful, like sorrow or desperation. Working together, Catherine and Wallace had laughed a great deal, excited by one another's wit.

She told Hank at supper that it was a stroke of luck, Wallace volunteering to work for nothing more than a meager supply of groceries until they could afford to pay him a wage. Hank's agreement was less than wholehearted. He said Wallace would never be a grocer. She argued in Wallace's behalf: he would help them get acquainted with the villagers. He knew every last person in town, everything about them. Seeing a car go by, he could tell you where it was going and who was driving. Smelling a funny smell, he knew where it came from.

"That's silage," he had explained to her when she inquired about the odor drifting over Main Street. She and Wallace were removing stock from the shelves in preparation for scrubbing and painting.

"What's silage?" she had asked.

"Rotting vegetation—cornstalks and pea vines, for instance. A lot of farmers keep a pile in their yard for feed."

"Feed?"

"Cattle feed."

"It's putrid. It's worse than smelling smoke in the city."

"I agree," Wallace exclaimed. "I'd love to be smelling smoke instead of this rot." He faced out the front window with his hands on his hips. "I despise this town!"

His vehemence cast a temporary cloud over Catherine's hopes. Of all days to be told that Plum was despicable! Coaldust covered everything in the store including the cobwebs. There were rats in the basement. Hank was finding empty wine bottles in the drawers of his desk. Their customers for the day numbered twelve. Their proceeds amounted to $4.36. And as though defying fate, they had gone into debt for new stock, placing an enormous order with a wholesaler named Bob Donaldson from Minneapolis. He had pulled up in front of the store in a 'forty-two Ford, the newest car on Main Street, had spent half an hour in Legget's Grocery and then crossed over to Kermit's. He was a freckled man of about forty-five who smelled of the samples he carried on the road, primarily sage. He was effusive in his greeting. He said he had always believed Plum to be a two-market village waiting for its second good market. He explained that for an order of four hundred dollars or more he would allow Hank and Catherine to delay payment until after their Grand Opening. Hank looked at Catherine, they looked about them at the mess and they decided to shoot the works, sending Bob Donaldson away with a thousand-dollar order.

4

O _N THE SECOND DAY_ of school Dodger was distant. Brendan passed him a note by way of Lorraine Graham. The note said, "Boomerang after school?"

Dodger read it and crumpled it. He didn't look in Brendan's direction. Brendan was grieved. He spent arithmetic period (fractions) totalling up the friends he had left behind in the city. They came to seven. During current events (a new death in Belgium, a new Gold Star Mother in Plum) he tried memorizing the names of his classmates as the teacher called on them. He noticed which ones responded with indifference to his uncertain smile, which ones with a sneer of disdain, and which ones— there were two or three—with smiles of their own.

During noon hour as the others hunched against the misty wind and chose teams for softball, he followed Dodger across the wet sand to the swings and told him there was nothing to fear from the broken window. His father had already replaced the glass.

"No kidding?" Dodger squinted, lifting his lip on his unclean teeth. "Didn't you catch heck or nothing?" He looked doubtful. His own errors had always led to punishment, never pardon.

My dad just said to throw it from out in the field farther. Come back this afternoon and we'll throw it some more." He almost said please.

Dodger examined his face for deceit. Was this a trap? "My dad would have strapped me for breaking that window." Then he added, with relief: "My dad's in prison for taking money from a plumber he used to work for." Then, fearfully: "He had a leather strap he used to use on me." He gazed far off, scowling thoughtfully, and Brendan respectfully gave him a few moments with his memories before asking:

"Will you come over after school?"

Dodger spoke decisively. "Yep, but we'll go to my house first. I've got something for you."

After school they walked along the alley of puddles behind Main Street. "See that door?" said Brendan, pointing. "That's the back room of our store. And this is our car. We drove this morning because it was raining." The boys saw Wallace Flint standing in the doorway, watching them. Brendan waved, but Wallace did not.

"You know Wallace?"

Dodger nodded.

"Doesn't he give you the creeps?"

Dodger shrugged and changed the subject. "See that door over there? That's the back door of Gordy's Pool Hall. And see that door there? That's the fire exit from the theater. Sometimes it's not shut tight and you can get in and see a free movie."

In the next block Dodger said, "Let's look in here," and led Brendan through the back door of a furniture store. The place was gloomy and smelled of cigars. There seemed to be no one minding the store. They zigzagged through the disorderly display of chairs, tables, lamps, and bedsteads and went out the front door. "Sometimes there's a dead body to look at, but not today."

Brendan was horrified. "In there?"

"Yeah, in a coffin."

Brendan read the sign over the door: KIMBALL'S FURNITURE AND FUNERAL HOME.

They walked several blocks and came to the wide, sagging rooming house on Hay Street where Dodger lived with his mother. Its ash-gray paint was peeling. In the entryway were five mailboxes and the smell of fried onions. "Ma?" he called as they climbed the stairs, but his mother wasn't home. He led Brendan into number six and showed him around the three-room apartment. Brendan saw a hot plate and a toilet but no sink or refrigerator or bathtub. He asked where they took baths, where they kept their food cold. They washed in a basin, Dodger explained, and kept their milk on a windowsill overlooking the blacksmith shop across the alley.

In the sitting room, Dodger opened a drawer of the dresser that stood beside his cot and took out a cap gun fresh from the five and dime, a snub-nosed pistol of heavy steel, a wartime rarity. He said Brendan could have it. Brendan took it and admired it. The silvery barrel was untarnished, the crosshatching of the grip pleasingly rough to the palm, the trigger stiff. He had outgrown cap guns, but he said thanks.

Dodger nodded, leaning over him, his hand on his shoulder, admiring it himself. "I'll get you some caps for it tomorrow."

Then they went to Brendan's house and took the boomerang out into the plowed field, where Dodger perfected his delivery. Moving about the classroom and schoolyard, Dodger's insecurity made him ungainly and hesitant, but here in the open his movements were swift and certain, and at least three times out of four he sent the boomerang sailing farther than he had yesterday. "Unnnnn," he sighed each time it left his hand. "Yeaaah," he whispered as it curved into its wide arc and started back. Its return was erratic because of the wind, and as they ran this way and that to retrieve it, the heavy soil built up on their shoes and they had to pause every few minutes to pare it away, using the edge of the boomerang as a blade.

Brendan studied Dodger's style. He was throwing it sidearm, with a vigorous snap of his wrist. Brendan tried that method but was only half successful. Although it sailed a good long way, it didn't come back; at the point where it should have made its midair turn it was already falling to earth.

"Maybe you should try it like a discus," said Dodger, demonstrating how a discus thrower uncoils like a spring before letting go. "You get more power that way."

Good advice. Brendan's next throw climbed high into the wind, turned and came back like a shot and stabbed itself into a hummock of wet earth.

"Who taught you to throw a discus?"

Dodger squinted, trying to remember.

"Your dad?"

It came to him: "No, I saw a guy throw one once in a newsreel."

They threw till their arms ached, and they kept on throwing. They couldn't seem to get enough of watching the boomerang turn in the air. By what miracle did something you cast away come back to you? Fire off anything else in life—a bullet, a tantrum, an insult—and there was no hope of retrieving it; you let it go and hoped it did or didn't hurt somebody. But time after time this crooked stick steered itself around to its starting point and gave Brendan a curious sense of consolation, suggesting that not every law of the universe was immutable, that you *could* rethink your impulses. He chose this afternoon to tell Dodger about certain regrets from his city life, words and actions he wished could be undone. The time he took incense from church and packed it in Grandfather's pipe, causing him to be very sick when he smoked it. The time he went to a friend's birthday party bearing as a gift a tiny toy motorcycle so wonderfully mechanical that he couldn't stand to give it up and stole it back when the party was over and took it home and hid it in his room. The time he bawled and carried on, fearing the move to Plum.

Dodger got the drift. Out and back the boomerang flew as he told Brendan about the day his mother took him to the Winona County Jail to see his father before he was shipped off to prison. "He told me he was being sent up for five years, but he'd be out on parole in less than two, and I said, 'I hope not.' And he wasn't even being mean that day. He was acting pretty nice."

Out and back the boomerang flew. "It was that leather strap I was thinking about."

At dusk Catherine drove home from the store with Grandfather, who was now under close surveillance. Hank followed later on foot. Brendan was called in to supper. Dodger accompanied him up onto the back porch, and when Brendan slipped off his muddy shoes so did Dodger.

"Don't you have to go home?"

Dodger said he didn't. He went into the kitchen and said hello to Brendan's mother and was already sitting down at the table when she invited him to eat with them.

Brendan went to wash his hands and face.

"Are you sure you wouldn't like to wash up before you eat?" she asked Dodger.

He said he was sure he wouldn't. He poked a knife into the honey pot and lifted out a gob.

Hank and Grandfather came to the table. "This is Dodger, Brendan's new friend," she told them.

"Are you one of the Brooklyn Dodgers?" asked Grandfather, taking his place at Dodger's right hand and playfully jabbing him in the ribs.

"No," said Dodger, ticklish, squirming, twirling his knife to sever the trailing string of honey.

Hank sat on Dodger's left and said, "Maybe he's the Artful Dodger from—what was that book, Catherine? You aren't a pickpocket, are you, Dodger?"

Dodger's eyes narrowed. How did this man know?

After the dishes were washed—Grandfather and Brendan drying, Dodger looking on—the Fosters groomed themselves for the priest. That Brendan should wash his face and hands a second time within an hour and change his shirt and comb his hair struck Dodger as ridiculous. Lying on Brendan's bed, he asked, "How come you're going to church at night?"

"We're not. We're just going to the priest's house to register." He took his sixth grade blazer from the closet, hoping Dodger would be impressed with the brass buttons. On the breast pocket was the crest of St. Bonaventure's, where he had been schooled by nuns for six years.

"Register for what?"

"Just register, so the priest knows we're Catholic."

"How come you're Catholic?"

He considered the easy answer—we were born Catholic—but settled on the scholarly one: "The church is one, holy and apostolic." At St. Bonaventure's he had advanced to Book Four of the Catechism.

"It is?"

"Yep."

"Is it true you pray with beads?"

"Yep."

"And tell your sins to a father?"

"Yep."

"And what else?"

"We dip our fingers in holy water." Buttoning his three brass buttons, he led Dodger downstairs.

"I heard you don't eat meat on Friday."

"We don't."

It was a moonless night. Dodger walked with them for a block or so, then angled off toward home. Watching him go, Brendan felt suddenly very grateful for the boomerang instruction. But all he could think to offer Dodger in return was more religious instruction. "And we don't get divorced either," he called after him.

Under a distant streetlight, Dodger turned and considered this for a moment, relieved that his parents hadn't been Catholic and forced to stay together. Then he went on.

"And we don't join the Masons," Brendan shouted.

Approaching the church grounds, the four of them checked their buttons and shifted into a churchly frame of mind, which didn't mean quite the same thing to any two of them. No one was so taken with the outward forms of Catholicism as Brendan was— the rituals, the candles, the Latin. The nuns had put him through a rigorous course of worship. Processions. Chants. Long silent vigils on his knees before the Blessed Sacrament. But what portion of Brendan's piety was devoted to God? Not very much, he realized, and it was God's fault entirely. God was so evasive, so hard to know. Brendan planned to get better acquainted with God when he was older.

Brendan's religion at twelve was strangely ascetic compared to Grandfather's at eighty. Brendan's was meditative. Grandfather's was social. At Mass Grandfather carried on a kind of restrained dialogue with those around him; he smiled, nodded, winked and whispered. Bored with prayers, he might turn and pick lint off the clothes of strangers. He rose to his feet while others were kneeling. One time at the Consecration he had struck a match to light his pipe.

Church for Brendan's mother was a place to evaluate actions—hers, Brendan's, everybody's. Life was a contest between good and evil, the Church was umpire, and Catherine helped God keep score. In a typical week she acquired a full load of moral questions to ask her confessor: Was I wrong in doing this? Was my family right in thinking that? Like her father, she had a long memory, and if there was nothing close at hand to make judgments about, she would reconstruct a problem from the past. Was Cousin Fred justified in leaving his old and irascible parents alone on the farm and going into the Navy even though he had been declared exempt from the draft? Such were the puzzles she presented to the priest, and to her family later at supper, together with the priest's response. Fred, it turned out, *was* justified, given the Navy's need, if not Fred's.

Hank's faith resided in the marrow of his bones. He never spoke of doctrine or morality. He simply accepted whatever the Church asked him to, and he went about his life accordingly. If he was expected at Mass on August 15 every year to commemorate the Blessed Virgin's disappearance from earth, then he would be there dressed up and on time. He believed, of course, being a practical man, that much of what he believed was unbelievable, but this caused him no misgivings because another of his beliefs was that there was more to life than he could understand, more ways of looking at things than the one afforded him by his human and therefore limited sight. Avoid meat on Ember Days and Fridays, decreed his Church, and so he did.

Register with the priest when you move, and that's why he was leading his family up the dark sidewalk to the front door of Holy Angels Rectory.

The house was dark. Hank, having phoned ahead, rang the doorbell. They waited a long time. They turned and looked across the wide lawn at the church. Behind him, Brendan heard Grandfather breathing moistly through his wet pipe. There was a sound beyond the door. An inner door opening. A light coming on under the eaves. A key rattling in a lock. The outer door opening. A dark human shape behind the screen.

Hank said, "We're the Fosters."

"Except me," put in Grandfather. "I'm Michael Mc-Mahon."

The priest's Roman collar caught the light as he unlatched the screen and held it open, but his face remained in shadow.

Catherine was first to step into the glassed-in porch, which despite the dank weather was oppressively warm and smelled of stale sunshine. The priest led them single file across the inner threshhold and down a dim hallway to his office, which was lit by a glaring light in the ceiling.

"Be seated," he said, standing behind his desk. He was old; the creases around his mouth and eyes were as deep as Grandfather's. He was tall—well over six feet—and nearly bald. His collar was tight to his throat and its square of white moved with his Adam's apple when he spoke. "I'll need your names." From a bookcase he drew out an enormous record book with metal corners. He opened it on his desk. He sat. He dipped his pen and looked at them.

Grandfather said, "I'm Michael McMahon, what's your name?"

"Father O'Day."

"*Father* O'Day? Don't you have a first name?"

The priest closed his eyes. Such impertinence. Opening them, he picked a pair of wire-rimmed glasses off the desk. He ran them up and down his shirt-front, cleaning them. He hooked them over his ears. His ears and nose were freckled. His thin fringe of hair, apparently red in his prime, had faded to an ivory-rose. There was aggression in the jut of his jaw. There was ice in his blue eyes.

"Foster, you say?"

Hank said yes.

"It's a rare thing, moving to Plum, bringing your family. I haven't registered five new families since I came here. The parish grows, but the growth is mainly brides from somewhere else marrying our farmers' sons and then having babies." His voice was husky. It didn't rise and fall but scraped along at the same dull pitch. "How does it happen you're not in the war, Foster?"

"I'm too old by a year and a half."

"Were you in the first one?"

"I was too young."

The priest smoothed the open page with a freckled, sinewy hand. "And your first name?"

"Hank."

"You mean Henry?"

"Yes."

The priest clenched his teeth as he wrote.

"Middle name?"

"Richard."

"Where were you born?"

"Minneapolis."

"What do you mean *Henry*?" said Grandfather. "You mean to say your name is Henry?"

"It was to start with."

"You knew that," said Catherine. She was sitting near the priest on the chair drawn up to the side of the desk. The others were on the couch.

"If I did, I forgot, probably on purpose," said her father. "I never cared for that name. I once had a neighbor named Henry, an unfriendly chap. He kept bees. They always came zinging across the yard like they meant to sting you. Sometimes they did."

"Minneapolis," said the priest, writing it. "What's your business in Plum?"

"I bought Kermit's Grocery."

"Where do you live?"

"We're renting from Mrs. Ottmann, her big house."

The priest nodded. "Good woman, Mrs. Ottmann. Hard to say what will become of her son when she dies. He's feeble-minded, you know."

"Yes."

Grandfather cleared his throat. "My uncle Albert's daughter was feeble-minded." He emptied his pipe into an ashtray. "But then, so was his wife." He opened his tobacco pouch. "And so was Uncle Albert, come to think of it."

The priest's stern eyes came to rest on Grandfather, and the look the two old men exchanged reminded Brendan of the classroom diversion known as the staredown. But this was more intensely inquiring, like the look between long-lost enemies, one old Irishman measuring himself against another. Measuring what? Facial erosion? Lifespan? Depth of soul? Father O'Day lowered his eyes; Grandfather won.

"And you, Mrs. Foster."

"I'm Catherine."

"With a 'C,' I assume."

"Yes."

"'K' is an affectation. Middle name?"

"Lynn."

"That's not a saint's name."

"Oh?"

He didn't write it. "Maiden name?"

"McMahon."

He wrote that. "Where were you born?"

"Minneapolis."

This filled the heavy page, which trembled noisily as he turned it.

"When did you get married to Mr. Foster, what year?"

"Nineteen thirty-one."

The priest wrote this, pressing the page flat.

"What's your boy's name?"

Brendan piped up confidently, certain that both his names had belonged to saints: "Brendan Richard, and I was born in Minneapolis."

The pen scratched jerkily across the paper; the characters

were sharp and illegible. Upside down the line looked to Brendan like a stem of thorns.

"Does he serve Mass?" Father O'Day asked this of Hank, a twelve-year-old being too insignificant to consult.

"No."

"I'm short of servers. Send him to me for early Mass on Sunday."

Brendan, shy of the limelight, had been afraid of this. An altar was like a stage.

The priest turned to Grandfather. "What's your name?"

"Michael McMahon. Born in November of 'sixty-four, went with the railroad the spring of 'eighty, married Sadie Crocker June of 'ninety-three, had two daughters, Catherine here and Mae. Mae went into hats, but left the hat business when she married a Navy flier. She lives in Florida and has no children, so the lad here's my only grandchild. His mother had female trouble a few years ago, had the sort of operation that puts a stop to babies."

Catherine blushed.

"I rose as high as conductor once, but I lost that job and went back to brakeman. It might interest you how I lost it."

The priest clapped the book shut, and they all stood.

"Give as much as you can every Sunday," he said, leading them out of the office. "Sunday Masses at eight and ten. Send me the boy at eight. Confessions between two and four on Saturday."

In the hot porch Catherine said, "We're told the Catholics in Plum are at odds with the Protestants." Wallace Flint had said so.

"I've been told that myself. The priest here before me said so."

"Do you find it's true?"

Father O'Day cupped his chin in his hand, meditating. "Mmmmmm, no."

"You're friendly with the Lutheran minister?"

"No, I haven't met him."

"He's new here?"

"No, he was here when I came."

"You're new here?"

"Yes, I've been here only seven years. Go home now, it's late." He unlatched the screen door for them.

Outside, Grandfather turned to speak through the screen. "To make a long story short, I lost my job as conductor because I let my friends ride free. I could have lost all my rights and seniority, but they let me go back to being brakeman. I'm just too damn likable to be treated harshly, is what it amounts to. But I never got the good runs anymore. No way-freights. No passenger runs. Only spurs. Twin Cities to Wells. Twin Cities to River Falls. All the godforsaken places."

The priest latched the screen. "At least your fault was on the side of charity, Mr. McMahon." He switched off the light.

5

$E_{ARLY\ THE\ NEXT\ MORNING}$, working with
Wallace Flint at the produce display, Hank told him about Dodger's visit. Wallace's initial reaction was amusement. "How
incongruous," he said, chuckling, imagining the no-good,
dimwitted son of a jailbird being the Fosters' first dinner guest.

But when Hank went into the back room and left him alone
to pick through the apples, checking for bruises and rot, Wallace
quit chuckling and began to smolder, jealous that Dodger should
be present where he himself wished to be. For two days now
Wallace had been trying with all his might to attach himself to
this family from the city. Picturing himself as Hank and Catherine's indispensable confidant and advisor, he had been waiting
for an invitation to their house. Hank and Catherine, he sensed,
were bleeding hearts, suckers for anyone needy.

In a few minutes the front door opened and Brendan, on his
way to school, stepped in to pick up a pack of gum. Unwrapping
a stick, he said hello to Wallace, who had found a bad apple and
was holding it daintily by the stem.

"I have some advice for you," said Wallace, smirking, dropping the apple into the box at his feet. His glistening eyes were penetrating.

"Yeah?" Brendan stood in the open doorway, ready to run. The school bell was ringing, and he had three minutes to be present in his homeroom desk.

"If you know what's good for you, you'll quit hanging around with Dodger Hicks."

Brendan bristled, sensing that Wallace seldom had an idea that wasn't self-serving.

"If you want to fit into the seventh grade, you can't start out by having Dodger Hicks over to dinner. Hang around with Hicks and nobody else will come near you."

Brendan replied defiantly, "What do you know about it?" and he ran off to school. Being uncivil to Wallace made him feel good. Wallace asked for it with his superior tone, his smug expression. What did Wallace know?

Perhaps quite a lot, he decided later in the morning as he studied the cliques of the seventh grade. The more thought he gave it, the clearer it became that in order to be accepted by his more glamorous classmates he would have to put distance between himself and Dodger.

During noon hour Brendan and Dodger sat suspended on adjacent swings watching a softball game. Sam Romberg punched a single into centerfield, Philip Crowley scored from third and Pearl Peterson and Lorraine Graham jumped up and down and cheered, Pearl holding her carefully curled hair in place. These four made up the inner circle of the seventh grade. Pearl Peterson used lipstick and got nothing but A's. Lorraine Graham carried cigarettes in her purse and had what the music teacher called perfect pitch. Philip Crowley was said by the girls to be cute; his father owned the movie theater. Sam Romberg wore a self-confident expression beyond his years, he excelled at athletics. Brendan sensed that these four, while holding him at bay, were keeping an eye on him, watching to see if he could somehow unlock their trust.

The key, it occurred to him, was his boomerang. Having fascinated Dodger, wouldn't it fascinate others as well? Maybe not Pearl and Lorraine, but surely Philip and Sam? With twenty minutes remaining of the noon hour he ran home for the second time and returned with the boomerang. He carried it across the softball diamond, interrupting the game and for the first time in his life purposely drawing attention to himself. He ran down the long grassy slope to the high school football field. Dodger left the swings and came loping after him. Brendan paused under the goalpost and made sure Sam and Philip and the rest of the boys were watching, and then he unleashed what he hoped would be his mightiest throw. Alas, it was one of his worst. In his eagerness he had forgotten to snap his wrist as Dodger had taught him and the boomerang flew scarcely forty yards before falling to the ground like a stick of firewood. He ran to retrieve it, but was outrun by Dodger, who in a single motion of great beauty, like a dancer's, snatched the boomerang off the grass and sent it flying sixty yards at least; sent it out over the far goalpost, out over the edge of the hayfield beyond, and then—a magic moment—he stretched forth his arms and beckoned and the boomerang turned and came back and glided to rest at his feet. A multitude came rushing down the slope. They scuffled for turns. Dodger and Brendan stood aside, watching them experiment with various deliveries. Although the boomerang did now and then return, no one's throw was nearly so grand as Dodger's. The next best throw was Brendan's when he finally stepped in and threw it forty yards out and forty yards back. Everyone cheered. They devised a system for taking turns, Dodger excluded, and they followed the boomerang off the football field and through the standing hay and by the time the schoolbell rang they were clustered in a field of oat-stubble.

Brendan returned to the schoolyard surrounded by new friends. They made a chant of his name. They clapped him on the back. They asked him where he came from and why. From Minneapolis, he said, and that was impressive. Kermit's Grocery, he said, and they made faces. No brothers or sisters, he said, and they thought that very odd. An uncle in the war, he said, and that made up for a lot. He caught glimpses of Dodger at the edge of this crowd, slouching along with a faint smile on his lips, thinking perhaps that by his skill with the boomerang he had won acceptance along with his only friend; but of course he had won nothing of the kind, and Brendan knew it if Dodger didn't.

The extent of Brendan's treachery wasn't clear to Dodger until after school when he began to follow Brendan home and was turned back. Standing under the elm near the swings, Brendan said, "We can't be friends any more."

"We can't? Why not?"

"Because." He chose not to accuse him of being a weight on his rising fortunes. "Just because."

"Because why?" The "why" was drawn out, a whine.

"Because my folks said so." Brendan averted his eyes, avoiding Dodger's squint. Brendan wasn't good at lying.

But good enough, apparently, to convince Dodger, for whom this rejection was nothing new. "Who cares?" he said, walking away from the swings and out of Brendan's life with the same surprising swiftness and grace with which he had mastered the boomerang.

6

W<small>ITH PAINT AND SOAP</small> and the help of Wallace Flint, Hank and Catherine gradually overcame the grime and gloom of Kermit's Grocery. They scoured and oiled the wooden floor and improved the lighting. They whitewashed and stocked the shelves and above the shelving they painted the walls tan and the high ceiling white. They acquired two cats, a gray and a yellow, to hunt in the basement. With a razor blade Hank peeled Kermit's name from the front window and hired a signpainter to letter his own: HANK'S MARKET.

A round, bald man named Stan Kimball, who came in every day to buy six cigars, became the Fosters' self-appointed mentor. Stan Kimball was Plum's undertaker and furniture merchant. Averaging only two funerals a month, he spent his days popping in and out of stores, inquiring into each proprietor's personal life as well as his business methods. He left his furniture display room unattended for hours at a time; if you wanted to buy furniture you tracked him down. It was usually late morning when he showed up at the market, lit a cigar, and let flow a stream of gossip and economic advice.

"You'll want to put on a big Grand Opening sale," he insisted. "You'll want to flood this town with circulars offering prices these tightwads can't resist. Ask your wholesaler to try and get you a shipment of something there's a shortage of—candy or coffee or detergent—and hold a drawing every hour and give it away like dirt. You'll have customers coming in here like pigs to a trough."

Although Stan Kimball had a few unclean habits which kept Catherine from being as fond of him as Hank was (his talk was peppered with vulgarities and he drooled juice from his spongy, malodorous cigars), she found his frankness disarming:

"This town will support your store just fine, once you get established, don't worry about that, but if you've got social aspirations, don't get your hopes up. There's two kinds of people living in Plum, the newcomers and the native born. My wife and I have been here seventeen years and we're still outsiders—except my wife's one close friend happens to be the mayor's wife, which makes Plum heaven on earth in my wife's opinion, never mind that the mayor's wife is a baboon."

Catherine was the first to sense that Stan Kimball did not care for Wallace Flint. She saw his eyes grow wary whenever they fell on Wallace. Before long she realized that Wallace was about the only person in town that Kimball didn't talk about behind his back. Only once did he bring up Wallace when Wallace wasn't present; Grand Opening was drawing near and Kimball was conducting an inspection tour:

"Your produce looks a little shopworn, Hank. Don't you refrigerate it overnight?"

"I can only cram so much in the compartments under the meat cooler."

"Then you'll have to build a walk-in cooler. There's space for one in the back room."

Hank nodded. "Someday, I suppose."

"Not someday. Do it soon. You'll get a jump on your competition across the street. Legget's never been known for good produce."

"Where would I get the money?"

"You could get rid of your clerk and save his wages."

"Wouldn't help much. Wallace works for next to nothing."
"That's more than he's worth."

One of Wallace's favorite topics was religion, especially Catherine's, which he teased her about. "You Christians have this ridiculous system of putting everything in categories. The Ten Commandments. The Seven Deadly Sins."

"Categories make sense out of things," Catherine replied.

"The Six Corporal Works of Mercy," he said. "Or is it five?"

Brendan was present for this exchange. Coming from school, he had found his parents and Wallace in the back room, Catherine brewing coffee on a hotplate, Hank sorting through window posters he had found in the basement, most of them still tightly curled in their mailing tubes, bargains from Kermit's Grand Opening of several years before and never displayed by Kermit.

"I've seen the Catholic Catechism." Wallace went on. " 'Who made me? God made me.' 'What are the two kinds of ignorance? The two kinds of ignorance are vincible and invincible.' " His smile was crooked and supercilious, and Brendan hated him for it. "You can't say there are two kinds of ignorance, Catherine, like two kinds of sugar—white and brown."

"Of course you can," she said brightly, pleased to have found a villager with a philosophical turn of mind. She handed him a cup of coffee. "Think of it like the night sky, Wallace. The Big Dipper. It's nothing but a few unrelated stars until somebody sees the pattern and gives it a name. Seeing the pattern in stars is like seeing the pattern in human actions."

She looked to Hank for corroboration, but Hank only smiled, content to let her handle faith and morals because she did it so well, leaving him free for other things.

"When you group stars and give them names, they're easier to understand," she continued. "Does anybody in this town even look at the stars?"

"I do," said Wallace.

"I do," said Brendan, competing.

"And your categories of life after death, Catherine. Hell and limbo and purgatory and heaven. They're straight out of fairy tales.''

She turned her back on him, pouring coffee for Hank.

"Do Lutherans go to heaven, Catherine?" Wallace asked.

"I don't know who's in heaven and who isn't. God knows.''

"But you must have a theory about it. You've got a theory about everything else. Hank, what do you think?''

"About what?'' Hank was rerolling posters, taking out the curl.

"Can a Lutheran go to heaven?''

"It's fine with me.''

They fell silent for a few moments. Catherine sat down on an apple box and blew on her coffee. She had spent most of the day peeling old paint from the wall behind the meat case. She wore an old blue smock, patched and faded. On her head she had tied a blue kerchief. In her forlock Brendan noticed for the first time a glint of gray.

"And what about atheists like me, Catherine? I suppose my goose is already cooked.''

"Nobody knows who's in hell Wallace. God knows.''

"What does God know? Does God know there's so much religious hate in this town that nobody deserves to be saved? Holy Angels Catholic and Emmanual Lutheran—they compete for places on the village council and the school board and they bury their dead on opposite sides of the cemetery.''

Another silence. His expression changed from sardonic to sour to hostile. "I'll tell you who's in hell, Catherine. We all are. Because Plum is hell.''

7

"*DID YOU NOTICE, LAD*, that poor wretch has done nothing since Labor Day but stare out the window of that crackerbox of a house over there?"

It was a scorching afternoon. Grandfather and Brendan had moved out onto the front porch for a breath of air. Brendan, sitting on the steps, was applying postage stamps to a stack of Grand Opening circulars, which would go out tomorrow on the rural-delivery routes. Stacked in the kitchen were four hundred additional circulars to be distributed door to door through the village. Brendan and Wallace would do that tomorrow after school. The three-day Grand Opening was to begin the following day.

"Hell of a way to spend your life, staring out a window like that."

Grandfather, just up from his nap, sat in his shirt and tie, smoking, perspiring and concentrating on the face across the street. He felt a strong need for diversion. Ever since boarding the train for Pinburg, he had been forbidden to leave the house on his own. Most days after his nap, Catherine accompanied him downtown, where he gave the market a brief inspection and then went next door to Gordy's Pool Hall and sat through the late afternoon under Gordy's watchful eye, nursing a beer and visiting with the other idlers; but today Catherine was too busy to pick him up and Brendan had come straight home from school to make sure he didn't wander. Sickening, thought Grandfather, to be a prisoner in your own house. Depressing to be put in the care of a twelve-year-old. No fault of the lad, of course. He was a fine young lad and the only grandchild but he never had much to say. Too much like his father in that regard—a listener, not a talker. And no great shakes as a listener, come to think of it. Ah, well, just so the war ended before the lad came of age and he grew up happy and healthy and found himself a pretty lass to carry on the good Irish line and didn't get her with child before the wedding.

"What did you tell me is the matter with that poor wretch?"

Brendan, tearing a sheet of stamps into strips, explained, "He's a moron."

"How do you know?"

"Everybody says so. Father O'Day says so."

"Father O'Day, now there is a case for you. A man off in his own world somewhere. The only time he speaks to you is from the pulpit, and then it's endless sermons you can't make heads or tails of. How would a man like that know a moron from a motorcycle?"

"You've seen Rufus in the store, haven't you, standing there like a moron?"

In order to go about her shopping unencumbered by Rufus, who couldn't turn a corner without being steered, Mrs. Ottmann sometimes deposited him in Gordy's Pool Hall or in Hank's Market. She would look in at the pool hall first because there Rufus could sit on one of the chairs near the card table, as Grandfather did, but if her card-playing son Orville was not there she would lead Rufus next door to the grocery store and place him in the care of Hank and Catherine.

Not that Rufus needed care. He was content to stand endlessly at the full-length window of the front door, looking out as though enchanted, his hands clasped behind him, his eyes directed vaguely at the people who passed on the street, his face locked in its customary grin. When someone entered or left the store, Rufus shuffled backward and allowed himself to be pressed for a moment between the plate glass in front of him and the glass-ine doors of the cookie display behind him. Then as the door went shut he shuffled forward, keeping his nose about six inches from the glass. Brendan noticed that most of the customers ignored Rufus as they entered the store—perhaps in a village as small as Plum the ordinary population didn't outnumber the odd by enough to make the latter seem rare—while a few gave him a fleeting smile.

Brendan wished he could do one or the other, ignore Rufus or smile at him, but he could do neither. When as an exercise in good will he tried smiling at Rufus through the plate glass, he found that he couldn't force himself to look upon the horrible hollowness of those eyes for more than a split second; and conversely when he tried to put Rufus out of his mind, he couldn't shake the haunting sense of his presence until Mrs. Ottmann came and took him away. Movies set in the desert or on the polar icecap triggered a similar vague terror in Brendan, a fear of any vast emptiness.

A week ago his aversion to Rufus had led Brendan to commit what the nuns at St. Bonaventure's would have called a shameful sin of omission. It had been very warm, like today. Brendan had propped open the front door of the market for a breath of air and Rufus, apparently thinking it was his sign to leave, went walking off down the street. Brendan saw his duty, but he couldn't do it. The very thought of running after Rufus and taking his hand and bringing him back made Brendan shudder. So he continued stocking shelves, assuring himself that when you were only twelve you weren't expected to be your brother's keeper, particularly if your brother was an imbecile going on forty. After a half hour of trying not to imagine Rufus stepping in front of a speeding car, he decided he'd better tell his father, nonchalantly, that he noticed Rufus was gone. But before he said anything, Stan Kimball showed up leading Rufus by the hand. Stan had found him sleeping on a mattress in his display window.

"You can never be sure about morons," said Grandfather, perspiring on the porch. "Some of them play the dolt for money. I've known of cases."

Brendan paused in his work, holding a strip of stamps over the moist sponge in the saucer. He had stamped two hundred circulars, and had a hundred to go. "What do you mean?"

"I mean they aren't always as dumb as they look." Grandfather pressed his thumb on the hot coals of his pipe, a habit which had long ago burned the pad of his thumb nerveless. "I'd like to take the measure of that boy's thickness. He might be playing the dolt for money. My cousin Albert was a case like that. Albert was no great shakes as a thinker but he was nowhere near as dense as the woman he married. Flo was her name. Flo was so dumb she didn't know if Christ was crucified or shot by the Indians. They had a daughter. Flo was the daughter's name, too. She was dumber than her father and mother put together, and she had to be taken away and put in an asylum for the feeble-minded."

An old story. Brendan went back to his circulars.

"Well, it so happened that Albert and his wife would go and visit their daughter at the asylum and eat a meal with her now and then, and they couldn't get over how good the food was. So pretty soon Flo the mother started to get dumber and dumber, if such a thing was possible, until she herself was put in the asylum. I knew, if nobody else did, that she was aiming to be taken care of by the State so she could get in on all that good food. See, lad, she was playing the dolt for money. Then wouldn't you know, when she and her daughter had been living in the asylum for a while, Albert himself went sort of mental. One day in December he started up his tractor and tried planting himself ten acres of corn in a field covered with snow. And you know why?"

"He wanted to live in the asylum, too."

"Right you are, lad, right as rain. But he wasn't playing the dolt for money, you see. Poor Albert was playing the dolt for companionship—he was lonesome as hell. But it didn't pan out the way he wanted. The State never took him in. He lived out his life on that farm, getting by."

Grandfather was silent for a long time, then he stood up, laid aside his pipe and straightened his tie. "Come along, we'll go over there and take the measure of that boy's thickness. Bring one of your handbills."

Brendan shuddered at the thought of being enclosed with Rufus in his tiny house.

"I can't, I've got all these stacks to do before supper."

"Then I'll go myself." He picked up an unstamped circular. "I'll be back shortly."

Rufus Ottmann, seeing Grandfather approach the house, broadened his grin. Grandfather nodded at him curtly as he passed in front of the window and stepped up to the screen door, which was latched. He stood back and made beckoning motions with the circular, but Rufus remained in his chair by the window, grinning. Grandfather went over to the window and said through the glass, "Get your mother," but Rufus stayed put. Grandfather pressed his face to the glass, trying to see deeper into the house, and he rapped on the window frame. At this, Rufus rose from his chair and pressed his face to the inside of the glass, centering his nose on Grandfather's. His smile was gay and toothless, his nostrils cavernous and hairy. As Grandfather moved from side to side to see around him, he could hear Rufus's throaty noises of delight as he, too, moved from side to side to block the view.

Mrs. Ottmann appeared behind her son, looking pleased, as though she and Rufus had been hoping for just such a playmate as Grandfather. She unlocked the screen and stood in the doorway with a dust mop in her hand. "What is it, Mr. McMahon?"

"It's the Grand Opening of Hank and Catherine's store, my dear woman, and they've got more bargains than this one-horse town deserves. Here, see for yourself if they aren't giving you a ring of bologna for nineteen cents, two cents below cost."

She reached for the circular, but he withheld it. It was his ticket indoors.

"Do you mind if I come in out of the heat for a minute? I've been wanting to meet your son."

Now she looked skeptical instead of pleased. Her face didn't say welcome. She was thinking of the old gentleman's train ride of three weeks ago, how quirky he could be.

"Coarse ground or fine, take your pick, nineteen cents a ring. This handbill is full of bargains and nobody else in town has seen it yet. You're the first."

A frugal woman, she couldn't resist a man whose talk was so full of reasonable bologna. "Come in." She held open the door. "You can have a snack with Rufus."

In the tiny front room she directed him to sit on a chair facing Rufus across a little table. Rufus resumed his accustomed place, a rocker with high wooden arms and a leather seat and back. On her way to the kitchen, Mrs. Ottmann said, "Will you take a cracker with your milk?"

"I will indeed," said Grandfather, "and thank you so very much."

In a minute she was back with a tray, which she set on the table. Rufus's milk was in a heavy unspillable mug, Grandfather's in a small glass, half-filled. On a plate were four saltine crackers.

"Mr. McMahon, what's your Christian name, if I may ask?" She stood beside Rufus's rocker.

"Indeed, why shouldn't you ask? My Christian name is Michael, after the archangel who protects us against the malice and snares of the devil."

"Rufus, this is Michael."

Arduously gumming a small bite of cracker, Rufus moved his wide jaw like a horse, his cheek muscles bulging, his eyes clamped on Grandfather, who had been so much fun at the window. Grandfather could see the family resemblance. The old woman had the wide nostrils and deep eyes of her son, but not his coarseness. She looked refined. She had once been pretty.

He felt the Ottmanns waiting for him to speak. He said, "I can see he's a true idiot."

She was outraged: "I beg your pardon!"

"No playacting in that boy, he's dense as a rock."

"He's not dense, Mr. McMahon."

"Not?"

"No."

"The priest says."

"Never mind the priest, Rufus is not dense."

"What is he then?"

"Happy."

Grandfather leaned forward. "How long has he been happy like this?"

"He was born happy."

"Does he talk?"

"Of course. Rufus, say hello to Michael."

There was a quick shift in Rufus's eyes as though a thought had flickered behind them and vanished. The smile remained.

"How old is he?"

"Five."

"Go on."

"He's been five for over thirty years. It's what he wants. He's decided he's very happy to be five."

Grandfather nibbled his cracker. He said, "Do you have any ice cream?"

"No."

"Vanilla's sixteen cents a pint at Hank's Market." He opened the circular to show her. He read on: fruit, cereal, spices, flour. He folded the circular and handed it to Mrs. Ottmann. He stood up and said, "Thank you very much for your hospitality."

"You haven't finished your milk."

He patted her hand. "The cracker was very filling, thank you indeed."

"Will you come again and be company for Rufus?"

"Well . . ." Grandfather was rarely stumped for an answer.

"Do you like celery soup? I'm making celery soup today."

"I can smell it."

"Do you like celery soup?"

"When it's creamy. Is it creamy?"

"I can make it creamy."

"Make it creamy, Mrs. Ottman, and I'll come and have a bowl."

"Rufus would be pleased." She followed him to the door. "He has no playmates, you see. Five-year-olds are ideal but they grow to be six and seven and then they make fun of him.

And most of the old men at the poor farm are no better. We take cookies out to the poor farm, where we once found an old man slipping back to the age of five and Rufus struck up a great friendship with him, but the next time we went out they didn't get along at all because the old man couldn't stay five. Old men keep slipping back to four and three and set bad examples for Rufus. When they're four and three they sometimes muss themselves.''

"Goodbye, Mrs. Ottmann, thanks a million for the snack.''

As he crossed the street, it flashed into Grandfather's mind that the more circulars he could snitch from Brendan the more households he might investigate in this odd little town. He climbed the steps onto the porch and sank into his chair. He slowly filled his pipe, lit it and puffed.

"Well?'' said Brendan.

"Hundred percent.''

8

*A*FTER SCHOOL THE NEXT day, Brendan went out with Wallace Flint to cover the village with circulars.

"That's the McDowell house you've just been to," Wallace called from his side of the street. "Next is the Newlanders'. Over here I've got the Lingles coming up next, and then the Underwoods." Thus Brendan learned to associate the surnames of Plum not with faces, but with front doors, front porches, and dogs. Youngren, Simpson, Howell—screen door, glass door, blistered wooden door. Sandberg, O'Brien—poodle, collie.

At several houses they were met by women tending their doorways like sentries, expecting the paperboy with the *Rochester Post Bulletin* and surprised that they should be handed a red and black circular:

GRAND OPENING
HANK'S MARKET
FORMERLY KERMIT'S GROCERY
THURSDAY, FRIDAY, SATURDAY

ALL FRESH STOCK
DRAWING EACH HOUR FOR FREE MERCHANDISE

Wallace was struck by the great interest these housewives showed in the bargains. Having worked nearly three weeks with Catherine and Hank, Wallace shared their pride in the refurbished store, but he never for a minute believed that their Grand Opening would be anything but a flop. In Wallace's experience, aspiration came to nothing. Success, on those rare occasions when it seemed to exist, was merely a prelude to failure. Hadn't Wallace's own success as a straight-A student in high school led to his dead-end life as a grocery clerk? Hadn't his teenage dreams of living in a city and moving in a circle of smart, sardonic friends vanished at graduation? Now at twenty-five he still half-regretted not enrolling in the state college in Winona when he'd had the chance. His high school teachers, speaking of scholarships, had encouraged him to do so, but he was terrified at the prospect of having seizures among strangers and was relieved when his mother had stepped in and made plain to the teachers (as for years she had made plain to Wallace) that for an epileptic there was no place like home.

Hank's Market, then, would fail because hopes were invariably dashed, and it would fail for other, more practical reasons. Hank's inexperience was appalling. Hank had never so much as candled an egg until Wallace showed him how. Hank didn't know debits from credits until Stan Kimball the undertaker spent an entire afternoon with him, setting up his books. Catherine's flaw was her city background. Talk to her five minutes and you knew she'd never last in Plum. As a misfit she would eventually implore her husband to move away, and with the store floundering they would have no reason to stay.

Brendan, approaching the gray rooming house on Hay Street, was tempted to leave a handful of circulars inside the front door rather than risk meeting Dodger in the doorway of his apartment. For nearly three weeks he had been avoiding Dodger in school, taking care that they shouldn't come face to face. While Dodger never approached him, he glanced at him a hundred times a day. Even looking the other way, Brendan felt the glances, and they made his face prickle with shame.

He pushed open the door. Cooking smells mingled in the entryway. He looked up the stairs. Seeing the door to number six closed, he decided he'd be safe dropping a circular at each doormat, four downstairs, four up. When he reached number six at the head of the stairs the door opened and Dodger, smiling, said, "Hi, did you come for your caps?"

"No, I'm delivering these." He handed Dodger a circular.

"The dime store's out of caps. A shortage because of the war."

"That's okay, I can wait." He hurried down the steps.

"Is there other stuff I can get you instead?"

"No, that's okay, Dodger. So long."

"How about marbles? I seen you guys playing marbles in the lumber yard."

"No, thanks."

Brendan slipped out the door. Caps. Marbles. Was it Dodger's purpose to pile more shame on him than he already felt?

Wallace stood out in front, having crossed the street while Brendan was inside. "It's time for us to change sides again," he told him.

"How come we're always changing," Brendan asked, obediently heading for the other side.

"Because the sun isn't good for my skin. This side's got more shade."

Wallace, whose dark, bearded face was unaffected by sunlight, was setting Brendan up for dogs. Until this afternoon Wallace had not realized how intensely he despised Brendan. He felt a thrill of satisfaction each time Brendan was set upon, particularly by the larger dogs that nearly knocked him to the ground. It was a hatred born of jealousy. Brendan had everything that Wallace at that age had been denied. Perfect health. A living, breathing father. A witty, attractive mother. In the next block, on Brendan's side, lived an irritable black Lab and a slobbering Saint Bernard.

Meanwhile the market stood ready. After three weeks of toil there was little to do but wait for the Opening tomorrow. Catherine, staring out the front window, sensed Hank's anxiety. All day he had been busying himself with small, unnecessary chores while speaking scarcely a word. At this moment, he was kneeling behind the meat case, tinkering with the refrigeration motor, trying to make it run more quietly. Catherine was annoyed by his reticence. She needed to talk. To dissipate her nervous energy, she had spent the afternoon dusting shelves—or rather interrupting her dusting to run errands. She had gone home and driven Grandfather downtown, she had gone to the post office for the afternoon mail, she had gone to the drugstore to buy a birthday card for her sister Mae. Now it was four-thirty, the dusting was done, all errands were run, and very little of her energy was expended. As she gazed at the storefronts across the street, she felt an acute longing for her sister.

They had not been especially fond of one another as girls— Mae was eight years younger than Catherine—but as adults they had become great friends. Their afternoons together in downtown Minneapolis became a weekly ritual; after shopping and seeing a movie they squandered an hour or more over ice cream at Cellini's on Hennepin Avenue. That was before Mae married Howard and went with him to Pensacola, Florida, where she now remained, clerking in the PX at the naval air station while awaiting his return from the North Atlantic. Catherine recalled their last afternoon together and how they had splurged. Mae needed a skirt and blouse for traveling; Catherine was looking for a scarf and shoes. When Mae found the skirt and blouse she wanted, Catherine bought a skirt and blouse just like it; then Catherine bought tan, open-toed shoes and a paisley scarf, and so—impulsively—did Mae. The sisters had never before worn identical outfits, but they did so on the day of Mae and Howard's departure; and walking along the platform beside the train, they shed identical tears.

It occurred to Catherine as she stood in the store window fidgeting with the buttons of the blouse that matched Mae's, that throughout her life she had had two friends at a time, never more, never fewer. Through high school and beyond, her two close friends had been Loretta and Patsy. When Loretta got married in her mid-twenties and moved away, Mae took her place in Catherine's heart. Patsy in due course was displaced by

Hank. Who would replace Mae? For a long time Catherine had supposed that her sister would return at war's end and fill the void she had left, but now she didn't think so. The move to Plum wasn't the only reason. They had been separated for two years and their letters were growing lifeless, perfunctory. Although they continued to write often, they couldn't get down on paper anything like the happy, headlong discussions they used to have over ice cream at Cellini's. Furthermore, there was a sour tone in Mae's recent writing that Catherine didn't care for, a veiled resentment that Hank, who, being too old for the draft by a little more than a year, hadn't enlisted anyhow.

She picked up her feather duster and made another circuit of the store without finding a particle of dust on any shelf or can. She hung the duster on its nail in the back room and said to Hank, "I'll be back in a few minutes."

"Where to now?" he asked, his head in the meat case.

"The public library."

"Fine. Take your time."

She stepped out the front door into the warm, hazy sunshine of late September. Plum's main street was perfectly silent, perfectly still. Three old men sat on the bench in front of the post office. Two were staring at her. The other was asleep. Above them the Stars and Stripes hung limp.

Passing the pool hall, she glanced inside, expecting to see her father sitting under his column of pipe smoke, but he was gone from his customary chair. She went in and stood at the bar, waiting for Gordy to come out from the enclosure that served as his short-order kitchen. Looking out of the corner of her eye at the cardplayers, she saw them directing guarded glances her way, heard them muttering. She and Hank had been coming in here for coffee almost daily, and as the only woman among Gordy's clientele she never entered the door that the men didn't fall silent and scowl. They regarded her as a desecration, she knew. There were certain words you couldn't utter with a woman in the place. Certain directions you couldn't spit.

Gordy, however, made her feel welcome. Turning from his fry table and peering over his swinging doors, he said, "Just a sec, Mrs. Foster." Gordy was a large, soft man, gentle, passive, maybe a little simple-minded. He had a dimpled face and bushy eyebrows. He said things to Catherine he couldn't say to men. He had told her one day that when he attended Emmanuel Lutheran and heard Pastor Dimmitburg read from scripture about the lion and lamb lying down together, he got a warm feeling and thought of his pool hall because this was one of the few places in town where Protestants and Catholics mixed with each other. Catherine's reply to this had become their private joke: "The Peaceable Kingdom Pool Hall," she would say, and Gordy would quiver with laughter.

He stepped out of the kitchen wearing a long, soiled apron tied high under the armpits. "What'll it be, Mrs. Foster? Anything with your coffee?"

"No coffee, thanks. Has my father gone out?"

"Gone to the toilet."

"You're sure?"

"I saw him go in." Gordy pointed to a door at the back of the room, beyond the pool tables. He was a little hurt that she should suspect him of negligence.

"I thought he might have gone out. He sometimes wanders, you know."

"Look, Mrs. Foster, settle your mind about that. I keep watch. And so what if he wanders? It's a small town."

"But he'll go from place to place and forget how he got there. In the city we used to get phone calls from bus drivers and policemen."

"That's because the city's got too many places." Gordy's laugh, like a child's, had a gurgle in it. "Here, the whole town is only one place."

She left the pool hall and continued along the street toward the village hall, in which the public library was situated. More than once Wallace, with a smirk, had urged Catherine to visit the library. "Why are you giving me that look?" she had asked him, but he ignored the question, insisting that if she loved books as much as she claimed she must get herself a library card without delay and take advantage of the holdings. "After Grand Opening I'll have more time," she told him, concealing her main reason for putting it off, which was her need to believe that somewhere in this village a pleasant discovery awaited her. All her life she'd found pleasure in books, not only in reading them but also in their physical presence. She had clerked in books at Dayton's. She had loved smelling them, handling them and regulating the heat and humidity for them. She was counting on Plum's library to help dispel her longing for Minneapolis, which was growing more intense by the day. She yearned for the sound of streetcars in the night, the clink of milk bottles on the stoop at dawn. Most of all, she missed the anonymity of the city. Step into the Plum Five and Dime and the clerks turned and looked at you like a freak. Try to strike up a conversation with the druggist or the postmaster and all they wanted to talk about were the weather and crops. Was she doomed for the rest of her life to dwell on bushels per acre and rain by the inch? What in the world was alfalfa? Paging through a magazine at the drugstore this afternoon, she had come across a series of photos of an abandoned movie set, street scenes shot from behind the flimsy facades, and with every page her heart had grown heavier. It was a stunning display of nullity and it stood, in her heart, for Plum.

Passing the barbershop, she would have collided with Stan Kimball as he came out of the door if he hadn't nimbly side-stepped her; for a squat, heavy man he was quick on his feet. He smiled and said, "Excuse me, Mrs. Foster."

"My fault entirely, I was a thousand miles away."

"More likely a hundred." He was well aware that Catherine's heart had not followed her to Plum. There were very few secrets in this town that Stan Kimball didn't know. "Where are you going? I'll walk with you if you don't mind."

"To the library. Please do."

Before they proceeded, Kimball took a cigar from his breast pocket, unwrapped it, licked it and lit it, sucking and puffing so deeply that Catherine had to move upwind from the smoke cloud. As they walked, he repeatedly ran a hand over his scalp, front to back, as though smoothing hair he didn't have. His baldness was not the gleaming sort; his scalp was bumpy, with discolored splotches.

"My wife and the mayor's wife like to take credit for our

public library. They make up two thirds of the board. Between you and me it's a very rotten library.''

She laughed. "What's rotten about it?"

"I'll let you see for yourself. Fortunately, from now on you won't have time for reading books. Tomorrow you're going to be swamped with shoppers.''

"Could you be wrong? I'm almost afraid for tomorrow to come.''

"Nonsense. It's been years since this town has been hit with a good, big grocery promotion. Already I hear people talking about your ad in the *Alert*. There's been a shortage of detergent and Jell-O and coffee ever since the war started, and they can't believe you have all that stuff in stock, much less at sale prices.''

"Hank is hoping to average three hundred dollars a day for the three days.''

"That's peanuts! A thousand a day is more like it.''

"You're dreaming, surely.''

"Wait and see.''

They came to the village hall, a cube of brown brick set between the bank and the Standard station. Stan Kimball sprang onto the step and held the door open for her. "I'd accompany you further, Mrs. Foster, but it would destroy my image as Plum's leading illiterate. As I tell my wife, I haven't read a book since the Bible I burned as a teenager. Goodbye, and be prepared for a land-office business tomorrow.'' He shut her inside.

Despite the summery weather the furnace in the basement was producing heat; she felt waves of forced air rushing up from the vents along the dark hallway. On her right was a door with "Constable" lettered on the frosted glass. This, according to Wallace, was Constable Heffernand, a disabled veteran from World War One who spent most of his on-duty hours putting together model airplanes because he had little else to do—crime was unheard of in Plum. The village ordinance assigned only one official task to the constable: the stopping of traffic to let funeral processions go by.

On Catherine's left, a door marked "Mayor" stood ajar. Inside she saw a man in his shirtsleeves studying a ledger. This would be Harlan Brask, whose illegal conflict of interest (said

Wallace) was both well-known and condoned. Wallace claimed that besides his municipal duties Mayor Brask carried on his private insurance business from this desk, seeing to it that all village property was overinsured—the road grader, the dump truck, the sewage plant, the village hall, the lives and health of all village employees, the drums and horns of a village band long defunct—and thus his most lucrative premiums came from the village treasury.

Facing her at the end of the hallway was a third door.

LIBRARY
Wipe Your Feet

It was locked. She retraced her steps and put her head in at the mayor's office.

"Excuse me."

The mayor, a gray-haired, gray-faced man in a starched shirt, raised his head from his bookwork, removed his glasses, and peered at her with ice-blue eyes.

"Will the library be open this afternoon?"

He shook his head.

"Tomorrow?"

"Saturday," he said, putting on his glasses and lowering his nose to his ledger.

As she backed into the hallway, chilled, the constable's door opened behind her and a tall, middle-aged man leaned out with a smile. "Hello, I'm the constable. Can I help you?" His back was severely bent—injury to the spine in World War One, according to Wallace. Offering Catherine his hand (knobby, arthritic knuckles, razor-nicked fingers) he said, "I'm Charles Heffernand, and you're the grocer's wife. My sister Melva pointed you out in church."

"Catherine Foster. And I'm also the grocer's partner."

"Are you interested in aeroplanes? Step in and take a gander at my Japanese Zero."

She went in. The upper half of his high-ceilinged office was thick with model airplanes hanging on strings. A long table was covered with blueprints and planes in various stages of construc-

tion. Taped to the walls were newspaper photos of planes and
their pilots. On his desk she saw tiny bits of wood he had been
shaving with a razor blade.

"Ever since Pearl Harbor I've been building Jap and German
aeroplanes and setting them afire. Bombers, transports, fight-
ers. It gives home-front morale a big boost. Here's my Zero.
There's this rubber band attached to the propeller so it actually
flies—see it here? When it's finished I'll put a notice in the paper
and at the appointed time I'll take her up on the roof of the
village hall and turn the propeller tight and set a match to the
wing and let her go. She'll zip out over the street trailing smoke
and flames and crash like the planes in the newsreels. You'll
want to see it, Mrs. Foster. There's always a good crowd. I do
it during noon hour so the school children don't have to miss it.
Jack Sims from the *Plum Alert* always comes with his camera
and puts the picture on the front page of the next issue. Last
year a reporter came from Rochester and covered it for the *Post-
Bulletin.*"

Catherine made several appreciative remarks, then asked
about the library.

"The library? You want to see the library? Here, I can let you
in this way." He opened a door at the far end of his office.
"Library's open only on Saturday from one till four, but I can
let you have a look-see. Watch your step."

The library was a small, stuffy room with one window. Its
holdings were a hundred books, a buffalo head, and a collection
of janitorial supplies—brooms, dustpans, buckets of paint and
detergent. A few books were laid out on a table beneath the
buffalo head; the rest stood in two small bookcases flanking the
window. Catherine recognized none of the titles on the table.
The two she picked up, *The Blind Jurist* and *The One-Armed
Apothecary*, were written by someone named Edward Hodge
Fleet.

"Oh, oh," said the constable, hurrying to the window and
pulling down the dark brown shade, "the janitor must have raised
the shade. My sister Melva says books hate the sun."

"They hate dryness too," Catherine told him, imagining all

the cracked spines in this airless room. "Why do you open only on Saturdays?"

"My sister Melva's librarian, and during the week she's telephone central. I take over the switchboard for her on Saturdays so she can open up the library, and on Sundays so she can sing in church. We've got the switchboard in our living room. It was our father who brought the telephone system to Plum back in the teens, and we've kept it in the family."

Crossing to the small bookcases beside the window, Catherine recalled the solo voice that emanated from the choir loft during High Mass, an off-key quaver which together with the croaks of the old priest made for an unholy mixture of sour sounds. Now that she thought about it, it was the same voice that said "Number please" when you picked up the phone. She asked, without much interest in the answer, "Who takes over as constable while you take over the switchboard?"

"Nobody. No need for it. Nothing much happening on weekends around here, or any other day either. Stray dog now and again. Or maybe somebody having a stroke and needing a ride to the Mayo Clinic."

She examined the titles in the bookcase on the left. The few she recognized were insipid romances of ten or fifteen years ago. The shelves on the right held the collected works of Edward Hodge Fleet. She drew out a volume and turned it over in her hands. "Who *is* this?"

"Ah, our pride and joy. We're one of the few libraries in Minnesota with a complete set of Edward Hodge Fleet. When we bought the twenty-fifth book his publisher awarded us that plaque." He pointed to a small copper plate hanging on the wall. "And this special bookcase to hold his books. He's an inspiration."

"I've never heard of him."

"That's because he's only now becoming known west of the Mississippi. Culture comes from the East, my sister Melva says, and it was Mayor Brask and his wife who brought the first Fleet books with them when they moved here from Chicago."

She examined the book. The embossed binding was elegant. The paper was cheap, the print coarse. She looked at the front matter. The Tisdale Press, Chicago. Dozens of titles by the same author, all suggesting physical impairment.

"A new volume is sent to us every three months and the Christmas volume is free. Last Christmas it was *The Hobbling Cobbler*. It's a particular favorite of the mayor's. Come with me, you'll want to meet the mayor."

"I think I've met him."

"He's a literary man, come with me."

She returned to the bookcase on the left, searching desperately for a name she knew—Hawthorne, Cather, Galsworthy—but there was none. She felt a little dizzy. The heat in the room was oppressive. She called to mind Wallace's smirk, which she now understood. Dropping the Fleet book on the table, she followed the constable out of the room.

The mayor, as before, raised his eyes reluctantly from his ledger and removed his glasses. He seemed no more pleased than last time. It occurred to Catherine that getting acquainted in Plum was like learning your way through a zoo—an odd new specimen at every turn, vertebrates like yourself but not the kind you can communicate with.

"Mrs. Foster, Mayor Brask," said the constable. "Mayor Brask, the new woman in town."

The mayor stood up from his padded leather chair. He was chunky, solidly packed, shorter than the constable by six or eight inches. "Will you be attending one of our fine churches?" were the first words out of his mouth. He was quite sure of her answer, but he liked to verify hearsay.

"Yes, we're Catholic."

Rotten luck, his expression seemed to say. He cleaned his glasses on his necktie. "How many others in your family, Mrs. Foster?"

"My husband, my son, and my father."

He was relieved when she stopped after three. Not quite enough to tip Plum's religious balance. Now the risky issue:

"Is your husband politically inclined, Mrs. Foster?"

"Not at all."

He nodded approvingly as he returned his glasses to his face, using both hands to hook the bows carefully over his ears.

"But I am," she added.

The mayor turned away, frowning. The constable, a peace-loving man, wished she had not said that. The mayor, he knew, was upset by the very idea of political-minded women. Whiling away long afternoons in the village hall, the mayor had often told the constable about his running for the school board in Chicago and being defeated by a woman. Political women were dangerous, and it was schools they usually tampered with. Besides being mayor, Harlan Brask was chairman, ex officio, of the five-member Plum school board, on which there were two Lutherans besides himself—a majority nearly off set by the influence of the superintendent, who was Catholic.

"The Fosters have taken over Kermit's Grocery," said the constable.

The mayor said, "I see," not admitting that on recent afternoons he had stood in Legget's Grocery across the street from Hank's Market and watched the Fosters at work. His friend Louie Legget, always one to put the worst face on things, cursed whatever fate had brought him this ambitious competitor, who was sure to drain off all the Catholic trade Legget had gained through Kermit's decline.

Because this too was obviously an unhappy topic, the constable shifted to books. "She's a reader, Harlan. I showed her our Fleet collection."

The mayor brightened, looking her over. "Pain is gripping, don't you think?"

"Gripping? Pain?"

"In books, I mean. Don't you like reading about pain?"

"No, not as a rule."

"Edward Hodge Fleet is a master of pain. There's pain in all his work. Sometimes even mutilation and dismemberment. And it's always followed by happiness."

"Yes," said the constable, "my sister Melva says Fleet's got the sequence correct. Pain comes first and happiness follows."

"Inspiring," said the mayor.

"You bet," said the constable. "His books have done wonders for the war effort nationwide."

There were noises from both men, upper respiratory noises

of satisfaction as they recalled passages of pain and the happiness that followed.

Catherine excused herself, claiming to be needed at the store. The mayor said goodbye, and the constable accompanied her down the hall to the front door.

"Tell the men in your family that most likely I'll burn my Zero two weeks from Monday."

As she returned slowly to the store, her shoulders drooping in discouragement, Catherine advised herself to forget about finding friends and books in this outpost and concentrate instead on caring for her family and building up the market. She would be satisfied with Plum, she vowed, as long as her men were satisfied, and as long as Plum bought their groceries.

Passing the pool hall, she looked in. Grandfather's chair was still empty. She went in and said to Gordy, "Don't tell me he's still in the restroom."

Gordy said, "Oh, dear," and went to look. He returned. "I'm sorry, Mrs. Foster, I should have been more watchful, but I'm sure there's nothing to worry about."

In the market, Hank said the same: "Don't worry. It's Tuesday—no train."

"I'm going to look for him." She went out the back door, started the DeSoto and roared off down the alley.

9

M EANWHILE GRANDFATHER FOUND the house he was looking for. The other evening he had been in the car when Hank and Catherine gave Wallace a ride home in the rain, and he was struck by how closely the Flint house resembled his own boyhood home in Prairie du Chien, Wisconsin. It was an old two-story house, not very large, with latticework under the eaves and a dormer window facing the street. In Prairie du Chien that dormer had stood out from the room he shared with his brothers. For old time's sake he was determined to go upstairs in this house and stand at that window and look out.

Crossing the brown lawn, he saw that unlike the house of his boyhood the Flint house leaned slightly forward as if to get a jump on its neighbors. Its green paint was flaking off. It had a sheer face; the front doorsill was three feet off the ground and there were no steps. Taking a circular of bargains from his pocket, he went around to the side, stepped up onto the low, slanting porch, and rapped on the screen door, calling, "Anybody home here?"

A woman came through the kitchen from another room. She was short, fat and unkempt. She had gray hair and intelligent-looking eyes.

"See here," said Grandfather, unfolding a circular. "These wonderful prices on groceries. Lettuce at fifteen cents a head. I saw it come off the truck, great whopping heads packed in ice." He guessed the woman's hair hadn't been combed today. He guessed she weighed two hundred pounds.

Through the screen the woman said, "I'm well aware of all that stuff. My son brought home one of those fliers day before yesterday." She was aware, too, of the old man's identity. Wallace had described him.

"He's a son to be proud of, madam. A steady-working young man, I've heard Hank and Catherine say it more than once. Though why he should be wearing all that hair on his face is beyond me. When I was with the railroad, beards were against regulations. It's too easy for a bearded man to go seedy."

She laughed and pushed open the flimsy screen door. "Would you like to come in? You look hot."

"Delighted."

It had been a long time since Mrs. Flint had invited anyone into her house, but here was a case where kindness might not go unrewarded. For Wallace's sake the good will of the Fosters was all-important.

Grandfather came to a stop in the middle of the kitchen and turned in a circle, studying the cupboards, the icebox with its two oak doors, the black cast-iron range standing on its six chrome legs.

"Sit down and take a load off your feet," said the woman. "How about a drink of something cold?"

Grandfather had no intention of sitting down. He was here to look for his boyhood. He glanced again at her alert, knowing eyes. In Grandfather's experience, women with eyes like that required very little cajoling, so he got right down to business, pushing open the pantry door. "Ah, just as I thought. My brothers and I grew up in a house like this, and it was here in this pantry when our mother wasn't looking that we ate jam out of jars."

Mrs. Flint opened the upper door of the icebox and chipped a few shards of ice into a very small glass.

"And when we were a little older we got into the wine. My father was a great one for brewing wine in vats which he kept in the pantry. I remember sitting right back there in that corner, twelve years old and tight as a tick."

She opened the lower door and took out a pitcher of lemonade.

Grandfather strode into the dining room, where he looked disapprovingly at the furnishings—a couch, two easy chairs, a radio, books all over the place. "Where's your dining room table?"

"We don't use that as our dining room."

"But it's your dining room."

"No, we use it as our living room. We eat in the kitchen."

"Then what's your living room for?" He passed through an archway into the sparsely-furnished room facing the street. The shades were drawn; the room smelled like dust.

She followed him, handed him the glass. "We don't use this room, it's too cold in the winter."

"But it's summer."

"It's easier not to be changing rooms with the seasons."

"We had drafty rooms in Prairie du Chien, but the living room wasn't one of them. It was the bedrooms where we froze our follicles. My guess is that you have two bedrooms upstairs."

"Yes." Mrs. Flint lit a cigarette and waved the match out forcefully. "Won't you come sit in the kitchen?"

"One bedroom facing the street and the other facing the back."

"Yes." She shifted her weight from one leg to the other as she waited for him to finish examining the room.

He pointed to a ridge of stained glass running along the top of the front window. "We didn't have that in our house."

She observed that although the man's suitcoat was worn with age, it was made of a sturdy, expensive material. She was impressed with his necktie as well; it had the narrow diagonal stripes the men of Roosevelt's cabinet wore in the newsreels. These newcomers were people of substance, and Wallace's boss had obviously been lying about being short of money. The boss's wife was decked out, too, whenever you saw her on the street. Yesterday on her daily trip to the post office, Mrs. Flint had seen the boss's wife wearing a pair of open-toed shoes of a style not available in Plum. How lucky that Wallace was attaching himself to this family. He liked them and admired them. Maybe now he would quit threatening to leave home.

Grandfather downed the lemonade in three swallows and smacked his lips. "Delicious," he said, handing her the glass, "and now, if you don't mind, I'll dash up to the front bedroom and have myself a look out the window."

She didn't object.

He climbed, pausing on every third step to catch his breath. Halfway up, he looked down on the woman and thought, My God, she looks exactly like a rubber ball from this angle, no taller than she is wide. "If this is an inconvenient day for me to be doing this," he said, proceeding up, "Just say the word."

She waved him onward and started up herself. It wasn't only his clothes, it was his way of speaking. Why had Wallace failed to tell her of the old man's charm?

At the top of the stairs she was close behind him, making sure he didn't turn left toward Wallace's bedroom. Not that he could get in if he tried, the door was locked. Not even she herself was allowed in to clean or change the sheets. Wallace did that himself.

The front room was hers. She remained in the doorway, smoking, as the old man crossed to one of the windows.

"You should have more shade trees in your front yard," he said, looking out. "But I don't recommend cottonwoods."

She felt suddenly sad at the sound of a man's voice in her room, at the sight of a man's silhouette against the afternoon sun. She hadn't shared this room with a man since her husband had died nearly twenty-four years ago.

"We had cottonwoods in our front yard and they shed like cats, dropping their twigs every time a breeze came off the river. Across the street was a woods. Hardwoods mostly. Wonderful trees for climbing, especially the oaks."

Mrs. Flint paid no attention to his words, but listened to the rising and falling of his voice as though it were music. It made her husband's death fresh in her memory. Luckily, the grief was no longer fresh. The memory of grief was not the grief itself, thank God. The grief itself had been unbearable. It had lasted for years. It was Wallace, of course, who had pulled her through. Wallace was two when his father died. By the time Wallace was six she was nearly herself again and had quit punishing him in physical ways. She stopped hitting him and biting his fingers. It was the most marvelous thing to watch him grow up. He was so full of determination, so smart in school. Teachers kept telling her he was quicker in class than anyone else.

"If you climbed high enough in the oaks you could see out over the other trees to the river," Grandfather droned, half to himself. "You could see trains chugging across to Iowa on the floating bridge."

Wallace never climbed trees as a boy. She had urged him to. Go out and climb a tree, she used to say when he was owly. Go out and play darts. Go out and make something out of all that old lumber behind the shed; make a fort. On his ninth birthday she had nailed up a dartboard for him at the back of the house, but he never threw a single dart, not even when she threw a few to demonstrate. Maybe *because* she threw a few to demonstrate. He was always negative when she suggested something, even though none of her suggestions entailed playing with other children, which she knew he hated to do. He liked doing things indoors—reading, drawing, listening to the radio, splashing paint on the walls of his room. The summer he was sixteen he actually plastered his room, learning how from a book. He did it piecemeal, applying paint to the plaster before it dried, and ended up with what he called frescoes. She never saw them, for that was the summer he declared his room off limits and began locking the door.

Looking down from the window, Grandfather stopped speaking and watched the DeSoto pass slowly along the street, an elbow out the window on the driver's side. Catherine's elbow. She must be looking for him. He watched the car until it was out of sight; then he turned to Mrs. Flint and thought how various were the shapes women developed into. At the very least this one was two axhandles broad in the beam. Good eyes though. Brains behind the eyes, you could tell. Doubtless a woman you could talk to about trains.

"Did you ever take the *Hiawatha* to Chicago between 1918 and 1926?"

She nodded, guessing the correct answer was yes.

"Ahhhhh." He stepped forward and took her hand. She let him kiss it. The kiss was firm and moist. He stepped back and said, "I punched your ticket."

She smiled at him.

Without speaking they went downstairs and through the rooms to the back porch, where Grandfather asked, "I wonder, could you tell me the name of the Lutheran pastor and where he lives?"

"Reverend Dimmitburg. He lives in the white house next to the church."

"And where would that be?"

She pointed. "On the other side of town. Eight or ten blocks."

"Will this street take me there?"

"No, the church is one street over. Do you have to go? Will you have more lemonade?"

"I'm sorry, I must go."

"All right, I'll show you." She stepped off the porch and went with him to the front walk. "See that steeple?"

"So that's it. Is the Reverend the sort of man you can talk to about the verities?"

"The what?"

"The verities. The meaning of life. The good old days. Trains."

"I don't know, I'm not Lutheran."

"What are you then?"

"I'm whatever's on the radio Sunday mornings."

Gazing at the steeple Grandfather realized that it was going to be nip and tuck covering that distance with Catherine out patrolling in the car, but he felt the need of a companion outside the pool hall. All they talked about in the pool hall was farming, and all they knew of railroads was that miserable puddle jumper that backed up from Winona. The minister might have a broad view of life, might have had years of experience riding trains.

He regarded the houses across the street, saw an alley behind them.

"Does that alley run as far as the church?"

"Yes, it will take you to the back door of the parsonage." She watched him hurry across the street. "Goodbye," she called, but he didn't hear.

He had gone only three blocks down the alley when he heard the DeSoto drawing near, so he stepped into the nearest doorway. It happened to be an outdoor privy, unoccupied, which he made use of as long as he was there. With the clatter of the engine fading, he set off again, but slower now, for he was tired.

Again the DeSoto sounded in a nearby street, and he ducked into the doorway of a garage, where he found a young woman standing over a bushel basket shucking corn. She was facing away from the doorway and was startled to hear Grandfather say, rather close to her ear, "I beg your pardon." She spun around and stepped back from him. She was dressed in a two-piece sun-bathing suit, and Grandfather admired her shapeliness, her bronzeness, her honey-colored hair. In her blue eyes he detected uneasiness, which he attempted to relieve by saying, "I'm on my way to church. I only stepped in for a moment to get out of the sun." From his pocket he drew the circular intended for the Lutheran pastor, unfolded it and held it by its top corners as if displaying a bath towel. "Do you like Iced Aunt Sallys?"

Seeing Hank's Market printed on the circular, she recalled her husband's saying that the new grocer's family included an old man. She said, "My husband likes them."

"And doesn't everybody! That gingery taste. I eat four at a sitting sometimes."

"Actually all that icing is a little much for my taste."

"I know what you mean. I've thought so myself. I like candy well enough but not when I'm eating cookies."

The woman giggled and resumed her work, bending over and picking an ear of corn out of a wooden box. Grandfather admired the curve of her haunch.

"And speaking of candy, let me tell you a secret. It's a lean time for candy as we all know, Hitler and Tojo having seen to that, but in the back room of Hank's Market is a box of Hershey bars, one of which I'd be honored to set aside for you.''

She giggled again, wrenching the shucks from the ear of corn and dropping them into the basket.

''I'll put it in a sack with your name on it and leave it with Catherine at the counter. What is your name?''

She said her name was Phyllis Clay, but Grandfather didn't hear her; he was listening instead to the DeSoto drawing near. It was coming down this very alley. He backed into a corner of the garage where he couldn't be seen, and when the car had passed he came forward.

''How far is the Lutheran church from here?''

''It's in the next block.''

''Will I find the pastor at home, do you know?''

''I have no idea. I thought you people were Catholic.'' Her husband, a crabby bigot twenty-five years older than she was, had complained about the influx of fish-eaters: today the grocer, tomorrow the Pope.

''I'm Catholic to my bones, but I'm looking for companionship among the educated class. I've given up on the priest. To see eye to eye with the priest in this town you have to get down on your knees. If the minister's no better, I'll go to the schoolhouse and meet the teachers. What about your husband, is he fond of talking about the verities?''

''The what?''

''The verities. Love and death and railroads.''

''No, all he knows is turkeys.'' There was bitterness in her expression, hardness in her voice. ''He's a turkey-grower. He's got turkeys on four different farms around here. He's rich.'' Until recently she had considered him too rich to divorce, but now she poured out to Grandfather what she had told her chiropractor in Rochester the other day. ''I met him at a turkey-growers' convention in Omaha. I was the entertainment for their stag party. He came back to Omaha three times to see me. He'd get drunk and ask me to marry him. The third time I agreed. He was a lot friendlier drunk than he turned out to be sober. I married him because he was rich and because I had this idea that small-town life was cute and happy, like in the *Saturday*

Evening Post, and he said he was one of the leading citizens of this town and we'd live like royalty." She picked up another ear and tore at it roughly, all the more angry now that she realized that this old codger with the grocery circular was making her feel more like a woman than her husband did. "What does he mean, royalty? We never go anywhere. We never see anybody. I'm more like a slave than a wife. All he wants me for is cleaning his house and shucking his corn and feeding him pot roast five times a week."

Grandfather gave her problem a few moments of thought and decided not to concern himself with it. He felt like a nap. He stepped over to the workbench and smoothed the circular flat, leaving it for her to read at her leisure. He would go and see the minister another time. He was dizzy with fatigue—he shouldn't have skipped his nap. He staggered backward and braced his shoulders between two studs of the wall.

"What's wrong?" cried Mrs. Clay, drawing the wooden box toward him and turning it on its side for him to sit on, the silky ears of corn sliding like fish across the concrete.

He sat heavily, his forearms on his knees, his narrow shoulders hunched beside his ears, his head bowed.

"Can I get you anything? Water?"

With effort he smiled sadly up at her and said, "Yes, a bit of water." As she hurried away, he added, "If you please."

She went to the phone in the kitchen and reported to Central that the old man belonging to Hank's Market was having a breakdown in her garage. Miss Heffernand, sitting at the switchboard in the front window of her house on Bean Street, said she had seen the man's daughter driving around in her black car. She would ring a few houses and ask that she be hailed.

It was Mrs. Brask, the mayor's large, officious wife, who stopped Catherine by standing in the middle of Bean Street and holding her arms straight out from her sides and moving her small hands up and down like fins. She wore an ankle-length, flowered dressing gown that billowed as she stepped up to Catherine's window and said, "Your father is over there." She pointed between two houses, indicating a garage.

"Oh thank you. I've been looking and looking."

"He's had a collapse."

"Oh, no!" Catherine let out the clutch and began to move.

"Just a second, I'm not finished."

Catherine stepped on the brake.

"I am Cora Brask."

"I'm pleased to meet you. I'm Catherine Foster."

"My husband is the mayor."

"Oh, yes, I've met the mayor."

"Perhaps he mentioned that we don't encourage noisy vehicles on Bean Street."

What a perfect wife for Mayor Brask, thought Catherine. She gunned the engine and roared off. She screeched around the corner and sped down the alley.

She found her father sitting on a box and conversing with a leggy woman without much on. The woman introduced herself as Phyllis Clay. In one hand Grandfather held an empty water tumbler and in the other an empty shot glass. He was feeling much better.

"I had a grandmother with spells," said Mrs. Clay. "Her doctor recommended a shot of brandy. It always seemed to help."

Catherine had never heard a twang quite like Phyllis Clay's. She would have been interested to know how long Mrs. Clay had lived in Plum and how she liked it, but this was hardly the time to inquire.

"Brandy cures many an ill," said Grandfather as they helped him to the car. He got in and immediately began to doze.

"I hope you'll be all right," Mrs. Clay told him through his window.

He raised a hand and weakly wiggled his fingers.

Catherine thanked Mrs. Clay and started the engine. As they moved along the alley, Grandfather leaned into the breeze coming in his window. It was very refreshing.

Catherine kept glancing at him. The brandy was bringing his color back. He looked well enough for a reprimand.

"You lied to Gordy," she said.

His eyes widened. "Now wait a minute, Catherine, I never lie to anyone."

"You told him you were going to the toilet."

"And so I did." He pointed to the outhouse they were passing. "Right there."

Brendan and Wallace distributed circulars for three and a half hours, and when they finished, Brendan was hungry, weak in the knees and lost. He was also proud of having accomplished the first job in his life for pay. Walking beside Wallace, who showed him the way home, he hoped there would be more special sales with circulars. Next time he would carry a stick from the start. From the moment he picked up a stick today, the dogs had kept their distance. He had never seen so many dogs in his life—growlers, snappers, waggers, leapers and lickers. Only one biter, fortunately, and that, by coincidence, was the only dog to which Brendan was formally introduced. "Don't mind Georgie," said a wan, gray-haired woman drawn outside by the strident yap of her ugly little mutt. "Georgie loves little boys and never bites." Georgie didn't love Brendan and tore his sock.

The streets were pitch dark under the massive elms. Hanging on a post at each intersection was a solitary lightbulb casting a glow so feeble it was absorbed by the night before it fell to the ground. Brendan found Wallace slightly less creepy in the dark than in daylight. In the dark you couldn't see his eyes, which held too many expressions in quick succession, hardly any of which seemed to wish you well. Next time there was a sale, Brendan resolved to ask his father to hire Philip Crowley or Sam Romberg as his partner. Working with Wallace, you got too little sense of doing a man's job. What you got instead, for some reason, was a sense of Wallace doing a boy's job.

Turning down a dark alley, Wallace pointed and said, "Cut between these two buildings and you'll be on Main Street. You'll know the way home from there."

Brendan saw a glimmer of light on Main Street and knew where he was. Wordlessly he left Wallace and walked through the shadowy space between the village hall on his left and the gas station on his right. He came to a scattering of tires and tripped and fell. He got up and moved forward more slowly, shuffling his feet, feeling his way toward the light. The ground opened up under his right foot and he drew back from a hole six feet deep—a grease pit for servicing the undersides of cars. As he walked carefully around it and continued on his way, it occurred to him that Wallace might have steered him toward the hole on purpose. By the time he reached home he was convinced of it, and he said so to his mother as he sat down to the supper she had been keeping warm for him. She made a few consoling remarks, none of which indicated that she believed him, and he resented her lack of faith in his word, her loyalty to Wallace.

Stepping into his dark kitchen, Wallace called, "What's for supper? I'm starved."

"Stew," said his mother from the next room. "It's on the range."

He struck a match, removed the glass chimney from the lamp and lit the wick. He went to the range and lifted the lid of a small pot. "It's cold."

"That's because you're late."

"How come you let it get cold?"

"It's been a hot day, Wallace. The whole house was heating up from that one little pot of stew."

"Couldn't you have waited and eaten with me?"

"You know I can't put off my meals, Wallace."

He removed the pot and lifted the stove lid. He stuffed crumpled newspaper down the hole and dropped in a few sticks of kindling. He lit the paper, waited for it to flare, then replaced the lid and the pot.

"There's mail on the table," his mother said. There was no home delivery in Plum, and because Wallace had been known to destroy his mother's letters, the postmaster held the Flint mail for her to pick up at the window each day.

He looked at the brown envelope standing between the salt and pepper shakers and knew that it contained his third draft notice in three years. He felt none of the fear that had swept over him the first time. When the first notice arrived shortly after Pearl Harbor, he and his mother had ridden the mail truck to Pinburg and showed the letter to old Doctor Rowan, who had been seeing Wallace once or twice a year since his first seizure at the age of eleven. Doctor Rowan had lost most of his practice along with most of his eyesight. His office was the tiny back room of a barber shop. Wallace recalled how his mother's hand trembled as she handed the letter to him. He remembered the doctor bending low over his desk, straining to read, and then finally explaining to them that draft boards put epileptics into the same category as invalids and idiots; they didn't even have to show up for the physical examination if a doctor verified their condition in writing. Which Doctor Rowan did. The second letter arrived a year later. Again mother and son traveled to Pinburg in a state of nerves, believing that the Allied setback in the Mediterranean might have made epileptics draftable, but Doctor Rowan assured them that it was normal for the selective service to repeat their summons every so often in order to verify a man's disability. He told them to go home and quit worrying— he'd write to the draft board—and when the next notice arrived to forward it to him through the mail.

Waiting for his stew to heat up, Wallace slit the envelope with a paring knife. *Greetings.* He had thirty days to put his affairs in order. He would report to the Federal Building in Minneapolis for his preinduction physical examination at 1:00 P.M. on October 22, 1944. Enclosed for his convenience was a Greyhound bus pass and a timetable. At 9:20 A.M. the bus to the Twin Cities would stop at the junction of Highway 61 and the road to Plum.

He slipped the letter back into its envelope and carefully sealed it with adhesive tape. He crossed out his name and address and wrote Doctor Rowan's and "Please Forward."

He went into the dining room and sank into the couch, his head low, his feet up on the arm.

"What kept you?" his mother asked. She was reading *Screen Romance.* A cigarette burned in the ashtray beside her mug of warm lemonade.

"Covered the whole town with circulars, the kid and I. Didn't have one minute to rest. I'm going to tell Hank I need more pay for work like that. At least in the store you get to sit down every so often."

"Wallace, you'll never guess who came calling today."

He turned his head to look at her. "Came calling?" Their

last callers had been a pair of young Mormons in suits and ties whom Wallace had tried to provoke with his atheistic views. "Who was it this time, Jehovah's Witnesses?"

"Guess again." She took up her cigarette and inhaled, looking coy.

He couldn't guess. Callers were unimaginable.

"Your boss's old gent."

"Catherine's father?"

She nodded, smiling through her smoke.

"What did he want?"

"He said the view from my bedroom reminded him of his boyhood home."

"You let him upstairs?" He raised his head off the couch and glared at her.

"He's a nice old gent. I told him to come again."

"He probably will. He's a pest."

She put down her smoke and sipped her drink. "I hope he does. It's important to your career that we treat him nice."

"Since when does stocking shelves qualify as a career?"

"Since the Fosters took over. They're up and coming, Wallace. You've got a future in that job."

Wallace laughed. "We're taking in ten dollars a day. They'll be bankrupt by Christmas."

He got up and went into the kitchen, imagining the pleasure of watching the business go belly-up. Failure was always so much more dramatic than success. The only bad part would be losing Catherine, the first kindred spirit of his life. He sat at the table with his bowl of stew and a spoon.

"Lux Radio Theater's on in five minutes," said his mother. He heard the creak of her rocking chair as she leaned forward to turn on the radio. "Claudette Colbert and Dana Andrews."

"I can't stand Claudette Colbert." He chewed with his eyes on the ceiling as he calculated how long the Fosters would last. Bankrupt by Christmas might be pushing it. They were a persistent pair, more stubborn than was good for them. They'd stick it out far too long and leave town under heavy debts. Next spring, probably.

When he finished eating he said, "I'm going upstairs to read."

"Read here. I'll fix you some cocoa."

"I can't read with the radio going."

"Yes, you can. You do it all the time. Come and sit down."
Her tone was the one he despised the most, tender and coaxing.
He went upstairs to his bedroom and slammed the door.

10

S TEPPING INTO THE MARKET after school the next day, Brendan found his parents and Wallace scurrying among a swarm of shoppers. His father put him immediately to work, sending him to the basement (ratless now, the cats on patrol) to bring up potatoes.

At closing time he was sent next door to retrieve Grandfather. Hank pressed the *Total* button on the cash register and lifted the lid to read the tape. He turned to Catherine and Wallace, who stood nearby removing their aprons, and said, "Guess."

Catherine wanted to guess five hundred dollars, but said four hundred to be safe.

Wallace said, "Three seventy-five."

He tore off the tape and showed it to them: $683.43.

Catherine said, "Oh, my God."

Wallace shook his head in wonder, recalling that Kermit, even years ago on his best day, had never hit six hundred dollars.

They still had deliveries to make to a few people who had called in their orders. Brendan and Grandfather rode in back with the groceries. Wallace, sitting between Catherine and

Hank, pointed the way down the twilit alleyways. Brendan carried the bags to the various kitchen doors accompanied by his mother, who made change from a drawstring bag and apologized for not showing up before suppertime. Their last delivery was Wallace himself, who had been excused from carrying bags because his feet hurt and his head ached.

"See you in the morning," said Hank, as Wallace got out.

"Get a good rest," Catherine told him. "Tomorrow may be even busier."

Wallace nodded and said goodnight. He stood on the curb and watched the DeSoto disappear down the street. Mingled with his fatigue was an odd sense of buoyancy such as he had not felt since his high school days when he was the class brain and imagined a bright future for himself. It was exciting to think that the Fosters might prosper in Plum. Until yesterday he would have bet his life's savings—all two hundred dollars of it—on the failure of Hank's Market, but now it seemed possible that they might remain in Plum indefinitely. They might go on and on, Wallace and Catherine, reminding one another of their superiority to this village, helping one another resist its downward pull.

Trade was even brisker on Friday. This was the day that convinced Wallace that the Grand Opening had transcended religious barriers. One after another as they left the store, he named for Hank and Catherine the Lutherans they had just waited on. Again Brendan worked after school, Wallace got sore feet and a headache, and there were deliveries to make at twilight. The proceeds for Friday were $804.20.

Brendan was in and out of the store all day Saturday, balancing the demands of his parents with the demands of his friends Sam Romberg and Philip Crowley. He managed an hour of marbles and boomerang throwing in the morning, and got away again later for the Gene Autry matinee.

After the movie, he was replenishing the bin of oranges when he overheard the observations of two women who had come into the store not to shop but to inspect. One was tall and square; she wore a circle of foxtails draped around her shoulders. Her companion was much smaller; she had a long neck, narrow shoulders and the overall shape of a bowling pin. They stood in front of the canned soup, like wallflowers at a dance.

"She seems very businesslike," said Small.

"Being businesslike never becomes a woman," Large declared. "Why isn't she home tending to her family?"

Catherine darted up to Brendan, whispered, "The one with the furs is the mayor's wife," and darted away again.

"She has only one," said Large.

"One? And she's Catholic?"

When they both turned to look Brendan over, he realized he was the one.

After a few moments Large added, "I spoke to her in that awful car she drives. It was the day her father turned up in Webster Clay's garage."

"Stanley says her father is in the pool hall nearly every day talking about trains."

Could Small, Brendan wondered, be Stan Kimball's wife?

They left the soup and strolled along the produce rack, checking prices.

"Look at Wallace Flint spruced up," said Small. "He's trimmed his beard."

"Yes, he looks downright useful."

"And handsome."

Just then, Wallace wore out. Having never worked so hard in his life, he went suddenly very pale and had to be helped into the back room, where Hank sat him down on his desk chair and Catherine gave him coffee and felt his forehead. Wallace said he'd be fine as long as he rested. Hank returned to his customers. Catherine felt his forehead once more, then left him alone. After a while Brendan, hurrying through the back room to fill a vinegar jug, noticed that Wallace seemed not to be resting but was sitting upright and tense, his eyes wide and distracted.

"Are you okay?" he asked him.

"Fine!" Wallace shot back resentfully, curling his lip.

"Just take it easy," said Brendan, repeating his father's instruction to Wallace. "Just sit and rest."

"Never mind!" Wallace snapped.

Returning with the gallon of vinegar, Brendan found his father and mother standing at the cash register reading the tape. "We did it!" his mother said gleefully.

Hank explained to Brendan, "Our income so far equals what we paid for stock and overhead. From now on it's all profit."

Brendan turned and saw his mother running through the store to tell Wallace. He ran after her, magnetized by her high spirits, but by the time he reached the doorway to the back room it was closed off by the two women who had been standing in front of the soup. Now they stood shoulder to shoulder peering into the back room. Brendan came to a stop behind them and looked over the smaller woman's shoulder. He saw his mother acting silly, chirping, "Good news, good news," as she flew toward Wallace with her arms flapping. He saw Wallace spring up from his chair and take Catherine tightly in his arms and at the same time make a curious growling noise in his throat. Catherine, laughing, gave him a peck on the forehead. Wallace, his arms locked tightly around her neck, began jerking along the entire length of his body. Catherine cried, "Wallace!" and broke free.

The two women turned away, looking as though they had witnessed the vilest sort of degradation and were outraged but not surprised. Setting off at a quick strut toward the front door, they missed seeing Wallace topple to the floor and roll onto his back, mucus oozing from his mouth and nose, his half-closed eyes showing all white.

Catherine's scream and Brendan's were a single note.

Customers came running. A man in overalls shouted, "Stuff something in his mouth or he'll bite off his tongue." Another man lifted Catherine's feather duster off its hook and tried to insert the wooden handle between Wallace's grinding teeth.

"No, not that," said the man in overalls. "You'll break his teeth."

Then Hank was suddenly there, holding a ring of bologna in his hand. He bent over Wallace, waiting for him to open his mouth.

Two dozen people stood entranced, watching Wallace writhe, froth and shoot his arms and legs about.

"I thought he was getting better," said a largely pregnant

woman holding two toddlers by the hand. "He hasn't had one in public for a long time."

"Not since the basketball tournament last spring," said her companion, a woman with her arms full of a baby in blue blankets.

"Were you there for it?"

"No, but I heard about it. They had to stop the game because he sprawled out onto the floor."

Three times Wallace snapped his mouth open and shut, and the third time Hank made his move and Wallace sank his teeth into the bologna. He lay rigid for a minute or more before his muscles began to relax. He whimpered unconsciously for a while, and then went limp. Hank gently removed the meat from his mouth. Sweat, saliva and tears came flowing out of Wallace. He shuddered. Catherine covered him with her coat, Hank's jacket and several empty potato sacks.

"He's all right now," said the man in overalls. "He'll sleep it off."

One by one the shoppers went back to their shopping. Catherine sat at the desk and kept watch. In a few minutes Wallace woke up. She looked down at his eyes and saw them gradually fill with the knowledge of what had happened. She saw shame and then anger. He turned his eyes away. His voice was a weak whisper: "Home."

She called to Hank, who carried him out the back door to the car unaided. Comparing him to hundred-pound sugar sacks, Hank guessed his weight to be about 130.

Hank drove him home, carried him up onto the side porch and kicked at the door. Mrs. Flint opened it and cried, "Oh, my poor Wallace. Oh, Mr. Foster, thank you, thank you."

So this is Wallace's mother, thought Hank. He had seen her short, heavy figure moving along Main Street toward the post office each day about the time the afternoon mail was distributed. It occurred to Hank that she was the only person who passed the store without being singled out and identified by Wallace.

"Please put him in there." She pointed to the room beyond the kitchen.

Hank laid Wallace carefully on the couch in the dining room as Mrs. Flint turned down, but not off, the fiddle music on the radio.

"Thank you ever so much, Mr. Foster. He'll be just fine by Monday. He'll be at work bright and early. You wouldn't fire him for this, would you?"

"Of course not." No such thing had occurred to him.

"Will you stay for a cool drink? I have lemonade."

"Thanks, I have to get back." He returned through the kitchen to the door.

"A hot drink?" she asked, following him. "I have coffee."

"No, thanks, we're very busy and my wife and boy are alone."

"Oh, that's wonderful—I knew you'd be busy. I said so to Wallace. He doubted it, but I said, 'Mark my words, these new people will make the business go.' Did you know your father-in-law came and paid me a call on Wednesday?"

"No, I didn't."

"A very gentlemanly old gent. I gave him a glass of lemonade."

There was a moan from the other room. Mrs. Flint went to the doorway and looked in. "Just a minute, Wallace, I'm seeing Mr. Foster off."

He moaned again, and his mother stepped in and covered him with an afghan.

Glancing around the kitchen, Hank saw that the appliances were a generation behind the times; in the late thirties, before the war made them scarce, most people had acquired electric refrigerators and gas or electric stoves, but not the Flints. Noticing the kerosene lamp on the kitchen table, he realized they were without electricity. He glanced again at the radio in the room beyond; it was cordless, battery-powered.

Mrs. Flint followed him out onto the porch, thanking him again and again.

"Call us if there's anything you need," he told her. "Medicine or anything." Having said this, he realized they probably had no phone.

"No, you're very kind, all he needs is rest. He'll sleep tonight and Sunday and be as good as new on Monday morning. He likes his job, Mr. Foster, he likes working for you and your wife, he told me so.''

Hank found Catherine and Brendan swamped, and the market grew even busier after supper when the farm population came to town after the day's fieldwork. The last customer left the store shortly after 10:00 P.M. The proceeds for Saturday were $1,460.96.

11

EXPECTING THE HIGH TIDE of Grand Opening to flood over into the following week, Hank was at the market before sunrise on Monday to take stock of his diminished grocery supply. He filled out a lengthy order form provided by Bob Donaldson and took it to the post office before eight o'clock so that it would go out on the morning mail truck and delivery of the stock would be assured before next weekend.

Wallace came to work at eight-thirty, looking restored if slightly bleary-eyed. Catherine showed up at nine. They worked quickly in preparation for the day's trade, Catherine sweeping and dusting, Wallace replenishing the shelves with the last of the storeroom reserves, Hank taking down the posters in the front window and washing it inside and out. The day darkened and a light rain began to fall. By ten o'clock Catherine and Hank were avoiding each other's eyes, not wanting to acknowledge that half the morning had passed without a penny of income.

The first customer came in at ten-fifteen to buy a pack of cigarettes. He was followed by a woman needing a small can of floor wax. The woman was followed by no one. At eleven Catherine cried desperately, "Where is everybody?"

"Mondays are always dead," Wallace told her. "Haven't you noticed?—not even Legget is busy on Monday."

As it happened, they turned their eyes across the street just as three shoppers were filing into Legget's Grocery and two were coming out.

"I see what you mean." Her tone was ironic.

"Well, it's been dead over there until just now."

Catherine recognized one of the women coming out as the mayor's wife. "Who's the woman with Mrs. Brask?"

"Mrs. Kimball."

"Stan's wife?"

Wallace nodded. "You hardly ever see one of those women without the other. They live on Bean Street, two doors apart. Mrs. Kimball is mousy. She listens devoutly to everything Mrs. Brask tells her."

"They're looking this way. Maybe they're coming over to shop."

"No, they'd never do that. They belong to Legget. Always have."

"They were in here on Saturday."

"No."

Catherine nodded. "In the afternoon, while you were resting in back."

"I bet they didn't buy anything."

"I don't remember."

They had bought nothing. They had come into the market on Saturday merely out of curiosity, and they had hurried away with the most stupendous gossip of their lives. They had gone straight to the village hall and told the mayor and the constable that Mrs. Foster hugged and kissed Wallace Flint in the back room of the market when Mr. Foster wasn't looking. Constable Heffernand, not much affected by the news, went on assembling the tail section of his Japanese Zero. The mayor, however, was agog. He locked up his office, said goodnight to the constable, and drove his wife and Mrs. Kimball home, muttering along the way that it was no surprise to him that a woman who had no time for the right-thinking books of Edward Hodge Fleet went in for hugging and kissing the help. Getting out of the car in front of her house, Mrs. Kimball was advised by the Brasks to point out to her husband how ill-advised his friendship with the Fosters was, how shortsighted he had been to associate with them without verifying their moral character beforehand. "I will," Mrs. Kimball said obediently. She went into her house and spoke baby talk to her dog, a white, high-strung pup with pointed ears and hair hanging in its eyes. Then she went into the living room and announced to her husband that Mrs. Foster had hugged and kissed Wallace Flint in the back room of the market when Mr. Foster wasn't looking. Stan Kimball sat in his easy chair with only the bumpy top of his bald head and a cloud of cigar smoke visible behind the *Post-Bulletin*. "Cora and I saw it with our own eyes," she told him as the dog barked and danced, catching at her coat and stockings with its claws. "They held each other tight, and Cora and Harlan wonder if you'll be thinking twice before associating with them in the future."

"What I'm thinking is, Cora and Harlan ought to mind their own business." He turned a page. "Can't you get that mutt to shut up?"

Two doors away Cora Brask phoned the Lutheran parsonage to tell Mrs. Dimmitburg the news, and Mrs. Dimmitburg agreed that the pastor must be told immediately, for it was a scandal with theological overtones, proving beyond a doubt that the union of Catholicism and atheism led to depravity. Wallace was known as Plum's lone atheist.

A block and a half away, Melva Heffernand, a slender, aging woman whose short, dyed hair resembled a black helmet, sat at her switchboard and listened to the conversation between the minister's wife and the mayor's wife. When it was over, she watched dusk gather under the elms of Bean Street and pondered the ethics of her profession. It was her policy not to use the facilities of Plum Telephone for broadcasting gossip except to her closest friends, and then only if the gossip consisted of verifiable fact. That Mrs. Brask had witnessed the hugging and kissing was verification enough, she decided. That she numbered over three dozen women as her closest friends accounted, in part, for the great number of curiosity-seekers who crowded into the market on Saturday evening.

Although the Webster Clays lived on Bean, across from the Brasks and the Kimballs, word of the affair did not reach Phyllis Clay until her husband came home for his noon meal on Monday. "I hear the new grocer's wife is carrying on with Wallace Flint," Webster Clay muttered around his mouthful of rump roast and potato. "People seen them smooching in the back room of the grocery store." Rump roast, boiled potatoes, turnips and cake made up the noon meal of Webster Clay five days a week, after which he napped for an hour and then returned to his turkey farms. "I heard it from Skeffington in the bank and Downie at the gas station."

Phyllis Clay was elated to learn of another adventuresome woman in town. Since arriving here a year ago as Webster Clay's bride and discovering very quickly that he had nothing to recommend him but his wealth, Mrs. Clay had had a couple of flings of her own. The first one, with Fred Butz, the high school shop teacher, hadn't lasted long. After two weeks the affair somehow came to the attention of the school board, and Fred Butz was threatened with the loss of his job if he didn't stop seeing her. Currently she was seeing a chiropractor in Rochester once a week for treatment of her lower spine and for dalliance as well.

After her husband finished eating and went upstairs to lie down, she picked up the phone and asked Central for Hank's Market. She asked Wallace for Mrs. Foster.

When Catherine said hello, she asked, "Does Hank's deliver?"

Catherine recognized the voice. "Yes, Mrs. Clay. Around three every afternoon."

"Oh, good, I need a few things. I need powdered sugar and ten pounds of potatoes."

Catherine wrote this down.

"My husband comes home from his farms with filthy overalls. Which soap is best for that?"

"I've always had good luck with Rinso."

"Then give me a big box of Rinso. And how is your father, Mrs. Foster?"

"He's fine. He had a good rest and is feeling himself again."

"I'm so glad. I was worried."

"Thank you for asking."

"Mrs. Foster, I get the feeling we've got a lot in common." She giggled briefly. "You and I."

Catherine tried to think what it might be. All she remembered of Mrs. Clay were her youth, her accent, and the scanty clothes she wore.

Another giggle came over the phone, followed by the rest of the list for delivery.

Putting the order together with Wallace's help, Catherine asked, "What do you know about Phyllis Clay?"

"She married Webster Clay for his money. He's the sourest man on Bean Street, and that's saying quite a lot considering Mayor Brask lives on Bean."

"She says she and I have a lot in common."

"Oh, really? What?"

"I'm asking you."

Wallace scratched his beard and smiled. "She used to come in and make suggestive remarks to Kermit."

"She's a flirt?"

"And then some."

By three o'clock there were two deliveries to make, and Wallace went out in the DeSoto. It was raining rather hard. His progress was jerky, for despite several driving lessons from Hank, his clutch-coordination was clumsy. Though his history of epilepsy made him ineligible for a driver's license, he had assured Hank and Catherine that he was to be trusted at the wheel because he could feel his seizures coming well beforehand.

The car coughed and shuddered as he brought it to a halt in front of the rooming house on Hay Street. He carried in a bag of groceries for Mrs. Lansky in number seven. At the top of the stairs he looked through the open doorway of number six and saw Dodger Hicks emptying clothes from a dresser drawer into a cardboard box.

"Dodger, how come you're not in school?"

Dodger turned and smiled. Two mismatched socks hung from his hands. "I quit."

Wallace stepped into the room. "You can't quit. You're not sixteen."

"I quit," he said again, because the words gave him such pleasure. Since grade one, nothing in Dodger's education had been quite so satisfying as quitting.

"They'll make you go back. Just wait and see."

"Not here they won't. We're moving to Winona."

"You are? Why?"

Dodger shrugged as he dropped the socks into the carton. "My ma wants to. We got a nicer place to live there." It was a worse place, actually—two rooms instead of three—but Wallace didn't need to know that. Nor did he need to be told that a number of roomers here had been complaining about the night noises in number six whenever one of his mother's men friends drove up from Winona to see her. A couple of them got a little wild when they drank. They hollered and smashed beer bottles and made his mother angry. The loudest noises of all came from his mother when she was angry.

Wallace said, "You'll have to go to school in Winona."

Dodger's smile weakened. "I suppose." It brightened. "If I lay low they might not know I'm there."

"Who is it?" called his mother from the next room.

"Wallace Flint."

"What's he want?"

"Nothing."

Mrs. Hicks emerged from the other room. She was tall, thin and round-shouldered. Her face was long like Dodger's, her hair the same light brown as his. Her features, however, were not large and open like her son's; they were small and pinched. She frowned. "You want something?"

"I was just taking groceries to Mrs. Lansky."

"You got the wrong apartment."

"I know it. I was just wondering why Dodger wasn't in school."

"So now you know." She returned to the other room.

The door to number seven opened into the kitchen. Mrs. Lansky, an old woman in bedroom slippers, was stirring something on the stove. She told Wallace to set the bag on the counter and asked how much she owed him.

"A dollar and eighty cents."

"Heavens." She put down her wooden spoon and dug through the bag, examining the price of each item. "How come crackers are twenty-five? I thought they were nineteen."

"That was just during Grand Opening."

"Take them back."

Wallace subtracted twenty-five cents from her slip and she paid him, carefully counting coins out of her purse.

Picking up the crackers, he said, "You're losing your neighbors."

The old woman looked suddenly sad. "Poor Dodger."

"Why poor Dodger?"

She said nothing. Shaking her head, she turned to the stove and resumed her stirring.

When he heard Mrs. Clay call, "Come in," Wallace opened her kitchen door and found her sitting at the table, her face heavily made up, a magazine open in front of her, an amber drink in her hand. Her blouse, thought Wallace, had too many buttons open to be modest.

"You can set them on the drainboard," she told him, smiling.

He put down the bags and handed her the sales slip.

"I'll have to pay you next time, Wallace; I don't have any money."

Wallace told her that was fine.

"How about having a drink with me?"

"No, no," he said. This woman had been making Wallace uneasy ever since she started coming into the store and batting her eyes at Kermit. It had been embarrassing to witness Kermit trying to look roguish while turning to jelly. As far as Wallace knew, there had been nothing between them beyond eye-batting and giggling.

"Why not have a drink? Webster buys Old Crow by the case and never keeps track. He has no idea how much I drink or give to my friends—just so his pot roast is ready at twelve and his supper at six."

Wallace folded the slip and tucked it into his shirt pocket. "I'll put this on your account," he said, staring at her as he edged toward the door. Uneasy as she made him, he couldn't take his eyes from her.

She put her glass to her lips, took a sip and licked the rim. "Wallace, would you tell me something if I promise not to spread it around?"

"What?"

She looked him over, smiling, thinking he was handsome enough in a miniature sort of way, but feeling her seductive manner wasted on him. "I hear you and the boss's wife are really hitting it off." She giggled.

"What do you mean?"

"Lovey-dovey stuff." She rolled her eyes. "Is it true?"

"Where did you hear that?"

"Everybody's saying so. Webster heard it from two different parties this morning. I called up and told Central and she said she knew it already."

There was a touch of hysteria in Wallace's laugh. "That's ridiculous."

"Central said she heard it on Saturday. Is it true?"

He told her there was nothing to it, but he spoke weakly and she assumed he was guilty and ashamed. She giggled when he said goodbye.

On his way back to the store, Wallace stopped at the post office and asked for the Hickses' forwarding address in Winona.

"What do you want it for?" inquired the postmaster from under his green eyeshade.

"We're billing them for groceries."

"I thought Mrs. Hicks shopped at Legget's."

"She did, mostly, but Dodger ran up a bill for candy."

The postmaster, referring to a note tacked to the wall, read off the address and Wallace copied it down.

Entering the store, Wallace laughed and called out, "I found out what Mrs. Clay meant on the phone." He saw that Catherine was dusting, Hank was working at the produce display, and they had been joined by Rufus Ottmann, who stood at the front door staring out. Wallace told the Fosters of the rumor in terms he intended as amusing, but they weren't amused.

"Is she crazy?" cried Catherine. "Is everybody crazy?" She picked up a jar of preserves, swiped at it with her feather duster and plunked it down angrily. "Are there nothing but lunatics in this village?" She closed her eyes and seethed.

Hank, checking grapes for decay, said, "Catherine, don't take it so seriously."

"Don't tell me how to take it," she flared. "It's our lives these gossips are playing loose with. How did we happen to choose the town with the highest percentage of lunatics, bigots, gossips, and . . ." She would have added "idiots" if Rufus Ottmann at that moment hadn't turned his magnanimous, empty smile upon her.

Hank took the feather duster from her and handed it to Wallace. "We need a good, long coffee break. Wallace, mind the store."

Left in charge, Wallace leaned on the cash register, his arms folded across its top, his eyes on the children passing along the wet street from the direction of the school. Rain fell in sprinkles. He felt strangely elated at having been accused of illicit love. It was a damaging rumor, for it worked against Catherine's adjustment to Plum, but it was delightfully bizarre. He was reminded of the rumors that had accompanied his graduation from high school. Somehow it started going around that he would attend the University of Minnesota on a full scholarship. Others said Winona State. A few had heard the University of Chicago. The rumors stayed alive for a year or more, while only Wallace knew he was going nowhere.

Brendan came angling across the street, having promised his parents he'd look in to see if he was needed before going off to play. He hoped he wouldn't be needed. Philip Crowley was waiting for him in the covered shed of the lumber yard, where they had dug nine small holes in the dirt floor and devised a rainy-day game combining the principles of marbles and golf. Loser paid winner a marble per hole, each marble being redeemable for a cigarette at such time as the loser came into possession of cigarettes.

Nearing the market, he saw Wallace and Rufus looking out at him. The faces put him in mind of the puzzle page of *Boys' Life*. For ten points, which face is the idiot? Which is the heartless villain? Stepping through the door and cringing under Rufus's smile, he said to Wallace, looking him in the eye as though he neither hated nor feared him, "Not very busy, huh?"

"Dead all day. Only the gossips are busy."

"What gossips?"

"All the gossips in town. They're saying your mother and I are having a love affair."

Brendan's eyes widened in wonder, then went shut as he laughed. "Boy, that's rich."

Wallace, having expected him not to take it so lightly, found his glee offensive and changed the subject:

"Have you heard about Dodger Hicks?"

"What about him?"

"He's moving away."

Brendan's expression turned serious. His betrayal of Dodger continued to nag him. After three weeks of turning it over in his mind, he had decided on Saturday that the betrayal was a sin, and following the Gene Autry movie he had gone to church and told Father O'Day about it in the confessional. The old priest hadn't seemed the least interested. He had assigned him a perfunctory penance of three Hail Marys, and his murmur of absolution had been followed by a yawn.

"Where's he moving to?"

"Winona, where he came from." A change came over Wallace's face as he spoke. His tone of contempt was such that Rufus momentarily lost his smile and shifted his eyes, and Brendan feared that Wallace was on the brink of another fit. But he wasn't. Immediately he eased up on his clenched look.

Brendan went off to marbles.

Wallace, gazing out the window, yawned.

Rufus, gazing out the door, did the same.

Catherine and Hank inhaled the odors of beer, smoke and hamburger grease as they stepped into Gordy's and slid into their customary booth along the wall opposite the bar. Gordy brought them two mugs of coffee and commented on the continued warm weather, but sensing Catherine's agitation, he did not linger to chat.

Hank ventured a consoling remark: "It's only gossip, Catherine, that's all."

"That's all?" she seethed. "It's people lying through their teeth. Whoever saw Wallace have that seizure saw the way he clung to me and they made it into a love affair."

"I know it's a lie and I'm sorry. We have to ignore it."

Catherine rolled her eyes at the ceiling and let them fall on her cup. She sipped in silence for a minute or more, then stated in a subdued tone, "Hank, I don't have any friends here."

"Give it time. We've only been here three and a half weeks."

"But I don't have any *hope* of friends."

He spoke softly, carefully: "Who were your friends in the city, Catherine? After Mae went to Florida, who did you have?"

"The city was different. In the city I had . . . the city."

"Well, here at least you've got Wallace."

She was startled. "What are you saying?" Her voice rose. "You believe that lie?"

"No, of course not. I'm saying you and Wallace get along. You seem to have fun at work."

"Hank, Wallace is our charity case."

"You don't think of him as a friend?"

"In a way a friend, but don't you see, it's a sign of how impossible this town is that my only friend outside the family is a man years younger than I am, with such a cynical view of life that I sometimes find myself taking on his bitter ways and hating myself for it."

"Ways like nicknaming our customers?"

She broke out in a laugh. "I have to take the whole blame there. Wallace didn't start that, I did." Her laugh quickly died.

"Catherine, it's very bad for business, those nicknames. When Mr. and Mrs. Dombrowski were in the store Saturday, I saw you and Wallace snickering behind their backs, and I think they noticed it too."

"I couldn't help it." She smiled, remembering. "They're so stodgy and serious looking, so Victorian, and Wallace came up to me and said, 'Will you wait on Marx and Engels, or will I?' "

Hank sat back, studying her. "I don't get it."

"See, their real names are Max and Enga."

He observed her attempt to quit smiling. He said, "I still don't see the humor."

She sat forward and lowered her head, cupping her face in her hands and staring down at her mug of coffee. Her shoulders were shaking with giggles.

But they weren't giggles; he saw this a few moments later when she raised her head. The tears she wiped away were not tears of amusement.

"I'm sorry," she said. "For being such a misfit."

He placed his hand over hers. "Catherine, there were times on Friday and Saturday when I felt like I'd never felt before. We had more customers than we could keep up with, and I felt a thrill almost like the day you said you'd marry me."

She gazed at him.

"Like we were having a kind of Grand Opening inside ourselves." He paused. "Like we finally got where we were meant to be in life."

He saw renewed tears in her eyes. He said, "But then I felt a letdown yesterday morning in church. I was thanking God for all those customers when I realized that no matter how well the store goes, it's no good if you're not happy here."

"I'll be all right. I'm sorry."

"Don't apologize. It could have been Brendan who had trouble moving. It could have been your father. It could have been me. I'm just saying it never occurred to me before we moved that there was more than one way for us to fail. I thought everything depended on how many groceries we sold."

"Give me time," she said. "I'll be all right."

"But I want you to be more than all right. I want you to feel what I felt on Friday and Saturday."

She nodded, smiling weakly.

"Because I can't feel it if you don't."

12

AFTER SUPPER WALLACE TOOK a long nap in his room. When he awoke he lit the kerosene lamp on the table beside his bed, and as the flame grew brighter he watched the purple faces materialize on the ceiling and walls. They numbered thirty-two. They were crude faces, applied with a wide brush, but with enough detail to be distinguishable one from another. He gazed at Emily Dickinson above the dresser. Her features were guesswork, for he had had no picture to go by, only her poems, which had gone unpublished until after her death. Next to her was Vincent van Gogh. Eyes slightly aslant, an ear missing. One painting sold in his lifetime. Above them was John Keats. Curly hair, jutting jaw. By the time he was Wallace's age, John Keats was dead. The faces consoled Wallace, belonging as they did to people whose genius had not been acknowledged in their lifetimes.

He read for a time, then went downstairs, where he found his mother listening to the ten o'clock news and snacking on Spam. He stood in the doorway for a minute as H. V. Kaltenborn set forth his nightly analysis: "The final blow at Germany is of course inevitable. Only two things might delay it: a new German weapon of unforeseen effectiveness or an unbridgeable rift in the Allied Coalition. The victory over Japan appears to impose greater problems. Measured in total size of forces alone, the task ahead is stupendous. Add to it the vast areas that must be conquered and it tries the imagination.''

"I'm going for a walk," he told his mother.

"But it's raining."

"No it isn't.'' He took his jacket from the coat stand next to the kitchen door and stepped out into the sprinkling rain.

No teacher or janitor ever stayed in school beyond 10:00 P.M., but to be safe Wallace walked the dark streets until 10:30; then he crossed the playground to the back of the school. The faulty latch was on the third window from the left, an opaque window at ground level, opening into the boys' physical education area. He made his way through the darkness to the coaches' office, his refuge whenever he couldn't stand one more minute under the same roof with his mother, an ideal place for night work, being an inner room with no windows to show the light. He closed the door, switched on the overhead light, and settled himself at Mr. Torborg's desk.

Wallace had never met Mr. Torborg, but he knew him by reputation and recognized him on the street. A wounded veteran of the Pacific campaign, Mr. Torborg had joined the teaching staff only a year ago. According to the *Plum Alert*, he had been awarded medals for heroism. He taught math and coached basketball and track. Watching a basketball game last winter, Wallace had perceived him as a kindly, patient young man, well liked by his students. He had a small blond moustache, which he habitually groomed with the thumb and forefinger of his right hand. His paralyzed left hand, hanging useless at his side, was the badge of his heroics in the Philippines, and more than once Wallace wished that he had come by his own disability in such a glorious way.

Wallace opened the drawer in which Mr. Torborg kept his school stationery. He found an envelope, rolled it into the typewriter and addressed it to the superintendent of schools in Winona. Next he rolled in a sheet of paper.

Dear Sir:

I wish to alert you to the fact that a student of ours, aged 15, is moving with his mother to 321 Broad Street in Winona. Being a reluctant student and the son of negligent parents, he might well pose a truancy problem. His name is Dodger Hicks.

Wallace was about to forge the name of Thomas Reinhart, the principal, when it occurred to him that administrators often ran across one another at meetings and this letter might come up in conversation. Instead, he closed the letter with an imaginary name and title:

Jeannette Horvath
Assistant to the Principal

He sealed the letter and cursed under his breath because he had forgotten to bring along a postage stamp. He wanted it to go out on the morning mail truck so that Dodger would be confronted by the authorities the moment he got to Winona. Searching through the desk, he found, along with stamps, an envelope containing three snapshots from Mr. Torborg's time in the service. In one he wore a dress uniform and looked very young; he was probably just out of basic training. In the second he stood with several buddies in fatigues under a palm tree; he was holding a water canteen in his left hand and laughing. The third picture showed him wearing white pajamas and sitting in a wheelchair; an officer stood at his side with his hand on his shoulder, and there was a nurse in the background.

Wallace placed the snapshots side by side on the desk and studied them for a long while, feeling envy for this man no older than himself who had gone halfway around the world and made friends and done heroic things and come home with medals. Serving in the military was amounting to a lot more than Wallace had foreseen when he had sought deferment early in the war. Papers and movies were full of stories in which the common sailor, infantryman or pilot did glorious things. By now, Wallace thought, were it not for his medical disqualification he might be wearing medals of his own. At this very moment he might be involved in a valorous act at the front, dying a valorous death. Dead or alive, he'd be shipped home to acclaim. Dead, he'd be given a hero's burial. Alive, he'd be given a parade down Main Street, after which he'd leave town and never come back.

He replaced the pictures in the drawer, sadly aware of how little he was affecting the course of world events. He switched off the light and left the office.

The next morning, waiting for the school bell to call them across the street, Brendan, Sam and Philip played marbles in the lumber yard. They were between the seventh and eighth holes when Brendan saw a pickup stop in the alley at the far end of the shed and a figure enter the wide doorway and come slouching toward them. Against the sunlight flooding the doorway Brendan thought at first it was an employee coming to work carrying a lunchpail, but as the figure drew nearer he saw, with a tinge of shame, that it was Dodger Hicks carrying a brand new bag of marbles.

"Hi, Dodger," said Brendan, getting down on one knee, ready to shoot.

"Hi." Dodger stepped boldly into the path the marble would take, and in a voice oddly authoritative he told Brendan to stand up and hold his pockets open.

Brendan stood and smirked at Sam and Philip, trying to make clear to them without words that this intruder was no friend of his. He held open his right pants pocket and Dodger poured marbles out of his bag until the pocket overflowed. Then he filled the left pocket. Brendan had been playing with a meager capital of about ten marbles, losing half a dozen a day, winning them back the next. Now suddenly he had this wealth of glassies, five or six dozen gems of swirling, brilliant design—amber, violet, crimson, green. What did they mean? Were they Brendan's reward for having eased Dodger's loneliness during the first two days of school? Or were they meant to deepen his shame?

Dodger didn't explain. He simply nodded when Brendan said thanks, and he turned and left the shed, his stride long-legged and lazy, his wrists dangling far out of his shirtcuffs, the back of his head carelessly barbered. Out in the sunlight he climbed into the cab of the pickup, in which a man and a woman sat waiting. As the truck moved past the doorway, Brendan saw that it carried a load of furniture.

"What was that all about?" Philip wanted to know.

"Beats me," said Brendan nonchalantly, getting down on one knee and feeling enormously relieved to have seen the last of Dodger Hicks.

13

"*Look at these books,* Hank. You've been in business two months, and you've had only one week when it was worthwhile to unlock your front door." Stan Kimball, undertaker, sat on an orange crate beside Hank's desk. Having just come from a funeral, he wore a large white carnation in the lapel of his dark suit. A short, spongy cigar smoldered in the corner of his mouth. "Turn back to that other page and let's have a look at your weekly totals."

The ledger told them that whereas weekly income averaged $48 before Grand Opening, it averaged $165 thereafter.

"It's an improvement," said Hank, concealing his fear that the market would never produce a living for himself and his family. After overhead, his net profit was very small. Now in the chill of late October he was burning coal like paper, particularly at home, where the walls lacked insulation.

"It's peanuts! You've got to hit these people with more sales. Your Grand Opening got you a hell of a flock of customers, but when it was over they mostly went back to Legget. You've got to hit them with one sale after another until they get the habit of coming in here even when there is no sale.''

"But here it says you can put on too many sales." Hank handed him the latest issue of *Independent Grocer*. "People get so they ignore sales."

Kimball riffled the pages. "Where does this come from?"

"Chicago."

"What the hell does anybody in Chicago know about Plum? Your Grand Opening was the first grocery sale this town has seen in this millennium. Kermit never put on a sale, and therefore Legget never had to. Hit these people with a sale a month and pretty soon you'll have this store so goddamn full of customers you'll have to double your staff."

Hank took the magazine back. "It says the best way to build trade is to be dependable day to day." During a sale his profit margin decreased.

"Dependable to who—Mrs. Ottmann and her idiot child? Listen, Hank, haven't I told you about the economics of groceries as compared to the economics of death?" Kimball held his handkerchief to his chin and dribbled brown cigar juice into it and returned it to his pocket. "I average twenty-four funerals a year in this town and there's no way short of murder I can change that number. If I offered a hot price on caskets, how many people would die to save a few bucks? Now you, on the other hand, you can mount a sale as often as you feel like it, and people will flock to your groceries like cows to a saltlick. You're in complete control of your business, Hank. My business is run by the angel of death."

They heard the DeSoto come to a stop at the back door, heard the engine die, cough three times and die again.

"Tell that to Catherine," Hank said.

"I will. Excuse me, I've got to take a leak." Kimball went into the basement.

Entering the back door, Catherine sniffed, smiled and said, "I smell Stan's cigar."

Hank nodded. "He's downstairs. Catherine, it's time to talk seriously about our next sale."

"Haven't we talked it to death?"

Indeed, they had gone so far as to name it Hank's Harvest Sale and to lay out the circular, but they had not carried through for fear of failure. Grand Opening, while a triumph in itself, had brought them very few permanent customers. If it was novelty and low prices that had made Grand Opening a success, could a second sale possibly succeed on low prices alone? Day after discouraging day in October, they had felt their hopes become stunted, their courage disappear.

Catherine hung up her coat and slipped the loop of a fresh apron over her head, tied the strings behind her. She saw Stan Kimball mounting the steps.

"Hi, Stan, how's your dog?" It was her standard greeting to him, for he had a complaint a day to get off his chest.

"Hello, Catherine. She's all mouth and digestive tract. If she isn't eating, she's eliminating, usually on the living room carpet."

"She? I thought it was a he."

"Maybe it is. You'd have to ask my wife."

"What a lovely flower you're wearing."

"Like it? I picked it fresh off a graveside bouquet. Catherine, I'm trying to convince your husband to mount another sale."

"We've talked about it."

"Do it. Call it a Halloween Sale and give away pumpkins."

"There isn't time before Halloween," said Hank.

"Then call it an Election Sale. Have a mock election where each customer gets to cast a ballot, and on Saturday night count them up and see if Dewey can take Roosevelt."

Seeing that Catherine looked interested, Hank cautioned, "I don't think we should mix politics with business."

"Well, how about an Armistice Day Sale? As long as we have to fight this goddamn war, we might as well take advantage of it. Advertise a big drawing for eleven o'clock on the eleventh of November—give away a lifetime supply of grapefruit or Brillo pads or some such thing."

"Lifetime?" laughed Catherine. "That could be seventy years."

"All right, birdseed for the life of some bird, but the main thing is to get yourself a gimmick and offer prices like you did the first time and print up a red, white and blue circular and you'll have shoppers crowding in here like you've never seen. What do you say?''

She looked at Hank. ''Should we do it?''

Before he could answer Wallace appeared in the doorway and said, ''Catherine, I'm starving.'' He pointed to his wristwatch.

''Go ahead, Wallace, I'll take over.'' She went to the mirror and straightened her hair.

Stan Kimball said, ''Wait a minute, Catherine, there's something else I want to say to both of you.''

Wallace remained in the doorway listening.

''The house next door to mine on Bean Street is going on the market next month. The name is DeRoche. He delivers auto parts and his company is moving him to Wisconsin. I think you ought to buy the place.''

''With what?'' said Catherine.

''With your profits on Hank's Armistice Sale and all the sales after that. DeRoche is asking less than four thousand. The bank will give you twenty years. There's not a doubt in my mind this town will support two grocery stores and support them damn well. Your house is an old ark on the wrong end of town and you're paying Old Lady Ottmann twice what it's worth. Get yourselves a place of your own on Bean Street before the war ends and prices go up. Don't you agree, Wallace?''

It made no difference to Kimball what Wallace thought, but he was careful never to ignore him entirely, sensing that to ignore Wallace was to turn your back on a poisonous snake.

Wallace, leaning against the doorframe with his hands in his pockets, did not reply. Kimball pressed him:

''What do you say for yourself, Wallace?''

''How's your dog?'' In this as in many other things Wallace followed Catherine's example. ''Is it trained yet?''

''People do not train dogs. They train themselves to accom-
modate dogs. My wife and I have trained ourselves to predict within one minute when this dog of ours will go to the bathroom.''

''Well, that's progress.''

''Yes. It's the minute after we bring her indoors.''

He removed his cigar and examined the ash. "Catherine, maybe you're thinking you'd prefer a house with more amiable neighbors, and I can understand that. It's not the happiest prospect having my dog on one side of you and the mayor's commander-in-chief on the other. But apart from the neighbors you'll love the house. Three bedrooms, all on the ground floor—no need for your father to climb stairs. DeRoche gave it a fresh coat of paint last summer. The yard is big and full of shade trees."

He put on his coat and made for the door. "Come on, Wallace, it's lunch time. I'll give you a ride home."

The red, white and blue circulars were delivered by Brendan and Philip Crowley on a cold afternoon. Sam Romberg had declined, saying he had to work for his father (Plum Bottlegas was the Romberg enterprise), which probably meant that Sam was out delivering cylinders of gas with his brother Andy in the family pickup. Brendan couldn't call Sam his best friend, but he wished it were so. As a companion Sam was unfaithful. He had time for Brendan and Philip only when his other friends weren't available, older friends mostly, whom he had come to know through his brother Andy, who was sixteen. Andy's friends were Plum's fast crowd. They knew girls as far away as Pinburg. They sometimes drank beer.

Philip Crowley had red hair, freckles and large teeth. He was taller than Brendan, but he seemed younger, given as he was to hijinks, giggles and whiny moods. The hijinks and giggles were fine with Brendan, but the whiny moods were not. Brendan distrusted moods, his own included. He considered the moodlessness of his father ideal behavior. He wanted to be like that himself, and not like his mother, who in recent weeks had become very peevish. This was a side of his mother he had never seen before. She was all right in the market, where she had her work and Wallace to divert her, but around home she was temperamental, and at the suppertable her talk was peppered with the word "disgusting." The smell of silage was disgusting, and so were the idlers who spat tobacco juice all over the sidewalk in front of the post office, and so were the school board members who had voted to double expenditures in the athletic department without adding a dime for badly needed facilities in music, home ec, and business education. "Twenty stenography students are taking turns on five typewriters," she would announce over dessert, and Brendan would try to knit his brow and show concern the way his father did, feeling quite certain that his father's concern, like his own, was caused by his mother's discontent rather than by the shortage of typewriters. Part of her trouble, he knew, was the nonsense going around about her being in love with Wallace. He had heard it first from Wallace, and then from Pearl Peterson in school. More than once he had overheard his parents discussing it in low tones as they did dishes together after supper. He wanted to speak up and assure his mother that he, for one, knew it was nonsense, but he was wary of his mother these days and he kept silent.

Distributing circulars along Bean Street, Brendan came to the houses of the mayor and the undertaker and the house in between that was for sale. It was painted creamy-yellow. It had two porches and a lot of bushes and trees around it. At the undertaker's urging, his parents had made an appointment to look at it. Brendan hoped with all his heart they'd buy it, for it stood directly across the alley from Sam Romberg's house.

Further along, he came to the Heffernand house. Here lived the lady who played the organ in the choir loft and sang through her nose. She lived with her brother, the constable. A few days ago Brendan had joined the crowd in the street in front of the village hall and watched the constable fling a burning airplane off the roof, and although he cheered with the others when it crashed in flames against the plate glass window of Plum Hardware and fell to the ground a cinder, he did not feel cheerful in the least. He felt instead a sense of war's ruination of all things fine and human, for he had put together enough model planes of his own to know how much intricate work they required. He felt, too, that the constable might be a little crazy.

The wind being cold on his hands and face, Brendan was relieved to enter the rooming house on Hay Street. He left circulars at the various doors and smelled the various suppers cooking. Upstairs the door to number seven stood open, and

Brendan saw old Mrs. Lansky tending two pots on the stove. He stepped in and handed her a circular.

"Is it Hank's again? Are they having that good price on crackers?"

"I'll look." He unfolded the sheet and they examined it together, finding not crackers but three or four other items the woman was interested in.

She thanked him, and as he turned to leave, she said, "What grade are you in?"

"Seventh."

"Then you knew Dodger Hicks. Have you heard about poor Dodger?"

"No."

"Mrs. Slocum downstairs heard it from her sister-in-law in Winona. Dodger robbed a gas station and was caught and sent to the Home School for Boys in Flensboro. Think of it, not sixteen and already a convict."

The news stung Brendan. He pictured the red-tiled roofs of the Home School, the flower beds, the boys working on the grounds, the guard raising his stick to a boy. It was Labor Day in this picture; they had just eaten a restaurant meal with Uncle Herman. "Poor Dodger," Mrs. Lansky said again. This was the first tender word Brendan had ever heard ascribed to Dodger. Her saying it made him feel sad. Slowly descending the stairs, he realized that it had been easier to be indifferent toward Dodger when everyone else was indifferent.

Making his way across town by way of the alleys, Grandfather turned up the collar of his long black coat and pulled his gray fedora down tight to his ears. He wished he had worn gloves. The cold wind stung his fingers and made his eyes water. He patted his coat pocket, making sure it contained the red, white and blue circular intended for the Lutheran minister. He recalled that the original Armistice Day in 1918 had been warmer than this. News of the Armistice had reached Minneapolis just as his train was pulling in from Chicago. Crowds poured out onto the streets and he had some difficulty making his way from the depot to the carline on Hennepin, for along with his grip he carried a large box containing a flowered pitcher and bowl for Sade's birthday. He boarded the Bryant-Johnson streetcar and looked down on the people moving deliriously along the street. It was stop and go for several blocks until they reached the Basilica of St. Mary, where the way was completely blocked. Caught up in the rejoicing, everyone on the streetcar including the motorman and conductor pushed his way out onto the street. Grandfather would have joined them had it not been for his grip and his box. Looking toward the Basilica, he saw Monsignor Murphy in his cassock and biretta standing in the portico and motioning with his arms for the people to come and thank God for peace. Grandfather leaned out the window and shouted, "Go and thank God for peace!" to those milling around below him. He repeated it several times, pointing to the priest, and soon the mass of people began moving out of the street and up the steps of the church. With the tracks more or less cleared, Grandfather sat down at the controls and confirmed what he had suspected after years of watching motormen at work, that compared to a train driving a streetcar was easy as pie. He moved it along as far as Hennepin and Lake, where he encountered not only another mob but also a confusing junction of tracks. This being only eight blocks from home, he picked up his grip and his box and walked. He found the house empty. Sade and the girls, he learned later, were over at the neighbors, toasting the Armistice with apple juice. He changed out of his uniform and hurried to his favorite saloon on Lyndale and drank and sang songs till midnight.

Windchimes tingled pleasantly over Grandfather's right ear as he let himself into the enclosed back porch of the parsonage, slamming the door behind him and taking out his handkerchief to wipe his eyes. Almost immediately the inner door was opened by a very tall young man in his twenties who scowled and blinked as though he found daylight painful. He wore thick glasses and clothes so dark Grandfather took them for clericals.

"Are you the minister?"

"No, that's my father," said the young man in a soft, deep voice. "Can I help you?"

"I was hoping to talk to the minister himself."

"He's out, probably until this evening, but I can give him your message. Are you a parishioner?"

"Yes."

The young man put out his hand and Grandfather shook it, adding, "But not of this parish. Michael McMahon, section hand, brakeman and conductor with the Milwaukee Road for forty years."

"Paul Dimmitburg," said the young man.

"Paul's a fine name. If we'd had a son, my wife and I, we'd have named him Paul. With our second daughter we were expecting a boy and Paul was the name we'd chosen. Paul Mc-Mahon, now there's a name for you. I see a man with a name like that coming in off the road after a few years and taking an office job. I see him directing the railroad's affairs from behind a desk in St. Paul and going home to a house on Summit Avenue in the same block as James J. Hill's, a house with a stone fireplace in every room." From his coat pocket he took out the circular. "I want the minister and his lady to see these wonderful prices on groceries." He unfolded it shakily, turned it right side up. "See here, fresh carrots, Lava soap—all of it under cost at Hank's Market in honor of Armistice Day."

The young man's face registered no interest. It was the sort of face you couldn't open without a key, thought Grandfather, the sort of face you ran into all over this town. What the hell was on the minds of all these farmers and villagers that they should be so hard-shelled and unforthcoming? Aside from Gordy there was scarcely a soul in the pool hall with an amiable manner about him. They all had a way of hooding their eyes and speaking in monosyllables. Cold. Hot. Rain. Snow. Yup. Nope. Well, at least the pool hall was warmer than this porch, and this tall young man with glasses obviously wasn't going to invite him in.

"I'd be much obliged if you'd give this to your father." He handed him the circular. "Tell him I stopped by." Opening the outer door, he paused. "Perhaps you can tell me. Does your father enjoy talking about the verities?"

"Of course, it's his vocation."

Grandfather laughed happily. "In the words of the great Mac-Arthur, I shall return."

Paul Dimmitburg returned to the kitchen, where he had been sipping tea and reading. When the temperature fell below freezing, the kitchen was the warmest room in the parsonage. He dropped the circular next to the two books open on the table, a volume of Kierkegaard and a carpentry manual. He turned the heat on under the teakettle, and as he waited for the water to boil he stood at the window with his arms crossed, watching the old man walk away with his head cocked against the wind and relishing the stillness pervading the house. He was enjoying his first day of solitude since arriving home from the seminary a week ago. Not that he wasn't fond of his parents and his brother John, but they had been paying him altogether too much attention, his mother acting as if his problem were a physical malady and treatable with enormous helpings of food, both during and between meals; his father pretending he had no problem and treating him as if he were a colleague, drawing him into conversations about his parishioners and asking advice about next Sunday's sermon; John proudly bringing home troops of his high school friends to meet Plum's all-time high-scoring basketball player. Today his parents had driven to Red Wing on church business and John was occupied after school by the first basketball practice of the season.

Paul Dimmitburg went to the stove and held out his hands, warming them over the spout of the teakettle. Having progressed six weeks into his third year of post-graduate training, he had suffered a nervous collapse in late October from an overdose of moral theology. In Paul's case, fear of the Lord was not the beginning of wisdom, as Scripture claimed, but of neurosis. His professors diagnosed his problem as overscrupulosity. The very thought of God's majesty and man's sinfulness filled him with trepidation. Falling so hopelessly short of God's perfection, the human race would have been better off if God had not made His covenant with them, but had instead left them to grovel in their iniquity. When Kierkegaard suggested, perhaps in jest, that all of Christianity ought to carry their Holy Bibles to a mountaintop and plead with God to take them back and relieve humanity of its terrifying responsibility, Paul Dimmitburg murmured to himself, Yes, dear Lord, yes, turn to your angels, make them your chosen people, for we mortals are too weak to offer you anything but disappointment. His fear of God's punishment was at its most acute on Sundays. Sitting in church and listening to the preacher call down God's blessing, he cowered, aware that when you asked for blessings you sometimes got curses, much the way when you prayed for rain you sometimes got hail.

And so, late last week, on the advice of his professors, he had packed up and left St. Louis. They had advised him to go home and look for a job that would not tax his moral sensibilities and maybe next fall he could resume his studies. They told him that if he could learn not to be quite so hard on himself and on the rest of humanity, if he could learn to relax, then he would be free to develop into one of the most brilliant ministers that the seminary had yet produced. They said they'd pray for him.

With his fresh cup of tea, Paul Dimmitburg sat down at the table and resumed reading, alternating every fifteen or twenty minutes between his two books. He had trained himself to study this way, to interrupt his heavier reading with a few pages of something unrelated. It helped his mind stay sharp. In fact, theology and woodworking, his two favorite subjects, weren't as unrelated as they seemed, Christ having grown up in his father's carpentry shop. Paul picked up a pencil and underlined:

Sermons as we know them today constitute a form of communication in complete disaccord with Christianity. Christianity can be communicated only by witnesses, i.e., by men who existentially express what they proclaim, realize it in their lives.

A few minutes later he underlined again:

The wooden spline, inserted in a saw kerf, is a sure and simple way to strengthen miter and butt joints. A spline's width should be slightly less than the combined depth of the kerfs, allowing for a layer of glue.

After a while, leaning back and stretching, Paul let his eye fall upon the red, white and blue circular, and it came to him that Hank's Market must be Kermit's Grocery under new management. In searching unsuccessfully for work this week, he had avoided Kermit's Grocery, assuming it to be the same squalid operation it had always been. He had applied to several Lutherans for work (Louie Legget, Mayor Brask, Len Downie at the Standard Station, Russell Romberg of Plum Bottlegas) and against his mother's wishes he had even gone to a couple of Catholics (B. L. Skeffington in the bank and Ben Crowley at the movie theater) but he had found nothing.

He looked at the clock on the kitchen wall. Hank's Market would be closed. He would apply first thing in the morning.

Walking door to door with circulars was the hardest work Philip Crowley had ever done in his pampered life, and when he came near his own house he crossed to Brendan's side of the street, handed him his sack of circulars and said he had to go in.

"You can't go in. We're not done."

"I've got an earache and a stomachache."

"But we've got all of Clover Street and Corn Street to do yet. And that bunch of houses out by the poor farm. You're getting paid for this."

"When my ear feels like this I have to lie on a heating pad so I don't get mastoiditis."

"What's mastoiditis?"

"And when my stomach feels like this, it might be appendicitis, and I think I've got a blister on my foot. I get infections from blisters."

He limped across the street and into his house.

Alone, crisscrossing streets, the job took three times as long. Nearly an hour later, crossing Clover Street in the dark, Brendan ran to avoid a pair of headlights bearing down on him. It was the Romberg Bottlegas pickup, which, after passing him, screeched to a halt and backed up. Sam Romberg called, "Hey, Bren, want a ride?"

Looking into the cab, Brendan saw five faces reflecting the dim lights from the dash. He saw the red glow of at least three cigarettes. Pearl Peterson sat on Sam's lap. Against the far door Andy Romberg was at the wheel, and next to him was Norma

Nash, a blonde from the junior class who, it was said, went all the way with boys. Squeezed in the middle was Lorraine Graham, who said, "Hi, Bren, what are you doing in this end of town?"

"Delivering circulars."

"Aren't you done yet?" asked Sam. "You've been at it since school let out."

"I'd be done if Philip didn't get sick."

"What was it this time? Appendicitis?"

"I guess so."

"He always quits games when he's on the losing side. It's usually appendicitis."

"Why don't you get in and ride with us?" said Lorraine.

"Yeah, get in," said Andy. "We're taking a tank of bottlegas out to the poor farm."

"He'd have to ride in back," said Pearl sourly. "It's too crowded in here."

"No," said Lorraine, "it's too cold in back."

"You just wish you had a lap to sit on," Pearl told her. "You're always begging some boy to hold you on his lap."

"I am not. You're the one who's always pushing yourself on boys."

Norma Nash said, "Let him in and close the window, it's cold in here." She raised a bottle of beer from between her legs. "Want a swig of beer, Bren? Warm you up?"

"I've got to finish Clover Street and then do the houses out by the poor farm."

"Hell, we'll do those houses for you," said Andy. "Give us a bunch of them bills."

Lorraine said, "Why not do Clover Street too? Come on, let's get out and help him."

Sam threw open his door. "Pick us up at the end of the street, Andy." He slipped out from under Pearl and hopped to the ground.

"Wait," said Pearl, "I'm not delivering any old bills."

"Don't be such a crumb," said Lorraine. "Let me out."

"Let me out too," said Norma Nash. "I've got to pee."

The girls pushed Pearl out the door and got out themselves.

"You're all horrid," said Pearl, climbing back in and slamming the door.

Brendan and Lorraine took one side, and Norma Nash, after pausing behind a bush, joined Sam on the other. They finished Clover Street in ten minutes and packed themselves into the truck, Brendan next to the door with Lorraine on his lap.

Andy gave the bottle to Norma and reached into the tangle of legs to shift gears.

"You drank it all," said Norma.

"There's a swallow left."

"Here, Bren, you get to drain it."

He took it from her and gulped it down. It was warm and fizzy. As the truck bounced over a rut he belched loudly in Lorraine's ear. Lorraine laughed wildly and so did Brendan. He brimmed with happiness. What could be better than fitting tightly into the Romberg pickup with a girl on your lap and fizz in your nose? In abandoning him to this, Philip had done him a great favor.

"Should I open the other bottle?" asked Norma Nash, feeling under the seat.

"Why not," said Andy, picking an opener off the dash and handing it to her. "How come nobody's smoking?"

They all helped themselves from a pack on the dash.

Dragging cautiously on his cigarette, Brendan watched Norma Nash open the bottle. "Where do you guys get beer?"

Norma said, "We always keep a bottle or two under the seat, don't we, Andy?"

"Yep, always. Ever since yesterday."

"They only started going together yesterday," Lorraine explained to Brendan. Her voice was birdlike, twittery with giggles. Her hair brushed his forehead.

"My dad drinks beer by the case," said Norma, "and Andy's dad smokes like a chimney, so that's why we decided to go together. I snitch a bottle or two and Andy supplies the smokes. Right, Andy?" She gave Andy a loud kiss on the cheek and passed the bottle around.

Brendan, seeing Pearl and Lorraine decline, asked, "How come you aren't drinking?"

Lorraine said, "We've got to go home for supper pretty soon."

Pearl said, "Our parents would smell it."

"Don't your parents care?" he asked Sam, who was guzzling.

"Dad's not home tonight."

"How about your mother?"

"My mother can't control us."

Andy laughed. "We jolly Ma up with a few jokes and then we get away with murder."

Brendan could picture it, for although he didn't know their mother he knew Andy to be the clown of the Romberg household. Sam was the serious one. They had a little brother called Larry-the-Twitch, a nervous wreck.

Speeding out to the west end of Main Street, they rolled down the windows for oxygen and shivered in the wind.

Brendan and the girls waited in the truck while Andy and Sam attached a full cylinder of gas to the fittings under the kitchen window of the poor farm. Through an adjacent window they saw heads of white hair bent over a meal in a dimly-lit dining room: institutional living at its gloomiest. The sight put Brendan in mind of Dodger.

"Guess what I heard about Dodger."

"Who's Dodger?" asked Norma Nash.

"A classmate of ours who got F's all the time," Pearl told her.

"He got caught robbing a gas station, and they sentenced him to a year in the home school."

"What's the home school?"

"A prison for boys in Flensboro."

Lorraine sighed, "Poor Dodger." Mrs. Lansky's very words. Though they caused Brendan to grieve for Dodger, he loved Lorraine for saying them.

The dozen houses in the neighborhood of the poor farm stood well back from the road. Andy roared up each driveway in a low, grinding gear and turned the truck around while Brendan ran to the door with a circular.

"Can't you guys hurry up?" Pearl kept asking. "I'm late for supper."

"Me too," said Lorraine. "I was supposed to be home ages ago."

Andy took this as a challenge. He cut corners, driving across lawns and flowerbeds. Careening up the drive to the house of the banker, B. L. Skeffington, he nearly ran over a cat. Lorraine screamed, Norma Nash laughed hysterically and Pearl Peterson ordered him to slow down. On his way out he clipped several boughs off a spruce tree and sideswiped a stone pillar. They sped back to the center of town.

At home Brendan's mother told him he smelled like Gordy's Pool Hall, and he said he had spent some time there warming up.

Business was booming the next morning when Paul Dimmitburg found Hank behind the meat counter. He introduced himself and asked for a job. Hank, looking up from the wedge of cheese he was cutting, replied, "Don't you realize I'm known as the Catholic grocer in this town? Won't your father's parishioners say you've sold out?"

Paul Dimmitburg's smile was world-weary. "Please don't think I'm bound by the bigoted ways of this village, Mr. Foster. I'll give you a full day's work for a full day's wages, and religion won't enter into it."

Hank looked him over. Six foot three. Hunched shoulders. Dark, serious eyes behind thick glasses. Hank would need another clerk if this trade held up throughout the sale, particularly if Wallace continued to work at half speed, afraid of dropping in a fit if he exerted himself. Further, mightn't the minister's son attract Lutheran shoppers? "Okay," he said, "if you'd like to try me out as a boss during the sale, I'll try you out as a clerk. Get yourself a fresh apron from the shelf in the back room and I'll show you the ropes."

While learning the ropes of the grocery business, Paul Dimmitburg also came to understand the ties connecting Wallace to the Fosters. He had been in school with Wallace and knew he required special handling, not only because of his seizures but also because of his smug, disdainful behavior calculated to fend off friendship. The smugness and disdain were still in force, he

observed—Paul himself was the target of Wallace's most with-
ering look—but the force was modified in the presence of Hank
and Catherine. That Wallace should respect Hank and work with
him in a grudging sort of harmony did not surprise Paul; Hank
was the father Wallace never had. What surprised him was the
closeness between Wallace and Catherine. It was a brother-sister
sort of closeness turned up a few degrees. Their habit of nicknaming shoppers struck him as reckless. He thought it in bad
taste for them to refer to the round-shouldered Charles Heffernand as Quasimodo. Worse, one day he heard them call Mrs.
Brask and Mrs. Kimball, who were passing by with a jittery
little dog on a leash, "sounding Brask and tinkling Kimball,"
blaspheming St. Paul in his letter to the Corinthians. Regarding
Brendan, Paul observed that whenever the boy turned up in the
store Wallace drew back in haughty repugnance. Wallace's remarks to the boy were designed to cut and wound, as though
the boy were a foe in possession of some fearful power. Paul
sensed that if Wallace would deign to speak to him it would be
in this same manner, and he resolved to react, if need be, in the
same way Brendan did, by paying Wallace only enough attention
to keep him from feeling ignored. Paul rather liked Brendan.
The boy gave you a level look that made him seem older than
twelve, his eyes settling on you and lingering, observing. His
disposition reminded Paul of his own at that age, quiet and
generally serious.

During the three days of the Armistice Sale, Catherine and
Hank were impressed by Paul. He was a dependable worker,
not speedy but steady and untiring. They liked his way with
customers; he was more accommodating than Wallace, less
brusque. His dark, heavybrowed eyes were thoughtful, sincere,
without guile. His speech was soft, devoid of all sharpness,
including wit. Catherine wondered if he ever laughed. There
was nothing spontaneous in his strange little chuckle; it sounded
like a subdued form of throat-clearing. She wondered, too, why
he addressed all his questions about the store to Hank, never to
her. Didn't he realize she was a full partner in this enterprise?
Or was he one of those men who didn't take women seriously?

"What are you majoring in?" she asked during a Friday-morning lull, her first opportunity to chat with him.

"Philosophy was my undergraduate major," he said, looking somberly down at her and straightening his tie as though for inspection. "My master's will be in theology."

"You'll be a minister like your father?"

"Yes." He waited in silence for additional questions.

She thought his formality odd, and assumed it was due to shyness, but in fact it was due to Wallace's presence not six feet away. Shut up, you flunky, said Wallace's hate-filled eyes.

She approached Paul again when Wallace had gone to lunch. "What's it like coming home to Plum after St. Louis? Isn't it horribly dull?"

He blinked a few times and replied ominously, "Plum is in danger of losing its soul, Mrs. Foster. I have never seen such sectarian bigotry. If I were God I'd be so sick of the prideful ways of the Catholics and Lutherans in this village I'd vomit them out of my mouth." He went on to describe his father, who, though virtuous in all ways and unbigoted, had so far been unable to erase the prejudice of his parishioners. It was Paul's ambition to devote his life to the cause of unity among Christians.

Catherine was intrigued. His speech was absolutely flat, and by the end of his sentences his voice faded to a whisper, as though he were losing strength. Here was a thinker after her own heart, a young man who would go out in the world and make a difference. His mind was bent to a purpose. Wallace's, by comparison, was haywire.

After returning from lunch Wallace Flint realized that he had been deposed in Catherine's heart. Through the afternoon he fumed and pouted and snapped at customers. He hated Catherine for being captivated by a gawky basketball player whose grades in high school were inferior to his own, a humorless stuffed shirt who planned to waste his life in the service of a nonexistent God.

When Catherine came to work on Saturday morning and went straight to Paul and said, "I had a dream about you last night," Wallace was outraged. He didn't hang around to hear about the

dream, nor did he attend to any of the several customers who
were waiting for help. He went out the back door and touched
a match to the pile of cardboard boxes and waste paper in the
incinerator. Warming himself at the flames, he came to the bitter
realization that as far as he knew Catherine had never dreamed
about him. He had had dozens of dreams about her. Most recently she had been his mother and taken him for ice cream at
that place with an Italian name she was always talking about in
Minneapolis.

Hank put his head out the back door and said, "Don't bother
with the trash now, Wallace. We're too busy up front."

Wallace came away from the fire reluctantly. He loved watching fire. He stomped indoors with his eyes cast down and his
mind made up to join the army. Removing his apron and putting
on his jacket, he told Hank he was going home. "If I keep
working I'll have a fit. I don't feel good."

Hank believed him. "Do you need a ride?"

"No, just rest. I'll see you Monday."

At home his mother asked him what was wrong and he told
her to shut up. He climbed the stairs to his room and searched
through his jumble of books for military biographies. He lay
down on his bed with the lives of Lee, Pershing and Genghis
Khan.

In the late afternoon he pulled his ironing board up to his bed
and wrote a letter to his draft board, volunteering for induction.
Until today he had dreaded serving in the military, but his jealousy of Paul Dimmitburg had jarred him out of his cowardice.
Soldiering seemed the opportunity of a lifetime. The army was
his ticket out of Plum, launching him into the larger world. The
army took care of its own, had doctors and nurses to help you
through your seizures. Certainly it was a better life than living
anonymously in some city where if you had a fit they'd just stand
there and let you bite off your tongue.

After dark, carrying the letter to the post office, he saw that
Legget's was not as busy as Hank's. The moment he dropped
the letter into the slot, he was relieved of his resentment of Paul
Dimmitburg. By the time Wallace came home on leave, in uniform, Paul would either be ordained a cowardly, draft-dodging

preacher or be still selling groceries for eighty cents an hour. Wallace returned to the market and said he was feeling much better. He put on an apron and worked until closing time.

Income for the Armistice Sale came to $3,155, ten percent more than Grand Opening.

WINTER

❖

14

I N   L A T E   N O V E M B E R   C A T H E R I N E was amazed
to open a letter from a woman who announced that she was
Uncle Herman's bride. She said she was looking forward to
meeting Herman's relatives and asked if the Fosters and Grandfather would come to Flensboro on the following Sunday afternoon and stay for supper. "We're living not on Herman's farm
but on mine, which is adjacent to his and easy to find if you stay
on Highway 61 through town and turn left just beyond the Home
School for Boys. We're inviting relatives from the Twin Cities
as well, and they will bring Nancy Clancy along if she feels up
to it. I want this to be what has been lacking in Herman's life
for too many years—a good old family reunion." She signed
her name *Virginia.*

Catherine passed the letter around at supper.

Grandfather chuckled. "Funny to think of Herman as a ladies' man. Why didn't he tell us about her when we stopped to
see him."

"He did, in his way," Catherine told him. "He kept talking
about the woman on the next farm."

"But he didn't mention romance."

"Can we go?" she asked Hank. "Can we get there and back?" The DeSoto had developed a serious cough, accompanied by a lurch, and the radiator, which had had its holes soldered shut several times, was becoming porous with rust.

"Let's see," Hank calculated. "Flensboro's forty miles. I could clean the spark plugs once more and see how she runs. We'll have to take six or eight gallons of water in the trunk."

After supper he and Brendan carried tools and a flashlight out to the back yard and, as they removed the plugs, reset the gaps and cleaned the points, Hank taught Brendan how pistons worked. "Hold the light steady," he said more than once. It was a chilly night, and the light wavered as Brendan shivered.

When they were nearly done, Brendan brought up what was troubling him. "Dodger Hicks is in the Home School in Flensboro."

"I know."

"Mom says I should visit him."

"Do you want to?"

"I suppose I should." His voice trembled with cold. "It's one of the corporal works of mercy, visiting prisoners."

Catherine's very words—Hank was vaguely irritated to hear them from his son. He wished his son were less fretful, a little less pious. "Hand me the smaller wrench, and try to hold the light still."

Watching his father wipe the last spark plug with an oily rag, Brendan recalled how often in the past weeks he had heard Dodger's name brought up around town, recalled the pang of guilt he felt each time, as though by rejecting Dodger's friendship he had somehow caused Dodger's trouble. It surprised him how much attention the arrest was commanding in Plum. It seemed as though after four years of discussing heroism, everybody found it refreshing to concentrate on vice for a change. The war was dragging on and valor was becoming old hat. Every hamlet had turned out its share of soldiers and sailors (Pinburg had produced an army colonel, no less) but how many towns could boast of a father-son team of convicts? In the pool hall Brendan had heard the men recounting the crimes of Dodger's father—embezzlement, extortion—and predicting what lay ahead for Dodger—armed robbery, murder. In the store, Wallace Flint went on about Dodger like a man obsessed, instructing shoppers that Dodger's downfall could be traced to three causes other than his father's criminal example; namely Dodger's inability to read and thus his humiliation in school, his mother's promiscuity and thus his feeling of rootlessness, and (here Wallace threw a meaningful look at Brendan) the insincerity of his so-called friends.

Replacing the spark plug, Hank said softly, "What do you feel like doing? Seeing him or not seeing him?"

Brendan steadied the flashlight on the fender. "I feel like not seeing him."

"Then don't see him."

A long pause.

"But I should see him."

"Then see him."

They arrived at the farm in the late afternoon. It was immediately evident that by marrying his neighbor, Uncle Herman had risen in the world. Virginia's farmhouse stood on a knoll commanding a view of the river, the fields and the town of Flensboro. There were a dozen cars parked in the drive. As Hank steered the rattling DeSoto around to the back of the house and parked near the stoop, so as to be handy to water, Brendan saw eight or ten children's faces looking out the hayloft door and other apertures of the barn.

The newlyweds came out onto the back stoop to welcome them. Married only a few days, his bride had already done a lot for Uncle Herman's appearance. He wore a new suit and a carnation in his lapel. There was no sign of the hair that used to grow out of his ears or the crack that ran across the right lens of his glasses. But she hadn't cured Herman of his shyness; he stood behind her, smiling off in another direction, while his bride introduced herself. "I'm Virginia, and I've been dying to meet you." She pumped their hands energetically. She was about Herman's age, maybe a year or two older, a broad-faced woman with a broad smile and broad shoulders. She wore a rose blouse and a figured apron over a full black skirt. "How wonderful to know you,'' she said to Grandfather as he bowed deeply and kissed her hand.

The house was jammed with strangers. Though Virginia had called it a reunion, it was actually a wedding reception, and she had invited her family and friends as well as Herman's. Grandfather plunged in, giving each woman in his path his brightest smile and a courtly bow. As though by instinct, he found his way to the place in the living room, where the ancient and diminutive Nancy Clancy was tucked into the corner of a very large chair. She had a translucent look, the flesh of her face paper thin, paper pale. Her dress was burgundy, tied at the throat with an enormous white bow, giving her the aspect of a small jewel wrapped as a gift. The instant her piercing black eyes fell upon Grandfather she rose weightlessly to her feet and held both of his hands to her breast. ''Michael, why don't you ever come to see me?''

Hank, Catherine and Brendan gathered around and bent over her. Catherine apologized for their neglect, explaining about their untrustworthy car. She asked how Nancy was feeling.

''I feel just fine for ninety-three, but I simply must see you people more often. When you're as old as I am, you feel like you're coming unmoored from the human race unless your dear ones stay in touch. Do you realize, Catherine—my, this boy of yours is shooting up like a weed—do you realize, Catherine, that your father is the last of his generation, and I'm his *aunt*? You know what that means? It means he's my last link with your generation. He's my bridge.'' She lowered her voice. ''Tell me frankly, Catherine, how has your father been getting along?''

''None of that,'' Grandfather broke in. ''You're the same today as you were when I was a boy, asking about me as if I wasn't old enough to answer for myself. I'm fit as a fiddle, thank you.'' He did two steps of a jig to prove it.

''But don't you miss the city, Michael? How do you occupy yourself in that little burg?''

''I'll tell you how I occupy myself. Mornings I sleep late. Afternoons I take a nap, and after my nap I visit the pool hall. Evenings''—he laughed, pinching her elbow—''evenings are given over to the digestion of my supper.''

Nancy Clancy said to Catherine, "Your cousin Marge is here, did you see her? She picked me up and drove me here. If you haven't seen her daughter Julie in recent years you're in for a delight. She's fourteen and a vision of loveliness."

Brendan brightened at this; he had expected to find no one his age at this affair. He remembered his cousin Julie from family get-togethers in the city. She had been a gawky nine or ten when he saw her last, and very likable for a girl.

Nancy Clancy laid a feathery hand on Brendan's arm. "You must make friends with her, my boy. Cousins must not grow apart."

Brendan searched the rooms of the farmhouse but didn't find Julie. He was about to go outside and look for her when she came in looking for him. She planted herself in front of him with her fists on her hips and said, "Hi, you're twelve this year, I've been keeping track. Come on outside and see the horses."

She was an inch taller than Brendan. She had black hair, dark gray eyes and freckles. She wore a rich-looking gray dress with a single red flower on the skirt. She had breasts.

They made their way through the chattering crowd and out the back door.

"So do you think seventh grade is harder than sixth, Brendan? I think eighth is easier than seventh. It's nice being in junior high, isn't it, moving around to different classrooms instead of sitting in the same old desk all day. In my school we got to take home ec in the seventh grade. Do you get to take shop? Are you out for sports?"

She made him feel important. Who else considered all these areas of his life interesting enough to ask about? Walking down to the pasture behind the barn where a team of workhorses were grazing, she asked him how many friends he had. He said he had three close ones; their names were Sam, Philip, and (fibbing to test her reaction) Pearl. She said she had twelve, none of them boys at the present time. Laughing, she twirled around so that her dress swirled at her knees. "Would you want to be my boyfriend if we weren't cousins?" He shrugged and blushed a little, thinking yes.

The horses were gigantic and old, their brown hides beginning to grow woolly for winter, their tails busily brushing flies. A number of younger children, their Sunday shoes soiled with manure, emerged from the barn where they had been tormenting the piglets, and joined them in the pasture. They hopped about picking grass and handing it to Julie, who held it out to the horses. "Here, Julie, take mine." "No, take mine." The horses chewed slowly, blinking and twitching their ears. Each time one of them dipped for another bite, wetting Julie's palm with its muzzle, she giggled.

Eventually the children grew bored and went off to play hide and seek among the outbuildings. As Julie wiped her hands on the neck of one of the horses, Brendan gazed across the pasture, searching his mind for something to say that would impress her. Her eyes fell upon the Home School for Boys at the edge of Flensboro.

"You know what this place is, those buildings?"

She said she didn't.

"It's a reformatory for criminals under the age of eighteen."

"Really? Is it a prison?"

"Sort of, I guess." He paused for effect. "I've got a friend in this one."

"You do?" She covered her mouth in trepidation. Her eyes, searching his, were wide. "A prisoner? What did he do?"

"He robbed a gas station in Winona."

"All those trees. It looks so pretty. It's scary to think it's a prison."

"Want to go and look it over?"

"You mean actually go inside?"

"Yeah. We'd say we're visiting Dodger."

She looked back at the farmhouse. "Should we tell our folks?"

"Let's go before the little kids follow us."

They ran across the pasture.

Inside the entrance, an archway of stone, they came upon a man sitting in a black pickup. He poked his head out the window and said, "Who you seeing?" He had small eyes and a crooked nose. He wore a khaki shirt with a small badge pinned to the collar. Beyond the pickup was a high hedge of lilac with its leaves turning brown. The hedge was full of sparrows, chirping and fluttering.

"Dodger Hicks," said Brendan. "Is he here?"

The man looked them over. "Where's your adults? Kids aren't allowed in without adults."

"Oh? We didn't know that." Brendan was relieved. Though he feigned disappointment, he thought it a great stroke of luck to have impressed Julie and tried to carry out a corporal work of mercy without actually having to see Dodger. What could he and Dodger possibly say to each other?

"Come on, we better go," he said to Julie.

She didn't respond. She was looking through the opening in the hedge at the main building. Five people stood on the front steps, visiting. Two adults and three teenage boys. One of the boys was bald.

"But it's okay this once," said the man in the pickup. "Hicks ain't had a visitor since he got there. Sign your names." He handed a clipboard out the window.

Brendan backed away. "No, that's all right. Dodger probably wouldn't remember me anyway."

But Julie was already signing her name.

"I seen Hicks on the grounds a few minutes ago, just look around. If he's not outside, ask at the desk in that first building."

Brendan signed his name.

As they came to the main building and turned left to skirt it on a pathway of sand, Julie whispered, "Look, he hasn't got any hair."

The bald boy, slouched in a posture of boredom and ignoring his visitors, was looking down at Brendan and Julie from the steps. Julie waved and said, "Hi," but the boy turned away.

Behind the main building they came to a fork in the path and stopped. They stood looking at the people scattered on the lawns. They saw a pack of boys in the distance playing leapfrog; their heads were all shaved. They saw a pair of hairless boys sitting under a tree reading a comic book. Another bald boy came toward them on the path surrounded by a crowd of visitors—parents, grandparents, brothers, sisters, babies. They saw a young couple in love, embracing as they strolled, the bald boy burying his hand in the girl's thick red hair.

They took the path leading off to the right and came upon a skinny, dark-skinned boy sitting on a glider that hung from a large wooden frame. He, too, was bald. His pants were too short for his long legs; his short-sleeved shirt was old and faded. His eyes kept darting toward Brendan and Julie and then shifting away. As they passed him, he got to his feet and fell into step beside Julie. Fearful, she leaned into Brendan, taking his arm. The boy was tall. He spoke, looking straight ahead:

"Say, did I ever give you caps for that gun? I don't think I did."

"Dodger!" Brendan gaped at him. He hadn't recognized him without hair.

Without breaking stride, Dodger said, "I'll bring you some caps first chance I get. You still live in the same house?"

"Yes." Brendan, holding Julie's hand, kept his eyes riveted on Dodger. Hairless, he looked much older than the boy who threw the boomerang, but he was Dodger all right—long teeth exposed when he pulled back his lip in that self-conscious smile, head hanging forward on that long neck, eyes shifting away when you tried to engage them.

"Or can I drop off the caps at the store? Your ma and dad still got that store?"

"Yep."

Dodger nodded approvingly. Some things, at least, were permanent.

Julie whispered, "Introduce me."

They stopped walking. "Dodger, this is my cousin Julie."

"Hi." He didn't look at her. "Brendan's an old friend of mine."

"Yes, he told me."

"How's your boomerang? Jeez, wasn't that fun?" Dodger's eyes lit up as he put out his hand and slowly traced the boomerang's arc through the air. "Damn if it didn't come back like it had a leash on it." He laughed with delight. "Damn if I ever saw another one. You still got it?"

"Yep, I have."

"You still throw it?"

"No, the ends got splintered and it doesn't fly so good." Brendan noticed tiny round scars and scabs on Dodger's forearms, a similar scab on his throat.

"Damn if this wouldn't be a good place for a boomerang." Dodger indicated the lawns and the fields beyond. "Damn if I wouldn't like to have a boomerang here—show these guys."

"Maybe we could find you one," said Julie. Brendan saw that she was entranced by Dodger. Her eyes were sad and serious. "Brendan, let's try to get a boomerang for Dodger."

"Okay."

The three of them walked on.

She asked, "How long will you be here, Dodger?"

He shrugged. "I guess I could get out any time."

"Then why don't you?"

"Well, see, I'd have to go live with my ma. My dad's still doing time in Stillwater, and my ma she's living with this guy in Winona and they only got two little rooms, and I'm not crazy about the guy, he's crabby. So this here's my home for now." His eyes fell on Brendan, shifted away, came back. "Maybe I could live in your house? Your folks could be my guardians."

To be so utterly homeless and needy—it took Brendan's breath away. He wished he hadn't come. Having no sooner bragged to Julie that this loser was his friend, he was now being asked to prove it.

"I don't know, Dodger, we've got my grandfather at the house, and he's pretty hard to live with. Gets up at night and talks out loud." A very lame excuse, as Dodger implied:

"Yeah, it gets sort of noisy here nights, too, sixteen of us to a room."

A bell sounded. Dodger stopped and said, "That's supper. Hey, how about if you eat with me? Visitors get to stay for supper on Sundays."

Boys ran past them on the path, heading for the door of the dining hall.

"No," said Brendan, "we've got to get back. We're having a family reunion over there at that farm."

Dodger looked where Brendan pointed. "Whose farm is that?"

"Relatives'."

"Boy, that's a big house. How many people live there?"

"Two. My Uncle Herman and his wife."

Dodger gawked at the farm for a few moments, his head hanging forward; then he sucked in his saliva and said, "Would you ask them if I could live there?"

Julie and Brendan exchanged a pained glance, and Dodger, seeing it, gracefully withdrew his suggestion by laughing as though he hadn't meant it. This was the Dodger of old, all right; at the first sign of rejection he backed off with something of apology in his manner. Sorry for needing you, he seemed to say.

The family they had seen on the front steps came around the corner of the building and went into the dining hall. They were followed by the boy with the large delegation of visitors. Last, slowly, came the two lovers.

They walked Dodger as far as the doorway, where Brendan said, "We'll be seeing you, Dodger."

"Can't you stay and eat?"

"We've got to get back."

"Okay, I'll go to the gate with you."

"Don't you have to go in and eat?"

"I ain't very hungry."

As they retraced their way along the path, Dodger scanned the grounds for someone to notice that he had visitors—he was feeling very proud—but everyone had gone in to supper.

Passing through the opening in the bird-filled hedge, Julie said, "How long will you be here if you don't go and live with your mom?"

"I don't know, till next summer, I guess. Or if my dad gets paroled I might go and live with him." He turned to Brendan. "Don't worry, I'll bring you some caps for that gun as soon as I get out."

"It's okay, Dodger. I can get caps at the dime store." Didn't Dodger realize that cap guns were for children?

"Yeah, but a guy always needs more caps than he thinks he does. I'll bring you a few rolls."

They said goodbye and Dodger left them.

As Brendan took the clipboard from the man in the pickup, Julie gripped his arm. "You've got to eat supper with him."

"I do?"

"Look at him."

Dodger was moving away with the same loose-jointed shuffle Brendan remembered from the lumber yard the day he filled his pockets with marbles.

"You're his only friend in the world."

He shook his head. "No, I was kidding about being his friend."

She scolded, "You told me you were his friend."

"Yeah, but that was a long time ago, and it was only for about three days."

"That's good enough for Dodger."

He gave her an impassive look, concealing his unease. Appalling, the magnitude of Dodger's need.

"He wants to eat with you, Brendan."

"What good would that do?"

"He wants people to know he's got a friend, don't you see?"

He turned away, stirred by jealousy that she should have so much room in her heart for Dodger. He was stirred by admiration for her as well.

"Please?" she said. It was a drawn-out, wheedling please.

"Will you eat too?"

"Sure." She smiled.

He handed back the clipboard. "Hey, Dodger, wait up."

A burly man wearing a white apron stood inside the door of the dining hall. He had a flat, scarred face and cold eyes. He said, "You're late, Hicks."

Dodger nodded agreeably.

"Who's your visitors?"

"Brendan and Julie." Dodger grinned crookedly.

"Sir!" the man in the apron demanded.

"Brendan and Julie, sir."

"They relatives?"

"Old friends, sir."

The man put out his hand. "Friends pay." Two of his fingers were half gone.

"I thought it was free for visitors on Sundays."

"Relatives eat free, but friends pay the fifty cents."

Brendan and Julie were without money. As they stood awkwardly in the entryway looking at each other, the man hooked his thumbs in his apron straps and drummed his fingers on his chest, the whole fingers and the fractions. "You sure they ain't related, Hicks?"

It was Julie who recognized the opening he offered. She said to him, "We're cousins."

"Yeah, cousins, sir," beamed Dodger, delighted at the thought of having cousins.

The man looked at Brendan, who echoed "Cousins, sir." It was true of two of them at least.

The man growled, "Hurry up then, before the food's gone."

The dining hall doubled as a small gymnasium. Trestle tables were set up on the basketball floor. Dodger led them to a hole in the wall where three trays of food were handed out to them from the kitchen. The main dish was a slice of meatloaf and a boiled potato; the other dish was melting ice cream. They found places to sit at the end of a table where a dozen bald boys were chattering loudly and throwing their shoulders into one another as they ate. The presence of Julie quieted them for a minute— there was something reverent in the looks they stole at her—and then it inspired them to greater horseplay than before. They punched one another in the ribs and belly; they cried out in pain, shouting insults. Watching them bounce on their benches, Brendan thought of the rising a_d falling of pistons in the DeSoto, energy pressing against confinement; compression and combustion. The burly man in the apron came across the room and restored quiet by roughly knocking six or eight shaved heads together. For several minutes thereafter the heads were bent low and silent over the table, the boys trying to conceal the tears of pain brimming in their eyes. Julie and Brendan ate very little— the meatloaf was cold, the ice cream warm—but Dodger ate swiftly and hungrily and went back to the hole in the wall and asked for more. He returned with a small, wrinkled potato.

A buzzer sounded and a small, important-looking man wearing a suit and tie came into the room and drew a paper from his vestpocket. He wore a fussy little moustache and goatee. He walked up and down between the tables until everyone was silent, then he read the day's announcements. His voice was shrill. Softball equipment would no longer be provided during free hour (a groan sounded along the tables) until it was discovered who had been stealing balls. Study would be extended by one half hour tonight (another groan) because of the mid-term exams beginning tomorrow. There was to be a lyceum program tomorrow at three o'clock; a penmanship expert would demonstrate how beautifully he could write with his right hand and left, frontward and backward; and his wife would show slides of historical houses in Massachusetts. But if the boys behaved as they had at the last lyceum program (the man's voice rose in anger), if they couldn't learn to shut up and sit still (the man glared so hard his face turned red), and if they had no more manners than monkeys and jackals (his anger silenced him for a moment), then there would be no more lyceum programs (a brief cheer), *and* no more Saturday night movies (a groan). He gave his emotions a few seconds to subside, and then he ran through the last few items, concluding with this, delivered with a chilling smile:

"It would seem there is no end to the consequences of the fight that occurred last week in the lavatory on the second floor of Building C. Whoever it was that struck Jerry Ludbeck in the face and broke his glasses, will no doubt be happy to know that at eight o'clock tomorrow morning a doctor in Rochester is going to remove Jerry Ludbeck's right eye."

An intense hush.

"All right, dismissed."

Everyone stood. Watched over closely by the man in the apron, they all lined up at the kitchen window to dispose of their trays; then they hurried outdoors.

"I'd show you around some more," said Dodger, "but it's the end of visiting hours now. When you coming back?"

"I don't know," said Brendan, hurrying them along to the front gate.

"If you come back again, I'll look in my trunk for something to give you."

The man in the pickup handed them the clipboard and they signed out.

Julie said, "Thanks a lot for supper, Dodger."

"Sure." He stood in the stone archway facing them, blocking their exit, one hand in his pocket, the other rubbing the top of his smooth head. "One thing I got in the trunk I could give you right now is a *Superman* comic. You like *Superman*? I could run and get it."

"No, that's okay," said Brendan, "we've got to be going."

For the first time since they were introduced, Dodger looked fully into Julie's eyes. "You like *Superman*?"

"He's okay. I'm not crazy about comics."

He thought. "Or I could give you *Blondie*. You like *Blondie*?"

She nodded, aware that accepting his gift was a gift. "I do like *Blondie*."

"Wait here." Dodger loped off up the path.

"Hicks ain't a bad kid," said the man in the pickup. "It's a shame the way he's picked on, but you know how kids are, they need to find one amongst them that won't fight back so they can pick and pick and pick to their heart's content." The man waited for them to ask for the brutal details, but they wished not to hear them. Which made him all the more eager to tell: "They come at him in his sleep and burn him with their cigarettes. If I was Hicks I'd wait for them sons of bitches to go to sleep themselves, and I'd take a knife and castrate them."

The sparrows in the bushes sang and sang. The family of five came down the path. The parents and two of the boys signed out; the other boy hurried back to the main building. The separation appeared a relief on both sides.

The lovers came down the path. The girl signed out, then held the boy's bald head on her shoulder. The man in the pickup said, "Scram now, and remember what I told you. Next time bring an adult or you don't get in."

The girl stamped her foot angrily. "I *am* an adult. We're both adults." There were tears in her eyes as she ran out the gate.

Soon Dodger was back with a tattered comic book.

"Thanks," said Julie, taking it from him.

"Yeah, it's okay."

"And I hope you get good grades on your exams."

Dodger laughed. "I never do. I always flunk everything. They say if I'm still here next term they're maybe going to take me out of school and put me in one of the shops."

"The shops ain't so bad," said the man in the pickup.

"I hope it's woodworking," said Dodger. "I hope it ain't the foundry. But maybe I won't be still here next term."

"So long," said Brendan, his eyes on the scab at Dodger's throat. "Be seeing you."

"Goodbye," said Julie. "Thanks again for everything."

They walked out through the gateway and across the road, and as they were about to step into the pasture, they looked back and saw him standing in the gateway, his bald head gleaming in the slanting sunlight. He called, "When you coming back?"

"We'll see," said Brendan.

The shiny head bobbed, nodding.

The sun set as they crossed the field in silence. Brendan, trying to rid his mind of the scars, wished he could relive the afternoon, leaving Dodger out of it.

Nearly everyone in the farmhouse had eaten, and some of the guests had left. Brendan's parents came up to him as he stood at the buffet filling his plate with ham and corn and scalloped potatoes. "Where have you been?" his father asked. "We've been waiting to start home."

"Julie and I went to see Dodger."

"Oh, good," exclaimed Catherine.

In his mother's eyes Brendan saw a sparkle he remembered from their days in the city. The afternoon away from Plum had obviously been good for her. "He must have been glad to see you," she said.

"I guess he was."

"What's it like there? How's he getting along?"

"It's okay. He's doing okay."

Because Julie was sitting at the dining room table, he took his plate to the kitchen. He didn't want Julie to overhear his false account of Dodger in the Home School, nor did he want his mother to know the truth. His mother's cheer must be maintained as long as possible.

"How long will he be there, did he say?" Catherine sat across from him at the kitchen table.

"He'll be there a year, unless he decides to go where his mother lives. He can get out any time if he does that."

His mother must have detected a false note, for the sparkle in her eyes was replaced by concern, like Julie's. "Are you sure he's all right? Virginia says it's a dreadful place. Boys get injured in fights."

"No, he's fine." He glanced through the doorway, making sure Julie couldn't hear him. "He's doing fine."

His mother looked skeptical. "Really and truly?"

He nodded emphatically, his mouth full of corn.

BOYS WITH RECORDS OF good behavior and homes to go to were released from the Home School for ten days at Christmas. Dodger was one of them. On the afternoon of Christmas Eve, two days after the other boys had left, he stood on the porch of the main building and watched for Mr. Cranshaw's car to turn in at the gate. In a cardboard box at his feet were a change of underwear and socks, a clean shirt, and several comic books. It was Mr. Cranshaw, his Winona County case worker, who had delivered Dodger to the Home School in October. He was a sharp-faced little man with a brusque manner and not much to say, but with a certain amount of compassion in his eyes. Dodger had been grateful when, after sentencing, Mr. Cranshaw assured the judge and the sheriff that Dodger did not require an armed guard on his way up the river.

The clouds of Christmas Eve were darkening to gunmetal blue and threatening to unload a heavy snowfall into the Mississippi Valley. Dodger wore no cap; his bald head was numb with cold. His jacket was a thin flannel shirt he had appropriated for himself in the laundry room, where he had been working half days since being declared uneducable by the teaching staff. On his feet were warm, sturdy work boots lent him by the barber who came out from Flensboro every second Thursday and shaved 109 heads. "Are those raggedy old things the only shoes you've got?" the barber asked him, "You can't go home for Christmas looking like a bum." The barber, whose name was Johnson, took a special interest in Dodger, more than once having spoken to the warden about the two cigarette burns near Dodger's hairline that were slow to heal. The warden finally relented and allowed Dodger to see the doctor during his weekly visit to the school. The doctor gave Dodger a tube of ointment for his burns and he gave the warden a piece of his mind for allowing physical abuse in the dormitories. "If you don't take action," the doctor threatened, "I'll report it to the governor and the state board of health." The warden's only action was to warn Johnson to quit meddling in the affairs of the Home School or else lose his barbering contract with the state.

In an office at the front of the main building, the warden looked up from his desk and saw Cranshaw's car turn in at the gate. He clapped a hat on his head and scurried out to the porch. "Come on, Hicks, we can't keep your man waiting." Dodger picked up his box and descended the steps with the warden. One of the few things Dodger had in common with the other boys was his dislike of the warden, whose eyes were angry and whose tiny moustache and pointed goatee reminded Dodger of drawings he had seen of the devil.

Dodger went around the car and got in on the passenger side while Mr. Cranshaw rolled down his window and greeted the warden.

"About time you got here," piped the warden.

"I told you I was tied up till today." Mr. Cranshaw handed him a document.

"It wasn't in our budget to feed the kid for two extra days. How come his mother didn't come for him?"

"She has no car."

The warden glanced at the signatures at the bottom of the document and said, "All right, take him away, and be sure he's back here by suppertime on New Year's Day. And while you're at it, give him a talking to about laziness. He makes no effort in his classes and he makes no effort in the laundry. He's well on his way to being a bum.''

Mr. Cranshaw rolled his window shut before the warden finished. He shifted gears and the car moved down the sloping drive.

''Well, how have you been, Dodger?''

''Not so bad.'' Dodger smiled. He sat holding his box on his lap.

''You sound like you've got a cold.''

''Yeah. It's real hot in the laundry, and then I go outside and my nose runs.''

''Haven't you got a cap? You'll freeze your head.''

''Yeah, I've got a cap but I keep forgetting it. It's hard to keep wearing a cap when you never did.''

Driving out through the gate, Cranshaw felt a sense of freedom almost as great as Dodger's. Over the years he had seen enough of the Home School to despise it. His work took him to prisons, hospitals, orphanages, insane asylums and schools for the blind and deaf, none of which made his skin crawl the way this institution did. The guards were thugs and the warden was a martinet with a treacherous look in his eye.

''Dodger, your mother isn't home. I called her last week to make sure she'd sign your release form. She said she'd sign it, but when I went to the apartment this morning the landlady said she'd been gone for a week or more. But she expects her home for Christmas.''

Dodger shrugged and nodded and shrugged again.

''I'm not supposed to take you home, Dodger, without your mother being there.''

Dodger said nothing.

''But I'm taking you anyhow. I forged your mother's name.''

Dodger chuckled.

They rode in silence for twenty miles. The highway was a narrow, winding shelf at the base of the bluffs. Below them the blue-black river was dotted with small ice floes. As they sped past the sideroad leading up over the bluffs and beyond, Dodger asked, "Have we got time to swing through Plum? I've got a friend there."

"Afraid not. I'm late getting home as it is. Maybe on our way back on New Year's."

It was dark when they reached Winona. Snow was dropping in large, watery flakes. Cranshaw drew up in front of a house facing the highway and said, "Okay, Dodger, I'm sticking my neck out for you, so return the favor by staying out of trouble, will you?"

"Sure."

"Starting the day after tomorrow I want you to call me up every day or drop in at my office. It's just like being on parole—you've got to keep checking in."

"Sure."

"You remember where my office is?"

"Sure."

"Your landlady said to tell you she wouldn't be home tonight but she's left your apartment unlocked."

"Okay."

"Merry Christmas, Dodger."

"Merry Christmas."

Snowflakes melted and ran down the dome of his scalp as Dodger carried his box into the tiny front hallway and climbed the stairs. He wished the landlady, Mrs. Wrobleski, were home. She had been nice to him during the short time he lived here, offering him a cookie or a cupcake every so often and letting him look at her stereopticon. He opened the door at the head of the stairs and entered the apartment. He switched on the light. His mother's bed in the living room was unmade. Standing on the table and the two windowsills were a number of empty beer bottles. He went into the kitchen and saw that his mother had been using his cot as a catch-all for clothes and groceries. He added his cardboard box to the clutter on the cot and went to the refrigerator for something to drink. Mr. Cranshaw's heater fan had been going high speed the whole trip and dried out Dodger's throat and nose. He uncapped a bottle of milk and took a big swallow before he realized it was sour. He went into the tiny bathroom, spat into the sink and drank a glass of water.

He returned to the living room and pulled a chair up to the window. He watched the headlights moving along the highway below him. He savored his solitude. After two months in the Home School, this was pure peace. There was no one to taunt you or hurt you or put you to work. He was glad his mother was gone. Christmases without his father were hard on his mother. She drank and got weepy, then drank some more and got angry, and then drank some more and slept. With his father present, come to think of it, her behavior wasn't all that much different, except the weepy part was shorter and the angry part was longer. "For them that can be merry," she'd say when anyone wished her "Merry Christmas." Wherever she was tonight, Dodger hoped she was with a man she liked, someone thoughtful enough to give her a present.

It dawned on Dodger that he had no present for her. He went to the closet and found a cap he hadn't seen before, a black watch cap probably left behind by a riverboat man. He pulled the cap down over his ears and left the house. Snow slanted into his face as he hurried along the highway toward the lighted sign of the Conoco Station. He feared it might close early because it was Christmas Eve, but he got there in time. He stopped in the shadows beyond the gas pumps and saw only one attendant on duty, luckily not the same man that had caught him stealing money from the till. The attendant was giving change to the driver of a pickup, and there were two cars waiting for service. Dodger unbuttoned the cuffs of his flannel shirt, then went up to the man and asked if he could use the toilet. The man said sure. Dodger went into the grimy, brightly lit station and looked around, making his choices, his heart beating wildly as it always did in the act of stealing. Keeping his eye on the man pumping gas, he slipped a Zippo lighter into the pocket of his flannel shirt and a candy bar up his left sleeve. He went into the rest-room while the attendant came in and rang up a sale and went out again. He emerged from the restroom and studied a standing display of windshield-wiper blades. He put a blade up his right sleeve and opened the door and left, the thrill of success washing over him, his heart beating faster and faster. Stealing was wrong, he knew, and most people were dead-set against it, but how could you resist doing the one thing in life you were good at?

He walked through the deepening snow, buttoning his shirt-cuffs and taking pleasure in the warmth of his feet in the barber's thick-soled boots. He walked to the neighborhood store where his mother bought groceries. A bell tinkled over the door as he opened it. The old woman proprietor came out from her sitting room at the back and said, "Merry Christmas" before she saw who it was. She replaced her smile with a stony glare. He saw at once that there would be no stealing from this woman. He asked for a bottle of pop, a sack of potato chips, and a tin of shoe polish the color of the barber's boots.

As she took his money, made change and put his purchases in a bag, he noticed balloons and jacks and other toys on a shelf behind her.

"Have you got caps?" he asked.

"This is a grocery store, not a clothing store."

"I mean caps for a cap gun."

"No."

He went home and put the Zippo, his mother's gift, on the dresser. When Mrs. Wrobleski came home he would ask her for a scrap of wrapping paper. As he ate his candy bar and drank his pop, he examined the windshield-wiper blade, disappointed in himself for having stolen it simply because it was available. He had no use for it. It was Dodger's policy to steal only out of necessity and never—or seldom—at random.

When he finished eating he put the wiper blade in his cardboard box and took out a clean handkerchief. He opened the tin of shoe polish and went to work on Mr. Johnson's boots, applying three coats of polish with his fingers and buffing them with his handkerchief. When he finished they gleamed like new. He resolved to pick up a new pair of bootlaces before he returned them to Mr. Johnson.

Then he sat by the window and watched the Christmas Eve traffic diminish to almost nothing. Snow fell thickly, like feathers, and he grew very sleepy watching it. He moved to his mother's bed and fell immediately into a deep sleep. Sometime after midnight he awoke with a cry, having dreamed that he was about to be burned with a cigarette. He lay with his eyes open for a minute, savoring the stillness and peace of the empty house; then he turned over and went back to sleep.

The falling snow enveloped Holy Angels like fog, piling itself high on the roof and window ledges and quickly filling the mass of footprints leading up the front steps to the wide oak door. Inside, Father O'Day slowly led his flock through Midnight Mass, periodically losing his place in the altar missal and finding it again, losing his place in the sermon and not finding it again. The ceremony was punctuated by his cries of *"Dominus Vobiscum,"* to which Melva Heffernand responded nasally from the choir loft, *"Et cum spiritu tuo,"* accompanying herself on the organ and adding an extra trill because it was Christmas.

During Communion, Brendan and Philip, vested in red and white, sat on adjacent stools in the sanctuary and gazed at the faces coming forward to receive the Sacrament. Ordinarily Brendan and Philip would have tossed a coin before Mass for the privilege of holding the paten under the chin of each communicant and watching their heads go back and their eyes flutter as Father O'Day placed the Host on their tongues, but tonight Deacon Gilbertson, a seminarian home on vacation, got to do all the glamorous things. Throughout the mass Deacon Gilbertson had carried the missal and rung the Consecration bell and lit the incense, while Brendan and Philip shared the merely decorative role of kneeling and standing on cue while looking devout.

The church was packed and Communion took a long time. Philip, growing impatient, leaned close to Brendan's ear and whispered, "How many presents did you get?"

"We don't open our presents till morning."

"I got eight."

Brendan saw Lorraine Graham kneeling at the rail with her two brothers and her parents. Lorraine wore a new coat of a nubby, dark-green material and a new dark beret tilted over her ear. She glanced at Brendan and immediately lowered her eyes and looked solemn. She was pretty, thought Brendan with surprise. Funny how you never looked twice at Lorraine Graham when she was hanging around Pearl Peterson, which was ninety percent of the time. Pearl's mouthiness and pushiness was the sort that contaminated everyone who came near. Seeing Lorraine by herself, though, you had to admire the blond hair and the small round face with the blue eyes.

"I got a football from my grandma and grandpa," whispered Philip. "I got a bunch of games and some clothes from my ma and dad."

Brendan saw Lester Higgins lining up at the rail with his wife and his scads of children. Once a week Mr. and Mrs. Higgins came in from their farm and bought more groceries from Hank than anyone else. It was the Higgins barn that stood beside the road three miles east of town with an ad for spark plugs painted on the wall. It was the Higgins pickup Hank would borrow next Sunday for the move to Bean Street. Higgins had offered himself as well, but Hank said no thanks; he had Wallace Flint and Paul Dimmitburg to help him with the heavy things, and Brendan and Sam and Philip would carry the lighter pieces. For Brendan the excitement of Christmas this year was far surpassed by the excitement of moving. On Bean he would be living about a block from Philip's house and across the alley from Sam's.

"I got a dumb book from my sister," Philip muttered. "It's never any fun opening my sister's presents. It's always a dumb book."

Among the next rank of communicants were Hank, Catherine and Grandfather. The hour being so late, Grandfather was fuzzy-minded and had to be steered to his place at the rail. Settled there on their knees, the three of them gave Brendan a glance— Hank winked—and then lowered their eyes as the priest approached them. He saw that his mother was wearing her severe look. It had nothing to do with her hairstyle or makeup; it was all in the tightness of the muscles around her eyes and the way she held her mouth. It was a look she had never worn in the city, but now he saw it almost every day. Brendan's heart had nearly stopped the other evening when she told Hank in the kitchen that instead of moving to Bean Street she wanted to move back to the city, that in Plum she felt like a prisoner banished to Siberia. "We can't move back to the city!" Brendan had cried, rushing into the kitchen and breaking in on the talk they had assumed was secret. "Not now," he added, on the verge of tears. Not now that he had friends in Plum. Not now that he had become accustomed to Plum school. Not now that basketball season was underway and he was out for the junior high squad. No, his father assured him; if they ever moved back to the city it couldn't be now, with all their money tied up in the market. His mother got hold of herself and said she had been kidding.

"I wish I didn't get a football from my grandma and grandpa," said Philip. "I've already got a football. What I need is a basketball."

Among the communicants Brendan saw Rufus Ottmann drifting sideways along the middle aisle like a rudderless boat in a stream. He had come unmoored from his mother, who knelt at the rail, and was turning left and right and casting his grin over the congregation. Philip Crowley's father left his pew and took Rufus by the hand and led him back to his place. As usual, the sight left Brendan full of questions. Why did the idiot's idiocy make Brendan fearful? What did Rufus have in his head instead of brains? Sam Romberg said straw. His brother Andy's guess was cold oatmeal. How, if the Catechism was correct in defining the human soul as understanding combined with free will, could Rufus be human? Where else but in Plum would Rufus be so well taken care of? Wasn't this village, despite the religious bigotry Paul Dimmitburg complained of, a kind of peaceable kingdom after all? By making a place for misfits weren't the villagers carrying out Christ's command to love one another? But why, Brendan wondered, hadn't Plum made a place for his mother?

Melva Heffernand began a fugue on the organ, and Brendan looked at his watch. It was one-fifteen. Philip went on about presents; the clothes he got from his parents were no more satisfactory than the football and the book; as for the games, they were all right, but not really the ones he wanted. The church had grown extremely warm, the air stale. Fighting sleep, Brendan turned his mind to the house on Bean Street and imagined how his room would be arranged. He asked God to speed up the time between now and Sunday. He thanked God for making the market a success. He asked God to make his mother happy.

Catherine, returning to her place after Communion, asked God to ease her mind concerning Bean Street. Hank had insisted that the property was a bargain and the interest rate of three percent was not unreasonable, but a house mortgage on top of a store mortgage struck her as an awful encumbrance. If the store failed, they'd lose both. Hank said it couldn't fail. He showed her the figures and said it was clear that their hard work was paying off. Weekly trade had doubled after the Armistice Sale, doubled again after the Thanksgiving Sale, and the Christmas Sale set a record for three-day income. He was so happy explaining this to her that she tried not to let her anxiety show. "We're established now," he said, "and there's nothing ahead but steady growth." She fought believing it because she was afraid to believe it. With a market thriving on Main and a comfortable house on Bean, she was afraid of being planted in Plum forever.

Hank's prayer, as he took his place beside her in the pew, was a prayer of thanksgiving for the many permanent customers he had won away from Legget. Bob Donaldson of Minneapolis Jobbing had been right; Plum had been a two-market town waiting for its second market. The only unfortunate thing was that all of Hank's new customers, except during sales, were the same people he saw returning tonight from the communion rail. He had thought that the combination of bargains and Paul Dimmitburg might have won him a few Lutherans, but it hadn't happened. Stan Kimball said it would never happen, no matter how superior to Legget's the market became. Kimball claimed that these villagers were never so happy as when they were at odds for the love of God, and when Hank came to town he restored to them their long-lost divisiveness in the area of groceries. But Hank wasn't convinced. If he and Paul and Wallace and Catherine remained steadfast in serving the public and absolutely noncommittal in matters of religion and politics, he foresaw the market becoming as neutral as Gordy's Pool Hall, patronized by one and all. Please let it happen, O Lord. And to this prayer he added the words he had addressed to heaven a thousand times in the past several weeks: Above all else, please help Catherine cheer up.

All his life it had been Grandfather's policy not to burden God with complexities, and tonight his prayer was as simple as usual: With all due respect, God, could you prevail upon your priest to move this along a little faster? I'm dying for my pipe.

In the alley between Hay and Bean Streets, Larry-the-Twitch Romberg turned his small face up to the thickly falling snow, shut his eyes, opened his mouth and screamed "Assholes" at the top of his lungs. Larry-the-Twitch and his brothers had been given a pair of skis by their parents, and now at one-fifteen on Christmas morning Andy and Sam were gliding down the sloping alley in the dark and ignoring their little brother's demand for a turn of his own. Mrs. Romberg opened the back door and called into the swirling snowflakes, "You boys get in here this instant, you'll wake up the neighbors. We're going to early service in the morning, and you'll be dead on your feet."

"Fart-blossoms," screamed the nine-year-old. "Piss-ants."

At the base of the slope Andy and Sam, who had just come to a stop in tandem, on one ski apiece, laughed until they couldn't stand up. They fell into the snow and shook with silent laughter, listening to their mother's futile calls interspersed with Larry's obscenities. Their laughter increased to the point of pain when they heard their father burst onto the scene, heard him chase Larry across the alley, heard his roars of anger alternating with Larry's piping pleas for mercy. Hidden in the dark, they laughed themselves breathless, confident that if they lay low long enough they would return to the house and find Larry-the-Twitch asleep and their father relieved of his anger and ready to laugh himself at the words the little twerp had shouted into the snowy peace of Christmas. "Oh, you men," their mother would say, trying to sound disgusted, but failing to conceal entirely her own amusement.

Henrietta Kimball turned over in bed and said, "I hear a ruckus, Stanley."

"I hear it too," replied the undertaker in the dark. "It's Russell Romberg chasing his kids."

The pup lying under the bed heard it as well and began to bark.

"Are you sure the doors are locked?" Mrs. Kimball asked.

"Yes, the doors are locked." Stan Kimball covered his ears and added, "I swear to God we're going to get a muzzle for that mutt."

"No, Stanley, Otto is our good little watchdog."

Otto continued to bark and Stan Kimball buried his head under his pillow.

"Hush," said his wife, reaching under the bed to calm the dog. "Hush, Otto dear."

Stan Kimball spoke through his pillow. "Either that or we'll have his voice box removed."

Two doors away Cora Brask, awakened by the voices of the man and the boy under her window, said to her husband, "The neighborhood goes down, Harlan."

The mayor, who had been listening to the Romberg noises for several minutes, agreed. "Families like that ought to be restricted to the other end of town, by the tracks." After a few moments he added, "You can always tell the riffraff—they're underinsured." He was thinking of the old pickup the Rombergs used for delivering bottlegas, and the careless way the oldest boy drove it, sometimes so loaded with youngsters the wheels rubbed the fenders.

"And to think the Fosters are moving in next door," said his wife.

"Yes. That rattletrap of a car they drive."

"She's nothing but a common grocery clerk. How can they afford a house with their store no busier than it is?"

"It's getting busier."

"Worse luck," she said.

They heard a shout and a howl as Mr. Romberg nabbed Larry-the-Twitch and dragged him home. They heard the Rombergs' back door slam shut. They lay in silence for several minutes, before Mrs. Brask said, "Must we go to early service, Harlan? We'll be short of sleep."

"You suit yourself, but I'm going. The boy is preaching."

"I can't respect a boy like that, dropping out of the seminary and going to work for a Catholic."

"It has nothing to do with respect. I want to hear firsthand what his ideas are. If he's a freethinker, he'll have to be nipped in the bud."

The Reverend Dimmitburg worked on the sermon he would deliver at the late service until one-thirty in the morning; then he switched off the light in his study and stood at the window in his pajamas and robe, watching the snow come piling down under the streetlight in front of the church. Whatever ailed his son in October was a thing of the past, he was sure of that. Perhaps Paul's mistake had been taking a job on campus and staying there all through the summer, allowing himself no time for refreshment between school years. He came home in October looking like a cadaver. His job in Hank's Market was a godsend. Got his mind off his troubles. Allowing the unordained to preach was highly unorthodox, but the Reverend Dimmitburg was eager to help his boy find his legs and send him back to the seminary with his confidence restored. Once back, he'd sail quickly through to ordination, no doubt about it. A peerless candidate for the ministry, so his professors said.

The minister left his study and went upstairs. Seeing a light under Paul's door, he rapped gently and said, "Put your sermon aside, Paul, and get your rest."

"Okay, Dad."

"Good night, son."

"Good night."

Paul's sermon, which Kierkegaard would have abhorred, had been dashed off hours ago. It was fifteen minutes of innocuous thoughts on the Nativity, for Paul had no desire to inflame people like Harlan Brask, whose ears would be cocked for heresy; he had no desire to stand his father's parish on its ear. He was lying in bed reading the four issues of *Independent Grocer* Hank had given him. As he studied the monthly article on store design, a new Hank's Market, vastly remodeled, began to take shape in his mind.

Long after Wallace had gone to bed, Mrs. Flint sat beside her radio and grieved, holding in her lap the letter Wallace had presented her as his Christmas gift. It was his draft notice. He had told her that instead of seeking deferment this time, he would answer his country's call. Seeing tears in her eyes, he had added, "I thought all mothers wanted their sons to be heroes. I thought this would make you happy." Of course he had thought nothing of the kind. And she knew it.

Constable Heffernand, minding the switchboard while his sister Melva attended Midnight Mass, was not able to connect Phyllis Clay with her party in Rochester.

"Nobody answers, Mrs. Clay."

She sobbed in his ear.

"I'm sorry, Mrs. Clay, shall we try again in the morning?"

"Morning will be too late, Mr. Heffernand. It's now I need to talk to him. It's Christmas Eve and Webster's been asleep on the davenport since eight-thirty. No kiss, no hug, not even a smile for Christmas. I've got nobody to talk to."

"Well," said the Constable, feeling pity for her.

"He went straight from his supper to the davenport and he's been snoring ever since."

"I'm sorry."

Another sob. A burp. He supposed she was drunk.

"I have this friend in Rochester. He's my chiropractor. I've got lower back pain. If I could talk to him for a minute I wouldn't feel so blue."

"For what it's worth, Mrs. Clay, let me say Merry Christmas."

"Oh, thank you, Mr. Heffernand. I suppose it's a happy season for you and your sister. It seems like everybody's got somebody, but all I've got is Webster. At home we always used to have mistletoe and my uncle would give us girls a kiss under it, and I've said ever since that a kiss means more at Christmas than any other time."

A long silence.

"Webster's"—a hiccup—"not a kisser."

The constable kindly held the connection open.

"Don't you agree, Mr. Heffernand? A kiss means a whole, whole lot at Christmas?"

"Yes, I suppose it does." He tried to remember the last woman he had kissed at Christmas. Or at any other time.

"Mr. Heffernand, would it be all right if you didn't cut me off quite yet? It's nice talking to you."

"I tell you what, Mrs. Clay. Could you step outside your house for just a minute?"

"Outside? It's snowing like hell."

"Just for a minute, I mean. There's something I'd like to give you for Christmas." He couldn't believe he was saying this. He never did romantic, spontaneous things. He was Plum's dependable drudge whose idea of fun was igniting model airplanes. He spoke fast now, afraid that his voice, already shaky, would fail him at any syllable. "If you came up the street toward my house, I'd meet you halfway."

He was trembling as he put on his coat. His heart was pounding. He hurried through the deep snow in the street and saw the bewildered Mrs. Clay materialize in the amber glow of the snowshrouded streetlight. Whether from drink or from slippery footing she was staggering. Her fur coat was open. When he saw the large snowflakes glistening in her hair and eyelashes, something dormant for decades fluttered to life in his breast. He took her in his arms rather awkwardly, for his trembling had grown to a kind of shudder, and he kissed her hard on the lips. As he tried to raise his head to say Merry Christmas, her mouth remained clamped on his; she held him tightly around the neck and didn't release him for several seconds. Then he blurted "Merry Christmas, I have to get back to the switchboard."

"You're an angel," she sighed.

"See, there's lots of long-distance calling on Christmas Eve, and my sister'd be mad as a hornet if she knew I was away from the switchboard." Overcome with shyness now, he was backpeddling as he spoke, and Mrs. Clay was becoming an indistinct form in the amber night, her arm raised in goodbye, her voice muffled by the snow as she called, "You're an absolute angel."

16

T HE MORNING AFTER THEIR move to Bean
Street, Brendan went out to clear the porches and sidewalk of
the snow that had fallen overnight. He began with the back
porch, which his mother called a veranda. It overlooked the
spacious back yard, and his mother said it would be pleasant
having their meals there on warm summer days. Brendan was
heartened by the effect of the move on his mother. From the
moment they carried in the first piece of furniture yesterday, the
lines of strain had vanished from around her eyes. She had gone
through the house exclaiming over her favorite features. The
veranda was one of many. She loved the living-room fireplace,
the built-in buffet in the dining room, the breakfast nook in the
kitchen. She said that as soon as they could afford one they
would buy a piano and put it in the sunroom. Asked what he
liked best, Hank named the automatic stoker attached to the
coal-burning furnace and operated by a thermostat. No more
days of eight trips to the basement to fuel the fire by hand. No
more fires going out when no one was home to tend them.

For Grandfather, this move proved easier than the last, though until the final piece was carried in and the help went home he was stirred up and confused, pacing from room to room and muttering, ''Who lives here and why aren't they home?'' Hank soon cured his disorientation by arranging a corner of the living room in exact imitation of their previous living room, placing the standing ashtray on the left side of Grandfather's armchair and the console radio on the right, with his rack of pipes on top of the radio. Grandfather sat down, fiddled with the radio, and was quickly pacified by the voices of Amos and Andy.

Shoveling snow from the steps of the veranda, Brendan saw the Rombergs' battered brown pickup come bouncing down the alley, Andy Romberg at the wheel. According to Sam, Andy was spending his Christmas vacation working for his father, and whenever he went out in the pickup to deliver tanks of gas he took Norma Nash along for the ride. If Norma was unavailable he took Sam.

The pickup came to stop in the Rombergs' back yard. The horn blared. Two seconds later the back door opened and Sam leaped out of the house with one arm in the sleeve of his jacket. He climbed into the pickup and slammed the door. Larry-the-Twitch came running after him in his stocking feet, carrying a half-eaten banana. He tried to get in as well, but his brothers turned him back with good-natured insults. Sam said, ''Stay home, garbage gut. If you don't get your twitchy little hands off the doorhandle,'' laughed Andy, ''we'll drag you to Pinburg.'' Larry-the-Twitch was enraged. He threw down his banana and turned purple screaming ''Shitheads!'' as the pickup backed out of the yard, its wheels spinning in the snow.

Brendan, shoveling, wished that Sam had noticed him and asked him to ride along. Not that he could have gone. In a short time he would be due at the market, where he was working two hours a day during vacation.

Finishing the steps, Brendan went around to the front of the house, and as he began to work on the sidewalk he saw Mrs. Brask step out of her house next door. She wore her circlet of red foxtails over a coat of black fur. She approached Brendan and said, ''How do you do. I am Mrs. Brask.''

''Hello,'' said Brendan. ''We're your new neighbors.''

"Yes, I know. Would you please go in and tell your mother that Mrs. Kimball and I are coming to call on her? She's not at the store, is she?"

"No, she's home."

"That's what I thought. I didn't see her leave the house." Mrs. Brask continued along the sidewalk toward the Kimball house.

"You're coming today?"

"Yes, in ten minutes."

Ten minutes gave Catherine scarcely time to set a pot of coffee percolating and, with Brendan's help, to clear the empty cartons from the living room. She was in a high state of nerves. "Are they out of their minds? Do they think we're settled and ready for visitors overnight?"

From his corner by the radio, Grandfather said, "This will not be a formal visit." He was getting out of his chair and brushing the tobacco from his shirtfront in preparation for being charming. "This will be only a moment's call to say we're welcome in the neighborhood."

When the bell sounded, Grandfather opened the door. "How do you do," he said, beaming with pleasure, for he thought the young woman before him exceptionally pretty. She had dark hair and large, lively eyes. In her hand she held a plate covered with wax paper. "I understand you're the mayor's wife."

"No, you silly man, I'm Phyllis Clay, don't you remember? I gave you a shot of brandy in my garage."

He remembered, and was doubly pleased. "And what a timely drink that was. I've been meaning to come by and thank you ever since. Please come in."

"No, heavens, you're not settled. I'll come back some other day. I only wanted to say welcome to Bean Street and give you these cookies."

He took the plate and lifted the wax paper. "Oatmeal with raisin?"

"Yes," she giggled. "Now don't be naughty and eat them all. Promise you'll share them with your family."

"I make no such promise."

By the time Brendan and Catherine came to the door from the

kitchen, she was already hurrying away. Catherine called, "Thank you." Mrs. Clay turned and waved cheerily, making room on the sidewalk for Mrs. Brask and Mrs. Kimball, who were advancing in single file.

Lumbering up across the porch and into the house, Mrs. Brask declared, "We're here only for a minute, Mrs. Foster, and we won't even sit down. I know what moving day is like. I remember the day we moved here from Chicago." Saying this, she removed her foxtails and coat, handing them to Brendan as though he were a butler. "We met the day you were looking for your father." She nodded politely at Grandfather. "But you may not remember. I'm Cora Brask and this is Henrietta Kimball."

"Of course, I remember," said Catherine.

Mrs. Kimball came stooping through the doorway so as not to snap off the enormous feather standing up from her hat. She did not remove her coat, but clutched it tightly as if fearing she might be forcibly disrobed. She said, "How do you do" to Catherine, to Brendan, to Grandfather, smiling kindly to each in turn.

Catherine was fascinated by her first close-up view of Stan Kimball's wife, her innocent expression, her tentative gestures, her meek eyes.

"Do sit down," said Catherine. "I'm making coffee."

Mrs. Kimball looked at her large friend for a decision, which turned out to be affirmative, Mrs. Brask lowering herself onto the couch and patting the cushion beside her to indicate Mrs. Kimball's place. Catherine went to the kitchen, and Brendan hung the heavy coat and the foxtails in the closet and went outside to finish his work. Grandfather pulled a chair up facing the ladies and asked the mayor's wife, "When you lived in Chicago, did you take the Milwaukee Road to Minnesota?"

Yes, she had done so, a time or two.

"In that case I may have been your conductor."

"I see. Well, if you're acquainted with Chicago you know the streets of large houses near the university. My husband and I lived in one of those houses. A perfectly lovely street. Wide boulevards. Elms." She withheld the fact that they had lived in a third-floor apartment of such a house while her husband tried and failed to establish himself selling life insurance to graduating seniors, who proved less gullible than he had been led to expect by his supervisor. Nor did she mention that their moving to Plum was actually a return home, both she and her husband having grown to adulthood here.

"I've never been to Chicago," said Mrs. Kimball timidly.

"Oh, how we miss Chicago," Mrs. Brask rhapsodized. "The hub of the nation."

"Yes, Stanley's embalming fluid comes from there."

Catherine came in with coffee, and Mrs. Brask addressed her: "Melva Heffernand says her brother showed you around the library. We're all so pleased that you're interested in books. What sort of books do you like?"

"I read *A Farewell to Arms* three months ago, and I haven't gotten over it yet."

"Yes, Shakespeare is wonderful, but we know someone better, don't we, Henrietta? Will you tell her the good news, or shall I?"

Mrs. Kimball asked shyly, "About the new book?"

"Yes."

Mrs. Kimball turned to Catherine. "Henry Hodge Fleet's new book has arrived."

"*Edward* Hodge Fleet, Henrietta."

"Yes, Edward Hodge Fleet. It's called *Heart Throbs.*"

"No, Henrietta, *Pangs of the Heart.* I'm halfway through it, and I can assure you it's simply wonderful. It's chock-full of tragedy, three heart attacks so far, but with Edward Hodge Fleet you know the sun will come shining through. Would you like to borrow it when I finish?"

Catherine did not say no. She said, "Well . . ."

Mrs. Brask concealed her disappointment at this tepid response and changed the subject: "Will you continue to work in your husband's store, now that you're living on Bean Street?"

"Oh, yes, we're in partnership, Hank and I."

Instead of stating outright that working wives were not approved of on Bean Street, that implicit in a Bean address was a certain elevation above the more sordid aspects of getting and spending, Mrs. Brask told Catherine a story. "Your predecessors in this house, the DeRoches, were lovely, lovely neighbors, Mrs. Foster, and so it always tugged at our hearts whenever we saw Mrs. DeRoche go out and help her husband on his auto-parts route. He traveled for a firm in Rochester, and sometimes when he stayed home to do his bookwork, she would take the truck out alone, delivering parts hither and yon.''

"And what was the problem with that?'' Catherine inquired.

"Well, you have to wonder, don't you, when you see a wife out in the working world, how she can properly care for her children and keep house and put wholesome meals on the table? The DeRoches never kept their yard up properly, as you'll discover this spring when the snow melts.''

Catherine was firm. "I help at the store, and my husband helps at home.''

"Well, of course it's entirely your business and Henrietta and I would be the last ones to advise people how to live their lives. Goodness, we've watched Mrs. Clay drink like a fish ever since Webster brought her home from Omaha and we haven't said a word to her about it. And speaking of drinking, we don't talk about it because they are two of the most respected residents on Bean, but there is a history of moonshine in the Heffernand family. Unavoidable perhaps, their being Catholic. And Charles and Melva have certainly overcome the shame. They've restored honor to the family name. A pity that the family will end when they die. When he was just out of high school in 1911 Charles Heffernand became engaged to a classmate named Mary Boyle, but she died of TB before the wedding. Their grandfather, Herman Heffernand, was the first mayor of Plum. He farmed what is now the west end of town. Their father, Hector Heffernand, established Plum Telephone Incorporated, along with bootlegging his homemade whiskey. Poor Melva, she suffers from psoriasis. The Woodruffs live just beyond the Heffernands. Who would have thought even ten years ago that Abraham Woodruff would be living on Bean, much less serving on the school board with Harlan? Ten years ago Abraham Woodruff mowed lawns and changed storm windows for whoever needed odd jobs done, and he and his wife and children went around in rags. Clean rags, of course—they've always had a good, healthy Protestant sense of cleanliness about them—but rags all the same. They used to receive food baskets from the church at Christmas. Then his brother in St. Paul somehow got him the postmaster's job, and he's been on easy street ever since. His wife's raisin pie is all the rage when we have our church bazaar in the fall. It seems like only yesterday Abraham came and asked Harlan to lend him money to pay his bill at Legget's. Harlan was left a nice little sum when his mother died, you see, and Abraham had the nerve to ask him outright for a loan. Poverty makes people so shameless. Abraham has a glandular disorder that makes him a little pop-eyed.''

There was no stopping Mrs. Brask once she got up her momentum. Not that Catherine wanted to; these thumbnail sketches were fascinating. Although they were conceived with a Lutheran bias, there was a perverse generosity in the way she delivered them, as though she were opening doors for Catherine and inviting her into all these lives.

''Do you know Mr. and Mrs. Philip Crowley? They have a son named Philip about the age of your boy. Mr. Crowley owns the movie theater and Mrs. Crowley is a Catholic of the most militant, disgusting kind. I hate to say it, but the whole family is a little bit loose in the area of morals. Mr. and Mrs. take separate vacations, their daughter who lives in Minneapolis was said to have borne a baby out of wedlock last year and Mr. Crowley one time brought a movie to town in which Henry Fonda used the name of the Lord in vain. The Peterson girl is also your son's age, is she not? The Petersons became well-to-do by selling Chevrolets and Buicks before the war, and they contribute generously to Emmanuel Lutheran. Mr. Peterson moved here as a young man to work in his uncle's gas station, and it was here he met his wife, a farmer's daughter. Besides Pearl they have two other children, a son in the navy and a daughter in nurses' training in Rochester. Mrs. Peterson is afflicted with bursitis. The Dimmitburgs are without a doubt the nicest people I have ever met, so kind, so intelligent, so well-dressed. It's regrettable that as a Catholic you will never hear the Reverend Dimmitburg preach. His voice is beautiful, his message always such a consolation. Mrs. Dimmitburg brought the money to that marriage. Her father was a contractor in St. Louis. How long can little old Emmanuel Lutheran hope to hang on to them? The smallest house and the largest family on Bean belongs to the Nicholis. Mr. Nicholi is the barber and his wife does sewing for hire. They have seven children—so Catholic—grown up and moved away. One of their daughters started college on scholarships and never quit, one degree after another. Her field is nutrition. She looks a fright when she comes home for the holidays, bags under her eyes and skinny as a rail. Mrs. Nicholi is burdened with an invalid sister who came to visit five years ago and never left. She's paralyzed in her limbs and her eyes don't shut. Well, Henrietta, don't you think we should leave Mrs. Foster to her housework? My, I like the upholstery on that chair over there. Next time we call we won't know the place, I'm sure. You'll have made this house your home. What will you hang over the fireplace? The DeRoches had a Biblical picture there, Geronimo battling the Philistines or some such thing. It was all reds and yellows and too active, I thought, for a living room.''

Grandfather helped Mrs. Brask on with her coat while Mrs. Kimball made her first attempt at conversation:

''Stanley and I have a dog named Otto. I named him after my doctor.''

''I've seen him,'' said Catherine. ''He's a handsome little thing.''

Grandfather opened the door and Mrs. Brask lumbered out, saying ''If there's anything we can do to help you get settled, just say the word.''

''Thank you so much, do come again,'' said Catherine. Then she called past them, ''Brendan, dear, it's nearly time.''

For his stint of work at the store, she meant. He whisked away a little more snow, then stood aside to let the two women pass.

Mrs. Brask said, going by, ''I suppose you'll grow up to take over your father's market, young man.''

His policy with adults was unswerving agreement. He said, ''Yes, I'll be a grocer.'' Actually he had no such intention. He would be a brakeman, maybe. Or a priest.

"Or perhaps you'll join the navy," said Mrs. Kimball. "I have a nephew who's very fond of the navy."

"Yes, that could be, too."

Catherine held the door open for Brendan, and for the woman who came hurrying along behind him. She was a small redhead with green eyes and freckles. She bounded onto the porch and said, "You're Catherine Foster, so happy to know you, I'm Bea Crowley. So sorry not to have been buying your groceries, but my brother is the grocer in Pinburg and we do all our shopping there. The ties of blood, you know. Now don't let me take you away from your work. I just wanted to say welcome to Bean Street and I'm so happy you're Catholic. The DeRoches were Catholic too, and when they moved away I was afraid we'd lose ground. This would be Brendan. My Philip talks on and on about Brendan, they're the best of friends."

"And this is my father," said Catherine, leading her into the living room.

"How do you do, I'm so happy to meet you." Removing her glove, she thrust her hand at Grandfather, who took it in both of his own and thought, Now this is more like it, neighbors in and out, a wise move leaving the Ottmann house at the lonesome edge of town, where the only neighbors were idiots and cows.

"I was saying to Philip yesterday when we saw you moving— Philip my husband, not Philip my son—that it's a shame we're in the middle of remodeling because we'd love to have a party and get you acquainted. We're doing over our whole ground floor, taking out partitions and brightening up the dark, old woodwork. Ordinarily one's parish church is the ideal place to get acquainted, but Holy Angels has done nothing but go downhill since Father O'Day took over. He discourages potluck dinners and teas and social occasions of all kinds. Philip and the rest of the Men's Club are planning a trip to the bishop to petition him to replace Father O'Day. He's old and forgetful and he lives in that rectory like a hermit. He ought to be retired. What did Mrs. Brask say about me? She's an awful gossip."

"Let's see, we talked mostly about whether I plan to go on working in the store. She doesn't approve."

"Oh, that woman. Just ignore her, if you can. I'm so glad

she's not next door to me. I can't believe she didn't bring up my name."

"She only mentioned the theater. She said your husband showed a movie one time with swearing on the sound track."

"How would she know? She never goes to movies, she says they're immoral. Well, I'll tell you what's immoral, her trashy taste in books."

"Oh, I'm so happy to hear you say that. I thought I was the only one who felt that way. Have you read *A Farewell to Arms*? I can't get over how sad it is."

"That's Hemingway. Philip and I don't read Hemingway, his philosophy's wrong. We read Catholic writers. Bernanos and Mauriac and people like that. I'll bring you some of their work."

"I think I've read most of Bernanos and Mauriac."

"And don't you agree, their philosophy's right?"

"Yes, I do, but then I don't read only for philosophy. I read to be moved."

"You don't find Bernanos and Mauriac moving?"

"Very. But I like variety. When I get our books unpacked you'll have to come and see if there's anything you'd like to read. I thought Wallace Flint was the only real reader in town."

Mrs. Crowley's eyes became suddenly clouded. She peered at Catherine darkly. "That awful man. We all wondered how long he would last with you. Philip didn't think he'd last a week."

"Actually, he's been a great help in getting us started. He's a walking Who's Who of Plum."

"But people despise him, you know."

"No, I don't think they do. Our customers deal with him just fine."

Mrs. Crowley shrugged. The lift of her eyebrows said, Wait and see. She took her leave, promising to have the Fosters over as soon as her house was presentable.

Catherine went straight to the phone and asked Central to ring the market. When Hank said, "Hank's," she told him, "I've just had four neighbors drop in to wish me well, Hank. Count them, four."

"Good for you. Good for them."

"Let's have a housewarming, Hank. Let's invite all our new neighbors and sort through them for kindred spirits."

"A good idea."

"And invite Wallace and his mother and the Dimmitburgs. We did nothing for our help at Christmas. Let's do it on New Year's afternoon."

"That's when the Rose Bowl's on."

"Those who want can listen."

"We can be ready by New Year's?"

"It will be very informal."

"I'm all for it."

"How's business this morning?"

"Humming right along. Send Brendan down. It's delivery time."

"He's on his way."

"How's unpacking?"

"I'm through in the kitchen."

"Don't overdo."

"No, I'm stopping now. I'm going to jot down our guest list."

Wallace poured a mixture of water and antifreeze into the radiator while Brendan carried bags of groceries out the back door and lined them up across the back seat. Then they got in and Wallace, starting the engine, said, "I've got something to show you." He reached inside his jacket and drew a brown envelope from his shirt pocket. "Read it and weep."

Brendan read it as they chugged along the snow-packed alley. It was a draft notice. It ordered Wallace to report for his induction physical in Minneapolis on January 16.

"I thought you always got deferred."

"Not anymore. I believe in taking up arms against Fascism."

"What have you been reading, *Joe Palooka*?"

"Don't take that tone with me, Brendan, dear."

"Don Winslow Helps the Marines?"

They came to their first stop, and Brendan ran in with the groceries. Hopping back into the car, he said, "But there's basic training."

"What do you mean, there's basic training? Of course there is."

"I can't see you crawling on your elbows and knees under a crossfire of live ammunition."

"I'll do what I'm asked."

Brendan imagined Wallace as a buck private. "The first time you're given an order you'll probably say, 'How horribly arch of you, sergeant.' " More than once he had heard Wallace accuse his mother of being horribly arch.

Wallace saw no humor in this. "When I'm given an order, I'll say, 'Yes, sir.' "

"You might get shot," Brendan pointed out.

"I might get shot and I might not." Wallace's voice rose. "I might come home a hero and I might not." His eyes shone zealously. "But at least I will have stood up and been counted when it counted."

17

T_{HE} GUESTS, ALL FOUR of them, stood visiting
at the dining room table, which was covered with sweets. Catherine opened the front door and welcomed Paul Dimmitburg.

"Happy New Year, Paul."

"And a blessed New Year to you," he said gravely, stepping
in out of the failing gray light of mid-afternoon. "Sorry to be
so late." He was followed by a heavy-faced man of great girth
and a lean, angular woman. The man wore a smile, the woman
a severe expression.

"I'd like you to meet my parents."

"How nice to know you."

"Our pleasure," said the minister. "Paul speaks highly of
you and your husband."

His wife mumbled something unintelligible. She was tall and
dark-eyed like her son.

"You must be pleased to have Paul home," said Catherine.
"He's a great help to us in the store."

"We were hoping he would return to school for spring semester," said Mrs. Dimmitburg resentfully. "We are sorry he's waiting till fall."

Paul directed his impassive gaze over his parents' heads, and when they had taken off their coats and gone into the dining room he said, "Please forgive my mother. She can't understand why God didn't create all of humanity Lutheran." He helped hang up their coats. "Have you given any more thought to my plan?"

"Yes, Hank is all for it."

"And you?"

"If we can afford it."

"It won't cost much. I'll do all the carpentry." With his ambition to transform the world temporarily thwarted, Paul was determined to transform Hank's Market; he had presented them with detailed drawings.

"I'm sure we'll go ahead," she told him. "The question is when."

Paul looked into the dining room. "My, a guest list of Lutherans. Isn't that Mrs. Peterson?"

"Yes, mother of Pearl."

"And her husband and the Kimballs."

"The Kimballs are only half Lutheran."

"Where are the Brasks?"

"Mrs. Brask said her husband devotes New Year's to his bookwork." Catherine said nothing to Paul about the poor turnout. The Dimmitburgs made seven. She had invited thirty-two. Bea Crowley had extended her regrets when she heard that Protestants had been invited. The Nicholis were entertaining family. Mrs. Clay was visiting a friend in Rochester. None of the other absentees had bothered replying to the invitation.

In the dining room, the Reverend and Mrs. Dimmitburg, declining Hank's offer of wine, greeted Mrs. Kimball, who thrust a photo of her dog at them. "Look at him, chewing on one of Stanley's shoes. Isn't he the most precious thing?"

"Perky-looking all right," said the minister, passing the photo to his wife.

"My doctor prescribed the dog to relax me."

"I'll bet he doesn't relax Stanley."

"What kind of dog is it?" asked Mrs. Dimmitburg.

"I can never remember. He's like a scottie, only white. His name is Otto."

The Dimmitburgs approached the table and greeted the Petersons, Stan Kimball, and Hank.

"Looks like more snow," said the minister.

"Too much snow," said George Peterson of Plum Chevrolet-Buick. He stifled a yawn.

"Saw your dog's picture," he said to Stan Kimball.

"Vicious little cur," said the undertaker, whose badly-chewed cigar hung from his mouth unlit. "Teeth like razors. Nips at my ankles all the time. I have to read with my feet up."

"Doctor's orders, I understand."

"The doctor's a quack."

"What kind of dog is it?" asked Mrs. Dimmitburg.

"The incontinent kind."

There followed an awkward pause while the group searched their minds for more to say about snow or dogs. Finding nothing, they turned to cars, the minister asking George Peterson, "How long after the war ends will General Motors start sending you cars?"

"My guess is six months, but there'll be a shortage for a long time. I expect to have a waiting list for at least two years."

Stan Kimball said, "Put Hank at the top of your list, would you? His car's got a death rattle if I ever heard one."

"The kickoff!" Grandfather announced, emerging from the bathroom and lifting the men instantly out of their tea-party torpor. Hank led them to the radio, where they pulled up chairs and stools and agreed that Tennessee would be too much for Southern California. Grandfather was delayed in joining them, stopping to apologize to the three female guests—"You'll forgive me, please, for listening to football, I have fifty cents riding on Tennessee."

When Catherine opened the door to Wallace Flint, it took her a moment to recognize him. He wore a crew cut, waxed and standing up straight. His beard was gone. His smile was a new one for Wallace—broad and guileless.

"Wallace, what have you done to yourself?"

"Government issue." He bounced his hand off his springy flattop.

"And your beard. Do you realize I've never before seen your entire face?"

He gave her his profile. "How do you like it?"

"Exquisite," she told him, though she thought his weak chin quite unattractive. Beardless and all but hairless, he put her in mind of the featherless baby bird she had found on the lawn last spring after a windstorm. Unformed. Vulnerable. "But why?"

"No beards in the military."

"Oh, Wallace." Her voice was plaintive, her expression tender. He'd never make a soldier. He'd wash out and come home depressed. Yesterday Mrs. Flint had come into Hank's Market for the first time ever and begged Hank to use his considerable influence on Wallace. She was near tears, Hank reported later to Catherine. Wallace was sure to meet with disaster, she said. His epilepsy would worsen. Her own heart would break. Hank had then tried to dissuade Wallace, had urged him to ask his doctor in Pinburg for another deferment, and Catherine did the same when she came to work, but Wallace was adamant. He was a changed man. In gearing himself up for induction, his mental machinery seemed to have slipped a cog. His military aspirations, begun in spite, were now apparently in earnest. Yesterday in the store he had talked about nothing but Robert E. Lee.

"They're staring at me, Catherine." His eyes were on the two groups of guests, women in the dining room, men at the radio end of the living room.

Indeed, all eyes were on him. Catherine saw her guests turning to one another with "It's Wallace Flint" forming on their lips.

He stayed a very short time. Outside, he drew a stocking cap from the pocket of his jacket and pulled it down over his ears, regretting what it would do to his waxed flattop. With longer hair he had never worn a cap, but the flattop provided no insulation. He didn't want to go to his physical exam with a cold; he must be in perfect health.

He walked with what he guessed was a military bearing—eyes ahead, back straight, arms swinging, It was mid-afternoon and daylight was already dying. A few grainy snowflakes were zipping about on the cold breeze. Turning into Main Street, he saw a car parked in front of the market, its lights on, its motor running. He saw a man behind the wheel. He saw a second figure get out and stand at the door of the market, peering through the glass. He approached the figure quietly from behind and said, "What do you want?"

The figure turned abruptly from the door. It was Dodger Hicks. "Ain't this the Fosters' store any more?"

"Of course it's the Fosters' store. Why wouldn't it be?"

"I been to their house and it looked empty."

"They moved."

"Yeah? Where to?"

"Bean Street."

"Yeah? Which house?"

"What do you want to know for?"

Dodger shivered. "I got something for Brendan."

The driver, a man in a gray overcoat and a black hat, got out of the car and spoke across the hood. "We're looking for the Foster family."

"They're out of town for the holiday," said Wallace. "Won't be back till tomorrow."

"All right, Dodger, let's run along." The man returned to his place behind the wheel.

Dodger took from his pocket a tiny parcel and handed it to Wallace. "Give this to Brendan, would you?"

Wallace nodded, taking it. It was a two-inch cube wrapped in Christmas paper.

"Tell him it's from me. It's for Christmas."

"Okay."

Dodger got into the car and it moved off through the flying snowflakes.

Wallace peeled the paper from the gift. It was a box containing five rolls of caps for a cap gun. He dropped the paper in the snow and started across the street toward home. Halfway across he saw a pickup approaching from his left. He stopped to let it go by. He tossed the caps into the pickup as it passed.

18

INCLUDED IN WALLACE'S DREAM of leaving Plum was the pleasure of watching the village recede behind him as he rode away. Though Plum was eleven miles from the nearest passenger train and bus route, the conveyance in the dream was sometimes a train, sometimes a bus, the time of departure was a brilliant spring morning, and the village was quickly lost in a fold of green hills. On the morning of January 16, in fact, his conveyance was the morning mail truck, which left town before first light. It was eight below zero and all was blackness except the frozen gravel in the beam of the headlights.

"I was in the first war," said the driver, a chain-smoking man whose route began in Rochester each morning at five. "That's how I got this job. Veteran's preference. Going to war's better than going to college. It's something they can't ever take away from you. It gives you first crack at government jobs. What branch you going into?"

"I haven't been told yet," said Wallace. "Probably the Army."

"How come you got no suitcase?"

"We're not called to camp until a week or so after the physical."

"They changed it then. In the first war we had our physical and left for camp on the same day. They sent me to a camp in Georgia. Cured me for life of ever wanting to live in a hot climate. Sweated off ten pounds the first four days. About died."

"Is basic training difficult?" Not being equal to the rigors of military life was Wallace's primary fear.

"Difficult!" The man laughed. "I about died."

Nine miles out of Plum the road tipped downward, beginning its descent through the densely wooded bluffs. In the dim gray dawn Wallace caught glimpses, between the bare trees, of the ice-covered Mississippi. The mail truck coasted down to river level and came to a stop at the intersection of Highway 61.

"You got quite a wait. The bus ain't through here till nine-thirty."

"I know." Wallace shut the door and the truck growled away. He crossed the highway to the gas station which served as the bus stop.

"Where to?" the attendant asked as Wallace stepped through the door. A layer of oily grime covered everything in the station including the attendant's jacket and eyeglasses.

"Minneapolis."

"Two-fifty, round trip."

"I've got a pass."

"Going for your physical, I suppose."

"Yes."

A car pulled in for gas. The attendant, going out the door, repeated the mail carrier's words, "You've got quite a wait."

With his handkerchief Wallace wiped off the top of a carton of oil and sat down. He might have avoided this two-hour wait if the Fosters had been more cooperative. Instead of consenting immediately when he had asked Catherine to deliver him to Highway 61, she had consulted Hank, who said it was doubtful that the car would start—it never started on subzero mornings. Rather than risk missing the bus, he ought to ride the morning mail truck. Hank said he would drive to the junction in the evening to pick him up—by afternoon the temperature invariably climbed above zero and the car came to life. At this point in the conversation, Paul Dimmitburg had stepped forward and offered to ask his father for the family car, but Wallace had declined with a wordless sneer. He hated Paul for having insinuated himself into Hank and Catherine's good graces. Especially Catherine's.

The attendant reentered the station and offered Wallace the morning *Tribune* to pass the time. Reading the war news, Wallace decided he'd rather be assigned to Patton in Europe than MacArthur in the Pacific. Patton was getting more press. *Events of the past two days in the Battle of the Bulge point to an eventual victory for the Allies. After exactly one month of the fiercest fighting yet in the European theater, Patton's Third Army is beginning to turn back what military analysts in Washington are calling the last German offensive of the war.*

Shortly before bus time a truck pulled into the station and let out a young man who held in his hand a pass like Wallace's. He had sandy hair, buck teeth and a crooked nose. He violated Wallace's concept of the military. Service personnel portrayed on billboards and in magazines were handsome, and it hadn't crossed Wallace's mind that he would be expected to serve side by side with homely people. The young man came into the station and said "Howdy" to Wallace, and when the bus arrived, the young man took the seat next to him. If he had tried to strike up a conversation Wallace would have changed seats, but the young man was shy and said nothing all the way to the city.

Among the people boarding the bus at each stop were two or three men of draftable age who handed the driver their government pass. Most of them looked to Wallace like stupid farm boys. Wallace himself was feeling very snappy. He kept bouncing his hand off his springy crew cut as he took in the sights he had heard of but never seen. Lake Pepin with clusters of fishhouses here and there on the ice. The pottery plant in Red Wing, and near it the factory where Red Wing Shoes were made. The Home School for Boys at the edge of Flensboro. The spiral bridge in Hastings.

By the time they disembarked in Minneapolis a dozen or more

recruits at the back of the bus had become friends, and they stood in the depot discussing what they would do until their one o'clock appointment at the federal building. They asked Wallace if he would like to go with them to find something to eat.

"No," he said sharply.

The buck-toothed boy seemed reluctant to leave Wallace's side. "Go eat with them," Wallace snapped, and the boy obeyed, following the group out the door.

Wallace left by another door, and, referring to the map in his brown envelope, he made his way toward the federal building. To be on his own among city people made his heart beat fast. He saw a lot of important-looking men in expensive-looking coats. He saw men and women in military uniform. He saw a policeman. He saw Negroes. He saw a Negro policeman. He saw a blind man selling pencils. He saw a midget. He was nearly pushed off the sidewalk by a swarm of young women emerging from the Minnesota School of Business. He was asked for money by a woman with *Salvation Army* stitched on her coat. His picture was taken by a man who handed him a card explaining how he might receive the picture in the mail. The city is my true home, he told himself as he stood at the corner of Seventh and Hennepin waiting for the light to change. These are all my people. Except the midget, he thought a moment later. Midgets aren't my people.

He stopped before a display window of Dayton's Department Store: imitation people lying on imitation sand with imitation drinks in their hands and umbrellas overhead. He went in and found his way to the book department, a quiet, dark-paneled alcove where a middle-aged woman with a pencil in her hair was taking books down from a shelf in the history section and showing them to her only customer, a small, white-haired man with a cane. "This covers the Civil War and after," he heard the woman say. "It's the 'after' that I'm particularly interested in," the man replied. "The presidency of Grant."

No wonder Catherine longed to be back in the city, thought Wallace. Who wouldn't feel dislocated having to give up this lovely room of books and intelligent customers and be surrounded by pickles and potatoes? He browsed in the drama and poetry sections until the woman came over and asked if she could help him.

"Do you remember a woman by the name of Catherine Foster?"

"Oh my, yes. She and her husband moved away. They went into the grocery business."

"They're friends of mine. I worked for them until yesterday."

"Well, how interesting. How are they getting along?"

"All right. Nothing sensational, but all right."

"Catherine was the most knowledgeable bookseller we had. She knew titles and authors like nobody else. Please tell her we miss her."

"I will."

"Is there something I could help you find?"

Wallace, in a moment of inspiration, saw an opportunity for vengeance. "The Fosters would be doing better if they weren't involved in a scandal. Catherine's been seeing another man, and you know how small towns are. You can't get away with a thing like that."

"No, not Catherine Foster."

"A thing like that affects your business."

"No," said the woman with certainty. "We can't be talking about the same woman."

"Are you calling me a liar?" he shouted angrily.

There was alarm in the woman's eyes as she turned away from him and went back to the elderly man with the cane, who had selected the book he wanted. Writing out the sales slip, she kept an eye on Wallace as he browsed, or pretended to browse, making his way to the hallway and then hurrying away.

"What do you make of that, Mr. Samuelson? Did you notice how distraught he was?"

The elderly man did not look up from the check he was writing. "Crazy as a coot."

Wallace, his anger cooling, was pleased by the classical lines of the federal building. He climbed the wide, granite steps, passed between two enormous pillars and entered the building through tall, heavy doors. It struck him as a fitting portal for a man about to take up arms against the forces of evil. Inside he found several recruits standing in a circle eating candy bars. He stood apart from them and looked out a window at the cars and trucks and streetcars going by. He regretted speaking angrily to the woman in the book department. What if she were the manager? What if she remembered his angry tone when he returned there after the war to apply for a job? He should have told her instead about the interest he and Catherine shared in books. But speaking ill of her gave him such pleasure.

A soldier wearing olive drab ordered the recruits down a hallway. The soldier's haircut, Wallace observed with satisfaction, was identical to his own. In a narrow room smelling of overshoes the recruits were ordered to take off their shirts and pants and shoes and socks and to proceed into the next room in their underwear. They made a comic procession in their shorts and union suits and Wallace, euphoric once again, laughed out loud. Then he was silenced by a shocking sight at the far end of the examination room. A grossly overweight doctor sitting in a chair with a cigarette hanging from his lips was probing and squeezing so roughly—it was the hernia and rectal exam—that the recruit standing before him cried out in pain. The recruits waiting in that line looked on in terror. Wallace broke out in a sweat. He couldn't stand anyone touching him there. He went from station to station—the hearing exam, the throat exam, the lung X ray—fighting off panic. He reminded himself that there were worse atrocities awaiting him in the military than having his groin poked at by a sadistic slob in a white coat. There were suicide planes in the Pacific. There was the story in the morning paper about the infantryman in Belgium whose stomach was blown open by a land mine and who staggered into the medic's tent carrying his intestines in his hands. Thinking these things made Wallace woozy. He stepped up to the eye chart and found the large black letters illegible. They moved fuzzily up and down. He heard himself utter a moan he hadn't intended to make, and then an animal sound like a growl. The last thing he remembered was throwing his arms out and tipping over backwards.

He awoke in the narrow room that smelled of overshoes. He lay on the floor with a blanket over him. He was wet. He lay in a pool of urine. The buck-toothed young man with the crooked nose got up from a bench and came over to him. Then a medic in a white coat appeared and the two of them raised Wallace to a bench and began to dress him. It took a long time. He was limp and shaky and he couldn't control his fingers and feet. With his suspenders twisted and his shirt buttoned wrong and a copy of his 4-F classification stuffed in his pocket, he was carried out the high, heavy doors and down the wide granite steps to a cab. The buck-toothed boy sat beside him on the way to the bus depot, patting him gently on the shoulder in an attempt to quiet his moaning.

The pool hall was crowded with farmers idling the winter away, the large front window opaque with frost. From the jukebox came Vaughn Monroe's furry rendition of "Racing with the Moon." Gordy, serving coffee to the Fosters, said, "Vern at the lumber yard says you folks've got a big remodeling job coming up."

"We start tomorrow." Hank took a folded sheet of paper from his shirt pocket and showed Gordy the sketch he and Catherine and Paul had been working on.

Catherine explained, "This is the new trend in grocery stores. We're going to open up the entire stock to the shoppers and they'll go around with baskets, serving themselves. The lumber's going into new shelving."

Gordy studied the sketch. "I was in a store like this in Rochester. They call it a supermarket. You going to change your name to Hank's Supermarket?"

Catherine said, "Let's."

Hank looked dubious. "Supermarket sounds like boasting."

Gordy handed back the sketch. "I told Louie Legget about the Rochester store. He says it's an idea that'll never catch on."

Hank smiled at this, pleased to know his competitor lacked foresight.

"Customers come into a store to be waited on, Legget says. They'll never take to serving themselves."

"Legget obviously doesn't read the trade magazines," Catherine said. "This new plan not only frees the help to do other work, it sells more groceries."

"It does?"

"It's been proven that people buy twenty percent more when they serve themselves."

Hank nudged her knee with his, and after Gordy left she asked, "Did I say something wrong?"

"Everything we tell Gordy, Gordy tells Legget. They're both trustees of the Lutheran church."

"But it's no secret we're remodeling."

"The secret's the twenty-percent increase. The longer it takes Legget to modernize the better off we'll be."

Hank recognized her gesture of frustration—casting her eyes at the ceiling while letting out a long, slow breath. He waited for the words he knew were coming:

"That's exactly what I can't stand about this town, Hank. Everything takes premeditation." She drilled him with her blue eyes. "Before I state a simple fact to Gordy, I have to stop and think what church Gordy goes to and what effect it will have on our income. Before I get dressed in the morning I have to think what effect my clothes will have on Mrs. Brask. Yesterday I saw a dress in the Sears catalogue that I felt like ordering, but skirts are going to be short this spring, and I decided I'm not up to being the first woman on Bean Street to be wearing a short skirt, not after all the nasty things Mrs. Brask says about Phyllis Clay's flashy clothes. It's no wonder Phyllis Clay sits home drinking herself silly. It isn't her husband she can't stand, it's the old biddies living all around her." She put her finger to her mouth, silencing herself. She had determined some days ago to try to spare Hank further complaining about her loneliness, about her dashed hopes for happiness on Bean Street. The New Year's tea had been the final straw. Two dozen people staying away without acknowledging their invitations. Soon after, as a palliative, she had accepted an invitation from Bea Crowley to go shopping in Rochester, hoping that in Bea, a reader of books, she would find a kindred spirit; but the woman's religious fanaticism proved insufferable. She blamed Luther and Lutherans for every ill including World War Two and her major purchase in Rochester was a set of soap dishes depicting saints of the Near East.

"Give me the pencil, Hank. I'll show you where the produce section ought to go."

He withheld the pencil. "I know it's not a happy time for you Catherine, but remember, it's Plum that's given us a house of our own, and the store we always wanted."

She made a helpless movement with her hands.

"And think how happy we are as a family." This was all part of Hank's formula response, repeated so often that he faulted himself for not being more original. "And remember," he added, "you've got me, and I've got you."

She nodded. Original or not, it always seemed to help. She took the pencil, smoothed the paper in front of her and began to draw. He reached under the table and gave her knee a tight squeeze.

They were on their second mug of coffee when the door opened and a man stepped into the pool hall brushing snow from his overcoat. Because he was a stranger, everyone turned to examine him, Hank and Catherine included.

The man stepped up to the bar and spoke to Gordy, who pointed to the Fosters' booth. The man walked swiftly over to them and put out his hand to Hank.

"How do you do, Mr. Foster, Mrs. Foster. Your man in the store said I'd find you here. My name is Cranshaw, I'm with the welfare office in Winona." He took off his overcoat and hung it on a peg. He wore a heavy green sweater under his tight suitcoat. "I'm sorry to bother you. My business might strike you as very odd, or it might not, depending on how much truth there is in what I've been told about you. May I?"

Hank made room for him to sit.

"So far, the roads aren't drifted shut, but I want to get home in daylight, they say there's worse weather coming." He rubbed his cold hands together—small, hairless hands, Catherine noticed—and he called to Gordy for coffee. Then he smiled shrewdly across the table at her; small teeth, she noticed. He had a foxlike face, a sharp nose, a thin smile. "What does the name Dodger Hicks mean to you, Mrs. Foster?"

"Dodger? Is he in trouble again?"

Ignoring her inquiry, he turned his smile on Hank. "And you, Mr. Foster?"

"Why do you ask?"

"I'll explain in a minute. I just want to know what the name Dodger Hicks means to the two of you. To your wife it obviously means trouble. What does it mean to you?"

Hank nodded. "Sure, trouble. He's in the Home School, isn't he?"

Cranshaw smiled up at Gordy, who brought him his coffee. He thanked him and held the mug in both hands for warmth. "Now my next question is this, Mr. Foster. Do you *like* Dodger Hicks?"

"Like him? I hardly know him."

"Hicks tells me you and your family are friends of his, Mr. Foster."

"That's laying it on pretty thick, considering we saw him probably twice in our lives."

"And you, Mrs. Foster? Do you like Dodger Hicks?"

"Pity him is more like it."

Hank tapped the man's sleeve impatiently. "Mr. Cranshaw, what's this all about?"

"I've just come from the Home School, where I've had a talk with Hicks and the warden—if you can call it a talk, the warden kept being called away, and Hicks is a boy of few words—but here's what it comes down to. The boy's serving a one-year term, which won't be over till next November, but they'd like to release him early and they're asking me to find him a temporary home till he goes to live with his father."

Catherine said, "I thought his father was in prison."

"So he is, but he's getting out in April. His parole board is convinced he's rehabilitated." He smiled cunningly at the Fosters. "It's been my observation that parole boards are wrong in their judgments exactly two times out of three, but here's a case where they might be right. In less than two years he's worked his way up to assistant foreman of the prison twine plant. He's told the parole board that he's set two goals for himself when he gets out. He wants to make an honest living, and he wants to make a home for his son."

"Would that be good for Dodger?" she asked. "I've heard he used to beat Dodger."

"His father's a better prospect than his mother these days. His mother has a number of men she lives with, one after another, and they all come from the bottom of the barrel. Besides that, Dodger's bigger than his father now. Hard to imagine him standing for any roughhouse. His father's puny."

"Dodger's willing to live with him?"

"Says he wants to live with him. Not hard to see why, compared to life at the Home School. They pick on him a lot."

Hank asked, "Where will they live?"

"Winona. I've lined Mr. Hicks up with a job at the box factory there, starting in the middle of April." His eyes darted from Catherine to Hank and back again. "Will you take Dodger till then?"

"Take him?" Hank drew back. "You mean to live with us?"

Cranshaw nodded.

"Why us?"

"He says you're his only friends. Wasn't it your son who went to visit him last fall?"

Catherine looked sad. "His *only* friends?"

"There have been ten visiting days since he entered the home school, and your son has been his only visitor. If you take him in, Winona County will pay you three dollars a day."

Catherine asked, "What do you mean, he gets picked on?"

"Has things done to him. He's a meek sort of kid, as you probably know. He needs to learn to stand up for himself, and he'll never learn it there. The place is a hell-hole. The warden's under a lot of pressure to stop physical injuries ever since one of the boys lost an eye in a fight. In Dodger's case the solution is simply to release him to custody. The judge who sentenced him agrees."

Hank said, "I thought welfare boards had families lined up to take in wards of the county."

"We do, but we're filled up. Besides, nobody wants to take in a fifteen-year-old with a record."

"So why do you expect us to do it?"

"Because you know what Hicks is like. He's not the criminal type."

"Exactly what is being done to him?" Catherine demanded.

Cranshaw looked at his watch. He looked at the wall. He looked at Catherine. "He has forty-some scars on his body from cigarette burns."

She shuddered and closed her eyes. "Hank," she breathed, turning it over to him.

"All right, Mr. Cranshaw, we'll have to see Dodger about this. You can't expect us to take a kid with a criminal record without making sure he'll live by the rules of our house."

Cranshaw nodded. "Why not go and see him during visiting hours on Sunday? My office will pay your mileage."

"I don't trust our car that far. They're predicting twenty below on Sunday."

"Okay, how about this? I've got tomorrow morning free. I can come and pick one or both of you up and take you to Flensboro, you can have your conference with Hicks, then I can bring you home. After that, if everything works out, I can deliver Hicks to your house on whatever day you designate."

"I'm tied up tomorrow. We're remodeling the store."

"I'll go," said Catherine. "What time in the morning?"

Cranshaw suggested nine-thirty.

"I'll bring our son along. After all, it's Brendan's life more than ours that Dodger will be sharing."

"Very good." Cranshaw sprang up and put on his overcoat. "I'll see you in the morning."

"You can pick us up at the market."

With a satisfied smile Cranshaw shook their hands. "It's a pleasure to know you both."

They watched him cross to the door and step outside, turning up his collar against the falling snow.

Catherine spoke, her eyes lingering on the door. "We really don't have a choice, do we, Hank?"

He said nothing.

"I mean, poor Dodger. How could we say no?"

"We couldn't, of course." He drained his mug.

She faced him, her eyes lively. "It's high time we made our

mark in this town by doing something large-hearted. Paul says the Christians in this town, for all their talk, hardly ever *act* like Christians, and he's absolutely right. Dodger may just be what this town needs to save its soul.''

She seldom spoke in such an inflated way, and Hank, folding the sheet of sketches and slipping it into his shirt pocket, was a little alarmed that she should pin impossible hopes on the likes of Dodger Hicks. Yet he realized, taking her hand as they left the booth, that she was never more appealing to him than when her eyes shone with purpose, never prettier.

Fortunately the wind diminished after dark, and so the snowfall wasn't blinding as Hank made his way across the farmland and down the winding road between the bluffs. At the gas station on Highway 61 he added a mixture of water and antifreeze to the radiator; then he and the attendant stood warming themselves at the oil stove as they watched the snow build up on the lighted apron surrounding the gas pumps. Soon a truck pulled in and a man in his sixties came inside and stood with them. His clothes smelled of a cow barn. ''I've got a son due back from his induction physical,'' he said to Hank. ''You here for the same reason?''

''One of my employees.''

''If they keep this up there won't be an able-bodied man left in the United States of America,'' said the farmer. ''They already got my two older boys, one in France and the other in the Solomon Islands, and who knows if they're alive or dead?''

''Hitler can't last much longer,'' Hank assured him. ''Then we'll throw everything we've got at Japan.''

''I got a younger one at home yet. He's seventeen. When he's drafted who's going to help me with the cows?'' The farmer turned to the attendant, who looked about thirty. ''How did you get out of it?''

''My left leg's shorter than my right one.''

''See what I mean? The home front's nothing but women and children and cripples and old guys like me.'' He looked more closely at Hank. ''What's your excuse?''

''Too old for the draft.''

"You could have enlisted."

So Catherine's sister had been implying in her letters. He nodded at the farmer, offering no defense.

"Not that I fault you for it."

The attendant spoke up. "I'd damsite sooner go to war than have a short leg."

Trailing a cloud of snow, the bus turned off the highway and came to a stop in the circle of light. The driver descended from his seat and asked, "Anybody here to pick up a guy named Flint?"

"Me," said Hank.

"He's pretty sick. You better pull your car up close."

As Hank brought the DeSoto around, Wallace was helped off the bus by the driver and the farmer's buck-toothed son. Hank opened the passenger door for them.

Wallace, shivering, his eyes fluttering, mumbled, "Back seat. Want to lie down."

"It's cold back there, Wallace. You'd better sit in front."

As they lifted him into the front seat and shut the door, the young man explained, "He was standing right in front of me at the eye chart when he threw a fit. Scared the bejesus out of me. He fell down and shook the way a hog does when you knock it in the head. The doctor said he'd be all right, but they hadn't no use for him. He's 4-F." The young man turned to his father. "I'm 1-A and I'm off to camp next Tuesday."

The farmer nodded sadly. "Come on, we'll go help Willie and your ma with the milking."

Driving home, Hank had all he could do to hold the car between the ditches, for the snow in the headlights dazed him—it was like driving through gauze.

"Hank," said Wallace, not loud enough to be heard over the roaring engine and rattling exhaust pipes. "Hank," he said again.

"Yes?"

"I can't go back to work, Hank. I can't go back to the store."

"No, you can take as long as you need to rest up."

"I mean ever, Hank. I can't ever go back." His voice broke.

"Why?" Hank searched the darkness beside him for the young man's face. He saw only the gleam of watery eyes.

"Because." This ended the conversation.

Driving, Hank kept seeing Wallace being helped off the bus and half-carried to the car. That very picture had appeared last week in the *Post-Bulletin*—a wounded G.I. supported by two of his buddies as he moved between a tank and an ambulance. It was the Battle of the Bulge and it was snowing. Wallace, too, was coming home from war. Never mind that Wallace's wound came not from a clash of armies but from an unfortunate mix of genes, he had volunteered for the service, which was more than Hank had done. Hank could imagine the incredible courage Wallace must have called up to overcome his unwarlike sensibilities. He experimented with one hand on the steering wheel, and when he found that he was able to hold the car between the ditches, he put his other arm around Wallace, who immediately began to weep, snuggling up to him like a little boy.

19

T H E   S U N   O N   T H E fresh snow was blinding as Brendan and his mother stepped out the front door of the market and got into the large gray car belonging to Mr. Cranshaw.

"Good morning, Mrs. Foster." He sat very low behind the wheel. Threads were unraveling from the brim of his black hat.

"Good morning. This is our son Brendan."

Cranshaw turned and offered his wily smile to Brendan in the back seat. "No school today, young fellow?"

"I'm excused."

"And not sorry about it either, I'll bet."

"Glad about it." In January the school year became eternal.

As the car pulled away from the curb, Catherine waved to Hank in the window. Hank waved his crowbar. Between customers, he and Paul were beginning to tear out the old shelving.

Three miles east of town the road took them up over a rise known as Higgins Hill, from which the view was unobstructed in all directions. Rolling fields deep in snow. Leafless trees a lifeless gray. Here beside the road was the red barn of Lester Higgins with an advertisement for spark plugs painted on its side. Horses and cows stood in a pen breathing steam. Ordinarily Catherine enjoyed the long vistas offered by high ground, but here, looking back at Plum huddled in a snowy hollow so remote that God Himself might overlook it, she shuddered, thinking of the twenty-five neighbors who had declined or ignored her New Year's invitation.

As the car descended Higgins Hill, cutting off the view, she took a piece of paper and a pencil from her purse and began making a list. "I think we can be ready for Dodger in two days," she told Cranshaw. "I've asked Hank to bring the rollaway down from the attic and put it in Brendan's room, and I'll empty out one side of the wardrobe in the hallway and assign it to Dodger." She knew, of course, that these household details were of no interest to Cranshaw, but she was elated by her mission and needed to talk. "Tomorrow I'll see about enrolling Dodger in school. That's something I'll have to bring up with him today— he'll have to agree to regular school attendance. And we'll have to come to an agreement about bedtimes and household chores."

Brendan, listening, wished his own preparations for Dodger were simple enough to put into a list. His preparations consisted mostly of suppressing his resentment. Dodger the ex-con was certain to be an even greater embarrassment than Dodger the mere outcast had been. Dodger was so tall and gawky and unhealthy-looking that everybody would stare at him—and at Brendan because Dodger would be at his side every moment of the day. Last night at supper when his parents proposed taking Dodger in, Brendan was shocked. He had turned to Grandfather and asked if he wasn't upset to think that a stranger was moving into the house, but Grandfather said no, he wouldn't mind another lad underfoot, the more the merrier. Before Brendan had a chance to register his dread, his father brought up Dodger's cigarette burns and said it would be heartless to turn their back on him, and his mother said there was more to Christian duty than the example set by Father O'Day; more important than prayer was doing good for others, and Dodger was their God-sent opportunity. How did you counter an argument like that without sounding selfish? Brendan kept his mouth shut.

By the time they reached Flensboro, Catherine's list covered both sides of the paper. "And I was thinking," she said to Cranshaw as he turned in through the gate of the Home School, "it will be good for Dodger to help out in the store on Saturdays—teach him the satisfaction of holding a job."

"There he is," Brendan said from the back seat.

Dodger stood smiling down at them from the steps of the main building, his baldness gleaming in the sun, his breath steamy. At his feet were two cardboard boxes.

Catherine said, "Does he think he's leaving with us? Mr. Cranshaw, didn't you tell him we were coming here only to talk?"

Cranshaw looked pained. "That's exactly what I told him, and that's exactly what I told the warden. Don't worry, I'll straighten this out."

He stopped the car at the foot of the steps, and they got out. Dodger came down to them.

"I've got a bunch of comics for you, Brendan." The pink scar on his throat was pale and barely noticeable. There were two new, bright red scars under his ear.

"This isn't the day you leave," said Cranshaw.

Dodger ignored him. "I've got a new *Superman*, Brendan. You said you like *Superman*." He set his boxes on the snow near the trunk of the car.

Cranshaw muttered angrily to himself as he climbed the steps and went inside.

Brendan explained, "You aren't supposed to come home with us today, Dodger. We're here to talk it over, is all."

Dodger laughed softly and politely, as though at an unsuccessful joke.

Catherine took Dodger's hand. "Remember me? I'm Brendan's mother."

"Sure." He averted his eyes.

"We're not taking you home with us today, Dodger, I'm sorry." Again he laughed quietly, looking at the ground to conceal his desperation. He'd been told at breakfast that the Fosters were coming to discuss the possibility of taking him home, and from that moment forward he knew that no power on earth could force him to endure one more night in the dormitory.

She continued: "We've come to tell you what it would be like to live with us, Dodger, and we want you to have a day or two to think it over." She opened her purse and took out her list, but she didn't look at it. She couldn't take her eyes off Dodger. His face had matured since last September—his eyes deep-set under ledgelike brows, his jawline long and bony. She tried to engage his eyes, but he wouldn't let her. They were fascinating eyes, shifty not out of furtiveness (she wanted to believe) but out of shyness. His smile, too, was fascinating. It came easily to his face and gave him a soft, kindly look. Catherine's heart, already full of pity, brimmed over with love.

Cranshaw came out onto the porch and down the steps, followed by the warden. Both men spoke at once, angrily, Cranshaw angry at the warden and the warden angry at Dodger.

"I went ahead and did the impossible, I found a place for this kid nobody wants, and you let him foul up my plans."

"I'll take care of this," seethed the warden. "I'll put him in solitary for a week." Brendan recognized his piping voice and his fussy goatee. He was the man who had come into the dining hall and made announcements on that Sunday last November. Though smaller than Dodger, the warden gripped him roughly by the arm and turned him so that he faced his two cardboard boxes. "Pick up your belongings, Hicks, and get back inside."

Chuckling softly, Dodger removed the man's grip, finger by finger, and climbed into the back seat of the car and shut the door.

Cranshaw railed at the warden, "You put him up to this to save the State money. You weren't supposed to unload him on us till we gave the word."

The warden looked through the window at Dodger, who sat staring straight ahead, smiling. "Give me a minute to find a guard, and Hicks will regret this to his dying day." The warden was livid. He turned abruptly and went up the steps and inside, slamming the door.

Brendan and Catherine had backed away from this encounter, alarmed by the ferocity of these two small men. Now Catherine stepped forward and said, "If you haven't any other business

here, Mr. Cranshaw, let's start back. We'll take Dodger along."
She motioned for Brendan to climb into the back seat.

"You're serious?" asked Cranshaw. "What about your list of
conditions?"

"We'll talk them over on the way." She got into the front seat
and shut the door.

Cranshaw loaded the boxes into the trunk; then he got in
behind the wheel. "You're sure?"

She nodded.

"Just a word of warning before we leave the grounds, Mrs.
Foster. It can be disastrous to let a type like Hicks win the first
round. You could find yourself spending the next twelve weeks
on the defensive."

"Dodger does not belong to a type, Mr. Cranshaw." She
turned and gave Dodger a reassuring smile, and Brendan, seeing
it, was jolted—a motherly smile directed elsewhere.

The door above them opened and the warden stepped out onto
the porch with the eight-fingered guard from the dining hall. As
they came down the steps, Dodger locked his door.

The guard rapped on Dodger's window and said, "Get out of
there, Hicks."

Catherine said, "Please, Mr. Cranshaw, let's go."

Cranshaw started the car, and as it began to move, Dodger
rolled his window open two inches and said, beaming up at the
guard, "Go piss up a rope."

20

THE NEXT DAY BEING Friday, a busy day at the store, Catherine hoped that Dodger might be enrolled in school immediately, but the principal was out of town and she was asked to bring Dodger in on Monday. She stayed home through the morning, therefore, and assigned Dodger chores, the first of which was shoveling coal. For this, she took him down to the basement and demonstrated how to fill the stoker; she left him to finish the job on his own, instructing him next to go out and sweep from the sidewalk the dusting of snow that had fallen overnight.

Alone in the basement, Dodger—dazed by happiness—worked very slowly. Lifting small scoops out of the coalbin and dribbling them into the stoker, he went over in his mind yesterday's wonderful liberation, beginning with the dazzling drive through the snowy countryside from Flensboro to Plum. His first sight of Plum from Higgins Hill had filled him with joy. When they arrived at the house on Bean Street, Brendan had helped him carry in his boxes and showed him the room they would share. It was a strange house to live in. You were assigned a certain towel in the bathroom. You spoke to God before meals. You hung your clothes on hangers. There was an old man who sat in the living room and listened to the radio all the time. Yesterday when Dodger was introduced to him, the old man shook his hand and said, "Welcome aboard, lad," and when he took his hand away Dodger found a fifty-cent piece in his palm. Then the old man ran his hand over Dodger's bald scalp and laughed, and Dodger laughed too. Later, Brendan's father came home from work and gave Dodger a handshake as firm as Grandfather's (but without the fifty cents) and a hardy pat on the back, as one man to another. By the time they sat down to supper, Dodger felt such a wonderful sense of well-being that when they paused after grace to be silently mindful of personal favors they wanted from God, Dodger was stumped. Supper was chicken, beans, potatoes and gravy, as much as you wanted and all of it hot. For dessert Brendan's mother served a cake with "Welcome Dodger" written in the frosting. After that, there were dishes to wipe (Dodger dropped and broke two saucers; no one punished him) and then there were three of Brendan's favorite radio programs, one of them exciting ("The FBI in Peace and War") and two of them sort of dull. After that, Brendan brought out a game played with dice and squares on a board. As the two of them played the game, Brendan talked a lot about Sam and Philip, boys for whom Dodger felt an immediate affection, not because he remembered them clearly but because Brendan was obviously so fond of them. Then it was bedtime. Both boys fell asleep quickly, but Dodger awoke with a start several times, expecting the searing pain of a cigarette burn.

Finishing in the basement, Dodger closed the lid of the stoker and slipped upstairs to the living room, where Grandfather sat in a deep chair between his pipe stand and the console radio. Dodger stretched out on the carpet in front of him and they listened to Don McNeil's "Breakfast Club" together. In a few minutes Catherine came into the room and reminded Dodger about clearing the sidewalk.

Looking out from her house next door, Mrs. Brask saw the tall young stranger lazily sweeping the Fosters' sidewalk. He was wearing the same red stockingcap she had seen on the Foster boy, and a jacket sometimes worn by Mr. Foster. She put on her boots, her hat and her fox tail and went outside to investigate.

"Are you hired help?" she asked, strutting toward Dodger in a manner he found vaguely frightening. He didn't reply. He leaned on his broom and gave the sky a tentative smile.

"Who are you?" she inquired, shaking him by his broomstick.

"Where do you come from? What is your name? What is your business in Plum? Are you a transient?"

He sorted through her questions for the one he could answer. He said, "Hicks."

"Hicks? Not the hoodlum Hicks! What are you doing here?"

He showed her his broom. "Sweeping," he answered.

"Don't talk smart to me, young man. Why are you sweeping this particular sidewalk is my question."

"Because it snowed last night."

She studied his face for insolence, but saw none. Perhaps he was retarded. "Are you Fosters' hired help then?"

He shook his head. "No, I'm just living here."

"You're living with the Fosters? I don't believe it."

He could hardly believe it himself. "For now," he added.

"When did you arrive? What can the Fosters be thinking?"

Dodger stood with his head politely bowed as she fired off eight or ten more questions. When she fell silent and waited for answers, he said nothing. She put Dodger in mind of the many schoolteachers who by scolding him for wrong answers had taught him not to open his mouth.

"Explain yourself," she ordered, but he raised his eyes to the overcast sky and kept them there.

She snorted, imagining the speedy decline and fall of Bean Street now that it was open to hoodlums. She gave up and went home.

When he finished sweeping, Dodger went back to the living room, lay down again near Grandfather's chair and listened to "Ma Perkins." At the funny parts, Grandfather laughed and slapped his knee and asked, "Did you hear that, lad?" Dodger nodded, chuckling contentedly and running his hand over his whiskery scalp.

Meanwhile Mrs. Brask phoned Mrs. Kimball and asked if she knew that a hoodlum was living next door. Mrs. Kimball gasped and went around the house locking her doors and windows and instructing her pup to be watchful; then she returned to the phone and called her husband at the funeral home. He told her not to be alarmed; Dodger Hicks was harmless. She then called Mrs. Brask and conveyed her husband's judgment. "He's a disgrace to the neighborhood," declared Mrs. Brask, "and I'll never speak another word to the Fosters as long as they harbor him in their house."

Catherine made ham sandwiches and called Dodger and Grandfather to the table. Hank was lunching at the pool hall, Brendan at school. Sitting across the table from Dodger, Grandfather decided to try him out as a listener. He told him two or three railroad stories and then, catching sight of snowflakes spiraling down past the dining room window, he called to mind a blizzard story he seldom told because no one believed it.

"When I was seven years old and living in Prairie du Chien, Wisconsin, a railroad town on the Mississippi, we had the blizzard of the century—the nineteenth century, that is—and the blizzard caused something to happen at our house that was too strange to be anything but a miracle."

They were finished eating now, and Catherine had left the table. Puffing and puffing as he lit his pipe, Grandfather rested his eyes first on Dodger and then—unfocused—on that day in 1870 when the sky grew heavy at sundown. "We lived in a house at the edge of town facing a hardwood forest, and shortly after supper a young deer came out of the woods and put its front hoofs up on the kitchen windowsill and looked in at my mother washing dishes. After she got over her shock and took a closer look, she saw in its eyes that it was afraid of something. She called us into the kitchen, and as soon as we all gathered at the window it got down on all fours and stood by the door. 'He wants to come in,' my oldest brother said. My father was off in Iowa with his section crew. He weathered the blizzard in a bunkhouse car sitting on a Great Northern siding near Dubuque. My brother opened the door and, believe it or not, the deer came indoors. It went straight through the house to a bedroom closet, where it curled up on the floor.

"Well, sir, we all stood looking into the closet, not believing our eyes. My mother told us it was a sign. She was always saying that about things, always on the lookout for signs, my mother. Signs of what, she never said. She said something was a sign and left us to figure out what it was a sign of. Do you understand my meaning, lad?"

Dodger nodded, enchanted by the tale of the deer indoors. So soothing was Grandfather's voice and so honored was Dodger to be the recipient of Grandfather's stories that his eyes stopped flitting and came to rest on Grandfather's face. With his head thrust forward, his mouth open, Dodger hung on Grandfather's every word. He had no memory of anyone taking the trouble to tell him a story.

Grandfather, for his part, was so pleased to have found an attentive listener that when Catherine prepared to go off to the store, he insisted that she let Dodger stay home. She phoned Hank and they weighed the alternatives. Bring Dodger to work with her? Leave him and Grandfather in charge of each other? They decided to risk the latter and she went to work alone.

Lingering at the table, Grandfather spun out the rest of the tale. "Not an hour after the deer came into our house it began to snow and blow," he said. "Never has a blizzard begun so suddenly. It took everybody by surprise and killed hundreds of people in the Mississippi valley all the way from Minnesota to Missouri. It caught farmers out in their fields and froze them to death. It trapped hunters in their duck blinds and buried them alive in snowdrifts with an icy crust. It stopped all trains. It raged on for two nights and the one full day in between, and all that time the young deer never budged from that bedroom closet. Three of us boys slept in that room, and now and then in the night we could hear it stand up and step around and find itself a more comfortable position, but that was all it did. We set a pan of milk and a pan of oats nearby, but it never ate or drank. For two nights and the day in between it stayed in the closet and never once ate or drank or peed or moved its bowels, now tell me if that's not a miracle. And then on the morning of the second day when it stopped snowing and the sun came out, the deer came out of the closet and went into the kitchen. My mother let it outside, and we never saw it again. We told our father when he got home and he didn't believe it. As long as he lived—and it was a long, long time he lived, the McMahons being a family of old, old men—he called it malarky. Now you'll excuse me, lad, it's time for my nap.'' He left the table and went to the couch in the living room.

Though he hadn't been directed to do so, Dodger went to Brendan's room and lay down on the rollaway in order to experience again the pleasure of falling asleep undisturbed by cigarette burns.

Arriving at work, Catherine was surprised to see Wallace Flint's mother carrying on what appeared to be an urgent conversation with Hank. The two of them stood at the back of the store—she short and squat and looking up at Hank with a supplicating expression, Hank staring at the wall and feeling the back of his head with the palm of his hand, as was his habit whenever he was nervous or perplexed—while at the front of the store Paul Dimmitburg worked as speedily as he could to keep up with the trade.

"Catherine, this is Wallace's mother.''

"Hello, Mrs. Flint. I've seen you going to and from the post office.''

"I'm so pleased to meet you, Catherine.'' She truly was—the Fosters could see it in her beaming smile. "I'm calling you Catherine the way Wallace does, I hope you don't mind.''

"Not at all.''

"My name is Margaret.''

"Is Wallace feeling better? We miss him in the store.''

"He'll come around.''

Did Catherine really miss him? Hank wondered. Though he felt a certain new tenderness toward Wallace since their drive home in the snow, he didn't miss him. He said to Catherine, "Mrs. Flint says he refuses to come out of his room.''

"Of course he's done this before," his mother explained. "He'll lock himself in his room a day or two at a time and tell me to go away when I try to get him to eat. I hear him go down to the kitchen in the middle of the night. Wallace can be *so* temperamental."

All this, Catherine noticed, was delivered with a placid smile; she might have been describing the night habits of a newborn baby. Catherine had never seen this woman up close before. Given Wallace's age, she had to be in her mid or late forties, yet she looked younger. Her round face was remarkably free of creases and wrinkles; her eyes were lively. She was obese; her tentlike coat of green and black plaid was stretched tight around her middle.

"But this time he's saying wilder things than usual." Her expression changed, grew serious again. "He's saying he's seen the last of the inside of this store. He's through working, he's saying, for life. He's saying it's my turn to go out and earn the money. I'm sure he doesn't mean it about never working again, but as I was telling your husband, if it's going to take Wallace a few more days to recover—his seizure in Minneapolis must have been one of his worst—then why shouldn't I go out and try to bring in some money? I'm not helpless. I know what work is. I used to wait on tables before I was married. I quit because my husband was against working wives. Then after he died he had two brothers who supported us until Wallace was eighteen, so I got used to the easy life." She laughed nervously. "I got spoiled and I got fat." Her laugh died. "Is there any chance you could give me a job?"

Catherine and Hank exchanged a look. Though unspoken, their thoughts, they knew, were identical. Without Wallace they were shorthanded, and if his absence continued into next week they had resolved to hire someone else, most likely a woman because of the wartime manpower shortage—but how much work would this overweight, flaccid woman be capable of?

"Could you come back?" Hank asked. "Say in an hour?"

"After we've talked it over," Catherine added.

"Sure," she piped cheerily.

But she wasn't feeling cheery. Walking the length of the store, she felt embarrassed and frightened and hopeless. She feared the Fosters were watching her ridiculous way of walking, the rolling, strenuous motion of great bulk set upon short legs. She feared she couldn't work at a job requiring her to be on her feet all day; at home she sank into a chair every so often to let her energy build. She feared this was no two-day snit Wallace was going through; she had never seen such fierce anger in his eyes as when, last night, when she rapped on his door with food on a tray, he burst out of his room and called her a repulsive sow and smacked the tray out of her hands. She would never erase from her mind the glimpse she caught of all those horrible faces. How could he stand to be in that room hour after hour, day after day, with all those bug-eyed, bruise-colored people staring down at him?

When Grandfather awoke at two-thirty, he went into Brendan's room and shook Dodger awake. "Come on, lad, we'll go to the pool hall and I'll buy you a soda pop."

Dodger sprang up and slipped into Hank's jacket and drew Brendan's stockingcap down over his ears. He waited by the front door while Grandfather slowly put on his vest, his suitcoat, his muffler, his overcoat, his rubbers, and his hat.

"Winters are milder than they used to be," he told Dodger as they stepped out into a chilly breeze. It had stopped snowing. The sun was low in the southwest, the shadows on the snow were deep blue. Gripping Dodger by the arm whenever they came to a stretch of snow-packed sidewalk, Grandfather rambled on. "We had a number of winters back in the thirties when it was below zero more noons than it was above, and I can remember one February when the cold spell broke and it snowed for a month. Why, the drifts were so deep on the prairie west of Fargo that my train ran three days late, creeping along behind the plow an inch at a time. Wind-driven snow can block your tracks like a wall of stone. Many's the time a sudden blizzard didn't give the ranchers time to bring their cattle in off the range, and we hitched a flatcar of hay behind our passenger train and threw off bales wherever we saw cattle along the tracks. I've seen it in the spring where the snow melts off a pasture and uncovers dozens of steers lying dead, their carcasses bloated like balloons.''

In the pool hall Grandfather introduced Dodger as a friend of the family, and although the cardplayers and everyone else in the place knew he was the outlaw son of an outlaw father they refrained from staring at him too openly and restricted their hostile remarks to mumbles Dodger and Grandfather couldn't hear.

Dodger watched a card game he didn't understand while he savored the bottle of cream soda Grandfather bought him. Though his head was hot, he kept his itchy wool cap on to hide his baldness.

The moment he finished his bottle, Grandfather bought him another. Sipping, he let his mind wander. He tried to remember when he had last drunk a bottle of pop, since it was either milk or water at the Home School, never pop. He tried to remember when he last had a companion as generous as Grandfather. Never.

He finished his second bottle and Grandfather bought him a third, which made him sick. He said to Grandfather, ''Save my place,'' and went out through the back room of the pool hall and vomited into the snow. Returning to his place at the card-table, he found a fourth bottle of cream soda waiting for him. He made this one last until five-thirty, when he and Grandfather left the pool hall and went next door to ride home with Hank.

They drove home by way of the Flint house. Hank, pulling up in front, said to Catherine, ''Come with me please.'' To Grand-father and Dodger in back, Catherine said, ''We'll be just a minute.''

They stepped onto the side porch and knocked. The door was opened by Mrs. Flint. Behind her the kitchen was dimly lit by a low flame in the kerosene lamp. There was no sign of Wallace.

''Why didn't you come back to the store?'' asked Catherine.

''Well, I got to thinking I'm not sure I could be on my feet that much. And I figured you didn't want me anyway.''

''But we do. We'd like you to work for a few days and see how it goes.'' She explained their plan. Mrs. Flint would work short periods at first, learning the trade, then possibly full time when the market was remodeled and they'd need a cashier at the checkout counter. They would devise a way for her to sit.

"Could you give us a few days?" asked Mrs. Flint, speaking for herself and her son. "Maybe in a few days Wallace will want to go back to work."

"We can give you till midweek," said Hank.

Catherine added, "We'll definitely need to know before next weekend because I've got more work at home these days and we'll need to hire somebody. We've taken in Dodger Hicks to live with us."

"Dodger Hicks!" cried Wallace, stepping around from behind the door. "Dodger Hicks in your house?" He laughed wildly. He was a ghost of himself, short-haired, beardless, emaciated.

Hank took Catherine's hand as they recoiled. They descended the steps.

"Catherine," called Wallace, leaning out into the moonlight. "I went to Dayton's where you used to work and talked to a gray-haired woman who wore her glasses on a ribbon around her neck and had a mole beside her nose."

"Marjorie Smith," Catherine said, halting and looking up from the snowy yard.

"I told her I knew you, but your name didn't register with her."

"Please, Wallace, that's not true." She set off with Hank toward the car.

"She said she works with so many clerks she has trouble keeping track of them all."

He was left standing on the cold porch feeling triumphant. He had never before tried to injure Catherine. It raised his spirits immeasurably.

After supper Brendan took Dodger to the Friday night movie, purposely arriving late so they could enter the dark theater unnoticed. Judy Canova played a hillbilly singer who traveled the Ozarks with a string band and outsmarted and brought to justice a pair of gangsters hiding in the hills. Brendan was bored by the singing, amused by the jokes, and excited by the railroad chase along a twisting track. Dodger, he noticed, was engrossed from beginning to end. He sat perfectly still with his head thrust forward and his lip lifted in half a smile. He emitted soft chuckles throughout. Only once did he break his concentration and turn to see Brendan's reaction and that was at the end of the railroad chase. Nudging Brendan with his elbow, he said, "We should have brought Grandpa."

After the movie, as Brendan feared, they ran into Sam and Philip outside under the marquee. To Brendan's surprise, the boys spoke to Dodger as though they cared for him.

"Hey, Dodge, how you been?"

"What's it like at the Home School, Dodge? Is it true they put you in solitary if you smart off?"

Dodger smiled at them and said, "I never smarted off."

Philip asked, "What's it like to be in jail, Dodge? We heard you were in jail."

"Yeah, the night I got arrested."

"What's it like?"

"Pretty nice, you get your own bed and your own toilet."

Sam asked, "Is it true all the guards at the Home School are ex-cons?"

Dodger, basking in their attention, said, "Naw."

Philip said, "I heard you're starting school on Monday, Dodge. Does that mean you know how to read?"

"Naw."

"What grade'll you be in?"

"I don't know, I was in tenth for a while this year. Then they put me in eighth. He laughed, "Then they put me in the laundry."

"How about coming out for basketball?" said Sam. "We could use some height."

"Think I should?"

"Yeah, you should. How tall are you?"

A shrug. "Five or six feet, I guess."

"You're close to six," Sam estimated. "If they put you in eighth grade you can be on our junior-high team. If they put you in ninth or tenth you get to play for the high school."

"I'd like to play with you guys."

The group left the theater and walked along the street, Philip dribbling an imaginary basketball, Sam miming hook shots over Dodger's head, and Brendan feeling elated, proud to be Dodger's host and to oversee his social debut.

But his pride was abruptly dashed. When they came to the pool hall, where Brendan and his friends customarily bought Fudgesicles after the Friday night movie, his friends ran inside and slammed the door, leaving Brendan and Dodger standing in the cold.

Dodger, hunched over, hands in pockets, waited for Brendan to make the next move.

"Want a Fudgesicle?" Brendan asked. He dug in his pocket for change.

"Sure."

"I've only got a nickel left. Can you pay for your own?"

Dodger showed him his fifty-cent piece.

They went in and stood at the end of the bar next to the peanut display, waiting for Gordy to serve them. Brendan saw his friends scurrying out the back door, ditching him, and he was considering running after them and assuring them that he was their friend, not Dodger's, when Gordy said, "What'll it be, the usual?"

Brendan nodded.

"How about you, Hicks?"

"Yeah."

"Boy, you sure got tall since last summer, Hicks. When you came in here this afternoon I didn't hardly know you."

Dodger said, "I'm close to six feet, Sam Romberg told me."

"How are you at basketball?"

"Never played it."

"How about other sports?"

"Never played them either."

They watched a pool game until their Fudgesicles were gone and Brendan said, "Let's go."

They walked in silence, Dodger now and again leaping and turning in the air, imitating Sam's hook shot, Brendan hanging his head and assuming, sadly, that it was his lot for the next three months to be ditched night and day by his friends.

At the corner of Main and Bean, Dodger said, "How about some peanuts?" He reached into his pocket and gave Brendan one of the small bags he had stolen when Gordy wasn't looking. They were salty and delicious.

"You've got to quit stealing stuff," said Brendan, chewing. "You'll end up back in the Home School."

"Yeah, I know it."

"If you know it, how come you took these peanuts?"

"I thought you might like some."

"But you didn't need to steal them. You've got money."

"Oh yeah, I forgot."

21

A *S A PROPONENT OF* diagnostic testing, Mr. Reinhart, principal of Plum Junior and Senior High School, gave
Dodger a written exam followed by an interview. His findings
were these: while Dodger read like a second grader, his acne
and dark whiskers looked like a senior's; therefore he split the
difference and placed him in the seventh grade. As a proponent
of remedial education, Mr. Reinhart gave him two study halls
instead of one.

Brendan was dismayed to find Dodger in four of his classes—
English, math, physical education, and choir. Brendan observed
that while Dodger was not as thoroughly ignored by his classmates as he had been last fall, he was still nobody's friend. By
robbing a gas station and getting caught, he had made himself
interesting, but the curiosity he aroused was morbid and mo-
mentary. Again and again on the way to school or between
classes, Brendan and Dodger found themselves drawn into an
encounter like that which followed the Judy Canova movie—
"Did they handcuff you, Dodger?" "Do you suppose someday

you'll go big time and kill somebody?'' It took only a minute or two to satisfy the questioner, who then hurried away.

Brendan wished he had the nerve to tell Dodger to quit hanging around. In September he had given Dodger the brush-off with ease but that had resulted in a serious case of guilt. Now he tried to ditch him by subtler means. He tried leaving for school earlier than usual, but Dodger was wonderfully adaptable. If Brendan got up an hour early, so did Dodger. If he skipped breakfast, if he set off for school at a run, if he lingered at the store and arrived nearly late for first period, so did Dodger. One morning Brendan said he felt sick and Catherine sent Dodger off to school while keeping Brendan home, but later when Brendan threw off his feigned illness and left for school he found Dodger at the corner of Bean and Main, where he had been standing for an hour, waiting. Brendan gave up then, reconciled to Dodger's constant presence. He thought of him as a kind of freakish appendage, like a third arm. Ten weeks and three days, he told himself, counting down. Nine weeks and four days. Eight weeks even.

For the first time in his life Dodger made headway as a student. That is, he maintained a D average in math. He achieved this with the help of Brendan and the math teacher, Mr. Torborg. Being an athletic coach as well as a wounded veteran, Mr. Torborg was enormously respected in the classroom. He deserved to be. He was a kindly, patient young man who took time to explain things to Dodger. So did Brendan. Each night they did their homework together, Brendan reading the story problems out of the math book and nudging Dodger toward the correct answers. This wasn't easy, because Dodger invariably became engrossed in the story and forgot about the numbers. Never mind the gas tank capacity of their cars, what was wrong with Mr. A's engine that he should run out of gas halfway between his house and his office while his next door neighbor Mr. B, who was driving the same distance, ran out at the three-quarter mark? Or, more to the point, what was wrong with the men themselves that they should forget to fill their tanks? And why, if a bushel of tangerines cost so much more than a bushel of oranges, did Mrs. X insist on buying tangerines? Didn't she like oranges as much as Dodger did?

Dodger got F's in English. No matter how Brendan tried, he couldn't get Dodger to understand the function of the preposition or to memorize "The Charge of the Light Brigade." Near the end of the six-week marking period, Catherine advised Dodger to ask his English teacher Miss Dale for extra help, and he did, but Miss Dale ignored him. Miss Dale was a dense, sentimental and slightly unbalanced young woman who thought of her junior high girls as a garden of lovely little blossoms and her junior high boys as noxious weeds. She particularly despised Dodger for being so tall and mature and lazy. She had assigned him a desk in the back row of her classroom, where the sun falling through the high windows made him happily drowsy, a condition she was unwilling to disturb.

In choir Dodger's fate was sealed the first time he opened his mouth. Plum's music teacher, Mr. Paulson, was a temperamental perfectionist. Whereas another teacher might send a student to the principal for misbehavior, Mr. Paulson did so for singing off key. Mr. Paulson had spent the fall and winter winnowing the frog-throats, monotones, and other repellent voices from his choir and banishing them to study hall, and he felt certain that he would bring home the trophy from the spring music festival in Rochester. This was before Dodger showed up. Heretofore "America, God shed His grace on thee" had sounded to Mr. Paulson like the ringing of small, clear bells, but with the addition of Dodger's growl it sounded like a dirge. He sent Dodger to Mr. Reinhart's office for assignment elsewhere. Catherine, hearing of this, was firm with Mr. Reinhart on the phone. Did choir class exist for the purpose of training students or for satisfying the enormous ego of Mr. Paulson? She had a mind to run for the school board (she told Mr. Reinhart) and look into any number of questionable practices in the Plum school system. The boys' and girls' toilets were not properly cleaned, she'd been told, and Miss Dale in English was positively batty. Mr. Reinhart, a proponent of harmony in the community, told her he'd speak to Mr. Paulson in Dodger's behalf, and he did, but he had uttered only a few words when Mr. Paulson drove him from the music room screaming, "His voice is disgusting!" and so Mr. Reinhart, a proponent of harmony among his faculty, withdrew Dodger from choir and assigned him to manual training.

Because of Dodger's height, Mr. Torborg urged him to come out for basketball. There were no junior high teams as such, but boys of that age were allowed to share the gym and put themselves through calisthenics and scrimmages similar to the high school team's. Thus Brendan, who had been out for basketball all winter, found himself allied to Dodger during the two hours of the twenty-four when he had expected to be free of him. For a few days Mr. Torborg stole time from his high school team to work with Dodger, and he observed that while Dodger picked up the individual skills of basketball very quickly, he was helpless when it came to teamwork. Give him a lot of room on the court and Dodger learned to dribble with either hand and to go in for layups with smooth footwork, but put him in a scrimmage and he fell over the lines painted on the floor. Mr. Torborg also observed that whenever he put Brendan in at guard instead of Sam Romberg (who was somewhat better at the position) Dodger settled down and made fewer mistakes. Not few enough, however, and Mr. Torborg finally gave up on him. Thus Dodger, sitting out of scrimmages but continuing to show up at practice because Brendan was there, lapsed into his customary role as a misfit.

In manual training Dodger became adept at sandpapering. He avoided the power tools (the scream of the band saw made his ears ache) and he was awkward with hand tools (it took him five minutes to drive a nail) but he never grew tired of standing at his workstation and sanding the rolling pin he was making for Catherine. When he took it home and gave it to her for her birthday in mid-February, her pleasure was everything he had hoped for. It had a curious shape for a rolling pin—oval rather than round—but it was smooth as a tube of glass and she hugged him and told him she loved it.

His birthday gift for Hank, in March, was a socket wrench for removing spark plugs. While assisting Hank in tuning up the DeSoto, he had watched him skin his knuckles on the engine block each time the pliers slipped off a plug, so he filched a socket wrench from the tool room at school, scrubbed off the grime and gave it to Hank. Later Brendan told his father where it came from; he recognized the identifying dab of red paint on the grip. Whereupon Hank invited Dodger into the kitchen, shut the door and sat facing him in the breakfast nook.

"Dodger." He laid the wrench before him on the table. "This belongs to the school."

Dodger studied the wrench and nodded, half smiling.

"You stole it, didn't you."

He nodded again, without hesitation.

"Don't you know that's bad? Wrong? A crime?"

Dodger pondered this for a while. "It didn't seem wrong at the time. They've got a whole lot of these wrenches."

"But now, when you think about it, doesn't it seem wrong?"

"I guess so."

"You have to quit stealing. You don't need to steal. We're giving you an allowance."

Dodger, nodding happily, agreed.

"I want to help you quit stealing. Will you let me help you?"

"Sure."

"All right, Catherine and I have a plan. But first, promise you'll take this back to school tomorrow."

"Sure."

"And you'll apologize to Mr. Butz."

Dodger scowled.

"Tell him you took it and you're bringing it back and you're sorry."

"Can't I just put it back and not say that?"

"No, you have to tell Mr. Butz. You have to make sure he understands that you're sorry and you'll never steal again."

Dodger sighed. Mr. Butz didn't like him very much.

"Will you do that?"

"Okay." He looked worried.

Hank patted his arm. "Good, now here's the plan. We're going to get you used to handling other people's property in an honest way." He leaned out of the nook, pushed open the door and called to Brendan in the living room.

"Boys," he said when they were both seated across from him, "we have decided you're both old enough to start taking on more responsibility at the store. We're going to put you in charge of the overnight change from the till." Leaning out again, he opened the silverware drawer and drew out a green drawstring bag. Coins clinked as he dropped it on the table before them. "Every evening after Paul checks out the till he puts forty dollars in this bag—a ten, three fives, ten ones, and the rest silver—and he gives it to me. I hide it overnight and put it back in the till in the morning. From now on Paul will give the bag to one of you instead of me. You'll take turns being responsible for it between closing time at night and opening time in the morning. You'll put the currency and coins back in their compartments every morning."

"Where do we hide it?" Brendan asked.

"That's up to you. I hide it in various places. Behind canned goods on a shelf. Sometimes down in the cellar in a potato bag. Sometimes I bring it home, like tonight."

"You mean we've got to be there every night when you lock up?"

"Yes, both of you. And while you're there I want you to sweep the floor and put the produce away in the cooler under the meat counter. It'll take you twenty minutes or so."

"And every morning when you open up?"

"Right. And get the produce out of the cooler."

"Geez, Dad, guys our age? Isn't Saturday morning enough? I mean, we've got school and everything."

"When I was your age I had to quit school to work ten hours a day."

"Yeah, but it's different now."

"Not so different. The Higgins kids spend an hour and a quarter milking cows before school every morning."

"Yeah, we smell cows on their clothes."

This irritated Hank—was his son a snob?—but he let it pass. "And they spend another hour and a quarter milking every night, and they're younger than you. I'll raise your allowance, both of you, to a dollar and a half a week."

Brendan looked mollified, Dodger pleased.

"Now remember, take turns with the bag. Change off every day or every week or however you decide. If you don't assign yourselves particular days, you'll get mixed up and maybe neither one of you will take care of it." He pushed the wrench toward Dodger. "Here, don't forget this in the morning." He pushed the bag toward Brendan. "We open at eight."

The next morning Mr. Butz saw the wrench protruding from Dodger's back pocket as he came to class. He accused him of theft, which Dodger did not deny. "I'm putting it back in the tool room. I'm through stealing stuff."

"A likely story," said Mr. Butz. He reported Dodger by memo to the principal and by phone to all five members of the school board. His motive was less to bring Dodger to justice than to improve his own reputation as an alert and discerning teacher. His reputation, because of his glum disposition and his dalliance with Mrs. Clay, was badly in need of enhancing.

At the next meeting of the board Chairman Brask moved that Dodger be expelled. He said that his wife was acquainted with scores of mothers who wished to see the young criminal banished from school before he contaminated their children, and the socket-wrench incident gave them just cause. Webster Clay agreed, muttering that if they didn't act fast crime and criminals would infiltrate American education the way pip ran through his turkeys. Abraham Woodruff, the postmaster, was undecided. The two Catholic members of the board, Nicholi the barber and Crowley of the movies, argued for leniency; their reason for defending Dodger was to ingratiate themselves with Hank, who they were hoping would file for the school board election and replace Webster Clay, whose term was nearly up. Thus the vote was split two to two, with Woodruff abstaining.

The next morning when the Fosters heard about Dodger's near-expulsion, it wasn't Hank who filed for the board, it was Catherine.

SPRING

❖

22

WALLACE FLINT, RESTING FROM his la-
bors, his hands and clothes spattered with green paint, lay on
the couch reading the *Plum Alert* and fuming with hate. He
could scarcely turn a page of the paper without seeing reference
to the Fosters. The lead article on page one was devoted to the
market's new design, with most of the credit going to Paul Dimmitburg. It was continued on page two, where Hank was quoted
as thanking his employees by name for their part in the market's
success. Wallace's name was not among them. Who had done
more than Wallace to get their precious market off the ground?
Who had scrubbed and painted and lifted and carried and been
nice to people when he hadn't felt like it? Who had been Hank's
right-hand man through thick and thin and cheered Catherine up
when she lost hope? Who but Wallace? And now he was cast
out like a leper. When he had asked for his job back in March,
the Fosters had had the gall to turn him down, claiming they
were fully staffed. But they were growing busier, he had argued;
spring and summer were always busier; they'd need more help.
No, they said, in addition to his mother they had hired Mrs.

227

Pelzer, a young woman whose husband had recently died in the
Pacific. They were selfish turncoats, and the simmering hatred
he felt for them was growing more delicious by the day. They
had usurped his place in Plum. From the time he was sixteen
he had overseen the goings and comings of the villagers from
the window of the grocery store; Plum had been his princedom,
and now he was overthrown and banished to the horrifying boredom of his mother's house. But he was not banished forever.
Sooner or later, he vowed, he would reclaim his rightful place
in the store.

The ad for the sale, which was getting underway this morning,
took up all of page three.

GRAND OPENING
HANK'S *NEW* MARKET
Completely remodeled.
New self-serve shopping.
New expanded produce department.
New shopping carts.
New low prices.

HOURLY DRAWINGS FOR FREE MERCHANDISE
FREE CUT-GLASS TUMBLER WITH $5 PURCHASE
FREE COFFEE AND COOKIES
Thurs., Fri., Sat.: April 12, 13, 14

Wallace had been told by his mother, who worked part-time at
the packaging counter, that he wouldn't know the place. Swank
was her word for it. New shelving. A new cash register and
check-out counter. A new red awning out front. New red aprons
for all the help with their names stitched in white on the bib.

On page four were a number of boxed ads from merchants
who had profited from the remodeling. Best wishes from Romberg Appliance and Bottlegas, suppliers of the refrigeration unit
for the walk-in cooler. Congratulations from Bob Donaldson of
Minneapolis Jobbing. Good luck from Plum Lumber.

Wallace hooted when he turned to page seven and saw the
photo of Hank and Catherine and their staff standing outside

under the new awning. His mother, who only ten minutes ago had come dragging home from work with the flu, bringing the *Alert* with her, called down from her bedroom, "What's so funny, Wallace?" but he didn't respond. He folded the paper and studied the picture closely. What a collection of misfits, his mother the biggest misfit among them. She stood in the middle of the group with Dodger on her left and Brendan on her right and peered shyly out over the shoulders of Catherine and Mrs. Pelzer, who stood in front. Under their aprons Brendan and Dodger wore white shirts and black bowties, as did Hank and Paul, who stood behind them. Wallace was incensed to think of a dunce like Dodger on the payroll. At Catherine's behest, Dodger was released from his late morning study hall each day for an hour of work at the store (vocational education was Catherine's term for it), and he spent most of that hour with Wallace's mother at the packaging counter. He wasn't a bad kid, she reported to Wallace. She enjoyed working with him. "That's because you're two of a kind," Wallace pointed out to her.

Peering more closely at the grainy photo, he saw that his mother was giving the camera her public look, her smile small and tentative, her eyebrows raised expectantly. That she had taken the job and stuck with it was a surprise to Wallace. For somebody who had spent over twenty years sitting by the radio reading magazines and smoking, she sure as hell got ambitious when the money ran out. They had been down to a few soda crackers and a Hubbard squash that day in January when she went back to the Fosters and accepted their offer. She'd been working fifteen to twenty hours a week ever since. She'd had a phone installed in the house so Wallace could call her home whenever he felt a fit coming on. She was in charge of the packaging counter, which formed an L with the meat case at the back of the store; she weighed and bagged merchandise as it arrived in bulk lots from Minneapolis Jobbing and other wholesalers. The perfect job, she reported to Wallace. She got to sit on a bench as she worked, and was not required to face the public. Wallace guessed it was a long-dormant social-climbing instinct that accounted for his mother's fondness for the market. She got a kick out of rubbing shoulders with the Fosters. She came home chattering like a schoolgirl about what Catherine said and what Hank said and what Brendan said and what Grandfather said until it made Wallace want to throw up.

After his army physical, Wallace had spent sixty days in a fog. He never left the house. He didn't so much as raise the shades and look out. He looked in the mirror instead, watching his beard grow back, and tried to imagine how he had ever mustered the energy to go to Minneapolis. He read very little; the printed word required mental exertion beyond his means. During those sixty days he never turned the radio off; fragments of programs wound in and out of his consciousness. Though he spent endless hours in bed and on the couch, sleep didn't come easily. He thought about things in a dazed sort of way. One of the things he thought about was suicide.

His depression lifted in March. He felt his energy gradually rising like liquid in a tank, felt his mind stretch itself and grow active. He wanted to talk. He wanted to see people. He wanted to resume his job at the market. He ordered his mother to stay home from work and let him go in her place.

She said no.

The shouting match that ensued was like nothing so far in their lives. It went on for a long time, his mother refusing, for once, to capitulate. She told him to find a job somewhere else. She said she was behaving like a normal human being after twenty years of avoiding people and she wasn't about to give up her job for anybody, not even Wallace. The battle ended in a draw, both of them stomping into their rooms and slamming their doors, their ears ringing, their throats hoarse.

The next morning he began painting the faces of seven Axis leaders on the walls of his mother's bedroom. These were to be murals, not frescoes, for he could find no plaster amid the clutter in the basement. The only paint he could find was half a can of the green enamel his mother had used years ago to paint the kitchen table and chairs. Tulip green it was called. At first he was dissatisfied to be working with such a fresh, happy hue, but after finishing Hitler and Tojo he was quite pleased with its effect against the background wallpaper of dark puce. It thrust the faces forward out of the wall.

Since he had only seven in mind, these were much larger faces—nearly four feet from ear to ear—than those in his bedroom. On the long wall opposite the window were Mussolini and Himmler and Hess.

"Get me back in the store," he told his mother when she put up a fuss. Her fuss took the form of shouting. The anger she'd been holding back for two decades came spewing forth every time she returned home from work and found a new green face. "Stay out of my room!" she screamed. But what could she do? She was gone from the house four mornings a week and her bedroom door had no lock, nor did it fit its frame snugly enough for a lock to be installed. "Get me back in the store and I'll stay out of your room," he replied with a smile as he went serenely forward with his next portrait. He enjoyed his mother's screaming fits. It was a much less boring household since she started blowing her top.

When Hank delivered her home sick this morning, Wallace was up on the stepladder, for the balloon face of Hermann Goering was going on the ceiling, looking down at his mother's bed. "A mate for you," he said. She was too sick to shout. She stood there looking dejected and feverish. "All right, go to bed," he relented, taking the *Alert* from her and leaving the room. "You look like death warmed over."

It took twenty minutes to read every word in the *Alert* from front to back. On the last page he saw Catherine's campaign ad.

Vote
For a New Voice
On the Plum School Board
CATHERINE FOSTER

In smaller print she set forth her intentions. She would redirect the flow of money for facilities, upgrading the business and home economics departments. She would promote periodic meetings between parents and teachers. Wallace was reading this list of promises when he heard footsteps on the porch. He got up and went to the door, pushing it open only an inch and peering out.

"Hello, Wallace."

It was Catherine. Her face, her voice, caused a surprising hitch in his heartbeat, a shudder such as a man might feel for a lover he hadn't seen for a long time. Or an enemy. He opened the door a little wider and looked her over. Her pale face was framed by her dark hair and the turned-up collar of a jacket he hadn't seen before. He thought her beautiful. He wanted to paint her portrait.

"Can I come in a minute?" she asked.

He made room for her to enter. He closed the door behind her. He didn't ask her to sit.

"We need help," she said, standing on the small rag rug by the door. "It's our Grand Opening and we've got scads of packaging to do."

His wish come true. But he hid his eagerness. He shrugged and turned partially away, hoping he looked aggrieved.

"Just while your mother is sick," she added.

"Why me?"

"Because you don't need to be trained. If we hire somebody else, by the time they get the hang of things the sale will be over."

"When would I start?"

"Now. As soon as you clean up. Is that paint all over your hands and shirt?"

He nodded. "I'm painting my mother's bedroom."

"That's nice." She smiled. "Will you come to work?"

"I'll be there in half an hour."

She thanked him and hurried away.

Stepping out onto the porch to watch the car drive off, he took his first breath of outdoor air in three months. He noticed it was spring.

Spring was unusually far advanced for mid-April. All across town songbirds were nesting in the budding elms. On the athletic field thirty junior-high boys in gym shorts responded to the whistle of Mr. McWhirter, who had been putting them through a series of track and field events, and followed him up the slope to the showers. Dodger brought up the rear, stalling, hoping to be too late for a shower. He hated showering with others. He was always asked about the scars on his arms and legs and neck and back. He wished he could go straight from the field to his hour of work at the market, but of course his clothes were in the locker room.

After the others entered the back door of the school, Dodger remained at the top of the slope, looking down at the football field surrounded by the oval grass track and thinking of the day he had sent the boomerang sailing so far and high that everyone came running from the playground and took turns. Never before or since had he done anything that attracted such admiration. He drew back his arm and brought it forward in slow motion, releasing an imaginary boomerang, aiming it at the high, warm sun.

His reverie was interrupted by Mr. Torborg, who came hurrying toward him, calling his name. He wore a blue suit and red tie and carried a math book in his good hand. "Dodger," he said, "you're a born runner."

"I am?"

"I've been watching you from up there." He pointed to his classroom windows on the second floor. "You've got long legs and a natural stride. You ought to be out for track. The Rochester Relays are having junior-high events this year, and I think you could win yourself a ribbon or two."

"A ribbon?" Dodger imagined the ribbons girls wore in their hair. "Shucks," he said, pretending more disappointment than he felt, "I'm moving to Winona. I'm going to live with my dad."

"So I've heard."

"Mr. Cranshaw's got it all set."

"Who's Mr. Cranshaw?"

"My case worker. He's got my dad a job at the Bemis Box Factory." This was a matter of pride with Dodger. Working at Hank's, he saw the Bemis trademark on many crates and cartons. "Me and my dad are going to live in the Hogan Hotel."

This didn't sound like a promising arrangement to Mr. Torborg, who knew the Hogan to be scarcely more than a flophouse. "When are you moving?"

"Monday."

"Well, at least you can run in the Rochester Relays. They're Saturday." No less than his interest in helping Dodger to a modicum of self-esteem was his interest in being well thought of by Catherine in case she became his superior on the school board, for along with his wound and his medals, Mr. Torborg had brought home from military service a strong respect for chain-of-command.

"Saturday morning?"

"Saturday all day."

"I work Saturday morning."

"I'm sure Mr. Foster would let you off."

"Think so? It's Grand Opening, starting today. It's busy."

"I could talk to him. I'm sure he and Mrs. Foster would be proud to have you on the team."

Dodger squinted. He could see that.

"There are other junior-high boys out for track. Philip Crowley's out, and the Holderbach twins."

Dodger nodded without enthusiasm. He didn't care for Philip. The Holderbach twins he scarcely knew; they were eighth-graders. He wished Brendan were out for track. Brendan, following Sam's lead, had gone out for baseball. Dodger had tried going out for baseball, but the owly coach, Mr. Butz, knowing he wouldn't be around to finish the season, had told him to forget it.

"What do you say, Dodger?"

He pictured himself in a PHS track uniform. It was gold. On the back of the shirt was a number, on the front a winged foot. He pictured Brendan in the uniform, standing beside him. "Do you think Brendan could come with me?"

"Brendan's out for baseball."

"Yeah, I know, but I mean just to Rochester."

"I don't see why not."

"You'd have to fix it with Mr. Foster for both of us."

"I'll fix it."

Phyllis Clay was washing her hair when the news came over the radio. She burst immediately into tears. She drew a towel over her head like a cowl, pulled on her bathrobe over her slip, and ran out the front door and across the street to the Fosters' house. She pounded on the door with both fists. It took Grandfather a minute to work his way out of his afternoon nap. He opened his eyes, rose up on his elbows and repeated the formula that usually helped him wake up: I am living in Hank and Catherine's house in the village of Plum and I have not been employed by the railroad since 1929. He got to his feet and opened the door.

"Oh, Mr. McMahon, the most awful thing has happened," sobbed Mrs. Clay on the threshold. "President Roosevelt is dead. It happened this afternoon. He was at his vacation place in Warm Springs, Georgia, and he slumped over dead in a chair. I just heard it on the radio." She covered her eyes and shook with grief.

Grandfather's heart grew suddenly heavy, his expression grave. He put his hand tenderly on her shoulder and led her into the living room and over to the couch, where she sat with her legs curled under her. Drying her tears, she asked if he would turn on the radio. "Webster's gone to his turkeys, and I can't bear to listen all by myself."

Her toenails, he saw, were painted red. He switched on the radio, and as they waited for it to warm up he asked if she cared for something to drink, some tea or coffee or whiskey.

"Oh, whiskey would be just the thing," she told him, smiling fondly.

In the kitchen Grandfather put the bottle of Southern Comfort to his lips and took a swallow, fortifying himself against the malaise that inevitably overtook him at the death of someone dear. For twelve years Roosevelt, by means of his Fireside Chats, had taken Grandfather into his confidence. Together they had eased unemployment, improved pensions, brought electricity to rural areas, insured bank deposits and put the Axis armies on the run. What would America do without FDR? God was great, but His timing was off. Ever since that summer morning when Sade fell dead in the garden, Grandfather was aware of God's terrible habit of taking people when they were needed most. The Germans were as good as licked, but the Japs vowed never to surrender, and how would the great MacArthur manage without his commander in chief? Grandfather had no confidence in the haberdasher from Missouri who would now move into the White House.

Returning to the living room, he found Mrs. Clay briskly drying her hair with her towel. He set the bottle on the endtable and pulled a chair up close so he could reach it too. He handed her a glass.

"You're so kind," she said. "And I'm so silly to come here crying like this over a man I've never met dying a thousand miles away, but the second I heard the news I thought of my grand-daddy and how he died without telling me how much he loved me. Of the three girls in my family it was me my granddaddy loved most, even though it was my two older sisters that got all his attention. We never knew our daddy and it was our grand-daddy we were with all the time, because he and Grandma lived on the next farm over from ours on the road running north out of Fayetteville. When he was plowing with his team and we took his lunch to him out in the field, he'd let my two sisters ride the horses a ways before he sat down to eat. When he took us to town on Saturday afternoons, my two sisters asked him for candy and soda pop and combs for their hair, and they were such pests about it that they got everything they asked for, but I knew he loved me best for not asking for anything. I hardly ever asked for anything and he hardly ever gave me anything, but I knew the reason was that if he gave me things I'd be no better than my sisters, and he knew I didn't want to be in the same class with them. I was away living in Omaha when he died. I wrote and asked my mama if he said anything about me before he died and she said not that she knew of. I cried for a week or more. I just couldn't get a hold of myself. I went around spouting tears like a pump, thinking how he didn't get it off his chest how much he loved me. My granddaddy didn't look anything like you, Mr. McMahon, he was short and wiry and hardly any bigger than a boy, but it's your hair that's the same. His hair was white like yours and he combed it straight back like you do. I can't explain it, but the second I heard President Roosevelt was dead I thought of my granddaddy and then I thought of you.

This is very good whiskey, Mr. McMahon. I'm feeling much better.''

They listened to a radio voice say that a cerebral hemorrhage was the cause of death. A funeral train was being assembled to carry the body to Washington. They sipped whiskey until the news report was replaced by somber music; then Mrs. Clay got up to go. They both spoke at once, she apologizing for breaking in on him and he saying reassuring things about her granddaddy's love. She said she had to go downtown and buy a ribbon for her hat. He said he was going downtown himself—would she do him the honor of walking with him?

"Oh yes, I'd love to. I'll go home and dress and be right back. It's a lovely day for a walk.''

Grandfather dressed as well, putting on a fresh shirt and a new tie and his Sunday shoes. He stepped out the front door just as Phyllis Clay was stepping out hers. She wore a short pink dress with puffy sleeves and carried a wide-brimmed hat of blue straw. She flew to his side emitting an intoxicated giggle, which she stifled by burying her face in his shoulder. Doing this, she dropped her hat.

"Your hat, Mrs. Clay, allow me.'' He bent over and picked it up. "A very pretty hat. I'm fond of a straw hat on a woman.''

"Isn't it posh? Montgomery Ward. In the catalogue it was pictured with a ribbon attached, so I planned to wear it hanging down my back, but it came without the ribbon.''

"Yes, I can see the eyelets where the ribbon would go.''

They set off, Grandfather strutting, proud to have a pretty young woman on his arm, Mrs. Clay swinging her hat in rhythm with her flouncy walk. They met Mrs. Kimball and Mrs. Brask.

"Don't forget to vote next Tuesday,'' Grandfather said, lifting his hat. "A new voice is needed on the school board, and Catherine is the one to provide it.'' It was his practice these days to plead Catherine's cause to everyone he met on the street.

Mrs. Kimball said, "I'm sorry, Mr. McMahon, but I've promised my vote to Harlan Brask.''

"Harlan Brask isn't running.''

"He's not?'' She frowned and turned to Mrs. Brask. "Didn't you tell me to vote for Harlan?''

"No, Harlan is board chairman ex officio by virtue of his being mayor," crowed Mrs. Brask, adjusting her foxes. "I said we must write in the name of someone who will cooperate with him."

"And who would that be?" asked Grandfather.

The mayor's wife appeared not to hear the question. She was looking contemptuously at the knees of Phyllis Clay.

"There are wrongs in our school that need righting, ladies. The toilets aren't clean and several windows are broken. Miss Dale in junior-high English is a dunderhead." There were a dozen other wrongs he had heard Catherine speak of, but he couldn't remember them at the moment.

Mrs. Brask said, "Come, Henrietta," and walked away. Her friend followed obediently.

"You must be proud of Catherine," said Phyllis Clay. "Webster says she just might win."

"She's always been one to set things right. Can we count on your vote?"

"You bet. Webster says I shouldn't vote for her, but you know what I say to that, don't you? I say to hell with Webster." They resumed their walk. "You want to know the real reason Webster's not running for re-election? He's afraid to be gone from the house nights. He's afraid I'll go out and find myself another man." Her laugh was throaty. "But I'll tell you a secret—the nights are the least of his worries."

Downtown Grandfather steered Mrs. Clay into the Plum Five and Dime, where he bought her a length of ribbon for her hat. They decided on pink, to match her dress. As the clerk slipped it through the eyelets and knotted the ends, Mrs. Clay's eyes filled with tears. "My granddaddy would have bought me things like this if my two older sisters hadn't been such pigs." She hugged Grandfather's arm. "You're just like my granddaddy, only nicer."

They continued along Main Street to the school. "Look at all those cute boys." She was pointing at the athletic field and the two dozen members of the track team. She led him across the playground and halfway down the grassy slope.

"Do you like my hat on my head or back on my shoulders?"

she asked as she went ahead a few steps with the hat on her head. Then she stopped and dropped it down her back. She turned for his judgment.

"When it's on your head I can't see your pretty hair."

"Oh, you're so sweet." She leaped to his side and hugged his arm again, causing him to tip over. She uttered a cry as she watched him go down very slowly and end up on his back, his head uphill. She knelt over him. "Are you hurt? Could you just kill me for being so rough?"

He sat up and waited for his head to clear.

"I'll kill myself if you're hurt, Mr. McMahon."

He wasn't hurt, but his pipe was broken. He fished it from the pocket of his suitcoat and tried fitting the stem to the bowl.

"Oh, look what I did. I'll buy you a new one. We'll go straight to the drugstore and I'll buy you a new pipe."

"Never mind, this doesn't happen to be my favorite. It's always been a little on the sour side."

So pleasant was the sun on the fresh-smelling grass, so heart-warming the sight of boys cavorting below them, so restful the view of farmland in the distance, that neither of them felt like moving. They sat for a time with their legs straight out in front of them. Mrs. Clay pulled her skirt up a bit, to sun her knees.

Grandfather, looking away, cleared his throat and said, "You have very pretty legs, Mrs. Clay."

Her laugh was melodious. "Shame on you, Mr. McMahon, at your age."

He chuckled contentedly.

23

H A N K ' S   N E W   O F F I C E ,   B U I L T high off the floor
at the back of the market, was designed so that by turning in his
chair and looking out over the soap display he could see at a
glance who his shoppers were and what his help was up to.
Catherine called it his crow's nest; Stan Kimball, his poop deck.
On this second morning of the sale—Friday—he was pleased to
see all his shopping carts in use. The wheeled shopping cart was
a new phenomenon in Plum and he was already planning to
double the size of his fleet. Thursday's proceeds had vastly ex-
ceeded his hopes, and it appeared certain that the sale as a whole
would bring in over twice as much income as the first Grand
Opening last September.

As shoppers passed below him he overheard their conversations, most of which had to do with the President's death.

The bell of the new cash register rang and Hank cast his eyes
upon Mrs. Pelzer at the checkout counter. The bell was shrill
and the drawer sprang open with such force that she had to step
backward to avoid injury to her ribs. The Fosters were more
than satisfied with Mrs. Pelzer. She was too tiny to lift much,

240

but she was quick on the adding machine and offered customers a line of sprightly chatter. She had applied for work in January after her husband, a sailor on his way back to the States to be discharged, had drowned while swimming off a reef in Hawaii. Mrs. Pelzer had confided to Catherine that she was grieved as much by her childlessness as by her widowhood; yet Hank, watching her carry on happily at the checkout counter, would never have guessed she was grieved. "Your change is two dollars, Mrs. Scott," he heard her say. "Thank you so much. Paul, will you carry Mrs. Scott's groceries out to her car?"

Hank watched Paul Dimmitburg rise from the low shelf where he was setting out cans of pork and beans and hurry to the counter. He bowed politely to Mrs. Scott as he took her groceries in his arms. Following her outside, he nodded politely at Rufus Ottmann, who had been standing in place for nearly an hour, backing up and coming forward as the door opened and closed. Seeing this, Hank was struck by the curious mix of people he had brought together under his roof. How peculiar that a scholarly would-be preacher should greet the village idiot. Or that Dodger Hicks should be working side by side with Wallace Flint.

"Listen, Dodger, how many times do I have to tell you to put fewer cookies in the bag to start with. Then when the bag's on the scale you can add what you need to make a pound."

"Yeah, that's what I been doing."

Both yesterday and this morning during Dodger's hour on duty, Hank had been forced to listen to Wallace Flint's relentless, fussy instructions at the packaging counter, which stood at the foot of the office steps. Never again, he promised himself, would he ask Wallace to work. Wallace had undergone a change since last fall. It was clear to Hank, and Catherine agreed, that the lighter side of his personality—the laughter, the joking—had vanished, and what remained was bitterness in its dark, pure form. He soured the atmosphere.

"If you've done what I told you, then why did I just see you taking cookies out of that last bag?"

"Because I had more than a pound in there." Dodger's voice was quietly adenoidal.

"But you just said you've been doing what I said to do."

"Yeah, I have been. But sometimes not."

"Now listen to me once and for all, Dodger. If you can't train yourself to be exact, train yourself to put less in each bag rather than more, and your work will go faster. It's easier to drop another cookie into a bag on the scale than it is to take a cookie out."

"Okay."

"You're as slow as molasses."

"I am?"

"It's not good for business, being as slow as you are."

"Why not?"

"Because time is money."

"It is?"

Hank's phone rang. It was Catherine.

"Is it busy, Hank? Should I come down early?"

"No, twelve will be fine."

"But you wanted to go out for a haircut."

"I'll go anyway. If you get here by the time Mrs. Pelzer goes to lunch, that will be fine. We're keeping up."

"Hank, I've been snubbed again by Cora Brask."

"Oh, my." He turned in his chair and faced the opening that had been cut in the wall to give him a view of the back room. Stock was piled against three walls. Against the fourth stood the enormous new walk-in cooler.

"It started raining and we both happened to be out bringing in wash at the same time and I spoke to her and she pretended not to hear me."

Hank said nothing.

"Isn't it a wonder the way the Brasks found each other, Hank—the world's most unenlightened man marrying the world's most priggish woman? I can still hear her saying, 'The neighborhood goes down, Mrs. Foster.' Wait till I'm on the board, her husband's lordly days will be over."

As Catherine paused to sigh and let her anger cool, Hank wondered if there had been a single day in the past two weeks when he hadn't heard his wife's imitation of Mrs. Brask's breathy falsetto: "The neighborhood goes down." She had said this to

Catherine in reference to Dodger's theft of the socket wrench
and his continued presence on Bean Street.

"How are you coming along with Dodger's things?" Hank
asked.

"His clothes are all clean and ready to pack. Mr. Cranshaw
just phoned. He said Dodger's father is going to phone here
tonight from prison. He wants to talk over last-minute details
with his son."

"What time?"

"Around seven."

"I'll tell Dodger."

"How are he and Wallace getting along?"

"Not so well." Hank lowered his voice so the two of them
wouldn't hear. "They can't work together five minutes without
Wallace getting his dander up."

"Then maybe they shouldn't work together. Why don't you
have Dodger work with Paul?"

"Because packaging is where we need him. Paul's almost
caught up."

"But isn't there something else he can do? Go out and wash
the front window?"

"Not in the rain. Maybe I should have Wallace and Paul exchange jobs until Dodger's hour is up."

"Oh, Wallace would die," she said. "He's above stocking
shelves." Hank swallowed his irritation. "Why did we ask him
back? He's impossible."

"Well, it's only for one more day. And tomorrow Dodger will
be gone to the track meet."

"One more day of Wallace Flint will be my limit. Never
again, Catherine."

"Whatever you say. I'll see you at twelve."

"Right." He hung up and turned to his bookkeeping, but was
again distracted:

"Dodger, did I just see you put a cookie in your mouth?"

A masticating reply: "Yump."

"Listen, Dodger, you can't be eating what the customer's
paying for."

"Hank said it's okay to eat a cookie once in a while."

"But you can't eat it out of a bag you've already weighed."

"I didn't."

"Yes, you did. I saw you."

"No, I didn't. I took it from the box."

"Like hell you did. I saw you take it out of that last bag you weighed."

"No, I took it from the box."

Wallace raised his voice: "Weigh that sack, Dodger, and see if it isn't a cookie short."

"You fellows pipe down!" Hank yelled.

"Damn him, Hank, he's eating cookies."

"Don't argue with me, Wallace, and quit being such an old hen!" Hank descended the steps. "I'll be back in a little while. I'm going for a haircut."

The moment Hank left the store Wallace left the packaging counter and went into the back room, where he lay down on the flour sacks. He savored his growing hatred for Dodger, for Hank, for Catherine, for everyone who had had a hand in changing this grocery store from the quiet, comfortable place it had been into a noisy, crowded shrine to the almighty dollar. How was a person supposed to keep his equilibrium with all this business going on, all this food to be weighed and packaged, all these stupid people cluttering the aisles with their ridiculous carts and lining up at the checkout counter where the parrotlike Mrs. Pelzer took their money and every so often had the nerve to call on Wallace to carry out groceries? With no lulls in the day, when could a person rest? When could a person talk to Catherine? Not that Catherine was worth talking to any more. Between mothering Dodger and taking up lofty thoughts with Paul Dimmitburg and spouting off to all the customers about tax levies and curriculum and teacher preparation, she had no time for the banter of their early days together.

But all in all, the rigor of grocery work was better than the boredom of staying home, and Wallace was determined to remain on the job. Come Monday at least Dodger Hicks would be gone to Winona. That nonentity. It was the ultimate humiliation to work side by side with an illiterate, thieving child who stood around with his mouth open and didn't know how to add. What's more, the child was on the payroll, earning nearly as much per hour as Wallace with his nine years' experience, and he was in charge of the overnight change bag. But Dodger had one attractive quality, and that was his vulnerability. This morning after Dodger emptied the change into the till and before Mrs. Pelzer came to work, Wallace had bought himself a pack of gum, ringing up a five-cent sale and filching a five-dollar bill. Unfortunately Mrs. Pelzer didn't notice that she was starting the day with two fives instead of three, didn't set off the investigation Wallace had imagined. Well, he had one more chance. Tomorrow he'd take a ten.

Hank peered in the window of Nicholi's barbershop and saw Stan Kimball lying flat in the chair with lather on his face. Stan Kimball spent a great deal of his idle time being barbered and shaved and watching others being barbered and shaved. Hank saw Phil Crowley sitting at the back of the shop, a newspaper in his lap. He put his head in at the door and said, "How about calling me when your chair is open?"

"Come in and sit down," ordered the barber. "We've been talking about you."

"No, I've got to get back. We're busy."

Nicholi beckoned with his shaving brush. "Stop bragging and come in and sit down. We've got something to ask you." The barber was a bald, wiry man who sent everyone away with the same haircut—clipped high on the sides and smelling of eye-smarting hair tonic. He kept a messy shop—wet towels hanging everywhere, the mirror smudged, clipped hair gritty underfoot.

Hank walked to the back of the shop and greeted Phil Crowley, whose jacket smelled of last night's theater popcorn. Above Crowley's head hung a calendar, a Navy Spitfire featured for April. Hank sat down and said, "What's up?"

The barber spoke across Stan Kimball's large stomach. "Tell him, Phil."

Crowley unfolded the *Plum Alert* and showed him Catherine's two-column ad.

"I've seen it," Hank said flatly, concealing his pride.

Crowley said, "A bunch of us men from Holy Angels have been trying for years to get another Catholic seat on the board and tip the balance." Crowley was a tall, unruffled man whose words came out smooth and unhurried. "When Webster Clay decided not to run for another term we figured this was our chance, and we figured on you as our candidate."

"My wife's your candidate."

"That's just the trouble."

"Trouble?"

"A woman can't win."

"Oh?"

"Nobody will vote for a woman. You're our only chance, Hank. We don't know how you do it, but you've got Lutherans buying your groceries and you just might get Lutherans to vote you onto the board."

Hank frowned. "What's religion got to do with a public school?"

Nicholi answered, his razor poised over Kimball's lathered face: "I'm on the board three terms and Phil's on two, and we can both tell you religion makes a hell of a difference when certain issues come up to vote."

"What issues?"

"Issues like whether to sell our old desks to the Lutherans for their school."

"What school? The Lutherans don't have a school."

"Then you haven't heard," said the barber. "If you'd poke your nose out of your store once in a while, you'd know what's going on in this town. Emmanuel Lutheran's got the idea of starting a grade school of their own next fall, and they're shopping around for a building and fixtures. We've got sixty old desks in Plum Elementary we're replacing, and unless we come up with one more Catholic voice on the board they'll go to the Lutherans."

"And if you get one more voice, where will they go?"

Nicholi waved his razor, slashing the air. "Into the furnace, out to the dump, who gives a damn as long as they don't go to the Lutherans, am I right, Phil?"

"Right."

Hank stood up. He paced quickly to the front window, saying, "None of this makes sense to me."

"Me neither," erupted Stan Kimball from his flat position. "Listen to these guys talk you'd think it was the Inquisition."

"None of your business," the excited barber told him, drawing the razor along Kimball's cheek, exposing a swath of florid flesh. "Just because you've got no beliefs of your own, Kimball, you can't understand people who do."

Kimball waited until the razor was safely lifted before he replied. "Is it your belief that Lutheran children shouldn't sit in desks?"

Nicholi silenced him by pinching his nose shut and shaving close around it. "Don't listen to this atheist, Hank."

Kimball gripped the barber's wrist and freed his nose. "How could anybody function as an undertaker in this town if he wasn't an atheist? The only reason I'm welcome in both churches is because I don't belong to either one."

Hank gazed out at the wet cars passing along the wet street and wished he could flee this small-minded carping; yet he felt obliged to stay and convince these men that even if Catherine couldn't win she was justified in running. Not that he was entirely convinced himself. It struck him as unwise of her to try to find her place in the community by seeking a place *above* the community. He had warned her that running for office might be asking for another, more damaging, sort of rejection; but of course there had been no dissuading her. She was caught up in this election the way she'd been caught up in the grocery business last fall, her energies poured into a cause the village deemed hopeless. What bothered Hank most was his suspicion that Catherine was striving for more than a seat on the school board, that all her disappointments in this village had come together in her drive for public office, and that defeat would leave her terribly embittered.

He spoke at the window, his back to the men. "Tell me this. Filings have been open a month, and my wife's the only one filed. If there's a religious war going on, why aren't the Lutherans running anybody to take Webster Clay's place?"

"Just wait," said the barber. "We figure they're going to run Len Downie."

"I'd be surprised," said Hank. "Len Downie's not the type."

"He's popular with the farmers."

Hank had played an occasional game of pool with Len Downie, proprietor of the Standard station. He was a man of mild opinions and few words, a man to Hank's liking. "He's not a leader. He's more of a follower."

"A faction only needs one leader, and that's Harlan Brask on the Lutheran side," said the barber. He slapped lotion and powder on Kimball's face and raised him to a sitting position. "You're next, Hank." He gave his barber cloth a vigorous shake, raising hair off the floor.

Kimball stepped to the mirror to examine his looks, then sat down next to Crowley and speculated aloud on who his next corpse might be. "There's an old codger named Foss at the poor farm who's got lung trouble and sinking fast. Father O'Day's nothing but skin and bones, but then he's always been nothing but skin and bones. The color isn't coming back into Mrs. Ottmann's face this spring the way it used to in years gone by. Did you know her big house is up for sale? She and her family are unloading it now, to avoid probate when she dies."

"Who'd buy that place?" said Hank, settling into the chair. "I lived in that house. It leaks heat like a tent."

There was silence for a time—the snip of scissors, the squeak of the rotating chair—and then Phil Crowley said in a slow, lazy tone, as if he weren't scheming, "Hank, you know about Harlan Brask trying to get your Dodger Hicks kicked out of school."

"Of course, it's one of the reasons my wife's running. Tell Brask the boy's transferring to Winona on Monday. That ought to make him happy."

"Well, that's not all there is to it. Did you know he's trying to get him sent back to the Home School?"

Swinging his head to look at Crowley, Hank was nearly speared in the ear. "What's the matter with him? Is he crazy?"

Nicholi and Crowley exchanged a satisfied look in the mirror. Arousing Hank Foster wasn't easy.

"Don't tell me it's the socket wrench. The socket wrench is back where it belongs. It was only gone overnight."

"But all the same, Brask has a point. When Hicks took the wrench he broke his parole."

"Who says?"

"The law says. Brask checked into it. If charges are pressed, Hicks automatically goes back to the Home School."

"And Brask will press charges?"

"He's thinking about it."

Hank understood then why Mrs. Brask had avoided speaking to Catherine this morning, and why Harlan Brask had avoided speaking to Hank last night when they both stepped out their back doors at the same moment. Brask had turned his back and pretended not to see him. Not that Hank minded. He had given up trying to be neighborly with the Brasks.

The barber took his turn. "There's lots of pressure to get the kid sent back."

"Pressure from who?"

"There's people living in fear."

"Nonsense."

"Mrs. Kimball is one of them, right, Stan?"

"You can't go by what my wife's afraid of." Stan Kimball was sitting low in his chair, picking hairs off his lapels. "My wife runs indoors when airplanes go over."

The barber continued, "But I think Phil and I could talk him out of pressing charges if we put our minds to it."

"Then put your minds to it," said Hank indignantly.

"If we went to the trouble of talking him out of it, would you do us the favor of running for the board? You can file till five o'clock this afternoon."

"My wife's already filed, remember?"

"Can't you get her to unfile?"

"No, damn it!"

The topic was dropped.

Later, his hair trimmed, Hank left the shop with Stan Kimball. They walked into arrows of wind-driven rain.

"We'll appreciate your vote, Stan. You and your wife's."

"Catherine's got my vote, but my wife will no doubt follow Cora Brask's advice and vote for the opposition."

"There is no opposition."

"There will be." As they drew near the market, Kimball added, "I hate to say it, Hank, but Catherine getting mixed up in politics is the worst thing that could happen to you. She's bound to alienate one faction or the other and your business is bound to suffer."

"I thought you knew her better than that. Do you think she's running for the board to take the Catholic side of things?"

"No, I don't think that."

"Do you think she'd vote to burn those desks?"

"Of course not. But what I think is that the more she keeps her opinions to herself the more groceries you'll sell. Say she votes to sell the desks—that makes the Catholics mad. Another issue comes along and she votes the Catholic side—that makes the Lutherans mad. As long as she's not a bigot you stand to lose *all* your customers, not just one side or the other. Come on, let's shoot a game of pool."

"Are you kidding? Look . . ." Hank pointed proudly through the window of the market. The aisles were crowded; a line of shoppers waited at the checkout counter.

"That's a pretty sight, Hank. Come election day, I'm going to hate to vote against it."

Hank assisted Mrs. Pelzer at the checkout counter until trade diminished as noon hour approached; then he went back to his office. Sitting over his ledgers, he tried hard not to believe that Catherine's emergence as a candidate for office—and worse, a woman of opinions—might be their downfall as grocers. He didn't have time to fully reject this depressing notion before he heard someone on the steps behind him. "Hi," he said without turning, assuming it was Catherine.

A man's voice said, "Hank, can we talk?"

It was Phil Crowley. Behind him on a lower step, was B. L. Skeffington, the banker. Skeffington was an emaciated man in his sixties wearing high-heeled boots and a loud sportscoat. Currently he was president of the Holy Angels Men's Club, an organization that met twice a month in the basement of the church. Hank paid his dues but never attended, having little interest in the two primary activities of the club—political scheming and cardplaying—and being too fond of his evenings at home.

Both men crowded up into Hank's crow's nest. Phil Crowley sat on the edge of the desk. B. L. Skeflington sat on the safe and looked out over the soap. He said, "Hank, you've got yourself a little gold mine here. When you first came to town last summer and took over from Kermit, I thought you must be the biggest sucker in the world, but, by Christ, look what you've done."

Skeffington's unctuousness made Hank uneasy. He turned to Crowley and said, "I'm not running for office, if that's what you want."

"No, no, we're here to talk property. B.L. is handling Mrs. Ottmann's big house and the Holy Angels Men's Club has decided to buy it. I'd have told you about it in the barbershop, but Kimball would have blabbed it all over town. B.L., give him the figures."

It took Skeffington a few moments to quit staring down at the market from this interesting angle. He turned, crossed his arms, crossed his boots, and said, "Mrs. Ottmann's letting the big house go for three thousand."

"I lived in that house," said Hank. "It's cold. It's got a wet basement and no insulation."

"But it's big and roomy and the framework is good and solid," said the banker. "Insulate it and seal the foundation and make some other improvements and we'll have ourselves a mighty fine piece of property. It's a steal at three thousand."

"I don't get it. Don't we have enough expense keeping up the church and the rectory without taking on a run-down house?"

"It's a money-making deal," said Skeffington. "The Men's Club buys it, refurbishes it, and then sells it for six thousand."

"Sells it to who? In this town a refurbished house for six will be a bigger white elephant than a run-down house for three."

Skeffington's voice was powerful: "There's a postwar boom right around the corner, Hank. It's going to be a seller's market in real estate."

"But six thousand for a house in this town? My own house was the most expensive on the market last year, and I bought it for four."

"You bought it just in time. Demographers say Plum's going to double in size. Our dear old farming village stands a good chance of becoming a bedroom community."

"What's that?" It sounded vaguely sinful to Hank.

"It's a town people live in who work in a city."

"But we're a hundred miles from Minneapolis."

"And only twenty from Rochester. Rochester's going to get real big."

"Twenty miles is a hell of a long drive to work."

"Not after the war, Hank. New cars. Paved roads."

Crowley unfolded a sheet of paper and gave it to Hank. "Here's what we've collected so far. We're asking each Catholic businessman for fifty dollars toward the down payment. When the house is sold you get your fifty dollars back and Holy Angels gets the profit and we use it for a new roof on the church and repairs to the rectory."

Hank scanned the list. Skeffington was down for fifty. So was Nicholi. Crowley was down for twenty-five.

"How come only twenty-five?"

"Are you kidding? On forty-cent movie tickets?"

Hank opened and closed his checkbook, looking at his balance. "Does Father O'Day know about this?" Hank distrusted the laity in church affairs.

"Yeah," said Crowley. "We went to see him about it."

"Does he approve?"

"I guess so, he said something holy."

The men turned politely away as Hank opened his checkbook again, intending to make out a check for twenty-five, fifty being too steep for such a dubious scheme. But as he wrote *April 13, 1945*, he saw in his mind's eye how attractive the Ottmann property might look with a fresh coat of paint and the yard trimmed. Standing empty this spring, it was becoming an eyesore, weeds standing high as the windowsills, rain gutters loosened by the wind. Perhaps he should contribute fifty after all, and help upgrade that end of town. Then, as he wrote *Holy Angels Men's*

Club, he felt a sudden compulsion to atone for his absence from meetings and decided that seventy-five dollars would buy the good will of the Catholic men and keep them and their wives as steady customers. And then he thought of something else to atone for—his wife selling desks to the Lutherans. He wrote the check for one hundred.

24

DODGER SAT IN THE breakfast nook ready to pick up the phone when it rang. Brendan had gone to the movie with Sam and Philip. Hank, Catherine and Grandfather were in the living room listening to a somber voice from Washington, where the train carrying the President's body was pulling into the station. It was a warm, cloudy evening. The rain had stopped. Through the open windows came the chirp of robins and the smell of wet earth.

Waiting, Dodger called to mind the Hogan Hotel, where he and his father would live. Mr. Cranshaw had arranged for them to have two rooms with a connecting door. The Hogan stood in the shadow of the big bridge across the Mississippi—a good location, Dodger thought. If his parents had to be in the same town at least they'd be twenty blocks apart.

In the Home School Dodger hadn't thought much about his parents, but since moving in with the Fosters he thought about them all the time. Sometimes he thought that if he could be more like Brendan, then his mother would be more like Catherine and his father would be more like Hank. His mother would quit swearing at him and getting drunk, and his father would quit being sneaky and having mean spells. But then common sense would break in and he'd realize this was too much to hope for. He could never be like Brendan. Brendan was smart and good-looking and had lots of friends. Dodger had overheard girls in school say that Brendan's dark eyes and dark hair were adorable and they loved his dimples when he smiled. What he'd overheard about himself wasn't so great. It was funny (he'd heard a girl say) the way Dodger's mouth hung open all the time and his ears stuck out.

But if he couldn't look like Brendan, why couldn't he at least *act* like Brendan? Brendan was better at everything. Work, for instance. After three hours of work on Saturday mornings, Brendan was never worn out the way Dodger was. To be a good worker, a good student, a friend to lots of people (Dodger concluded), you probably had to start early in life. To be like Brendan your parents probably had to be Catherine and Hank Foster.

The phone rang. His father's voice was faint over the wire: "How you been, son?"

"Okay, Dad, how *you* been?"

"Swell." There was a long pause. "Is it raining in Plum?"

"No. It was, a little."

"Yeah, it was raining a little here, too."

"Hey, Dad, are you and Ma thinking about getting back together?" It was his only serious worry and he held his breath. Hank and Catherine, too, held their breath in the living room as they tried but failed to concentrate on the President. To prevent eavesdropping, Catherine had turned up the volume on the radio, but there were long silent spells between the commentator's observations.

"No," said Mr. Hicks. "What ever gave you a crazy idea like that?"

"I thought maybe that's why you decided we should live in Winona. I mean, when we lived there when I was little, you never liked it."

"No, that's a crazy idea. The only thing me and your ma ever agreed on was splitting up. See, the reason I'm going back to

256 *GRAND OPENING*

Winona is because the county you go to prison from is the county you're supposed to go back to. It's where your parole officer is. You got a parole officer, Dodger?''

"Yeah. Mr. Cranshaw."

"Yeah, he's mine too. Kind of a sissy-looking guy, isn't he.''

"So you're going to like Winona okay this time?''

"It'll be swell, son. Bemis Box will be swell. It's a big enough operation so a guy can work his way up. See, when I was with Pierce Plumbing I couldn't go nowhere with my life. They had me in the back room all the time taking toilets out of packing crates. Speaking of jobs, Dodger, Cranshaw tells me you've been working at a job."

"In Hank's Market."

"That's swell. Are you going to have any money when you get to Winona?''

"Yeah, I might.''

"See, because when I get out of Stillwater all I'll have is a twenty-dollar bill from the warden, which isn't much considering even if I go back to work the very next day there's no telling when my first paycheck'll come through—I don't know how Bemis Box works their payroll.''

Dodger said, "I'll have a little money."

His father told him to speak up, this was a poor connection.

He said it again, louder. Hank and Catherine exchanged a look.

"Swell," said Mr. Hicks.

"Hey, Dad, how come we're staying in a hotel, Mrs. Foster wants to know. How come we're not getting an apartment?''

"We are. The Hogan's not really a hotel. They call it a hotel, but people live there like it was apartments.''

"You mean we got a kitchen and everything?''

"No, but there's a sink in the bathroom down the hall. Who needs a kitchen? Do you cook?''

"No, I don't cook."

"Neither do I. I like eating out, and there's a lunch counter next door. Don't you like eating out?''

"Sure.''

"By the way, son, how do you like the Fosters?"

"Like them fine."

"Yeah, Cranshaw says they're real nice. Got a lot of money, have they?"

"Yeah, I guess they've got money. They own a store."

"And a nice house, I suppose."

"A real nice house."

A long pause.

"Well, goodbye son. I'll see you Monday."

"Goodbye, Dad."

As soon as Dodger hung up, Hank took him outside. He handed him a screwdriver and asked him to take off the inside panel of the driver's door—the window roller needed fixing. It was brighter now, the western sky clearing, the sun going down in a blaze of orange. As Dodger turned the screws, Hank cleared his throat and said, "Are there going to be any problems, do you think, when you go and live with your dad?"

Dodger recognized this as the sort of question Hank wouldn't ask unless Catherine put him up to it. Hank always asked easy questions, like what are you working on in shop these days?

"No problems that I know of."

"No problems about money or anything like that?" Catherine had indeed put him up to it. Dodger's reference to money on the phone had aroused her fear that his father would lead him back into thievery.

"No, nothing like that."

Hank lifted the hood and checked the oil. He whistled a tune. He closed the hood and said, "We're going to miss you around here, you know that?"

Dodger stopped working and stared at Hank. "You are?"

"Yep."

Hank was held by Dodger's eyes, which were no longer so shifty and evasive. They were intensely hungry eyes. Three months with the Fosters had given Dodger an appetite for kindness. He stared hard at Hank, hoping to hear more.

"Yep, we will," Hank repeated. Now he saw more than hunger in the boy's eyes. He saw starvation, and he felt very sad. He turned away, lifted the hood again, and checked the

hoses and belts. He whistled another tune as he closed the
hood. He said, "What have you been working on in shop
these days?"

"I can't tell you, it's a surprise." Dodger removed the panel
from the door, exposing the window roller.

"A present?"

Dodger nodded. "For the house. I'm getting each of you
something else besides, but this is a present for the house." He
had shown it to Brendan. On a slab of wood designed to hang
over the front door, he had chiseled *THE FOSTER'S*. Brendan
would bring it home next week when the varnish was dry. Dodger
had argued against the apostrophe in order to leave ample room
for the *S*, but Mr. Butz was a purist albeit an unlettered one,
and the *S* ended up very thin.

"Catherine's rolling pin was sure nice," Hank said.

Dodger smiled at him with bald-faced love.

Returning from the movie at nine, Brendan said goodbye to
Philip and Sam and stood for a few minutes in the dark. Through
the kitchen window he saw his father and mother playing rummy
with Dodger in the breakfast nook, and the sight filled him with
a surge of ill will such as he seldom felt any more. Since January
he had gradually overcome his resentment of Dodger. Yesterday
and today on the track he had actually been proud to be Dodger's
teammate; in the 220 and the quarter-mile Dodger ran like the
wind and left everyone behind. Brendan could hardly wait until
tomorrow's track meet, where he and Dodger would represent
Plum in the quarter-mile. Coach Torborg had explained that
only Dodger would run in the 220 tomorrow because each runner was assigned a lane and entries were limited, but the quarter-
mile would be open to all, including Brendan. Yet now,
watching Dodger absorb his parents' attention as he picked a
card off the deck and pondered his discard, Brendan felt the old
resentment. Dodger was a very large pain in the neck. Not that
he asked for any favors. He asked for practically nothing, but
he needed everything. His very presence was an enormous demand. He needed food and clothes and a bed. He needed help
with his homework and he needed to be told that he needed it.

Worst of all, there wasn't a moment in the day when he didn't
need companionship. Brendan had come to resent how soft his
mother was on Dodger. She kept saying how touching it was
that Dodger and Grandfather should be such great friends,
Dodger asking again and again for stories, particularly the story
of the deer that came indoors during the blizzard of 1871. Okay,
so it was touching; Brendan could see that. More than touching
it was a relief to have help in listening to Grandfather's stories.
With Dodger tuning in, Brendan could tune out. But if Dodger
and Grandfather were such pals, why didn't they room together?
It was tiresome having Dodger in your bedroom night after night,
breathing around his adenoids. It was downright depressing
waking up every morning to the sight of that face looking at you
from the rollaway and knowing that this guy you didn't have
anything in common with wasn't going to let you out of his sight
for the rest of the day. Catherine praised Brendan for his patience
with Dodger, speaking of it in religious terms—Christian charity. She was right, of course—the nuns at St. Bonnie's had explained about Christian charity—but was there no limit to the
things God expected you to do for others? Didn't God ever let
you off the hook? Didn't God realize that while helping Dodger
learn to be normal Brendan was in danger of becoming an outcast?

Last Sunday Pearl Peterson had organized a picnic at Pebble
Creek, which Brendan didn't hear about until Monday morning
in school. Everybody had been there—Sam, Philip, and Lorraine from the seventh grade, as well as Andy and his girlfriend
and some other high-school students. Sam took along his fishing
rod and caught a big sucker. They roasted marshmallows and
drank pop. Brendan accosted Pearl in math class the next day.

"Pearl, how come you never told me about it?"

"Because you take your shadow wherever you go."

"What do you mean, my shadow?" He knew what she meant.
"I mean Dodger."

"So what? He just hangs around. He never bothers anybody."

"Listen, Bren, nobody wants to go to anything Dodger's at.
He's so . . . You know, he's so . . ."

As Pearl scanned the ceiling of the classroom for the precise word, Brendan felt as if his heart were being crowded by a hard growth in his breast. It was his resentment of Dodger, and it felt like a coconut.

Pearl smiled her prim smile, having found the word. "Dodger's such a goon."

25

On Saturday morning Dodger withdrew the money bag from the hiding place he had chosen behind the dog food, and because they were pressed for time he gave it to Brendan, who was much quicker at distributing the coins and bills into their proper compartments. He then wheeled the produce from the walk-in cooler to the display rack, and together they made short work of setting out the lettuce and celery and other perishables. They called goodbye to Hank and Paul and dashed out into the sunshine. On their way to school they met Wallace Flint trudging to work looking bilious and sleepy. They exchanged no greeting with him. In the locker room they slipped into their track uniforms and their maroon and gold warmup suits and followed the rest of the team out to the bus. Crossing the schoolyard, they met Mrs. Pelzer on her way to work. She wished them luck.

They were on the road an hour. Stepping through the gate of Soldier Field, Brendan beheld four hundred boys warming up for the Rochester Relays. The track was cinders, black and smooth. The football field it circled was lush and green. The sun was high. A stiff breeze made the new flag over the pressbox stand out straight. A few runners were practicing their starts, dashing short distances along the track; others did calisthenics on the grass; most stood idly in groups, waiting. Brendan picked out the ice-blue uniforms of the Pinburg team, the orange and black of Clarkville, the red and blue of Lewiston, the green of Haymarket. These colors seemed holy to Brendan and caused something like worship to stir in his soul, as if the feats he and these four hundred boys would perform today—the pole vault, the shotput, the quarter-mile—were the rites of a new and saving covenant.

Mr. Torborg blew his whistle, and his athletes gathered around to hear their instructions. The junior events, said the coach, would take place intermittently throughout the meet. He read aloud the day's schedule from his clipboard, and each time he came to one of Dodger's events he raised his eyes to Brendan, as if Dodger were his responsibility. At eleven o'clock Dodger would throw the discus. At one-thirty Dodger would run in the 220. At three Dodger and Brendan together would run the quarter-mile.

When he finished reading, Mr. Torborg tucked his clipboard under his arm and said, "It looks to me like Clarkville and Lewiston are the junior teams to beat. Each one of them's got about ten boys suited up to our five."

"Just so we beat Pinburg," piped Philip.

The coach turned to his senior team. "As for you guys on the varsity, if you end up anywhere in the top twenty you'll be doing good. Last year Plum came in twenty-fifth."

"If you guys come in behind Pinburg, I'll puke," Philip said to the older boys, who ignored him.

The public-address system came to life with a ten-count, a cough and a message of welcome from the Rochester High School athletic director. Then everyone on the field—athletes, coaches, bus drivers—stood at attention while a recording of the national anthem blared from speakers, and currents of wind swirled through the stadium carrying the melody off in one direction and returning it from another. When the music ended and the first events of the day were announced, Dodger said to Brendan, "Let's go up in the seats."

"What for?" The vast seating, which curved around three sides of the field, held a scattering of about thirty people.

Dodger shrugged. "So we can sit."

"Who wants to sit?" It was Brendan's intention to spend the day darting from one event to the next, learning all the skills of track and field.

"Just for a while, I mean." Dodger was pointing to the top row of seats. "Just see what it looks like from up there."

"Okay," said Brendan, for he had resolved to devote these final two days entirely to Dodger. He hoped that by resisting all of his anti-Dodger impulses, not once ditching him or ignoring him, he might forestall any twinges of guilt when it came time to say goodbye on Monday.

Standing on the top row of seats where the wind blew strong, Brendan regarded the spectacle from above. The cinder-black track with its bright white lines looked like the college tracks in newsreels. That he himself would run on it seemed a miracle. Perhaps he'd be faster on cinders. He regretted being something of a hindrance to Dodger during their two practice sessions in Plum. Running a quarter-mile with him, Brendan simply wasn't fast enough to keep up, and Dodger couldn't seem to resist turning his head to see how Brendan was doing. "Don't look back!" Coach Torborg shouted again and again, but Dodger kept doing it. "Promise me in Rochester you won't look back," pleaded the coach last night after practice. "You lose half a stride every time you turn your head." Dodger promised.

"Hey, Dodge, does running in a real track make you nervous?" Brendan asked.

Dodger didn't hear the question. He had moved away from Brendan and was looking out over the parapet of the stadium toward downtown Rochester, trying to spot a Woolworth store. He had certain presents in mind to give the Fosters and Grandfather before he left Plum, more expensive gifts than he could pay for, and he was partial to Woolworth stores because the Woolworth's in Winona had always been a pushover. And as long as he was at it, he'd pick up a greeting card for his mother, whose birthday, he guessed, was a week or so ago. He saw no Woolworth store from where he stood; trees obscured the west side of Broadway. He returned to Brendan and said, "I'm going downtown."

"What for?"

"Shopping."

"We aren't here to go shopping, Dodge, we're here to win ribbons."

"Yeah, I know, but we got all this time to kill."

"No, we haven't. You're throwing the discus at eleven."

"That's almost an hour, isn't it? I need to get my ma a birthday card."

Brendan looked at his watch. "It's not an hour, it's a half-hour. There's birthday cards in Plum."

Dodger didn't reply. It was impossible to pick things up in Plum. The storekeepers were laying for him.

The junior qualifying heats for the hundred-yard dash were announced. "Hey, look, Philip's getting ready to run—come on!" Brendan hurried down to ground level and reached the finish line of the hundred-yard dash in time to see Philip come in last. Philip had more talent as an actor than as a runner. Coming off the track he draped his arms around Brendan and another teammate and hung limp between them, his knees buckling, his tongue hanging out. Brendan knew he had picked this up from the recent movie about Jesse Owens and the 1936 Olympics: athlete winded. A moment later Philip broke away and ran vigorously in place, his knees nearly as high as his chin: athlete rejuvenated. He stopped running and said to Brendan:

"It's not fair having us run on cinders, Bren. Running feels funny on cinders. Wait till you try it. If we run on grass at home, how come we can't run on grass here? I would have won on grass."

"Cinders are supposed to make you run faster."

"They don't though." Philip dropped to the ground and lay on his back with his eyes shut: athlete spent. "I'm faster on grass than anybody. Cinders feel funny. I didn't come in last, did I? Wasn't there other guys behind me?"

"One or two," Brendan lied, knowing how annoyed Philip got when the truth went against him.

Coach Torborg, hearing this, looked down at Philip and said, "There was nobody behind you."

Philip rolled over and buried his face in the grass. "Oh, no."

"But don't feel bad," the coach added, "you were up against older runners."

Philip spoke into the sod: "I hate cinders."

Brendan watched a few qualifying heats of the hundred-yard dash and then wandered over to the sawdust pit and watched the pole vaulters. From there he went to the high jump. After a few minutes at the high jump he felt a hand on his shoulder. It was Coach Torborg. "It's time for the discus, Brendan. Where's Dodger?"

Dodger was shopping. Four blocks from the stadium Dodger had found a drugstore that carried watches, but they were kept under glass and so he left the store after picking up only a birthday card for his mother and a small tin of Union Leader for Grandfather and slipping them up under the front of his sweatshirt. Where else, besides a jewelry store, might he find watches? Catherine's watch was in need of repair and he wanted to get her a new one. Jewelry stores were tough to crack.

Further along Broadway he came to an auto-parts store. He went in and looked over the displays of tires and mufflers and other things in the showroom until a man came out from the maze of shelving behind the long counter and said, "What'll it be, Bud?"

"Have you got a gas cap for a DeSoto?"

"What year?"

"Twenty-eight."

"Nobody carries parts that old."

Which Dodger knew.

"Only place you'll find parts that old is a junkyard." The man returned to his maze.

Dodger opened and closed the door and remained inside. He continued to browse among the auto parts. He came upon a fan belt which he judged would fit the DeSoto. He slipped it under his sweatshirt and hurried away.

Across the street he stopped to tuck the waist of his sweatshirt into his warm-up pants. He walked down the street with his arms crossed, holding his loot in place against his chest. He came to a Woolworth's. He went in and walked the aisles. Passing combs, he picked out a small black one—Catherine had been urging him to carry a comb—and slipped it up his sleeve. He found watches. The more expensive ones were inside a display case, but the cheaper ones were on top, each one lying on a bed of cotton in its small, open box. He bent over and examined them closely. One looked nice enough for Catherine. It had a white face with small black Roman numerals and a black leather band. He took it, box and all, and slipped it up his sleeve.

He continued to walk the aisles until he decided that comic books would be Brendan's gift. On the comic book rack he saw at least three of Brendan's favorites (*Captain Marvel*, *Archie*, *The Katzenjammer Kids*) but the clerk facing him across the cosmetics counter—an elderly woman with a sour face—gave him no opportunity. He went outside, where he took the comb and the watch from his sleeve and slipped them down the collar of his sweatshirt. He tucked the waist more tightly into his pants, adjusted his load, and held it in place again by crossing his arms.

Passing a window of the Zumbro Hotel, he looked into the lobby and saw a newsstand. He went in. An idle bellhop, a registration clerk and an old man sleeping in a deep chair were the only people in sight. The clerk and the bellhop glanced at him without interest. He scanned the magazine rack and saw the new issue of Hank's favorite, *Popular Mechanics*. He considered picking it up, but decided that two gifts for Hank would be unfair to the others. He looked over the comics and found the same three he had wanted for Brendan at Woolworth's. He stood for several minutes waiting for his chance, and when it came—the registration clerk on the phone, the bellhop gone—he slipped his shirttail out of his pants and tucked *Captain Marvel*, *Archie*, and *The Katzenjammer Kids* up and under his armpit. As he did so, the fan belt fell out. He stiffened with the same jolt of fear he had felt last fall in the Winona gas station when the attendant came in and caught him robbing the till: cops, handcuffs, jail, Home School. But this time the jolt was a false alarm. No one was looking. The bellhop wasn't back and the clerk was still on the phone and the old man snored softly. Dodger gave himself ten seconds to relax and regain his light-fingered touch, then he picked up *Popular Mechanics* and tucked it under his shirt with the comics. He sauntered away, leaving the fan belt on the floor. Chances were it was the wrong size anyhow.

Out on the street, sensing that it was nearly time for the discus, he looked for a clock. In a jewelry window he saw a number of clocks and watches, but they all said different times. He set off toward the stadium, walking as fast as his shirtful of merchandise permitted and planning how he would wrap it all in his warm-up suit and hide it under his seat on the bus. He came to a clock over the entrance to a bank. Eleven-thirty already? How could it be eleven-thirty? It only proved what Grandfather always said at the end of the afternoon when Gordy reminded him it was time to go home: "My, how time flies when you're having fun." For this had been great fun. Stealing was his talent and his calling and it gave him a wonderful sense of accomplishment. It was wrong, of course, but when you walked into a store, how could you help casing it for clerks and floorwalkers and settling on the thing you wanted most and waiting for the right moment and then snatching it up and stashing it in your clothes in a single, natural, unhurried motion and walking out of the place in a casual way that hid your excitement? It was the best feeling in the world—ten times better than winning a foot-race—and it felt especially wonderful when the thing you took was a gift for a friend.

In the parking area beside the stadium, all the buses looked alike and it took Dodger several minutes to find the right one. He found it locked. He stood for a minute with his arms crossed, looking left and right down the aisle between buses, wondering what to do next. He couldn't very well enter the stadium with all this stuff under his shirt. He decided to hide it under the bus. As he was taking off his warmup pants, he heard the public address system announcing the winner and runner-up in the discus competition. He told himself that this was probably the senior competition; the junior event was yet to come. He tied one of the pantlegs shut at the ankle and filled the leg with his loot. He was about to push it under the bus when he heard Brendan calling to him:

"Hey, Dodger, where you been?" Brendan came running toward him between the buses. Behind him were the rest of the Pirates, senior and junior. It was noon and their sack lunches were on the bus.

"You missed the discus!" Brendan took Dodger's arm and gave him a shake. "You could have won, Dodger. Nobody came close to a hundred and twenty feet."

Philip came running, whining, "Hey, Dodge, what happened to you? Some guy won the discus that only threw it a hundred and ten. Boy, are you going to catch it from Mr. Torborg."

Dodger clutched his bundled-up pants to his breast and smiled warily at Mr. Torborg, who looked less annoyed than Philip, less disappointed than Brendan.

"We waited and waited for you, Dodger." The coach spoke softly. "I got them to hold up the meet while we all went around looking for you."

Dodger's eyes began to grow shifty. "I got sick."

"You did?"

"I threw up." Dodger pointed behind him. "Back over there, in the bushes."

"You don't look sick," said the coach.

"I'm okay again."

Brendan noticed how awkwardly Dodger was clutching his pants to his chest, and he realized where Dodger had been, what he'd been doing. Fearing that Coach Torborg, too, would understand, he stepped over to the bus and said, "Coach, could you unlock the door? I'm starving."

As Mr. Torborg drew out his keyring and unlocked the bus, he said, "He's your responsibility, Brendan. Promise you won't let him out of your sight this afternoon."

"I promise."

When the junior-high 220 was announced, Brendan accompanied Dodger to the starting line. Removing his gold sweatshirt, Dodger took his place in the third lane from the inside. He and the runner in the fourth lane, a redhead from Pinburg, were a head taller than the other boys. Standing nearby, Mr. Torborg turned to the Pinburg coach and Brendan heard him ask, "Who's the redhead?"

"Transfer student from Iowa." The Pinburg coach was a small, round man.

"What grade's he in?" asked Torborg.

"Eighth. Name's Jerry Franzen."

"Big for his age, isn't he."

"Yeah, about like that runner of yours. How old is he?"

"Fifteen."

"Is he the ex-con I've been hearing about?"

Torborg looked pained. "That's a little strong. It was only the Home School."

"What else you got him entered in besides the 220?"

"Quarter-mile."

"I've got Franzen in the quarter-mile too. Ought to be interesting."

The starter, wearing a jacket of vertical black and white stripes, shouted "On your mark!" and the eight runners got down on their hands and knees. Studying Jerry Franzen, Brendan was reminded of the athletes pictured in magazines. He was somehow more colorful than real life. He had short hair, a tan complexion and shoulders already muscular at fifteen. His brow was knit in concentration, his eyes riveted on the track ahead. Dodger, by comparision, looked limp. His head was hanging down, his eyes on the cinders. His shoulders were scrawny and his ears stuck out. "Get set," said the starter and the eight boys tensed, rising to their toes. At the gun Franzen leaped off to a quick start and was two strides ahead of Dodger at the turn. Brendan and the others ran across the grass to the finish line and saw them come out of the turn neck and neck, well ahead of the other six runners. He saw that despite Franzen's athletic appearance and fast start, Dodger was the better runner. Franzen had a jerky way of pumping his arms and his head, while Dodger galloped like a stallion and broke the tape two strides in the lead.

Brendan leaped to his side and slapped him proudly on the back, shouting, ''Way to go! Dodge, way to go!''

A Plum runner from the senior high shook his hand and said, ''At least we'll take home one blue ribbon today.'' There was great satisfaction in Coach Torborg's smile, which was interrupted by Philip pulling at his arm and insisting, ''I think the 220's my race, Coach. Next year I want to run the 220.''

Franzen, recovering his wind, sidled up to Dodger and hissed, ''You haven't seen the last of me.''

''Swell,'' said Dodger, assuming that Franzen was proposing a friendship.

''I won four blue ribbons already this spring.''

''You did?''

''In Iowa.''

''Gee, that's swell.''

''Just wait till the quarter-mile.''

The afternoon grew warm and beautiful. The wind had gone down. The sky was cloudless. What breezes wafted through the stadium from the prairie south of town carried with them the smell of freshly-turned earth. A growing number of fans were trickling into the stadium and milling among the athletes on the field.

Among these fans, to Brendan's surprise, were Pearl Peterson and Lorraine Graham. Lorraine was wearing pink lipstick and a fluffy new sweater the color of her fluffy blond hair. Brendan went up to her and said, ''Hi,'' proud to present himself in his maroon and gold warm-up suit. He greeted Pearl as well. Too long he had cultivated the image of the scholar. Though he didn't care much for Pearl, she was a girl nevertheless, and girls were impressed by athletes.

She looked him over. ''Aren't your pants a little big?''

''They're supposed to be. They're warm-up pants.''

''Have you won any races?'' asked Lorraine..

''I haven't run in any yet. Dodger just won the 220.''

The mention of Dodger caused Pearl's nose to wrinkle.

"You should have seen it. He beat that big guy from Pin-burg."

Pearl looked where Brendan pointed. "Wow, you mean him with the cute haircut?"

"His name's Jerry Franzen. He's a crumb."

"Gee, is he handsome! Look at his shoulders, Lorraine. Don't you love track uniforms on boys? Those little straps over the shoulders?"

Jerry Franzen, pretending not to be listening, preened.

"He's a crumb," repeated Brendan, removing his sweatshirt. "He doesn't know the first thing about sportsmanship. He said he was going to get back at Dodger for beating him."

"I would too, if Dodger beat me. Dodger's the crumb."

"Oh, don't be so mean," Lorraine said to Pearl.

Brendan saw Dodger coming and changed the subject. "Who did you come with?"

"There's a bunch of us. Lorraine and me and Andy Romberg and Norma Nash and Sam. Bren, would you introduce me to Jerry Franzen?"

"I never met him myself."

As Dodger came up and stood at Brendan's right shoulder, Pearl stepped over to Franzen, smiled up into his blue eyes and said, "A bunch of us from Plum are having a party at the creek tomorrow."

Franzen gave her a squinty, appraising look. "Yeah, what creek?"

"Pebble Creek. My name's Pearl." Brendan watched her put her whole face—lashes, lips, dimples—into a look that Franzen could not mistake for anything but adoration.

"Where's Pebble Creek?" asked Franzen.

"It's between Pinburg and Plum." There was a kind of music in her voice that Brendan had never heard before. "You leave Pinburg and go till you get to a big barn with a sign painted on it, and that's where you turn and go down the hill through the woods and there's the creek."

"Yeah? What time?"

"Two."

"Will there be beer?"

"Who knows?"

"How do you get there? You walk?"

"Some walk, some ride their bikes. A few of us have friends with cars. The sign on the barn is for spark plugs."

Brendan was annoyed by her refusal to see what an egomaniac Franzen was. But more than that, he was annoyed at being annoyed. Why couldn't he ignore Pearl and her party plans? Why did he feel that if he wasn't invited he would die of humiliation? What power did girls possess that by merely showing up with lipstick and curled hair they could set up this jealous competition in the otherwise pure hearts of boys?

Franzen told Pearl he might possibly show up at the creek, and he went jogging off to join his teammates.

Brendan moved over to her and said, "Don't tell me you're falling for him." Dodger moved with him.

"He's like a movie star," she said. "Lorraine, did you notice he's got whiskers and chest hair already? I'd love to see him run."

"He runs like a chicken." Brendan gave her a brief imitation of Franzen's jerky movements.

Dodger, to be of help, put in, "He runs at three o'clock. Me and Brendan run against him in the quarter-mile."

Brendan cringed, fearing he would cross the finish line far behind Franzen, far behind everybody, a sight Pearl and Lorraine shouldn't see.

Pearl said, "Come on, Lorraine, let's watch the hurdlers," and they set off across the field.

Brendan called, urgently, "Pearl, aren't you inviting me to the creek tomorrow?"

Pearl stopped and turned around. Dodger looked the other way, aware of what was coming.

"Consider yourself invited, Bren, if you come alone."

"Thanks," said Brendan with sarcasm.

For the quarter-mile there were no assigned lanes. It took the starter several minutes to arrange the twenty runners in three ranks. Dodger was in the second rank, with Brendan on his left and Jerry Franzen on his right. When the starter shouted, "Once around the track, boys," and added, "On your mark," snickering broke out as Dodger got down on all fours, having forgotten that in this race everyone started from a standing position. He got to his feet and nudged Franzen with his elbow to show he understood his mistake and could laugh at it, but Franzen wasn't wasting any energy on laughter. Franzen was biting his lip and looking nervous. It occurred to Brendan, witnessing this, that Franzen and Pearl Peterson were perfectly suited to each other, both of them so humorless. "Get set," the starter yelped, and the boys hunched forward, leaning from the waist.

The crack of the gun was followed by the scuffling noise of eighty shoes on cinders and a few grunts and curses as the aggressive runners fought for position by bumping the timid. Going into the first turn, Dodger moved ahead of Brendan and kept pace with Jerry Franzen in the lead.

"Go, Dodger, go!" Mr. Torborg shouted from trackside.

Brendan glimpsed Philip standing with Pearl and Lorraine. Philip hollered, "Step on it, Bren."

Coming out of the first turn Brendan was about halfway back. Ahead he saw Dodger lose a stride on Franzen as he turned his head to look back at Brendan. "Don't look back!" Brendan shouted to him, the words burning in his throat. The string grew longer on the straightaway, and though he gave it everything he had, Brendan fell farther behind. Jerry Franzen continued in the lead with Dodger losing ground. As they came out of the final turn the Pinburg coach shouted, "Start your sprint!" and this was where Jerry Franzen—his sprint full of wasted, jerky effort—would have lost the race to Dodger if Dodger hadn't cut his speed in half in order to let Brendan catch up.

Jerry Franzen, the winner, was cheered and clapped on the back until he pleaded, "Air, give me air!" and he moved off the track and strutted back and forth on the grass. Pearl Peterson stood at a worshipful distance watching him breathe.

At the finish line, meanwhile, Coach Torborg watched Brendan and Dodger finish side by side and gave his clipboard a despairing toss in the air. "Dodger," he said, "what the hell was that all about?"

Dodger ignored him. With his half smile directed at his long shadow on the grass, he went walking off across the infield. He ignored Lorraine, who asked why he slowed down. He ignored Philip Crowley, who told him that he and Brendan had tied for sixteenth place. He ignored Brendan who asked if he was feeling all right. What he was feeling was an enormous sense of relief at having remembered, in the nick of time, his mistake with the boomerang. In front of everyone in the schoolyard, he had picked up the boomerang and thrown it twice as far as Brendan had thrown it, and he had almost lost Brendan for life.

26

B RENDAN, TRUE TO HIS vow to be Dodger's ally all weekend, pushed open the door, and when he saw that the coast was clear he motioned Dodger to follow him into the back room. Dodger had wanted to take his warm-up pants full of loot straight home, but Brendan reminded him that they were expected to help out at the market as soon as they got back to town. It was already after sundown. While Brendan took off his jacket and tied on an apron, Dodger went down to the basement and stuffed his bundle into an empty potato sack and left it in a dark corner. Then he climbed the stairs, put on an apron and helped Brendan replenish the apple and grapefruit bins. Business was brisk: Mrs. Pelzer rang up sales while Catherine bagged groceries and Paul carried them out to cars. Hank worked the aisles, helping shoppers find what they were looking for. Wallace, looking tired and speaking to no one, toiled away at packaging. At the first lull, Hank and Catherine approached the boys and asked about the track meet. Dodger pulled his blue ribbon from his pocket and handed it to them. Catherine said it was wonderful and Hank said, "Congratulations," but neither of them looked happy. They looked heavy-hearted and a little angry.

"Dodger, was this your week with the money bag?" Hank asked.

"Yep."

"Come up to the office. We have to have a talk."

Brendan followed, thinking he was included in the "we," but his father turned him back at the office steps, ordering him into the basement to fetch a supply of paper bags for the checkout counter.

Downstairs, curious to know what Dodger had brought home from Rochester, he looked for the warm-up pants and found them in the potato sack against the back wall. He examined the watch, the magazines, and the tobacco. He guessed they were gifts for himself and his parents and Grandfather and he wondered if he, in Dodger's place, would have been so thoughtful.

As he started up the steps into the back room, his arms full of paper bags, he heard his father's voice coming through the opening in the wall high above him. "How much money do you have on you?"

"I guess about a quarter," Dodger replied.

"And how much at home?"

"I guess about two quarters."

Brendan laid his bundles on the step above him and stood with his ear cocked upward.

"Go through your pockets for us, would you?"

There was half a minute of silence before Catherine said, "Is that all?"

"Yep."

Hank spoke harshly: "We were five dollars short when we checked out last night and the cash register was another ten dollars short this morning when Mrs. Pelzer rang up her first sale. The five dollars could have been a mistake, I suppose, but when it happens two days in a row with you in charge of the money bag, it looks suspicious."

Brendan listened for Dodger to point out that he had not put the money in the till this morning—Brendan had done it—but he heard Dodger say only, "I never took it."

"Then how else could ten dollars disappear before a single sale is rung up?"

"And not only that," added Catherine, "didn't we hear you tell your father on the phone that you would bring him money?"

"Did I say that?"

"Yes."

"I don't think I said that. He asked me did I have any money and all I said was I did."

A long pause. If Dodger wasn't going to save his own skin, Brendan decided he'd better do it for him. He distinctly recalled putting the ten-spot in the till. It had to have disappeared after the two of them left for school. He was about to climb up to the office and explain this to his parents when he heard his father say, "You'll be staying in the house all day tomorrow, Dodger. No movie, no bike-riding until you level with us about the money."

At this, Brendan changed his mind. He picked up the paper bags and carried them to the front of the store. If Dodger was determined to cook his own goose, who was Brendan to interfere? With Dodger housebound tomorrow, Brendan would be free to go to Pebble Creek. After the party would be soon enough to clear Dodger's name. Unless, of course, Dodger or his parents spoke to him about the theft. Then he'd have to tell what he knew.

As the evening passed, it became obvious that his parents, as he expected, were discreetly keeping the theft a secret between themselves and Dodger. What surprised him was that Dodger, too, was keeping it under his hat—perhaps upon their advice. So Brendan allowed himself the luxury of imagining the fun he'd have at the creek.

During the next lull Brendan learned from Paul and Mrs. Pelzer, who were speaking in low tones at the checkout counter, that Dodger wasn't the sole cause of the trouble in the air. Wallace Flint, they said, had been acting moody and defiant. Ordinarily the packaging process was closed down on Saturday evenings, but Wallace, against Hank's wishes, had continued working.

Mrs. Pelzer told Brendan, "Your dad tried to give him his pay and send him home at suppertime, but he wouldn't go."

"He just kept weighing bags," Paul added, "and ignoring your dad."

"Look at him." Mrs. Pelzer nodded toward the back of the store, where Wallace was scooping something from a large bag into a smaller one. His movements were slow and mechanical, his eyes cast down. "He acts like he's in a trance."

Paul said, "Your dad told him he was caught up and not to open any more boxes or sacks of anything, but he's been opening them anyway."

"We're wondering how long before your dad blows up."

Wallace worked without interference until closing time; then he tidied up the packaging area and washed his hands. He wiped them on his apron as he strode up to the checkout counter, where Hank was counting the proceeds. "You can pay me what I was getting last winter," he said, "but eventually I'll want a raise."

"I'm sorry," said Hank, handing him his wages. "We've got all the help we need."

To Brendan, who was sweeping nearby, Wallace looked ghostly. His face was gaunt and white, his eyes hooded.

"Does this include tonight?" asked Wallace, counting the money in his hand.

"Yes, plus a tip for helping us out in a pinch." Hank turned back to the cash register. "Good night."

Wallace set his jaw, stood his ground. "What time on Monday?"

Hank spoke with his back to him: "Listen, Wallace, I can't hire help I don't need. Now please . . ."

"My mother might not come back to work."

Hank finished counting a handful of coins before replying, "We're expecting her back."

"She's not getting better. I might have to take her place."

Wheeling around, Hank raised his voice: "I do the hiring here! Don't plan on taking anybody's place!"

Brendan paused in his sweeping and stared, so rare was his father's anger. His mother, he noticed, was looking on from a distance. So were a couple of last-minute customers as well as Stan Kimball, who had dropped in to judge the success of the sale.

Wallace, untying his apron, said, "I'll come back in the middle of the week—give you a chance to change your mind."

"Don't come back, Wallace. Ever."

For several moments Wallace remained at the counter, watching Hank count quarters; then he turned and saw the several eyes upon him. A leering smile spread over his face as he took off his apron, dropped it on the floor and wiped his shoes on it. Still smiling, he walked out into the night.

Riding home with the Fosters in the DeSoto, Dodger had had no choice but to leave his bundle of gifts in the basement of the store, and now, lying in bed, he thought it just as well. He had not intended to present them in person anyhow. In order to avoid questions about where they came from, he wanted the gifts to be discovered after he'd left for Winona on Monday morning, and the store was as good a place as any. But he'd somehow have to bring them up out of the basement and put them on Hank's desk with a note explaining who got which gift. And he'd have to do it tomorrow. Getting a key was no problem; he'd take Catherine's key out of her purse. And sneaking away from the house might not be a problem either, if Hank and Grandfather took their usual long Sunday naps and Catherine spent the afternoon out in the back yard working on the shrubbery, as she had done last Sunday.

He turned and looked at Brendan in the adjacent bed. He was covered by moonlight and breathing softly, obviously asleep. Dodger was sorry to think that his time with the Fosters was ending on a sour note, but he simply couldn't squeal on Brendan. Brendan always had good reasons for what he did, and he must have had a good reason for taking the ten dollars. Besides, Brendan wanted to go to the creek tomorrow and he didn't want to go with Dodger. He hadn't said so, but Dodger knew it. A lucky thing, my being forced to stay home, thought Dodger. Now he can go without me and not feel guilty.

* * *

Brendan, feigning sleep so that Dodger wouldn't interrupt his thoughts, lay awake for a long time puzzling over the money. Having put the ten-spot and the rest of the change into the till, he had shut the drawer, which could be opened only by ringing up a sale. There had been no sales before he and Dodger left for the track meet. They had met Mrs. Pelzer on her way to work and they had met Wallace. Or was it the other way around? Yes, Wallace first. He would have arrived at the store five minutes or so before Mrs. Pelzer. On Friday morning Wallace had bought a pack of gum before Mrs. Pelzer showed up; Brendan had seen him ring up the five-cent sale and drop a nickel into the drawer. Had he taken out a five-dollar bill before closing it? This morning had he bought another pack of gum and taken out a ten—not only to line his own pockets but to get Dodger in trouble? Yes, of course. It was exactly what you'd expect of Wallace Flint. What a relief to be rid of him once and for all.

27

THERE WAS A HITCH in Catherine's voice as she called her family to the table for Sunday dinner. After grace, which they all said in unison, Catherine added, "And we thank you, Lord, for giving us Dodger." Immediately her eyes filled with tears. She left her place and stepped into the kitchen, where she wept in silence. Tomorrow Dodger would resume his directionless life in Winona; if under strict supervision he couldn't resist stealing from the money bag, how could he be honest on his own? She fought back her tears and returned to her place at the table. Hank and Brendan kept glancing at her with curiosity. To divert their attention she scolded Grandfather for the fresh tobacco stains on his new shirt.

Grandfather, ignoring her, turned to Dodger and asked if he would join the track team in Winona.

"No," he said. "Track's too hard."

"But you should," said Catherine. "Track is what you excel at." She pointed to the wall over the buffet, where Dodger's ribbon hung from a pin.

"Yeah, I guess you're right. I guess I should." Though it was sometimes difficult to conform to Catherine's expectations, it was more difficult not to. But he wouldn't join. It wasn't easy being on a team. Everybody expected you to be a standout. Dodger had spent too much of his life standing out—or standing off to the side. What he wanted most in life was what he had attained with the Fosters—the chance to blend in.

"I remember my schooldays with loathing," said Grandfather, startling everyone with his vehemence. "Aren't you glad it's nearly summer?"

"I sure am," Dodger replied. He was happier than he could say, for very little remained of his education. He would turn sixteen in August, and then he could legally quit.

After dinner, after dishes, Hank went to sleep on the couch while Grandfather studied the section of the Sunday paper devoted to Roosevelt's life and death. Brendan followed his mother out into the sunny back yard and asked if he might bicycle with Sam and Philip to Pebble Creek, where Pearl and Lorraine were hosting a marshmallow roast. Catherine, pruning a bush, said yes, and he rode away on his bike.

The Sunday matinee was *Wonder Man*, starring Danny Kaye and Virginia Mayo. Standing in line at the box office, Wallace Flint studied the posters and was disappointed to see dancers. What he liked in a movie was a tense, grim story without dancing or singing. *Wonder Man* looked insufferably airy.

Down the street the Romberg pickup was parked at the curb and Wallace saw a number of youngsters pile out of it—Andy and Sam Romberg, Norma Nash, Pearl Peterson, Lorraine Graham—and go into Gordy's Pool Hall.

Wallace bought a ticket, stepped through the doorway and handed it to Philip Crowley, Sr., who tore it in half. He lingered in the lobby until the show began; then he walked down the aisle to the fire exit. Stepping outside, he saw Brendan jump off his bike and enter the back door of the pool hall. Waiting a minute in case Brendan reappeared, he heard the engine of the pickup come to life. He hurried through the passageway between the buildings and watched the pickup pull away from the curb with Brendan, among others, riding in back. He returned to the alley and let himself into the back room of the market, using a key he had stolen years ago from Kermit.

The two cats had been dozing in a pile of excelsior beside the walk-in cooler. During the sale Hank had given away six dozen cut-glass tumblers, which had been shipped to Plum in boxes filled with this excelsior. The gray cat rubbed against Wallace's leg; the yellow one remained at a distance and yawned.

He gathered up an armful of excelsior and went into the basement. He switched on the light and dumped the excelsior on the floor next to the rear wall. He looked at the four large hooks above him in the ceiling, from which stalks of bananas were sometimes hung, and judged them to be almost directly beneath the walk-in cooler—exactly where he had seen them in his mind's eye as he lay in bed this morning planning the fire. Sifting through the embers and tracing the fire to its starting point, the firemen would blame it on faulty wiring in the cooler.

He went upstairs and brought down another armload of excelsior, then looked around for empty potato bags. He found three. He stuffed them with excelsior and hung them from three of the hooks. Searching for a fourth bag, he picked up the one containing the comic books, the watch, the can of tobacco, the birthday card and the current issue of *Popular Mechanics*. Such an odd collection, Wallace realized, could be only one thing, a cache of Dodger's stolen goods; therefore it gave him special pleasure to add excelsior to the bag and hang it from the fourth hook. He touched a match to the bags. The dry burlap crackled like kindling and the excelsior burned with a blinding, white-hot flame. Retreating to the steps, he paused to watch the flames cup the ceiling joists and lick at the floor above; then he hurried upstairs with the cats at his heels. He slid the remaining excelsior across the floor so it covered the wisps of smoke coming up between the floorboards next to the cooler. Then he went to the back door and opened it a crack. He cursed. Two men were pulling up to the rear of the pool hall in an old gray car. They were engrossed in a conversation that delayed their getting out. Wallace waited. The gray cat stood beside him, making hissing noises; the yellow cat paced the room, its tail twitching. When the excelsior beside the cooler suddenly went up in flames, ignited from below, the gray cat stood on its hind legs and planted its claws in Wallace's thighs. Stooping to smack the cat, he saw that his pants and shirt were covered with bits of excelsior. He brushed frantically, but the bits clung like lint. As the pile of excelsior turned quickly to ash, he saw that the wide floorboards beneath it were no longer so wide; gaps of flame were opening up between them. The smoke was thickening. The room was growing hot. The cats, he noticed, had vanished. Again he peered outside. The two men were gone. He slipped out and locked the door.

The cats, sensing someone at the front door, had streaked through the market, and the moment Dodger pushed the door open they shot outside to safety. Dodger shut the door and looked out the window to see if he'd been noticed. He had hoped to enter by the back door, but the only key in Catherine's purse was this one. Apparently no one had seen him. He turned around, sniffing, and assumed that the stoker in the basement was emitting smoke, as sometimes happened when it ran empty of coal. But why was the stoker running on such a warm day? Then he heard the crackle of burning wood. He ran to the threshold of the back room and saw flames opening a hole in the floor. He started down the basement steps, but stopped, realizing that retrieving his bag of gifts was less important than putting out the fire. At the sink he filled a basin with water and threw it on the flames—to no effect but a thicker billow of smoke. Again he started down the steps and again he changed his mind: first he'd better phone for help. He rushed up to Hank's crow's nest and picked up the phone. There were ten or fifteen seconds of silence on the line, during which he watched the fire through the opening in the wall. The smoke at this level made it hard to breathe.

"Number?" said Constable Heffernand.

"Hank's Market's on fire!"

He dropped the phone and descended into the basement. He had to pass through a shower of fiery ash to reach the point along the back wall where he had left his bag of loot. The bag wasn't there. He was turning in a circle, looking for it, when the walk-in cooler leaned sideways into the disintegrating floor, tore itself loose from its wiring and crashed into the basement.

From his switchboard Constable Heffernand activated the fire siren atop the village hall. When Catherine heard it, she went indoors and woke up Hank, who had joined the volunteer fire department last October, recruited by Stan Kimball. He tied his shoes and hurried out to his car. Stan Kimball came over from next door and climbed into the front seat with him. Russell Romberg crossed the alley and got in the back.

"Where is it?" asked Hank, driving out of the yard.

"We'll find out when we get to the fire hall," said Russell Romberg.

"Where's the fire hall?" Since October there had been no fires.

Kimball directed him to a small, clapboard garage, where they found Len Downie already sitting behind the high steering wheel of the red truck, racing the engine, and Woodruff the postmaster and Legget the grocer climbing aboard. They wore helmets and rubber coats. Nicholi the barber was on the phone.

"Hank, it's your store," said Nicholi, hanging up and hopping onto the back step of the truck as it began to move.

The DeSoto followed the truck to the alley behind the market. When Hank unlocked and threw open the back door, a cloud of white and black smoke came pouring out. Next door the theater was being evacuated, moviegoers spilling through the fire exit into the alley. They were joined by the pool hall crowd, led by Gordy, who as a member of the department helped Nicholi pull the hose off the spool and tug it through the passageway to the hydrant on Main Street. Russell Romberg buckled climbing spikes onto his legs and ascended a power pole to cut off electricity to the store. Legget went around breaking windows with a small hatchet—more windows than necessary, thought Kimball, who told him to stop. Hank peered through the smoke and located the flames. They were climbing the wall where the cooler had stood. They were licking the ceiling. He backed out, making room for Woodruff and Downie, who braced themselves in the doorway and trained the water on the fire.

In ten minutes the flames began to diminish. In thirty the fire was out. Russell Romberg set up a large fan in the doorway, running the cord next door to the pool hall. When the smoke had cleared enough to breathe, Hank went inside. He stood at the edge of the hole in the floor and looked at the hole in the ceiling. He felt raped.

Constable Heffernand conferred on the stoop with Len Downie; then the two of them explained to Hank that unless the cause of the fire was obvious the deputy state fire marshal in Rochester had to be notified. It was Downie's theory, given the location, that the fire was caused by faulty wiring in the new cooler.

"The hell it was," said Russell Romberg. "I did that wiring myself and it was all up to code. Look at the floor—the size of that hole. Fire doesn't burn down, it burns up. It had to start in the basement."

They went downstairs with a flashlight and sloshed through the two inches of water standing on the concrete floor. It was the constable who first saw the arm and leg protruding from underneath the walk-in cooler.

"God almighty," Hank whispered, "it's Dodger." He recognized the checkered shirtsleeve and the tennis shoe. "It's Dodger," he said again as he tried to move the cooler off the boy, but it weighed at least half a ton and it took all four of them to tip it on its side. Hank knelt in the water and rolled Dodger over on his back. He felt splintered ribs through the bloody shirt. Lifting Dodger's head, he felt the spine bend in the middle as though hinged. Dodger was dead.

Downie called up through the hole, "Send Kimball down here."

Constable Heffernand climbed to Hank's office, where he found the phone off the hook. He told his sister to call the fire marshal in Rochester and the sheriff in Winona.

Hank went out to his car and drove home.

Catherine looked up smiling from the Sunday paper as he came into the room, his light Sunday pants begrimed, his eyes in-

flamed. "I was worried. I wish you hadn't agreed to fight fires."
Then, reading his grim expression, she asked, "What is it?"

"The fire was in the store."

She put her hand to her mouth. The paper slithered to the floor.

"It burned the back room. We got it out before it spread to the front."

Grandfather turned off the radio—an account of this morning's burial at Hyde Park.

"But there's something worse," Hank said.

Catherine, seized by fear, grimaced and asked, "Dodger?" All day she'd entertained a series of fears about Dodger. They'd grown more insistent after she'd come in from the back yard and discovered that Dodger had sneaked away.

"We found him in the basement."

When Hank turned silently away, she sprang out of her chair. "You mean he's burned?"

He faced her. "He's dead."

"Dead?"

He nodded.

"Dodger's dead?" Her eyes shone with terror.

"The lad?" asked Grandfather, getting to his feet.

"The walk-in cooler fell through the floor into the basement. It landed on top of him." Hank moved to embrace his wife, but she stepped back.

"What was he doing there?"

"I don't know. I have to get back and meet with the sheriff and the fire marshal. Will you come?"

She nodded and strode through the house and out to the car.

"I'll come too," said Grandfather. On his way out he paused in the kitchen for a swig of bourbon.

Riding to Main Street, Catherine sat touching shoulders with Hank and trembling as she stared through the windshield.

"I'm not crazy about the way the Lord is running things," muttered Grandfather from the back seat.

Hank parked in front. They found the front door unlocked, Catherine's key in the keyhole. They stepped inside. Smoke hung from the ceiling like a layer of cirrus. None of the stock on the shelves had been burned or sprayed with water, but the stench of smoke and wet ash was pervasive. "I believe I'll go next door for a beer," said Grandfather, taking his leave.

"He's in the basement," Hank said to Catherine. "Do you want to come down?"

"Yes," she said. Then, "No."

"I'd better go down."

She nodded.

He found Stan Kimball alone with the body. He was standing on a wooden crate to keep his feet dry. His shoulders were hunched, his hands in his pockets, his gaze absent. Dodger, covered with a sheet, lay on a stretcher.

"Shall we carry him up?" asked Hank.

It took Kimball several seconds to gather his thoughts. He turned to Hank and said, "No, the sheriff will want everything as is. But I had to at least get him out of the water."

Reliving this Sunday in months to come, Hank would remember this picture: the man on the box, the boy under the sheet, smoky light filtering down through the hole in the ceiling, the floor of water below, the walls of stone.

"How's Catherine taking it?"

"It's hard to tell.'

Catherine, crossing the back room, avoided looking down the hole. Kimball's black hearse, open and empty, was parked at the stoop with two dozen people clustered around it. The movie had resumed, but some of the moviegoers, preferring real-life drama, remained outdoors waiting for the sheriff and the fire marshal to arrive. Gordy, standing in the sun, nervously wiped his hands on his dirty apron as he watched Catherine approach.

"Terrible for you," he said, giving her elbow a consoling squeeze. She was stiff to the touch. Her eyes were dry.

Constable Heffernand said, "He wasn't a bad kid, was he, Mrs. Foster? There's some that couldn't say a good word for Dodger, but I wasn't one of them. Nor my sister either. We always said, Where would any of us be if we started life out with parents like Dodger's?"

Catherine pinched the bridge of her nose and stared at the hearse.

"I can't remember what Dodger's voice was like," said the Constable. "Did he sound like he had a cold?"

Catherine didn't answer.

"I'm trying to place the voice that called in the fire. It sounded like a teenager, and it sounded like his nose was plugged."

Catherine nodded. "Adenoids."

Legget the grocer, a sallow man with big ears, joined them and said, "I'm sorry about Dodger and I'm sorry about the fire damage."

She thanked him without moving her eyes from the hearse.

"I was changing my window display and I saw Dodger let himself into your store. It wasn't a minute later the whistle blew. If you want to bring your perishables across the street, I've got more refrigeration than I need."

She thanked him again, shifting her gaze from the hearse to a gray car that was pulling up beside it. It had an emblem on the door. Two men got out. Constable Heffernand shook the driver's hand and called him "Sheriff." He was an overweight, elderly man wearing a black suit and cowboy boots. He introduced his passenger, a red-haired man in shirtsleeves, as Doctor Burke, the county coroner. The constable led them inside.

The crowd of spectators increased. They waited for the body to come out, their voices subdued, their eyes on the doorway. The two cats showed up. The gray one purred at Catherine's feet. The yellow one kept its distance, sitting on Gordy's back step and looking distrustful. Paul Dimmitburg came walking down the alley. He went directly to Catherine and looked solicitously into her eyes as he listened to Gordy's account of what happened. He made some consoling remarks, to which Catherine responded with a mechanical smile. Her gaze had returned to the hearse.

In a few minutes Stan Kimball appeared on the stoop lighting a cigar. He was followed by Hank and Dr. Burke carrying the stretcher, which they slid into the hearse. Kimball got in behind the wheel and the doctor got in beside him. The hearse glided off down the alley, raising a thin trail of dust, as a red car pulled into the alley and parked in its place. This was the deputy fire marshal, a pudgy young man in a baseball uniform. He had been called away from a game. The crowd watched him confer in the doorway with the constable, then follow him inside. He limped. His number was twelve.

Stepping over to Catherine's side and taking her hand, Hank felt shock setting in. He felt giddy and cold. "Are you all right?" he asked.

"I'm all right." It was true. She felt strong in a wooden sort of way. She felt, to her surprise, that if she allowed herself to shed tears there might be no tears to shed.

"How did it start?" asked Paul.

"The excelsior must have caught fire. There's a hole in the floor where we piled it, next to the cooler."

"What was Dodger doing in there?"

"God knows. Maybe hiding things. We found a watch in the basement, and a can of tobacco."

"Damn shame," said Legget. He repeated his offer of refrigeration.

"Thanks," said Hank. "We'll see what's worth saving when we open the cooler."

"Lucky the front end wasn't touched," added Legget.

Hank's "Lucky all right" was barely audible. Standing in the sun, he was shaking with cold.

Minutes passed. Grandfather came out and sat next to the yellow cat on the back step of the empty pool hall, sipping a beer he had drawn for himself. A procession of cars crept through the alley. A few moviegoers returned to the theater by way of the fire exit. Philip Crowley, Sr., remained outside, helping Nicholi and Woodruff feed the hose onto its spool. Russell Romberg taped up the severed cooler wires and restored electricity to the building.

The sheriff led the marshal and the constable out onto the stoop and asked the crowd, now numbering about forty, to gather close around. "Whatever you folks might know about this fire, I want to hear about it." He held a small, tattered notebook and a stubby pencil, ready to write.

Constable Heffernand spoke first. "I was tending the telephone switchboard. It was a boy's voice calling in the fire."

"Dodger Hicks," said Legget. "I saw him let himself into Hank's front door. I was working on my window display."

The sheriff, writing, asked Heffernand, "What did he say—his exact words?"

"Hank's Market's on fire."

"And he's the boy you found dead?"

The firemen nodded. Gordy added, "He's a ward of the Fosters."

The men stole glances at Catherine, whose eyes were far off.

"So Dodger didn't start it" Gordy continued. "I mean he'd hardly report a fire he started."

"Unless he started it by accident," said Russell Romberg.

"Wouldn't have been time," said Legget. "He went in the door and right away the whistle started blowing."

The fire marshal spoke up: "It doesn't look like an accident to me."

"Foster," said the sheriff, "what business did the boy have in your store on a Sunday afternoon?"

The constable answered for him: "We figure he was hiding stolen goods. He was a petty thief from the time he was a tyke."

"He had a key?"

"He took my wife's key," said Hank.

As the sheriff made notes, Catherine suddenly lost her distracted look and scowled sharply at the man in the baseball uniform. "Why did you say it wasn't an accident?"

"I said it doesn't *look* like an accident. There's the remains of burned excelsior in the basement. Somebody could have touched it off. That stuff goes up like gasoline."

Paul Dimmitburg said, "It must have fallen through the floor. We left a pile of it in the back room when we locked up last night."

"But that isn't all. There's a trail of it leading down the steps. Did you carry any of it into the basement?"

Paul looked at Hank, at Catherine. "No."

The sheriff turned a page in his notebook. "Now let's talk about keys, Foster. Who else has keys to this place?"

"Paul here. Myself. That's all."

"I doubt if that's all," said a voice from behind them. Everyone turned. It was Stan Kimball, who had left the body and the coroner in his embalming room and returned to the market on foot. "I'd be surprised if Wallace Flint didn't have a key from Kermit's time."

When Wallace left the kitchen and hurried through the dining room saying, "We've got company," Mrs. Flint imagined Grandfather dropping in.

"Will you see who it is?" she asked, straightening the pillows on the couch, but Wallace was already climbing the stairs. Then she heard a rapid pounding on the door that could hardly be Grandfather's; it was too loud, too impolite. She sensed trouble before she opened the door.

"Sheriff," announced the large, white-haired man who stepped inside without being invited. He was followed by three others, and she shrank back as they advanced. The fourth man, she saw to her relief, was Hank. The other two were Constable Heffernand and a stranger dressed in a baseball suit. Standing in the kitchen, they craned their necks to see into the rooms beyond while the sheriff asked her questions. Was Wallace home? Had Wallace been out earlier? How long ago had he returned? Would she go get him so they could talk to him? Answering, she thought it odd that Hank said nothing to put her at ease.

She went into the living room and called upstairs to Wallace, who said he'd be down in a minute. The men moved into the dining room. As she answered more questions, she wondered why on earth the baseball player was examining the pillows on her couch, the seat of her chair, the rug. Wallace had been to the movie, she told them. He always went to the movie on Sunday afternoon. No, he hadn't told her about any fire. No, he didn't have a key to the market. Nor did she. No (she lied, growing wary) she hadn't noticed any white particles on his clothing. She kept her composure until Wallace came down, then she retreated to her chair by the radio and sat facing partly away from the men so they wouldn't see her distress. Wallace, stepping boldly into the room, asked Hank, "Who are these men?" But Hank appeared not inclined to talk to him. It was the constable who answered:

"The law, Wallace. They've got some questions to ask you about the fire."

His mother, trembling, listened to enough of the interrogation to understand why her son had come home only a half hour after the movie began and why he had stood so long in the kitchen picking white crumbs off his clothes and dropping them into the range. As Wallace delivered his answers without the slightest trace of defiance or uneasiness, she turned and studied the faces of the four men and saw with great relief that they appeared to believe every word. Yes, said Wallace, he had gone to the movie. Yes, he had stood for a time in the alley with the rest of the moviegoers and watched the firemen at work, then he had gone home—the movie was too insipid. No, he had not told his mother about the fire for fear of aggravating her illness, for it looked to him as though most of the back-room stock was destroyed, which would put her out of work.

Because his setting the market afire was too horrible to think about, Mrs. Flint shut out the men's voices and let her mind slip back to that other Sunday afternoon when outsiders invaded this room and a confrontation ensued. It was twenty years ago. Her dead husband's two brothers and their wives drove over from Wisconsin to visit. Wallace was whining and making a fuss during dinner (he was four) and without thinking she bent over and bit his hand. Her in-laws were shocked and angry. They talked of nothing else for the rest of the meal. They looked him over and found other bite marks. Since these in-laws were her means of support, she half believed them when they told her they had the legal right to take Wallace away from her. Leaving, they said they would report her to the authorities and return often to check the boy for signs of abuse. Later, she doubted if they told anybody, and it was nearly a year before their next visit, but they succeeded in scaring her. From that day forward she stopped biting him. She doted on him instead. She discovered that impatience and anger were much less gratifying than the remorse and love that replaced them.

"Look here!" sang out the man in the baseball suit. Startled, she turned and saw him holding up a curlicue of excelsior he had picked off the floor. As the men handed it from one to another, she despaired. She saw her son imprisoned for arson. Having made him so dependent upon her all these years, was she to blame for his terrible frustration? Should she have given in to his pleading and allowed him to join the high school debate team and go off to other towns and have his fits among strangers? Should she have permitted him to accept those scholarships and go off to Winona State and bite off his tongue in a dormitory room?

But her despair was unfounded. Wallace explained to the four men in a steady, relaxed voice that he had come home both Friday and Saturday with excelsior on his clothes, having unpacked the tumblers Hank had given away as Grand Opening gifts.

Brendan, sitting on a rock beside the water, was starting on his third beer. So was Jerry Franzen, the track star from Pinburg, who was sitting beside him and proving more amiable than he had been in Rochester. Both he and Brendan, as it happened, had read *Gone with the Wind*, and they were comparing their favorite parts, agreeing that for great writing it was hard to beat the leg amputation performed in a field hospital with a crosscut saw and no anesthetic.

Sam had waded upstream alone, carrying his cane pole, a can of worms and a bottle of beer. Philip, halfway up a pine tree, was making noises like Tarzan. Lorraine and Pearl were gathering sticks to build a fire. Norma Nash and Andy Romberg stood in the creek holding hands and laughing at how funny their feet looked underwater. It was Norma who had supplied the beer, having been snitching from her father's supply for weeks in preparation for this party.

Though Brendan was where he had longed to be, he wasn't altogether happy. Besides the queasiness caused by the beer, he was feeling acute pangs of guilt over what he had done to Dodger. Or not done. He shouldn't have left him home unjustly punished. He should have come clean about the moneybag and brought him along to the creek. Sam, in fact, had asked on the way out from town, "How come you didn't bring Dodger?"

The noises in Philip's tree changed to groans, then to retching.

"I'm sick," he cried faintly. Philip, too, was full of beer. He was hidden by pine boughs but his vomit began to be visible, seeping down through the needles. Philip himself came down next, dropping in stages, and when he let go of the bottom branch and fell to earth, his face was smeared with pine tar and tears. He lay in a ball with his eyes closed, moaning. Brendan turned away, somewhat nauseous himself, and was astonished to see his father advancing toward him through the bushes.

Everyone froze, caught holding beer. But Hank appeared not to notice. He fastened his eyes on Brendan and said, "Come with me." Brendan smiled a weak, puzzled smile at his friends and departed, following his father through the brush. Halfway to the road Hank halted and said, "There's been a fire at the store, Brendan." His eyes were inflamed, his lips thin and taut. "Dodger is dead."

He turned and resumed walking. Brendan, almost too stunned to move, followed slowly. They climbed up out of the bushes to the gravel road, where the DeSoto, leaning into the soft sand of the shoulder, was parked behind the pickup. His mother got out and threw her arms around him. Grandfather sat in back, wearing no expression behind the smoke of his pipe.

"Where's your bike?" asked Hank. "We'll put it in the pickup and let your friends bring it home."

"It's in town. We all came out in the truck."

Hank's reaction was a flash of anger. "I don't want you riding in that pickup. Ever." His biting tone frightened Brendan. "Andy's a reckless driver."

Brendan got in with Grandfather. Hank started the car, turned it around and climbed up out of the ravine in second gear. When they stopped at the hilltop intersection, Brendan asked, "You mean Dodger burned to death?"

They sat with the engine idling, facing the giant spark plug on the barn across the road, while Hank told him what he knew of the facts. He said the fire marshal suspected arson, and Stan Kimball suspected Wallace, but there was no way to prove it.

"Do you think they're right?" asked Brendan.

"I don't know what to think."

"Mom, what about you?"

Catherine shook her head slowly, inscrutably.

"Have you any idea what Dodger was doing in the store?" His father was looking at him through the rear-view mirror.

"He brought home some things from Rochester and was hiding them in the basement."

"Hiding them because they were stolen?"

"Because they were presents, I think. Going-away presents for us."

Catherine, turning her gaze out her side window, saw Plum tucked into its fold of hills three miles away, two steeples, a grain elevator, and a water tower protruding above the elms. She said, "I can't believe we live in that town. It's like having a nightmare and never waking up."

Brendan, along with Grandfather, was dropped off at home, and his parents continued on to Kimball's Furniture and Funeral Home. Grandfather fell asleep on the couch. Brendan went out and sat under a tree in the back yard, waiting for the pickup to return from the creek; he was frightened—if Dodger could die then Brendan could die—and he wanted friends to divert him. He heard a snapping of twigs and looked nervously about him, sensing death's presence nearby. His eyes fell on the large brush-pile his mother was adding to week by week as she pruned the shrubbery. He imagined death taking up residence there. The brushpile was a short leap to any house in the neighborhood. Whose house was next? Would death strike Brendan's house twice in a row? He felt a powerful urge to run indoors and see if Grandfather still breathed, but he was paralyzed by a renewed snapping of twigs. The brushpile seemed to be moving. After a moment of terror he saw Larry-the-Twitch come crawling out from the midst of it. He hopped toward Brendan on one foot and threw himself on the ground. He scratched his chest and ankles and head and picked at the grass. "Dodger got killed."

"I know it."

Larry gave him a disgusted look. He had the sort of pinched face that comes from amounting to nothing in the eyes of older brothers. For once he knew something before his brothers knew it, but his brothers weren't home to tell and it wasn't news to anybody else.

"My dad says you'll probably keep Dodger in your house because it's expensive to keep a body at Kimball's."

Brendan was horrified. Death in the house?

"My dad says he'll be okay to look at. His ribs are mashed but his head is okay."

"Your dad saw him?"

"My dad's a fireman. He put out the fire. If it wasn't for my dad the fire would have burned down your store and the movie house and the pool hall. It might have burned down the whole town." He rolled over on his back and probed his nose with a twig. "What's it feel like to get killed?"

Brendan went indoors. He lay on the floor of the living room, paging through the Sunday paper while keeping an eye on his sleeping grandfather and listening to him breathe. When Grandfather awoke, he told him what he was afraid to tell his parents:

"They think Dodger stole money from the store. Dodger didn't steal it. I think Wallace stole it."

Grandfather, drawing on his pipe, opened and closed his hand in a beckoning way, as if asking to hear more.

Brendan told him that he had wanted his parents to think Dodger stole the money so he could go to the creek without him. He said that if he had come out with the truth right away Dodger might be alive. They might have gone to the creek together no matter what Pearl Peterson said. Who cared what Pearl Peterson said? Did she own Pebble Creek? Saying these things, Brendan realized that never in his life had he felt so close to Grandfather. Never before had he opened his heart to Grandfather in exchange for the five hundred stories Grandfather had told him. Listening to Grandfather over the years, Brendan had always been aware of the man's great age, but now, their roles reversed, the six decades between them fell away to nothing.

"No, it can't be tomorrow," said Stan Kimball, sitting behind a walnut desk at the rear of his furniture display room. "The grave won't be dug."

"Then Tuesday," said Catherine. She and Hank were facing

the undertaker on dining room chairs with orange price tags dangling from their ladder backs. The chairs were $48 apiece, the walnut desk was $179. "At Holy Angels," she added.

Kimball searched his pocket for a cigar. "You know as well as I do, Catherine, that a non-Catholic can't be buried from a Catholic church."

"Dodger went to Mass with us every Sunday." The memory of him beside her in the pew brought tears to her eyes.

"But he wasn't a Catholic."

"Not yet. We didn't want to press him. It would have come about."

"I'm sorry, Catherine." He lit his cigar. "You'll have to have the funeral here."

She turned in her chair, scanning the display room, the furniture standing in crooked rows, the upholstery smelling of cigars, framed prints of flowers and windmills hanging on the walls, everything adorned with an orange price tag.

"I'll talk to Father O'Day."

"He of all people, Catherine. In seven years I've never known him to bend a rule."

"I'll talk to him."

While Hank went into the basement with Stan Kimball to select a coffin, Catherine used the phone on the desk. Waiting for the priest to answer, she looked at her watch. They had spent nearly an hour on these arrangements. It had taken the Winona police most of that time to locate Mr. Cranshaw, who was away on a family outing, and when he returned Kimball's call it was too late to reach Dodger's mother, who according to her landlady had gone out for the evening. Cranshaw next phoned Stillwater and broke the news to Dodger's father, who crumbled, making sighing and sniffing noises over the phone and saying "No, no, no," when asked if he wanted to be consulted about funeral arrangements. Cranshaw, phoning Plum for the second time, advised the Fosters to make the decisions and he would try to round up Mr. and Mrs. Hicks for the funeral.

"Hello. Holy Angels."

"Father, this is Catherine Foster. The boy who has been living with us was killed this afternoon."

"What's his name?"

"Dodger Hicks."

"Are you calling for the last sacraments?"

"No, it's too late for that. I'm calling to ask if you'll have the funeral at Holy Angels."

"What did you say his name was?"

"Dodger Hicks."

"He belongs to the parish, does he?"

"No, but he came to Mass with us every Sunday."

"Catholic, is he?"

"No."

"Then you can't have the funeral here."

"But my husband and I are Catholics, and we're his guardians."

"Nobody's Catholic by association. Every soul is separate in the sight of God."

"Father." She swallowed her rising indignation and tried to sound less fiery than she felt. "I'm appealing to you as my fellow Christian."

"What did you say your name was?"

"Catherine Foster."

"You're new in town?"

"We moved here last September."

"Then why haven't you registered?"

"Father, don't you remember us? We have the store. Hank's Market."

"The precepts of the Church are very clear on this. It's your duty to register with the priest as soon as you move into a parish."

Catherine hung up and set about rearranging Kimball's furniture for the funeral.

28

O N M O N D A Y E V E N I N G T H E four of them took
their places in the DeSoto and drove to Kimball's for Dodger's
hour of visitation. They wended their way through the furniture
to the back of the store, where Stan Kimball was switching on
a few floor lamps and table lamps and Dodger lay in creamy
satin. Brendan had not expected Dodger dead to look so much
like Dodger alive. Yesterday morning Brendan had awakened
and seen him exactly like this, lying on his back on the rollaway,
snoring lightly. Catherine wept and Grandfather turned away.
Brendan wandered up and down the rows of furniture, death
riding his shoulder and whispering into his ear about people
going into the ground in sealed boxes. He heard his father and
Kimball reciting a litany of groceries. Flour. Cereal. Cookies.
Butter. Meat. The day after tomorrow the market would reopen
for a week-long fire sale, and they were enumerating products
that might have absorbed a smoky smell and should be sold well
below cost. Sugar. Cheese. Dried fruit. Bread and rolls.

Visitation brought only three visitors. Mrs. Lansky of the
rooming house patted everyone on the arm and moaned, "Poor

Dodger, poor Dodger.'' Paul Dimmitburg stayed the whole hour, saying little. Coach Torborg endeared himself to Catherine and Hank by offering to bring members of his varsity track team to the funeral to act as pall bearers. Leaving, he said to Catherine, ''Good luck at the polls tomorrow,'' and it was a moment before she remembered that she was running for the school board. When the hour was up, Kimball switched off his table lamps and floor lamps and locked the door, leaving Dodger alone among the dining room sets.

At home Grandfather went straight to the radio, turned on *Doctor IQ*, picked up a section of the evening paper and divided his attention between the quiz show and the news from the Pacific. Hank, too, was silent, sitting across the room from Grandfather and opening another section of the paper. On an inside page he found a short article about the fire: arson was ruled out after a suspect, unnamed, had been questioned but not arrested. Catherine, her eyes moist, settled into the couch and asked her father for the page with the daily recipe and dress pattern, both of which she studied at length. Sometimes even the roomiest house lacked enough partitions for family living, Brendan observed, and on such occasions in this house the *Rochester Post-Bulletin* became a folding wall. He asked his father for the sports page.

The next morning Catherine and Hank went driving in search of blossoms for the funeral. A mile or so beyond Higgins Hill they spied a crabapple thicket at the far end of a grassy meadow. Hand in hand they crossed the meadow. They broke off armfuls of sweet-smelling, white blossoms. On the way back to the car Catherine said, ''I have to leave town, Hank.''

He walked beside her with his head bowed, waiting for more. He was not surprised. He had feared this very thing.

''I want to go and stay in St. Paul with Aunt Nancy.''

They came to the road and stood in front of the car. He did not look at her. He looked at a bird perched overhead on the power line. He listened to frogs croaking in the wet ditch. He was afraid to ask how long she would be gone.

''You see why, don't you Hank? Ever since the first time I

stepped into the store and saw the mess Kermit left behind, I've wanted to run away. I wanted to run away when the rumor went around about Wallace being my lover. In the winter when we moved to Bean Street and Mrs. Brask began instructing me on how to behave and hardly anybody came to our New Year's tea, I wanted to leave and never come back. There hasn't been a day in the past seven months that I haven't wanted to go back to the city. And now this."

"Not one day?" He swept his eyes over a field of new grain, a field of new corn, a pasture. Did she intend to leave forever? If so, he must follow. He felt like weeping.

"Not one," she said with conviction.

In the fields each stem of grain was a small blade of grass, each corn sprout the size of a tulip. In the pasture stood a herd of brown and white steers. Never before had he been so deeply impressed by the rich look of this farmland. He saw prosperous years ahead, the war ending, young men returning to the farms, price ceilings no longer imposed by Washington, Hank's Market reaping greater profits. "Not even the day we moved into our new house?" he asked.

She didn't answer.

"Think what we have here, Catherine." He faced her. "The house and the market. The way your father and Brendan have taken to the place."

"It's not enough, Hank. Nothing's enough now." Her cheeks were pale as bone. Her eyes were slits. "Dodger meant something different to me than he did to you."

The bird overhead warbled a long, arduous melody. The steers in the pasture faced the road with their ears perked, as though listening to Hank plead, "How can you say that, Catherine? You have another boy besides Dodger."

At this she dropped her blossoms and threw herself at Hank, sobbing, "He won't die, will he, Hank?" She shuddered in his arms.

"Of course not."

"If Brendan died, I couldn't go on living."

He patted her on the back.

"And you won't die, will you, Hank?"

"I'm healthy as an ox."

"I have this feeling everyone is going to die." She shook with loud, choking sobs.

After a long embrace, he picked up the blossoms and they got into the car. After they drove away the steers continued to stare at the place where they had stood. The bird on the wire fell silent. The frogs in the ditch croaked on and on.

Entering Kimball's twenty minutes before the funeral, they found no one present but the undertaker, no names in the visitors' book since last night. Grandfather chose a soft chair and sat down while Brendan and his parents stood at the coffin—briefly this time, the sting of death blunted now, the shock gone, nothing more to be learned by gazing down into Dodger's face, which was taking on the look of a museum artifact, waxy and ancient. Brendan drifted to the front of the store and looked out the window while Stan Kimball helped his parents arrange the apple blossoms in vases at Dodger's head and feet.

Next to arrive was Mrs. Lansky. She spent a minute at the coffin, then she took a seat next to Grandfather and said to him, "Poor Dodger."

"Yes, quite the good lad," he replied, and considered going on at length about Dodger, how agreeable the lad was to live with, but he lacked the gumption. He was feeling low. He had felt this way when Roosevelt died. When Sade died. Whenever one of his fellow trainmen died. When relatives and friends died. Oh, was there no end to it? His spirits rose when he saw Mrs. Clay come in wearing her wide straw hat and her pink dress. She plopped into the chair on his right and patted his arm. He picked up her hand and gave it a kiss.

Paul Dimmitburg arrived carrying a Bible. He conferred with Catherine and Stan Kimball about the service he would conduct.

An old car louder than Hank's pulled up to the curb and backfired as the engine died. The driver, a man wearing a soiled Stetson and a baggy blue suit, got out and went around to the passenger door, which required all his strength to pull open. A tall, long-faced woman got out. Mrs. Lansky, turning in her chair, identified her as she came through the door: "Dodger's mother, poor thing."

Dodger's mother was drunk. She lurched up to the coffin, where she uttered a searing, bone-chilling shriek that quickly softened into a whimper. Her escort, too, had been drinking, as was apparent in his studied manner of walking; he picked up his feet and put them down as though trudging through snow. Coming to a stop at the coffin, he removed his large hat and held it over his stomach, and when Mrs. Hicks turned to him and said, "Christ almighty, my Dodger!" he led her to a matching set of dining-room chairs. Catherine and Hank went over to her and said how sorry they were, which caused her to wail anew. "Here," her companion said, handing her a small flask. She took a swig and was consoled. She looked up at Hank and said, "Who do we sue?" Hank froze. The possibility of a lawsuit had not entered his mind. Stan Kimball stepped between them and told Mrs. Hicks that whatever litigation might ensue, this was neither the time nor place to bring it up. As he patted her on the shoulder she clutched his arm and wiped her eyes on his pinstriped sleeve. Then she took another swig from the flask and said, "Where's the preacher? Let's get on with it."

Coach Torborg and his runners came in and sat on two sofas. It was time for the service to begin, but Catherine, expecting a larger turnout, asked Paul to wait a minute or two. Brendan, still at the window, doubted if anyone else was coming. There were many cars parked along Main Street, many shoppers crossing from store to store, and no one was heading for Kimball's. Plum wasn't pausing to mark Dodger's passing.

Stan Kimball closed the coffin. Hank stepped up and placed Dodger's blue ribbon on the lid. Brendan took a seat between his parents. Paul solemnly cleared his throat and said, "Dear friends." He was interrupted by the arrival of Mr. Cranshaw and Dodger's father, a pale, wizened man who looked nothing like his son except for his long teeth and his way of exposing them as he smiled apologetically. He took a seat behind the Fosters. Cranshaw sat in a distant armchair.

It was then, as Paul began reading from Luke, that Brendan achieved his breakthrough to God. Dear God, he thought, let people live! They were his most earnest words to God, ever. Until now he had mustered this sort of urgent feeling only for certain saints—Mary, Bonaventure, Brendan—but this was high-intensity prayer straight through to God Himself. He was certain God was listening—he could feel the current. In a flash every-thing he'd been taught by the nuns seemed confirmed: every human voice, though a whisper, though a silent thought, had reverberations in a world apart from this one. God, he pleaded again, his eyes on the dark gray coffin, let people live.

Paul put down his Bible and stated, to the amazement of most of the mourners, that Dodger had been a lot like Jesus Christ, and with this he embarked on the daring sort of sermon he couldn't get away with in church, his father's parishioners being (in his view) too hidebound and smug to understand Christian-ity's challenge to love one another. "Dodger's ways were not our ways, and our ways were not Dodger's ways," he said, his voice low and resonant, his eyes roving the faces before him. "Like Christ, Dodger passed through the world wanting next to nothing for himself. All he asked was to be accepted." (Here Brendan lowered his head, afraid that Paul's accusing eyes would fasten on him.) "For all we know, God might have sent Dodger on the same mission as His Son—to put us to the test, to bring us the message about loving one another to see how we reacted to it. True, Dodger was a thief, but he did not steal to accumulate the goods of this world. He stole out of need and he stole out of generosity. He stole in order to keep his body and soul together and he gave away the rest. His heart was larger than most, and he deserved better than he got from us. If the people of Plum, including myself, had been more open-hearted with Dodger his life though short, would have been happier and we would feel much less guilty today as we carry him to his grave. Take at least one thing home from Dodger's funeral: my assurance that each time we fail to care for one another we carry out, one more time, the act of crucifixion."

Paul picked up the Bible and read a psalm. Then he asked everyone to recite with him the Lord's Prayer. They got to their feet and did so. As he concluded by calling down God's blessing on everyone present, Dodger's mother wailed anew.

Stan Kimball asked Mr. Hicks if he'd like the coffin opened so he could look at his son. "No thanks," he said, smiling in a dazed, bleary way. Having been released only yesterday from Stillwater, he had not yet fully comprehended his freedom, much less his son's death. He wore a dark suit that had evidently belonged to somebody else, somebody shorter and heavier. When Hank and Catherine introduced themselves and offered their condolences, they were amazed by his gracious response. "You people deserve the condolences," he said. "You were better parents to Dodger than I ever was."

Dodger's grave stood open and waiting on the non-Catholic side of the cemetery. Nearby was a fragrant lilac hedge full of chattering sparrows. Mr. Torborg and his athletes settled the coffin on the taut straps over the grave and Paul, in the briefest of terms, commended the body to the earth and the soul to God. Paul was undemonstrative by nature, but because one of his professors in St. Louis had recommended the graveside embrace, he turned to Dodger's father and gave him a hug. Dodger's father wept for a moment in his arms. Then Paul turned to embrace Dodger's mother, but she fended him off by swinging her purse and shouting, "Keep your hands off me, Buster." Mrs. Clay stepped in and served as her substitute, slipping her arm around Paul's middle and laying her cheek on his chest.

The polls were open from four to eight. On her way to the school with Hank and Grandfather, Catherine tried to picture herself on the board and couldn't do it. She couldn't imagine living in Plum long enough to serve out her term. Or even begin her term. The woman who had filed for election was someone else, someone capable of sitting through biweekly meetings with the likes of Mayor Brask and maintaining her optimism about the village school system. About the village. About herself as a villager. So why was she voting? For Hank's sake? Yes. She wasn't ready to tell Hank that she'd given up on Plum forever.

The polling place was the school gymnasium, and the election officials were the principal's secretary and Constable Heffernand. They sat behind a trestle table at midcourt and handed out ballots with Catherine's name printed above a space for a write-in candidate.

"How's the turnout?" Hank asked.

The constable tipped back his chair and put his feet on the table. "Pretty slow. It's going to be a long four hours."

The secretary consulted her tally marks. "Your three votes make eighteen so far. We've only been open half an hour."

They marked their ballots and dropped them into a scoured lard bucket with a slot in the cover.

In order to appear indifferent toward the election, and thus inspire indifference in the Catholic electorate, the mass of Lutheran voters waited, by prearrangement, until seven-thirty to begin crowding into the school and writing Leonard Downie's name on the ballot, and when the results were announced shortly after eight o'clock, Catherine was defeated by nearly two hundred votes.

Stan Kimball carried the news to the Fosters. He was surprised by how little it seemed to matter to Catherine, who smiled in a mysterious way and thanked him for his vote and his concern. Leaving the house by the back door, he drew Hank outside and said to him on the veranda, "You're a babe in the woods, Hank. You're too innocent for life in this town."

"What are you talking about?"

"You put up money for buying Mrs. Ottmann's big house."

"Part of the money. A hundred dollars."

"And you have no idea why the Catholic Men's Club bought that house, do you?"

"To raise money for church repair. We're going to fix up the house and sell it at a profit."

"You had no idea, did you, that the Lutherans intended to buy Mrs. Ottmann's house and convert it into a parochial school?"

"No."

"As soon as your Men's Club got wind of the Lutheran school, they put together enough money to take the house off the market. And that's why the Lutherans ganged up on your wife today." Kimball went home.

Hank stood at the railing for a few minutes, looking out over the dark lawn, then he went in to break the news to Catherine. He found her ironing a dress for her trip to St. Paul. He told her about the hundred-dollar check he had given B. L. Skeffington and Philip Crowley and about their ostensible reason for wanting it as opposed to their real reason. He said he had helped bring about her defeat. He said he felt awful.

She shrugged. "Don't feel awful, Hank. It makes no difference." And when he saw in her face that this was the truth, he felt worse.

29

CATHERINE WAS GONE A week when she sent home a breezy account of her progress through Aunt Nancy's four-bedroom apartment—cleaning, papering, painting. She said she had gone to Dayton's and had a long, happy chat with her former co-workers. Also she had spent a day with her cousin Ann and Ann's daughter Julie, who asked about Brendan. She said Uncle Howard was on his way home from the North Atlantic and after a ten-day leave, which he and Mae would spend in St. Paul, he was to take up a new assignment in the Pacific. Howard was in touch with Northwest Airlines in Minneapolis about a postwar job as a pilot. Catherine would remain in the city a while longer in order to see her sister. How was Brendan? How was Grandfather? How was Hank? How was business? How was the repair work coming along? Was she missed?

Brendan, caught up in the novelty of bachelor life, didn't miss her very much. Weeknights he and his father took turns preparing supper, and on weekends they went with Grandfather to Gordy's and ate the evening special, usually hamburger steak and fried potatoes. Brendan had remained on the track team and participated in another meet, winning no ribbons but at least outrunning Philip in the hundred-yard dash. A senior-high teammate was tutoring Brendan in the discus.

Grandfather was slow to emerge from the malaise that had begun on the afternoon of the President's death. Day after day he stayed home from the pool hall and listened to the radio news, as though Roosevelt had left him (along with Eisenhower) in charge of the European front. His grief was somewhat mollified near the end of April when Mussolini was captured, shot, dragged to a public square in Milan and strung up feet first to the beams of a gutted gas station. His spirit quickened in the first week of May when, after a seven-week siege, Berlin fell to the Russians. A few days later when he heard that Germany had surrendered and Hitler was dead, he put on his light spring coat and resumed his daily trips downtown. Japan he would leave to MacArthur.

Hank missed his wife day and night. He spent all his waking hours at work, trying not to speculate about her intentions. "Awhile longer," her letter said—that meant she was coming home, but for how long? While Mrs. Pelzer and Mrs. Flint cleaned the smoky residue from the shelves and stocked them with fresh merchandise, Hank worked with Paul Dimmitburg and Russell Romberg, repairing the back room and installing a new refrigeration unit. His few minutes of leisure each day were spent over a cup of coffee in the pool hall, and that was where it became apparent to him that while the authorities had not seen fit to arrest Wallace and charge him with arson, the village at large had convicted him and passed sentence. There wasn't a merchant along Main Street who hadn't been convinced by Stan Kimball that Wallace had started the fire. Never as long as he lived, they vowed, would Wallace find employment in Plum.

Hank was more perplexed by this than gratified, for he was far from certain of Wallace's guilt. Lacking clear evidence, he found it hard to imagine Wallace capable of a crime so grave. Further, he found it conducive to his peace of mind to blame the fire on the wiring. "Do you fellows know something I don't?" he asked Stan Kimball. "How can you be sure it was Wallace?"

"What you're seeing here is small-town justice," Kimball explained. "Oftentimes a town as remote as Plum gets overlooked by the law, and the citizens have to be their own judge and jury. The sheriff decides there's not enough clues to make a case against Wallace, but the people who've known Wallace all his life find more than enough clues in their hearts. For the rest of his life Wallace Flint is going to be known in this town as the man who set fire to Hank's Market, and everywhere he looks he's going to see accusing eyes and he's going to live out his days in a kind of solitary confinement. Tell that to Catherine when you see her. Maybe it will help."

Catherine was gone for three weeks. On a Friday afternoon in mid-May, Hank drove to Highway 61 to meet her bus, and when he saw that she had only one suitcase (she had left with two) his dread was confirmed: his days in Plum were numbered. On the drive home she was full of city news. Howard had come home from the Atlantic and left for the Pacific. Mae and Catherine were staying together at Aunt Nancy's. There was a terrific housing shortage and Catherine felt obliged to return to the city and help Mae find an apartment, for Howard would surely be discharged within six months; it was everybody's opinion that Japan couldn't last longer than that. Coming up over Higgins Hill, she glanced ahead at the village without the slightest interruption in her talk. There was a lilt in her voice such as Hank hadn't heard for a long time, an excitement in her eyes, a radiance in her smile. This was not the Catherine of the past winter and spring. This was the Catherine he had married. This Catherine would never be a villager. And thus neither would he.

Grandfather and Brendan were overjoyed to have her back where she belonged. Bachelor life had very quickly grown stale; the house without its heart had grown lifeless.

The next day, Saturday, Catherine helped at the market. Paul Dimmitburg's greeting was as warm as his grave manner would allow. "How are you?" he asked, sincerely wanting to know. "Never better," she told him. "The city is my tonic." She was greeted cheerily by Mrs. Flint and Mrs. Pelzer, who had become the closest of friends. When asked about Wallace, Mrs. Flint spoke of him in a light, dismissive manner, saying that a house could accommodate only one recluse at a time and Wallace had taken over where she left off. His hobby, she added, was painting portraits of movie stars.

Neither Paul nor the two women got much of Catherine's attention while she was in the store. What time she stole from clerking she devoted to Hank, engaging him in hushed, urgent conversation in his office. Their manner together made Brendan uneasy. He recalled their talking like this last summer, before their decision to move to Plum.

Because Father O'Day was gone on vacation, the priest celebrating Mass the next morning was a stranger. He was a large, handsome man scarcely thirty years old, and he opened his sermon with a joke. The Crowleys were instantly crazy about him, as Bea reported to Catherine on the way out of church; she said that she and her husband planned to lead a delegation to see the bishop about putting Father O'Day out to pasture.

After their midday meal, Catherine picked the six or eight tulips that had come up on the sunny side of the house, put them into a Mason jar of water and drove with Hank and Brendan to the cemetery. There were no words at the grave, only the low sounds of Catherine's sobbing as she placed the flowers beside the headstone, and the chattering of the sparrows in the lilac hedge. Later Brendan went to the matinee with Sam: Esther Williams in Technicolor.

In the evening Catherine asked Grandfather and Brendan to come away from the radio for a few minutes—she had something to tell them. She said it wasn't definite yet, but she and Hank were thinking about moving back to the city. They were quite certain of selling the market and house at a profit, with which they might buy a store in the city. She had been offered part-time work at Dayton's. They would try to find a house in the same neighborhood they had left, but because of the housing shortage they might have to rent an apartment temporarily. They hoped to find one within biking distance of St. Bonaventure's. Speaking, she looked frequently to Hank for support and he nodded agreeably, but his eyes were far off. He was trying hard, and without much luck, to see himself in a city market.

When she finished, she turned to her father, whom she expected would be as hard to uproot as he had been last summer, but he put forth no objection. He said, "Give me a day or two notice," and he went back to Jack Benny.

It was Brendan who protested. He asked his parents to think of what he would have to give up. St. Bonaventure's had no athletic program, no coaches, nothing but fussy nuns on the faculty. He said he loved Plum. In arguing against the move he was not being entirely sincere, and he knew it. There were things he missed in the city—the occasional evening with his father at Nicollet Park, watching the Millers play baseball; learning his way around the city by streetcar, which he had begun doing before they moved; the vast choice of movies. And surely Uncle Howard, home from the war, would take him up in planes.

On the day the July issue of *Independent Grocer* appeared Bob Donaldson, the Minneapolis wholesaler, made an unexpected appearance at the market, arriving as Hank was locking up.

"What's going on, Hank? I saw your ad. Why are you selling the store?"

"Family reasons. We've decided to move back to the city."

"Come on next door, I'll buy you supper. We've got business to discuss."

"No, come home with me. My wife's gone to St. Paul and it's my night to cook supper."

Over pork chops, with Brendan listening and Grandfather half listening, Bob Donaldson spoke of his dream of adding a chain of half a dozen stores to his wholesale enterprise.

"And you want to start with mine?"

"I want you and your store both. I want you to come into partnership with me. We'll use the profits from your store, along with some money of my own, to buy a second one. Then when the second store's on its feet we'll use the profits of those two to buy a third. You'll handle the retail end of things and I'll continue as supplier."

"How could I run half a dozen stores?"

"You won't run them. We'll hire managers, and you'll go around and oversee them."

"I'm not crazy about living out of a suitcase."

"You'll be on the road less than I will. Two, three nights a week. A couple of the stores I have in mind are close enough to the city so you can make day trips. Have you got a map of Minnesota?"

Brendan went out to the car and brought in the road map. He watched Bob Donaldson pinpoint the towns.

"You know what I want to call our chain, Hank? I want to call it Hank's Markets. It's got a good, honest ring to it."

Hank smiled, picturing his name on the front of six stores. He guessed he'd be proud of that, though not as proud as he had been last September when his name went up on the store in Plum.

"Now here's the clincher, Hank. I know where I can pick up a car just like mine, except it's got fewer miles on it. It'll be yours, on the job and off."

Hank looked as if he didn't believe it.

"Mint condition, Hank. Just come to the city and we'll draw up the papers for our corporation and you'll take the car home with you."

Grandfather excused himself and went to his chair in the living room.

"Of course you'll want a few days to tell your wife and think it over, but don't wait too long. The postwar boom is right around the corner."

Hank was surprised to feel no obligation to consult Catherine, surprised to realize that by leaving town she had opened a rift, not in their marriage but in their partnership as breadwinners. Instead of his wife he consulted his son.

"What do you think, Brendan?"

"What year is your car, Mr. Donaldson?"

" 'Forty-two."

"Jeez, Dad, a 'forty-two Ford."

SUMMER

❖

30

SADLY TAKING HIS LEAVE of Sam and Philip and the other boys on the sun-scorched athletic field, Brendan said nothing about this being his last day in Coach Torborg's summer recreation program. Playing baseball and soccer all summer, he had become bronzed and muscular and grown two inches. His friends knew he would be leaving town before school started, but they had no idea which day. Sam would know it tomorrow morning when he awoke and saw the moving van across the alley.

He climbed the slope to the playground, hopped on his bike, and detoured around several blocks in order to suppress his sadness before arriving at the store. The late-summer elm leaves hung dusty and still. The houses he passed, which had seemed so novel last September when he and Wallace went door to door with handbills, were now too familiar to notice. Without looking left or right he knew every cornice and eave and window curtain. He knew all the people inside.

He entered the store perspiring. He greeted Mrs. Pelzer and Mrs. Flint at the checkout counter. They were loading the day's deliveries into two shopping carts for him. Mrs. Flint, having lost weight and gained stamina, was working longer hours now, and not exclusively in packaging. She took the place, more or less, of Catherine, who, though home from the city for most of the summer, had been working very little in the store. Now and then Wallace, feeling a fit coming on, would phone the store and his mother would rush home. No one but his mother had laid eyes on him since the day of the fire. No one brought up his name in her presence.

On his way to the back door, pushing a cart, Brendan saw his father and Art Nicholi taking inventory of the back-room stock. Hank and Bob Donaldson had chosen Art Nicholi as their manager because he met their four criteria: he was husky, ambitious, polite, and Catholic. An infantryman home from France, he was the eldest son of the barber and married to a daughter of Skeffington the banker. He had black hair, a swarthy complexion, and the military habit of saying "Yes, sir" and "No, sir" more often than necessary—to women and children as well as to men.

"Hot out," said Brendan.

"Yes, sir," said Art Nicholi.

Paul Dimmitburg followed Brendan with the second cart. They carried the orders out the door and lined them up across the back seat of the DeSoto, which was now parked permanently behind the store, delivery its only function. The family car these days was the 'forty-two Ford. They got in, Paul behind the wheel, and set off for the Standard station, the engine popping and coughing.

Len Downie was approaching the pumps and Paul was saying "Two gallons and check the oil," when the fire siren came wailing across town from the post in the Heffernands' back yard. Paul and Brendan got out and looked up and down Main Street for smoke. They saw none.

The Holy Angels churchbell began to ring, and Paul asked Brendan, "What's that all about?"

He was perplexed. Today being August 14, he made a guess: "Tomorrow's a holy day."

"So?"

"So this is the Eve of the Assumption of the Blessed Virgin." Which satisfied Paul, but not Brendan. He had never known of bells to ring on the eve of holy days.

Across the street a man stepped out of Plum Hardware, reached into an open car window and pressed the horn.

The Lutheran bell began to peal.

Downie said, "Call Central and see what the hell's going on."

Brendan went inside and picked up the phone. Melva Heffernand's voice: "Number please?"

"Why are the bells ringing?"

"The war is over."

He ran outside, his stomach turning a somersault. "The war is over," he crowed ecstatically.

Len Downie tossed his long-billed cap into the air and shouted, "Peace at last!" A breeze wafted the cap over the pumps and dropped it into the grease pit.

"Peace at last," Brendan repeated. This was the happy ending he had been urged to pray for since he was eight. It was for this moment he had collected scrap iron, bought war stamps, made novenas and gone without Hershey bars. Now America was in charge of history once again, the enemy crushed forever and every last complication removed from the face of the earth.

"Thank God," said Paul.

With the car fueled and adding its clattering noises to the ringing bells and honking horns, Brendan talked Paul into driving around town to spread the news. Through his open window he shouted, "The war is over!" to a cluster of men outside the pool hall. Gordy waved his bar rag. Next door Hank and his shoppers came spilling out of the market. "The war is over!" Brendan called, and his father clenched his hands over his head. They met Stan Kimball advancing slowly along Main Street in his hearse. He was leading a procession consisting of the county dump truck and the village fire truck, all with their horns blaring. The fire truck was driven by Mayor Brask, who was bowing his head left and right as if taking credit for the victory. "The war is over!" Brendan shouted into the ear of Nicholi the barber, who stood in the middle of the street holding his scissors and comb.

He asked Paul to drive down the alley behind Bean. His mother, airing out curtains and rugs and blankets in preparation for tomorrow's move, was conversing under the clothesline with Mrs. Kimball. Otto was tugging on his leash, digging a hole in the grass. "The war is over!" he called, and his mother threw him several kisses. Mrs. Kimball cupped her ear, not having understood. Behind them, he saw Grandfather, bewildered, groping his way out onto the veranda, mystified by the horns and bells apparently, or by something he had dreamed.

Along Hay and Corn streets people were coming out and standing in their front yards, as though, having heard of the Japanese surrender over their radios and telephones, they were waiting for Brendan to make it official. When he shouted, "The war is over!" they laughed and waved.

Their first stop was the Dombrowski house. "The war is over," he said to the Dombrowskis as he set their carton of groceries on a kitchen chair. The old couple didn't reply, but looked at him warily, like frightened birds. He said they owed him two dollars and ten cents. They looked aghast, as they always did when he said what was owing. Waiting them out—it was like a game each time—he noticed how much the Dombrowskis resembled one another. They were both lean and ruddy from a lifetime in the sun and wind. They seemed not to have drawn an easy breath since giving up the rigors of farmwork and moving to town. Community life made them tense and suspicious—all this human contact: neighbors passing on the front sidewalk, the delivery boy every few days.

Brendan asked, "Do you want to charge it?" and this horrifying proposal set them in motion. Together they counted out coins.

"The war is over," he said again as he left, but nothing, not even peace on earth, could trick the Dombrowskis into opening their mouths.

Next stop was Holy Angels. Through the open door of the church they saw B. L. Skeffington pulling on the bellrope. As Father O'Day's departure drew near—he was retiring on the first

of September—his otherworldliness was becoming more pro-
nounced: he never thought to feed himself, and Mrs. Skeffington
came in once a day to fix him a meal. It was she who had phoned
in the order which Brendan now carried through the back door
of the rectory. The old priest, stalled in the process of packing
his belongings, sat at his cluttered kitchen table reading old
letters. He ignored Brendan. Setting the groceries on a chair,
Brendan noticed that the letters were gauzy and limp from years
of handling. The stamps, he noticed, had cost a penny. Who
had written them—an angel? Surely this man had never been
attached to another mortal.

"Three dollars and thirty-six cents," said Brendan. The priest
turned to him, drew out his billfold and paid him. His hands
were blue with veins, his face was deathly white. Brendan
thanked him and added, "The war is over, Father."

"Oh, I've heard that before," he sighed.

"This time it's true."

He nodded impatiently. "Yes, it was true in 1918 as well."

First the Dombrowskis, and now the priest—would no one
rejoice with him? At least Mrs. Clay was on his route today.
Mrs. Clay was constantly happy of late, constantly inebriated.
When she drank heavily she tended to be careless about her
clothes, as Brendan learned two weeks ago when she opened
her kitchen door to receive her groceries dressed in a scanty
nightgown that revealed more female skin than Brendan had ever
seen in movies or magazines. He had caught sight of a whole
breast. He had hurried away to tell Sam and Philip, who accompanied him on his next delivery, but that time she wasn't home.

Paul drove from one church to the other. Waiting in the car
while Paul carried groceries in to his mother, Brendan saw Paul's
younger brother John pulling on the Lutheran bellrope and
thought that peace was proving much more exciting than he had
expected it to be. *Dona nobis pacem.* At mass when those words
were spoken he had always imagined peace to be quiet and dull,
not this loud and exhilarating.

Paul's mother and father followed him out the door. "The war
is over!" Brendan called to them. The Reverend Dimmitburg
said, "Thank the Lord, Brendan," and raised his arms in a

liturgical manner. Mrs. Dimmitburg nodded heavily, as though bestowing her queenly approval on the terms of the armistice.

Next they drove to the Flint house, where the method of delivery, at the request of Wallace's mother, was to set the bag on the porch, knock on the door and leave. Wallace wanted to see no one, she said; he would take in the groceries when no one was looking. Now in his fourth month of seclusion, Wallace was beginning to take on mythic proportions in the collective mind of the village. He was the mad recluse, the bad seed of the unfortunate woman who worked for Hank. All summer Brendan had been glad to leave the groceries and flee, for the house was vaguely spooky, but today he knocked and waited. Even a recluse, it seemed to Brendan, deserved to know the war was over. Also, he harbored the suspicion that Wallace had started the fire; one last glimpse of the man before leaving Plum might help him make up his mind.

There was no sound from inside. He knocked a second time. A third. When Paul honked again he gave up, for surely Wallace would not come to the door knowing the DeSoto was idling in the street. He set down the bag and stepped over to the kitchen window. Shading his eyes, he looked inside. Facing him from the wall over the range were half a dozen enormous faces—popeyed, leering faces painted in shades of red. Were these the movie stars Mrs. Flint had spoken of? The wide, half-smiling, heavy-lidded face next to the stovepipe might have been Peter Lorre, but the others were unrecognizable. Some, in fact, looked scarcely human. One had large pendulous objects hanging from her cheeks—tears perhaps. Another had cavernous nostrils and vacuous eyes, like Rufus Ottmann's. Paul honked a second time, and Brendan pulled himself away from the window, but not before catching sight of a face that might have been Catherine's. She had snakes for hair.

In the rooming house on Hay Street Brendan finally found someone whose ecstasy matched his own. Mrs. Lansky in number seven was weeping for joy. "It's over," she sobbed in her kitchen, "and now I won't have to imagine my grandchildren dead every day and night. My grandson is in the Seabees and my granddaughter is in the Waves." To the cost of the groceries she added an extra nickel. "That's for my granddaughter who will now live on and on," she said. "Now put out your other hand, this is for my grandson." In his other hand she placed a dime, a Seabee running twice the risk.

Turning to leave, Brendan faced number six across the hall and his joy was interrupted by the memory of Dodger bringing him up here to give him the cap gun. Brendan had never fired it. He didn't know where it was any more. On that same misty afternoon they had gone out into the sticky clay of the plowed field behind Brendan's house and thrown the boomerang until their arms ached. That was when Brendan first saw life as a circle, saw that things came round again. Yet he hadn't foreseen that a year later he would be returning to live in the city. Nor had he foreseen that Dodger would keep coming back, even after death. Not a day passed that Brendan didn't feel Dodger's needy presence at the back of his mind. It had taken him several weeks to understand what Dodger needed. For one thing he needed his name cleared. A whole summer had passed and Brendan had not yet told his parents that Dodger was innocent of the moneybag theft, that he had known about it all along but had said nothing so he could go to the creek with his friends. Would he ever work up the courage to tell them?

Dodger's second need was even more discouraging because it might take a lifetime to fulfill. Dodger needed Brendan's promise never again to be as unkind to anyone as he had been to Dodger, his promise to go through life more openhearted toward others and less concerned with himself. *Atonement* was the term the nuns of St. Bonnie's had been fond of using in cases like this. They said it was never too late to begin making amends. Unfortunately you never knew when your amends were complete. You could go on atoning all your life and never be sure you were off the hook. But Dodger was giving him no choice, was expecting him to begin atoning at the first opportunity. Luckily Plum, since Dodger's death, seemed to offer no opportunities.

"I know what you're thinking," said Mrs. Lansky behind him.

He turned and saw that the armistice glow in the old woman's

face was now overlaid with melancholy. He heard the words
before she spoke them: "Poor Dodger."

The Clay delivery was last. Brendan carried the bag around
to the back door, knocked and heard Mrs. Clay sing from a
distant room, "Who is it?"

"Brendan. Delivery."

"Bring it right on in. I'll be right there." Her melodious voice
meant she was pretty well plastered.

He stepped into the kitchen and set the bag on the drainboard.
Waiting, he scanned the several clippings pinned to the wallpaper beside the window. Most of the photos came from movie
magazines, men and women embracing. They stirred Brendan
in the same erotic places that Esther Williams affected when she
was wet. After a minute or so he felt a change of atmosphere.
He heard no footstep, all was still, yet it was the stillness of a
silent human presence. He turned. There across the room, smiling at him with her bathrobe hanging loosely open from her
shoulders and wearing nothing underneath and thus revealing to
him all her wonders from throat to thigh, was Mrs. Clay. Her
feet were bare, her toenails painted the same luscious red as her
lips. Her smile was impish. He stood there stunned and learning, absorbed in her flesh until she drew her robe together, tied
the belt and said, still beaming, "Charge it please."

Breaking out of his enchantment by force of will, he backed
slowly out the door, and his voice was subdued as he left her
with the news that no longer seemed so momentous: "The war
is over, Mrs. Clay."

He said nothing of this to Paul, but rode beside him in silence,
memorizing her rosy contours.

They found Main Street filled with tractors and cars and trucks
parked every which way and people milling among them. Villagers were streaming downtown and farmers were coming in
from their farms. The honking horns were deafening. Paul
stopped in front of the Standard station, for their way was
blocked. Brendan climbed up and sat on the roof of the car, his
feet on the hood. He followed the raised eyes of the crowd and
saw Constable Heffernand on the roof of the city hall releasing
a fiery plane. It made a loop over the street and disintegrated in

midair, its wispy remains falling like charred leaves. He sent out another plane and then another. To the delight of the cheering crowd he was launching his entire collection. Only the enemy planes were on fire. The Allied planes circled and dipped and climbed until their rubber bands went slack and they drifted into the outstretched hands of the crowd; most were scuffled over and crushed. Brendan saw Sam in the crowd. He saw Lorraine and Pearl in front of the drugstore, Cokes in their hands. He saw Philip Crowley with his mother. He saw Mrs. Ottmann on the far side of the street under the awning of the hardware store. He saw half a dozen farm children standing in the bed of the Higgins pickup. He saw Norma Nash kissing Andy Romberg. He saw several old men from the poor farm. Edging toward him along the front of the city hall was Rufus Ottmann. Following the example of those around him, Rufus had turned his eyes to the sky without knowing the reason. He was grinning at the sun and making excited little movements with his left hand while trailing the fingers of his right hand along the brick wall to keep his balance. There were cheers and laughter as a Flying Tiger climbed across the street and landed on the roof of the hardware store. For once, thought Brendan, everyone in town looked as happy as Rufus. He watched the idiot reach the corner of the village hall and leave the sidewalk as he followed the side wall back toward the alley. He saw him stumble over one of Len Downie's discarded tires. He kept his balance and continued moving along, heading straight for the grease pit with his eyes still lifted to the sky. "Hey, somebody catch Rufus!" cried Brendan, standing up on the hood of the car and pointing. "He'll fall in that hole!" But his voice was lost in the cheering as a German Fokker climbed to a peak and dropped, trailing smoke. He jumped to the ground and ran to Rufus, who teetered at the verge of the grease pit; he clutched his hand and wrenched him around. He avoided looking into the idiot's repellant face—the gaping nostrils, the cavernous mouth—as he led him back to the street. How docilely he followed. How large his hand was. How soft. The hand tightened painfully on Brendan's as he picked his way through the jostling crowd in the direction of Mrs. Ottmann. Seeing her son advancing toward her, she signaled him with a lavender handkerchief. As Brendan stepped into the shade of the awning and brought Rufus to a halt at his mother's side, he felt virtuous and mature, felt that Dodger—at least for the moment—was satisfied.

"Thank you very kindly," said Mrs. Ottmann.

"You're welcome," said Brendan, struggling to pry himself free of the idiot's grip.

Jon Hassler

❧

"A WRITER GOOD ENOUGH TO RESTORE YOUR FAITH IN FICTION."
—*The New York Times*